Humanity Abides

Book two

Emergence

A Post - Apocalyptic Novel

By Carol Bird

Cover art Copyright © 2013 by David Bird

Special Thanks to:

Christine L. Temple – Editor
Sherian S. Miller – Contributor

Books by Carol Bird:

Humanity Abides – Book One – Shelter

Humanity Abides – Book Two – Emergence

Humanity Abides – Book Three – The Search for Home
(Coming soon!)

Comments about Shelter on Amazon:

*One of the best books I've read in years. The characters
and locations are so well developed. I would recommend it to
everyone.*

*I love apocalyptic books, but it is hard to find
something unique. This book is unique and the characters are
fully fleshed out. The science is believable, without becoming
preaching. Read this book and you will not be sorry.*

*I loved this book! Can't wait for the next one in the
series. In the beginning it feels like a little too much
information but it all comes together in a great way. The story
sucks you in and you don't want to put it down till the very end.
My only complaint is that now I have to wait for the rest of the
story! Please write fast!*

Purchase at Amazon.com
Purchase at Createspace.com

Table of Contents

Chapter 1

Red eyes glared from under shaggy brows as the creature shifted position. It squatted behind jagged boulders at the edge of the cliff, looking through a gap in the rocks and remaining hidden from those it spied upon. Behind it, a small cave led into the side of the hill. The beast's clawed hands scratched suppurating wounds inflicted by blasts from a Remington 12 gauge shotgun, and reddened, decaying skin and hair sloughed off as it rubbed its chest. From its perch, a few hundred feet above the valley floor, the creature looked down through the fog and rain on a group of humans that stood around an open hole in the ground. It was hungry, but it remembered the pain of its wounds and it had gained respect for the long sticks many of the humans carried. It had learned patience and would bide its time until a kill was assured.

"Ashes to ashes, dust to dust..." Brian Morrison tossed a handful of dirt into the open grave containing the body of William Hargraves. Will's daughter Chris stood at the graveside, crying softly, as others of the assemblage slowly filed by and added their own handful of dirt to the growing pile on the shroud.

Low clouds blanketed the valley and a cold drizzle fell, further dampening the mood of the crowd that had gathered to bury their father, mentor, savior and friend.

My God, thought Mark Teller, *how will I live without his counsel?* He put his arm around the woman beside him and pulled her close. The morning chill caused her to shiver against him and she pulled her collar higher and tighter around her neck trying to keep the rain from running down her back. The long wet grass was only now beginning to turn from brown to green, as the spring had been delayed due to the nuclear winter.

Mark glanced around at the small crowd that numbered just under two hundred people, individuals who had become his friends, his family. He rubbed his eyes with his free hand as he tried to recall the events of the previous few days. They were understandably blurred. He'd had very little sleep, with intermittent bursts of frantic activity... adrenaline coursing through his veins, and most of the time spent in darkness, semi-darkness or in the eerie glow of the red emergency lights. The shelter, their home for almost eight months had been wracked by a series of earthquakes, and flooded by the water escaping the damaged penstocks that had provided hydroelectric power for the shelter. The tremors had caused massive cave-ins and destruction on every level of the shelter. Mark had barely escaped the collapse of the stairwell leading to the control room. Will Hargraves hadn't been so lucky. The rock fall had crushed the back of his skull, delivering what would be a fatal injury. Living long enough to see his charges escape to the cave at the rear entrance of the shelter, he was elated when they opened the blast door and looked out upon the beautiful valley that would be their new home.

During the chaos created by the quakes, the monsters had appeared out of nowhere. No one knew what they were, where they came from or how they had entered the shelter... but suddenly they were there, killing everyone in their path. Then the real horror began, as they devoured all those they had slaughtered.

It was almost too much to bear, with their shelter torn apart and friends lost to the terrifying creatures. Most of the residents and all of the children, along with quite a few of the animals, had escaped the carnage and entered this valley at the back entrance to the shelter.

When the survivors had left the cave the day before, they had followed a path that lead down to a moss-covered, rock bridge spanning a river that originated at the base of a waterfall on their left. Sheer cliffs embraced the waterfall, extending for two hundred feet toward the sky. Mist from the falls drifted around them as they crossed over the bridge. The path entered a forest of evergreens and aspens, the aspens just beginning to leaf out, and the air redolent with the scent of wet pines. There were patches of snow alongside the winding trail and newly grown grass sprouted up through the dirt between rocks embedded in the path. It was very cold and they were still dressed in the lightweight clothing they had worn in the shelter, so they quickly moved forward, herding the animals ahead of them, not knowing where the path led.

Lori's tug on Mark's arm brought him back to the present, and as some of the crowd turned toward their camp in the forest, he called out to them, "Hold on...I'd like to say something." He raised his voice to be heard above the sound of the rain and the wind that had sprung up out of nowhere. "I'd like to acknowledge all the others we've lost."

They didn't have any bodies to bury. Those had been abandoned in their mad race to escape the creatures and the rising water.

"Even before these last few terrible days, we lost Faye Claret. She was like a mother to us all. And Karl Dohner, who had his own private demons. And some of you knew Old Pierson. He was the first to be buried." They had found the remains of the first caretaker in a hidden cave outside the shelter's walls. He began to choke up as he recited the names, "Richard Krieg, Bud Nagle, Manny Ramirez, and... and Lenny Ralston." Some of the people in the crowd began to cry as the names went on.

Mark stopped to collect himself and Lori, standing beside him, raised her voice and continued, "Vernon and Jennifer Richenour, Bernie and Joyce Palmer and Jill Monroe...Karen Stroup and Doug Kraken." The latter two had been part of Chris's farm team and Lori knew them well. Now she choked up.

Mark spoke again. "Bill Jamison, Micah Lowell and Amy Zoren. Some of them we know were killed by the creatures, and a few others never arrived at the escape tunnel. I... I know we probably won't ever recover their bodies, so I just wanted to remember them too." The crowd, once again began to shuffle toward the trail leading back to camp.

Mark walked over to the grave and looked down at the body of the man that had been like a father to him. He thought of things in the past that were now becoming distant memories in this new world they existed in. Like going to live with the Hargraves as a teenager. Mark's father had died years before, and his mother, an alcoholic, was unable to care for him or his sister. They lived with their aunt and uncle until Mark was sixteen. His mother had sold the family aeronautics business to William Hargraves, who had turned it into a multi-billion dollar business. Will took Mark in and treated him as one of his own. Mark's sister Jill had continued to live with their aunt and uncle. She, her husband and their two children were presumed to have been killed in the nuclear holocaust just eight months before.

Eight months ago on August 21st, China, for reasons unknown, had unleashed a devastating nuclear attack against the United States and the other countries of the world. An overwhelming retaliation followed, with thousands of hydrogen bombs, most of them in the megaton range, detonated over every country. Anyone not under cover had perished, either from the thermonuclear blasts or from the radiation that permeated the atmosphere in the aftermath of the war. An untold number of neutron bombs, containing Red Mercury, had been delivered as well, and the deadly effects of this compound were only now becoming apparent. The small group of humans that had survived The Great War wasn't aware of the connection, but the unusual radiation created by the Red Mercury had created creatures heretofore unknown on this planet.

Hargraves, being a major defense contractor, had served on a civilian advisory board for the President of the United States and was aware of the danger posed by countries in the Mideast, China, North Korea and others. After his wife had died, he constructed a bomb shelter in the Sangre de Christo Mountains in New Mexico to protect his children from these dangers. His foresight had provided sanctuary for over two hundred individuals, who had barely made it to the shelter when the missiles were launched.

Mark was pulled from his reverie by a distant call.

"Hellooooo… " A shout came from behind them and everyone turned as one and squinted up at the sheer cliff where the voice emanated from. Through the mist, they could barely see a distant figure waving at them from a jumble of large boulders alongside the top of the waterfall.

A shout went up from the crowd, "Hey, it's Micah!"

Everyone started shouting at once, smiles lighting up their faces for the first time, after the deep sadness of the previous day and this morning. The figure on the cliff looked back over his shoulder and quickly sat down, scrunched forward and dropped to the ledge below him. "What's he doing?" Mark asked Lori. "Those rocks have got to be slippery that close to the falls. The last thing he said to me was 'I'm a great rock climber,' but this is going to be suicide."

"I don't know what he's thinking," she replied. "He should just follow the ridge south until it reaches the valley floor. It's the long way around but it's safer than trying to climb down that cliff." No one had ventured south beyond their camp as yet, but they could tell that behind the trees along the top of the ridge it gradually sloped down to a lower elevation.

The sun was just coming up over the top of the bluff and the brilliant rays suddenly silhouetted another figure, a huge misshapen form that appeared above Micah. The crowd, puzzled, quieted down and then someone yelled, "Oh God, it's one of those things!"

As though choreographed, the crowd began shouting and pointing to the south. Micah turned his back to them and quickly began to climb farther down the rock face. Mist from the falls swirled around, enveloping him. His foot slipped and he hung momentarily by his fingers, his feet scraping against the rock wall as he desperately tried to gain a foothold. He found purchase and lowered himself another few feet to an even narrower ledge. The figure above him tried to climb down, but its great size frustrated its attempt and it soon desisted. It stood back from the edge, disappeared for a moment, and then returned with a boulder the size of its head. It flung it over the edge and narrowly missed Micah as he hugged the cliff for dear life. He scrambled to the right where a small outcropping gave him at least a small amount of protection. He waited until the thing above him threw down another boulder and then made a dash, moving sideways, crab-like, trying to get to the edge of the cliff where it became less vertical and blended with the tree-covered mountainside. The creature was back with still another rock and it threw it at the man trying to escape him. They heard a yelp and Micah's left arm fell to his side. This seemed to bring the crowd out of its stupor and Mark began to shout orders.

"You guys with the rifles, fire at it!"

"We might hit Micah," one yelled back at him.

"Fire high and to the left. You're just trying to scare it."

Suddenly, every one of the armed sentries they had posted around the funeral was firing everything they had at the beast.

"Not all of you!" Mark yelled. "Don't waste the ammo." The thing screamed and backed away from the edge just as Micah reached the slope. He jumped over to the ground, slipping and sliding down the steep hill. They could barely see him through the rain, but they saw him grab a bush with his good hand just before the slope turned into rock and became vertical again, a few hundred feet above the valley floor. The crowd cheered as he gained his feet and took off to the south, through the pines, as if the hounds of hell were after him.

Mark shouted for attention, "I need some of you to stay here as guards until they finish filling the grave. The rest of you come with me. We have to get to Micah before that thing does. Jimbo, Keith, Mike… you guys stay here and watch closely. There may be more of them."

Jimbo swung about in a complete circle. "We'll watch for them, Mark. Get Micah."

Mark and Lori and most of the rest of the mourners took off running for their camp.

At the first shout from Micah, the thing that had been Arby Clark turned from its hiding place, and on all four extremities, and quick as lightning, scrambled up the hill behind it onto the plateau. It was on the north face of the cliff and was approximately a mile from the point where the second creature had attacked Micah, but it quickly set out in pursuit of its next meal.

***

Chris Hargraves watched Mark and the others disappear into the forest. Mark, Lori, David Cunningham and most of the others were all out sprinting, but a few of those that hadn't kept in shape while confined to the shelter had lagged behind. One of the armed men fell back and followed the last person who entered the trees, looking over his shoulder and peering intently into the dense forest to the right and left.

Jimbo raised his voice above the rain that was now coming down hard and ordered the other two men to take up positions around the small party that had stayed behind. "Mike, to the East. Watch the cliffs above for any sign of those things. Keith, you take the west side. Keep a close eye on the other side of the river. I'll circle the perimeter. Aaron, you guys should hurry and get that grave filled." He glanced over at Chris, "Sorry to rush you Chris, but we should get back to camp as soon as we can, to help out with defense."

During the war, Jimbo had arrived at the shelter on his Harley. At the time, he had been a weekend warrior, clean shaven, with a conservative haircut and twenty extra pounds around his waist. Now, his light brown hair was pulled into a pony tail and he sported a goatee that grew long below his chin. He hadn't shaved since the trouble started a few days before and his cheeks were covered with rough stubble. Wearing hunting garb, with an O.D. green jacket, camo pants and an old Astros baseball cap, he looked like he'd spent his life in the woods. He had a slight southern accent and a habit of squinting when he spoke.

"It's okay Jimbo, we'll hurry." She sniffed and reached for a shovel they had laid on the pile of dirt alongside the grave. Looking down at her father's shrouded body, partially covered by the dirt the mourners had tossed in the grave, she whispered softly, "Oh Dad... I will miss you so much." She began to cry again and fell to her knees in the mud, her tears mingling with the rain. Aaron Brown, a young African-American, one of the camp's two doctors and Chris's lover had stood back to let her pay her respects, but now he stepped forward and raised her up by her elbow. He enfolded her in his arms as she shook with renewed sobs. Samuel gently took the shovel from her.

"Chris, you go on over there by Mike. We'll take care of this." Samuel was one of the people that had worked daily with Chris in the shelter's hydroponic gardens. He had tremendous respect for her skill and knowledge, and had grown very fond of her.

Aaron led her over by Mike. He held her close and stroked her long, dark hair. "Stay here Baby. We'll finish up." She nodded and tried to stop crying, but failed miserably. Through her tears, her eyes swept the cliffs above for any sign of the creature.

Aaron, Samuel and Lucas James used the only three shovels they had found at the camp to fill the grave. The mound of dirt was turning to mud and the grave beginning to fill with water. They worked quickly and were soon sweating, despite the cold and the rain. Samuel, in his sixties but hardened by years of farming, worked just as hard as the two younger men.

Although she maintained her alertness, Chris's mind drifted back and she thought about her life and family. She had lost her baby sister to a hit and run driver when Chris was a teenager, and a few years later her mother Katherine had died of cancer. Her father was devastated and began to build the bomb shelter to protect Chris and Clay, his remaining two children, in the event world tensions deteriorated into war. Mark Teller had spent summers with them and had moved in permanently when he was sixteen. Chris had always thought of him as an older brother.

While in the shelter, her spoiled and arrogant younger brother Clay had tried to rape another resident and had been banished from the shelter by their father. Hargraves had personally placed his son in the elevator that led to the front entrance cave, and had given instructions that the elevator be locked at the cave until Clay exited. Clay remained in the cave for over a month. They sent him food and water using the elevator and he'd had to sleep on the floor and dig a latrine for sanitation. One day the instrument panel in the control room indicated that the front airlock door had opened and Clay used the intercom to tell them he was leaving. The surveillance camera showed him exiting the shelter.

Will hadn't been the same since the day he'd put his son in that elevator. He became withdrawn and reclusive and seldom left his room. Only in the last couple of days, with the earthquakes and the creatures, had he become his old self, taking charge and informing the residents about the escape tunnel to the valley at the back of the shelter. Even though mortally injured, when they had all reached the safety of the cave and he had seen the outside world, knowing that his daughter and the others were safe, his face had shown great joy. Now he was gone, killed by a cave-in during the last terrible flight from the monsters and the rising flood waters. She turned and looked at the low mound of dirt now covering her Father. She stopped crying and walked over and took Aaron's hand.

"Don't worry," he told her. "We'll set a proper headstone when we get Micah and kill that bastard from hell. And when this rain finally quits," he added ruefully.

"Alright guys, let's get back to camp." Jimbo's eyes swept the cliffs one more time as he fell in behind Lucas, Chris, Sam and Aaron. Mike and Keith led the way into the forest, Mike looking left with Keith watching their right flank. "Okay, let's double time it." Jimbo called out. The camp was over a half mile and they hustled along hoping their companions were able to reach Micah in time.

Chapter 2

The runners came streaming out of the woods, stretched out in single file as they entered the wide clearing. It was strewn with rocks, ranging in size from a few inches to several feet in diameter. Colorful tents, dimmed by the rain and fog, filled the meadow all the way to the thin tree line that separated it from the open grassland to the west. There were several teenagers, and three men with weapons, standing before a huge, metal storage building at the far side of the meadow. A covered porch extended in front of the double doors and the guards were all clustered under it trying to stay out of the rain. Although the morning was still cold, all the residents had found jackets in the building behind them that fit reasonably well. The children had not been allowed to attend the funeral and a few of the adults had remained to care for them. Since the gravesite was over a half mile from the camp and the residents had been outside the shelter for only a day, their parents weren't certain what dangers might be present. The sentries were startled by the runners coming toward them across the approximately two hundred yard meadow.

Sixteen year old Tucker Smith jogged toward Mark and Lori. "Hey, what's going on?" he asked.

Mark called to him, "Get some of the guards around to the other side of the building. We saw one of those monsters up on the cliff!" He ran right past Tucker, up to the building and threw open one of the doors. The people that had been at the funeral entered the building as they arrived from across the meadow, tracking mud and dripping water. The children and their babysitters came from the play area they'd created at the back of the building to see what was happening. Parents immediately sought out their children to reassure themselves they were okay.

Yelling above the noise of the crowd, Mark issued orders. "Everyone that has a gun, get it and follow me. Some of you need to join the guards out front and get this building surrounded. Stay in pairs, back to back. Can someone give me their rifle?" He had lost his shotgun in the battle with the creatures before they exited the shelter the day before. A semi-automatic rifle and a couple of magazines were thrust into his hands as he turned back to the entrance of the building.

Barbara Thompson, one of the young mothers who had remained to babysit, pushed through the crowd to Lori's side. "Lori, are they really out there? Are we safe here?" Lori had left her Uzi on a shelf half way across the room and as she ran to get it, with Barb running behind her, she told Barbara about seeing Micah on the cliff and the creature attacking him.

"Keep the kids inside, and after we leave, lock the door. We'll be back as soon as we get Micah, but he was running toward the far, south end of the valley and we may be gone awhile. And Barbara, I know it seems like I've asked you this a hundred times," she hugged Barbara and whispered in her ear, "please, take care of my kids."

Quite a few of the Remnant, as they had started to refer to themselves, had run throughout the building where they had stashed their weapons and were regrouping outside under the portico. Dave had already positioned sentries around the building and was assembling a group of men and a few women to form the rescue party.

Jean Carlin joined the group, and her new husband Ron grabbed her pistol from her hand. "You are not going with us!" he told her.

She reached for it but he held it over his head. "That's my gun, and I want to help," she said. He handed the weapon to one of the men that stood out in the rain. The man shoved it in his pocket under his coat to keep it dry.

"You stay here, inside the building." He reached out and stroked her cheek. "I want you to be safe, Jean."

She looked down with a brief nod. "Okay, but be careful," she told him.

Lori hurried up to Mark. "Let's go! I think Micah was hurt, and those things are really fast."

Mark didn't even bother trying to tell Lori to stay behind. He had learned better in the shelter, when she had been instrumental in getting the kids away from the creatures and to the safety of the rear cavern.

Mark glanced north and saw the last of the stragglers enter the meadow. He frowned as he realized that things would be different outside the shelter, more difficult and dangerous, and that all the residents would need to get in shape and contribute to the survival of the community.

He shook his head and told Lori, "We didn't even get one day of peace before it's all started up again."

"We'll just have to make it safe," she responded. "For the kids… and for us." She smiled up at him. "C'mon, let's go."

There were almost twenty people in the rescue group that took off running along the trail leading south, reentering the forest behind the building. A dozen more who were armed, stayed behind to guard the remaining residents. Chris and the others who had stayed behind to finish the burial weren't back yet, but the rescuers couldn't wait. Every minute that passed, lessened their chances of reaching Micah in time. They hadn't taken more than a few minutes to get organized but Mark was worried they might still be too late.

***

Adrenaline pumped through his system and Micah felt like his feet hardly touched the ground as he sprinted along the ridge line, jumping bushes and careening around trees. His left arm hurt like hell and he held it close to his body to lessen the jarring. The rain was turning the ground to slick mud, and even though he had reached an area that wasn't as steep, he was sliding downhill as much as moving forward. He could hear the creature crashing through the brush behind him, and was gratified it too was having trouble with the footing, and judging from the infuriated screaming, had fallen once or twice.

The ground leveled out somewhat, and Micah was able to run faster. But he knew the creature could now pursue faster, as well. Up ahead, he saw an outcropping of rock about fifteen feet tall and extending from as far as he could see on the left all the way to the cliff's edge.

"Oh no," he moaned out loud, "what now?"

As he approached the wall he could see, not only was it completely vertical, but it didn't appear to have any handholds. Due to the rain, it looked slicker than snot. He skidded to a stop in front of it and whirled around to see the creature approaching like a freight train, bearing down on him. Its eyes were so bloodshot they were completely red and stared out from a protruding Neanderthal brow. It was at least seven feet tall and its skin was mottled yellowish-green and looked putrid. Amazingly, it wore the remnants of pants, ripped at the seams and barely covering its nakedness. Only thirty feet away, it slowed down and slid to its left to block his path in the only direction he could go... east. Micah looked wildly about for a weapon, or an escape route. The wall was at his back, the cliff to his left and the creature in front. He didn't have time to try and climb up the wall or down the cliff.

Realizing it was over, Micah suddenly became calm. As the thing came closer, he decided he wasn't going to let it have him... he couldn't imagine a worse death than being eaten alive. Even as far south as he had come, with the elevation lessening as he ran, the cliff to his left was still two hundred feet high... high enough to kill him if he jumped over the side.

Just as he decided to leap from the cliff, and made a move in that direction, a tremendous roar emanated from the left of the creature in front of him. The bushes shook wildly, and another of the monsters, much larger than the first, leaped out upon that one that threatened Micah. They crashed to earth, thrashing about, with the screaming so loud Micah was momentarily paralyzed. Mud, rocks and branches flew everywhere obscuring his view.

As the larger beast clamped its fangs in the neck of the other, Micah realized he had very little time and snapped out of his paralysis. Knowing he would never outrun it along the rock face, and he only had a few seconds to act, he edged over to the cliff and gingerly slid over the side, his feet feeling for cracks or ledges below the brink. His foot found a crack and he inched his body over the precipice. Holding on with his good hand he lowered himself, feeling for the next foothold. As his eyes reached a point just above the edge of the cliff, he saw bright blood shoot into the air and knew the thing would be coming for him soon.

A rock jutted out at waist level, and he let go with his right hand. For a split second he didn't have hold of anything, but he balanced on his toes against the wall of the cliff and grabbed the lower rock. *How the hell am I going to climb with one hand?* He wondered. Frantically lowering his foot, he found a tiny crack to slide it into. He heard the beast above him coming closer. His other foot slid down onto a forty–five degree angle, two inch ledge. Now he was in a pickle. His feet were not that stable and his one arm holding the rock was slipping. He instinctively grabbed a small outcropping with his left hand, and screamed from the pain shooting up his arm and into his shoulder. But it held for that instant necessary to allow him to re-grasp the handhold with his right hand. Lowering himself another foot, he felt something swipe through his hair and risked looking up.

He wished he hadn't! The terrifying appearance of the creature almost caused him to freeze again. It was staring at him with those red, insane eyes. Lying at the top of the rock face, it stretched out as far as it could, reaching for him, two inch claws coming within an inch of his face. Micah ducked and flattened himself against the wall, lowering another foot. Now he was out of reach of the monster bellowing at him from above.

He remembered that the other one threw rocks at him so he continued as quickly as possible to climb down and to his right. The rock wall that had blocked his path had broken down somewhat on its south side and created a rock fall that enabled him to scramble more quickly across the rocks and back up the other side using just his one hand. The creature suddenly jumped to its feet and disappeared.

Back up on the ridge, Micah headed south once more. He figured the thing was heading east to a point where it could either get around or scale the wall. He had no idea how much time he had bought, and his energy was starting to flag. He still had on the lightweight shoes they had all adopted in the shelter. Due to their flexibility, they actually made adequate climbing shoes, but they weren't made for the abuse they were taking in this mad dash. The right shoe had split when he forced it into a crack and he had cut his foot badly. He was leaving a trail of blood that he knew would make it easier for the creature to follow him… and he was beginning to limp. His arm throbbed. He didn't believe it was broken, since he was able to use it briefly on his climb down the cliff, but he thought he had possibly dislocated his shoulder. Continuing southward he wondered when he would reach the valley floor and if help was on its way.

***

The rescue party had settled into an easy jog, not knowing how far they would need to run. The trail to the south wound through the forest and was entering thicker underbrush than they had encountered farther north. It sometimes curved to the west and Mark knew they were taking too long. He called for the group to halt and gave new instructions.

"Split down the middle." He waved half of them left and half to the right. "You guys stay on the trail so you can go faster. If it keeps going west, you'll need to leave it and head back toward the cliff. My group is going east to the cliff and then south."

"You're gonna really be slowed down going through that vegetation," Ron told him.

"I know, but the trail is going the wrong way. You stay on it awhile till you know whether it curves back. Hopefully one group will find Micah in time."

They left the trail and started through the brush. It was much slower going but Mark's group came to the cliff after ten minutes, and turned south once more. There had been rock falls from above, probably caused by the earthquakes, and the rain had made the rocks slippery, but they climbed over and around them and continued along the base of the cliff. The rain had finally lessened and after another quarter of an hour they heard a tremendous caterwauling from the top of the ridge. The cliff had enough growth of stunted pines and brush that they couldn't see more than half way up, but Lori looked stricken. "Oh God, Mark. Do you think it got him?"

"I don't know. It could just be making noise to flush him out. It sounds like there's more than one."

They all stood craning their necks, trying to see the top of the cliff. It was much lower at this point than it was at the camp. Mark figured another mile and it would reach the level of the valley.

Dave Cunningham said, "We need to keep going until we can get up on the ridge. Even if it got Micah, we have to kill it."

"Yeah," Jerry Thompson agreed. "We can't let it get away." Dave towered over Jerry by a foot but both men were tough, and didn't shrink from the idea of hunting the creature.

"Okay, let's keep going." Mark started off again moving quickly over the rocks.

They heard the creature scream again.

***

The ridge took a sudden dive after another half mile, and in ten minutes Micah was able to scramble down the rocks and start back along the base of the cliff toward the north, and he hoped, toward help. Moving slowly now, his foot was swelling and the pain was becoming almost unbearable. He heard a noise and looked up... and there it was.

He let out a whimper. He'd tried so hard to escape but this was too much. The thing was fifty feet above but quickly moved southward to get onto the level with Micah. He only had minutes before it would be back. Climbing up onto the rocks that had fallen along the base of the cliff, he looked around desperately, spotting a crack between two boulders. He forced his body between them down into the crack. Micah was not a big man, five-nine if he stretched real tall, and he wedged himself down as far as he could get. The rain helped by making the rocks slick. He heard the thing coming and pushed himself down hard but he was stuck, facing down, his good arm pinned under him and his other arm useless.

The creature made slobbery, snuffling sounds as it approached. Micah knew he had been discovered when he was assailed with an unbelievable stench. It smelled like death. The trail of blood had led it directly to Micah's hiding place and looking down through the rocks it spotted the man a few feet below. It quickly flopped down on the rocks and reached into the crack. The thing had once been a man, and during its transformation into this hellish creature its nails had grown into razor-sharp, two inch claws. It stretched out its hairy arm as far as it could and scratched Micah's back from his right shoulder down to his hip, completely ripping the shirt off his back. The claws were able to penetrate only about an eighth of an inch but blood oozed into the furrows and Micah screamed in pain, trying to wedge himself further down into the crack. But he was stuck and at the mercy of the beast. It would cut him to ribbons. Pulling its arm out of the crack, it licked the blood from its claws and raised its head to emit a blood-curdling scream.

Then it plunged its arm between the rocks and raked Micah's back a second time. It drooled vile, mucoid saliva onto his back, where it mixed with blood welling out of the gashes, turning the blood pink and green. The Arby-thing wasn't happy with small tastes of blood and tried to reach farther into the crevice to grab the man and drag him out. Micah had passed out from the pain and his limp body slumped lower. Jumping up, the monster grabbed one of the boulders, and with massive muscles bulging, it wrenched the boulder up, dragging it off to the side.

It had a clear path to the helpless man.

***

As Mark and the others heard a human cry out in pain they leaped forward with renewed speed, crashing through the underbrush. Then their senses were assaulted by an otherworldly scream and they feared for the worse. They came crashing out of the forest into a small open space. Large boulders had fallen from above and one of the monsters from the cave was lifting a boulder that would have taken three normal men to move. The creature cast the boulder aside and looked down into a crack in the rocks. In its bloodlust to get at its prey it hadn't heard them approach. They stood frozen for a minute as the smell assailed them, then reacted and began to fire wildly in the direction of the Arby-thing.

The creature swung on them and swatted the air as a bullet or bullets slammed into it. So fast they couldn't react quickly enough, it turned and slithered up the rock fall and disappeared over the ledge above.

Dave jumped up on a rock, his rifle pointing where the thing had disappeared. "Get him out of there! I'll cover you. Lori, help me here."

Lori ran beyond Micah and scrambled onto the boulders, swinging her Uzi left and right, her eyes as wide as saucers.

The others gathered around the crevice that held Micah's shredded figure.

"Jerry, can you get down there and pull him free?" Mark asked him.

Jerry slid over a boulder into the crevice and placed his feet on either of Micah. His brother always teased him that he was built like a fire plug; he was short, but well-built and very strong. He wedged his hands into Micah's armpits and squatting down and using his legs, he heaved. Several of the others reached down and grabbed as Micah came out of the hole. They wrestled him out and carried him to the ground.

A rustle of brush and shouts brought Lori around facing west and she almost blasted away the second group of rescuers as they ploughed headlong into the clearing.

"We heard shots! What's happening?" yelled Ron.

Mark stood and gestured them over. "Micah was hiding in the rocks but it got to him. He's hurt pretty bad but he's alive."

"Where's the thing?" Greg asked, fanning his weapon as he searched above them.

David had never stopped scanning the cliff above and Lori had kept a watch to the south.

"We scared it off, and I think we hit it, but it didn't seem to be hurt all that bad," Mark told him. "We need to get Micah back to the doctors and we can get together a hunting party later." He looked up the hill and said, "I'm sure it was the big one that almost got me in the shelter. It seems almost indestructible."

"How're we gonna get him back?" Lori asked

"We can use a fireman's carry," Jerry said. "There are enough of us so no one has to carry him far."

"I can run back to camp and get a stretcher," Ron offered.

"Are you crazy?" Dave asked him. "Nobody ever goes off alone until we're sure we've killed every one of those bastards."

Mark told them, "I'll go first. Pick him up and hoist him onto my back."

They lifted the unconscious man. Mark grabbed Micah's arms over his shoulders, crossed them across his chest and bent forward. "Okay, let's go."

Armed men formed a circle around them as they started back toward camp.

Chapter 3

The cold rain continued to fall and a number of residents were huddled under the porch extension trying to stay warm and dry. A sudden, faint volley of gunshots caused them to run out into the rain, around the corner of the building, staring toward the south in the direction of the shots.

"Shall we go out there to help them?" Chris asked.

"We don't want to spread our defenses too thin," Jimbo replied. "But I guess we could send a couple of guys with a stretcher in case they found Micah, and he or one of the others is hurt."

"I'll get it." Lucas ran back to the building and disappeared within, coming back a minute later with a rolled up stretcher.

Jimbo gestured to the trail. "Let's go Chris. Aaron, they may need you too if someone's hurt." Chris and Lucas were armed with rifles, and Aaron carried the stretcher as they trotted off into the woods. Chris scanned right and Lucas left as they moved along the trail that was quickly becoming a quagmire. They kicked up mud as they followed the trail, winding through the trees in a southerly direction until the pines began to thin and the path took a turn to the right, heading in a westerly direction. They heard sounds of a group moving through the brush ahead and, weapons at the ready, slowed to a halt.

Lucas called out, "Hey Mark, is that you?"

"Yeah, we need help!"

The three moved forward and found the rescue party, with Micah being carried on David's back. They lowered Micah onto the ground. Aaron unrolled the stretcher beside Micah and they moved him on to it, covering him with one of the men's jackets to try and keep him warm.

"How bad is he Aaron?" Chris asked, forcing her way through the others to get a look.

Mark and David helped Aaron roll him on his side. "Wow, he's cut to ribbons. I can't tell how deep the cuts are though." He looked at his hands. "Ew, what is this stuff?" He wiped the slime on the grass beside the stretcher.

"The creature drooled all over him," someone said.

"Uh oh. That could be bad. We'll get him on antibiotics. No telling what pathogens those things have in their mouths. It looks like his shoulder is dislocated and you guys were carrying him by his arms. Good thing he's unconscious or he couldn't have withstood the pain. Let's get him back."

Ron and Lucas each grabbed one end of the stretcher and they started off north. The others, all armed, fanned out ahead and behind. They were quickly learning that they could never, ever, let down their guard in this valley beyond the shelter.

As they entered the clearing with Micah, dozens of people surrounded them, all asking questions at the same time. "Hang on," Mark told them, "we need to get him to the doc. Then we can tell you what happened." He pushed through the crowd and through the open door as the team rushed into the building with the stretcher. A makeshift medical ward had been set up in the far left corner of the building and Dr. Jim and his nurse, Carmen, were arranging medical supplies alongside a bed. The men carrying Micah had to move down aisles between large shelving units to get to the back. They lifted Micah onto the bed and Dr. Jim put a screen between the bed and the crowd. Aaron scooted around the screen to help with the exam. "We'll examine him and let you know as soon as we can," he told Mark.

The crowd of people moved back to the front of the building which reminded Mark of a large wholesale, warehouse store with open metal beams at the top and the shelving stacked high with supplies almost to the ceiling. In addition to an open area in the center, there was a space just inside the doors with three long couches surrounding a square coffee table. The rescue party flopped down on the couches even though they were wet and dirty. They had been used to being so clean in the shelter, but they were too tired to care.

Ron starting filling everyone in about the rescue and Mark closed his eyes and leaned his head back against the cushion. He knew he should be doing something, but he was exhausted from the emotional morning at the funeral, and the physical tiredness resulting from the chase to get to Micah and the long trek back. He sat there thinking about their arrival at the camp yesterday and realized they had actually accomplished quite a bit since then.

When they arrived at the clearing, and saw the building against the trees at the far side of the meadow, Mark realized from the size of it that it must contain a huge amount of goods and supplies that they would need to survive. Glen Mitchell, the head caretaker of the shelter had moved to the front of the crowd and led them across the meadow to the front doors. They were unlocked and he just threw them open to allow everyone to enter. The outside temperature was in the low fifties and the parents were holding the children and hugging them to try and keep them warm. As soon as Glen entered the building he turned on a thermostat to warm the immense structure. Mark heard a motor start up and assumed it was a generator.

"Why aren't the doors locked?" Walter Thompson asked him.

"We had a camera at the entrance to the valley that we could monitor continuously, and there's a fence with a 'no trespassing' sign down there. Will owns this whole valley so we were aware if anyone came around. We didn't want it locked in case we had to exit the shelter in an emergency and no one had a key. Kate and Marilyn came out here once a week to check on things and to rotate the supplies."

They had all streamed into the structure and moved to the center of the building where there was an open space that accommodated the entire group. Glen stood on a box and called for attention. "It's going to take a while to warm up in here," he told them. "Over on aisle one there's shelves full of work shoes and boots. Since Will thought there would be more of us that made it to the shelter there should be plenty for everyone. There are all different sizes. The lightweight shoes we had in the shelter will fall apart out here. On the same shelf you'll find jeans and wool pants, long sleeved shirts and jackets. Everyone just go over there and get what you need. Don't take anything extra until we know what we have left. There's an outhouse on the west side of the building with solar toilets and showers. You will definitely need to take turns since we only have ten of each."

"How about the kids?" Lori Arnaud asked him.

"There are kids' shoes and clothing over there with the adults' stuff, and in the back corner, on the right, is a play area. Maybe the parents can leave the kids there and bring them warm clothes.

Some of the residents started toward the front left corner and others took the children to the back. Mark and twenty or so others approached Glen. "Where are we all going to sleep?" Jimbo Pierce asked him.

"After everyone is dressed more warmly we can get tents and set up a camp. We have sleeping bags, pads, lanterns and other equipment. Mark, do you want the kids and the injured to sleep inside?"

Mark once again realized he was still in charge without having asked for the job. The others were all looking to him for direction. He didn't fight it and began to give instructions. "Yeah, that's a good idea, Glen. I'll need to meet with you and the other permanent staff to find out what supplies we have here." He looked around for David and saw him standing at the back of the group with his big arms crossed.

"Hey David. Can you organize security? Inventory our weapons and ammo and get with Marilyn to see what they've stocked here."

"Sure, Mark. Do you want me to set out more sentries?"

"I'll leave that up to you, but we have no idea what's out here, and we know for damn sure what broke into the shelter." David gestured for Jimbo, who had occasionally helped him and Lenny in the Dojo, to follow him.

"I'll need a detail to retrieve Will's body for burial. I wish we could get the others, but the remaining creatures are locked in the shelter and we can't risk it."

Some of the other residents were returning, dressed in street clothes. The women had gone around to the far side of the shelf unit and changed there, and the men had all just stripped in the hallway and changed clothes without any modesty. Mark asked Tom Galloway, who stood six-foot three-inches, and Lucas James, who was the same height, to accompany him to the cave. Aaron, Chris and Gregory Whitehorse volunteered to go as well. They would use the gurney that Dr. Jim used to carry Sandy and her newborn daughter to the camp. The trail down from the cave was too rough to roll the gurney, but the wheels folded up and it could be carried.

"Glen, please get everyone busy setting up their tents." He waved over Kate Barkley. "Kate, can you get some people to prepare food? Almost no one had any breakfast and we're past lunch."

"Of course, Mark." Kate, always happy and accommodating giggled and hustled off toward the kitchen area.

During the afternoon the group slowly got organized as all the residents found warm clothes and decided where they would set up their tents. Most of the tents were two or three person backpacking tents that were easy to pitch and tie down. There were a couple of large ten man army tents that took several people to figure out how to pitch. These could sleep a group of single men or women. Now that they were busy accomplishing something, the mood of the group lightened up slightly. These were people that had already survived The Great War and had learned to cope in their new environment. Now they were forced out of the shelter prematurely and needed to adjust all over again, but Mark thought they were up to it.

Mark and the others took a linen body bag they located with the medical supplies, and headed back to the cave. Tom and Lucas carried rifles, as they had no idea what dangers there might be in this valley in addition to the creatures.

It was one of the hardest things Mark had ever done. He fought back tears the entire time and Chris wept openly.

They placed Will's body in the bag but decided to leave him in the cave. The small meadow on the opposite side of the river, between its south bank and the beginning of the forest, made a perfect graveyard. They would dig the grave in the morning and would only have a short distance to transport the body. Dejectedly, they returned to camp.

Things were running smoothly in the meadow. Tents were going up and people had plates of food. Some folks actually smiled at him and he felt his spirits lifting. The sun was shining brightly in the west and the sky was clear. He found Lori and the children inside the building and filled her in about their trip to the cave. She had set up canvas cots against the far left wall in the hallway and informed him that she and the kids would sleep inside. "It's warmer in here," she explained. "We'll move outside when we know how safe and secure it is and when the weather warms up."

"I'm glad. I'd prefer you guys stay in here. I'm going to pitch a tent but I'll stay here until time to turn in, if that's okay."

She smiled and assured him, "Of course it's okay." They hadn't had a chance to talk about the moment in the cave when he had told her he loved her. They would wait until they could be alone. The kids had been terrified of their encounter with the creatures in the shelter and Mark, sitting on the floor, his back against the wall, held first Ashley and then Kevin. Lori was at his side.

"You guys know Mommy saved you from the scary thing and we will always be here to protect you?"

Both children had nodded their heads but Mark knew they were far from convinced. They would feel safer staying the night in the building. The lights had been turned off to save fuel for the generator and after the children were asleep, Mark hugged Lori and kissed her for the very first time. She clung to him until he had to leave for his tent to spend the night.

The band of survivors had turned in early that first night. Mark felt naked sleeping in the tent without a weapon and he vowed he would get something the next day. They had assigned a few sentries to patrol the area but didn't realize how lucky they were to have had no problems that first night.

After the events of today, their second day outside, Mark knew they would have to increase their security, especially at night.

Having had a few minutes rest, the rescue party began to get up and move away. Mark went out to his tent, crawled in and immediately fell asleep.

***

Mark awoke after about an hour to someone calling his name. "Hey Mark, Dr. Jim wants you." Remaining still for a few minutes, to come fully awake, he then crawled from the tent into a light mist… all that was left of the morning's rain. He was almost as stiff as he'd been that morning, after sleeping on the ground all night. At thirty six, and used to a soft bed, the thin, thermo pad just didn't cut it. He was refreshed, though, from the brief nap. A shower and a shave would have felt great, but he'd been too busy for either of those luxuries. They would have to wait. His tent was about a hundred yards from the building and he quickly crossed the rocky ground, entered the structure and made his way to the medical area.

"Hi Doc. How's he doing?"

"Well, we had to cut away some of the flesh and disinfect the whole area. Then we sewed up the worst of the cuts and fixed his dislocated shoulder, but he's still unconscious. That concerns me. We have some I.V. supplies and he's getting antibiotics so I guess we just need to wait for him to come out of it."

"So what kind of supplies did you find here?" Mark looked around the screened off area and compared it, in his mind, to the well-equipped medical areas they'd had in the shelter.

Dr. Jim gestured at some cabinets along the side and back walls. "There are quite a few meds, but since we were in the shelter for eight months, many of them are getting close to expiration. That bookshelf over there contains books on surgery, general and internal medicine, and pediatrics. The thing is, they're mostly meant for non-medical personnel. I guess in case there were no experienced doctors and nurses. There's 'Where There is no Doctor' by Werner and 'Where There is no Dentist' by Dickson. That one's an old edition but since we don't have a dentist, it may come in handy."

"How about instruments?"

"It's all pretty primitive. We have stethoscopes and blood pressure cuffs and there's a laryngoscope and some other simple instruments. I feel very fortunate that we had good equipment in the shelter. You know… our people are pretty healthy and well-fed. Most of the folks worked out in the gym, lost weight and got fit. If there are other survivors out here, they probably aren't in as good a shape as we are. That's a definite advantage if we have any problems with them." He turned and lifted Micah's eyelid. "I feel like we got an eight month reprieve."

Mark sat on a stool and looked around the small med room. In the shelter they'd had an entire suite of exam rooms and a small lab and X-ray area. They had even had an operating room. "I guess we're lucky we have the stuff that's here." He stood up. "How about all the people that were injured when the shelter collapsed? Are they okay?"

"We pretty much got them patched up. There were two broken arms. One is Janet Spears and with Darian having a broken leg it really impacts that family. Al has his hands full, but there are plenty of folks wanting to help. Three concussions and a dislocated shoulder, and lots of cuts and abrasions. Only two that had to be sewed up. Johnny Jay has a badly twisted ankle but he'll be fine. Sandy and the baby are doing well and she's got Sarah and Pete looking after her. They're staying indoors."

"Okay, Jim. Thanks. Keep me informed and send someone after me if Micah wakes up."

"Sure Mark."

Mark started back toward the front of the building but he got bushwhacked by several individuals that wanted an update. He told a couple of them to round up the others and they would have a meeting before dinner. Thinking about the auditorium, where they'd held meetings in the shelter, he was reminded of how great it had been in their protected, artificial environment over the past eight months.

Life was about to get a lot harder.

Chapter 4

"I'm only going to ask you one more time!" The infuriated man backhanded Terry again, smashing his head sideways and spraying spittle and blood across his chest. Terry's hands were tied behind the back of the chair, the zip tie cutting into his wrists and impairing the circulation. Blood ran from his nose and the corner of his mouth, and his right eye was swollen shut. His right cheek was purple. The chair jounced backward, almost tipping over from the force of the blow. It had already moved backwards five feet from the repeated blows.

"Lay off him Clay. You're gonna kill him." Jinx grabbed Clay's arm to hold him back from another blow. Clay whirled and sucker punched Jinx in the abdomen, sending him to his knees.

"Who's in charge here?" He glared at the man on the floor.

"You are, Clay," he moaned through gritted teeth. "I'm sorry. But if he's dead, he can't tell us where they are. That's all." That calmed Clay down and he glanced at the man that had lost consciousness and had slumped in the chair.

"Get him out of the chair and chain him to the bed," he ordered the man who was standing in the corner watching the interrogation. Clay opened the front door and slammed it back against the wall. A blast of cold air blew in from the outside. Walking out into the bright, late morning sunlight he angrily kicked a scrawny dog that had been sleeping on the old wooden porch. The animal yelped and limped down the steps to the dead, brown grass. It slunk across the lawn, out through a gate that hung from a single hinge and down some old wooden steps to the street, its ears flattened against its head and its tail between its legs. The dog belonged to Jinx, and hung around the old house living on scraps thrown from the table, when the men took pity on it.

Clay never did. He was thinking about butchering it for food.

Monroe came out on the porch. "Ya know, Clay, he's never gonna to tell us where they're hidin'. We're just gonna have to search the whole damn town till we find 'em. Hell, with that Jeep they mighta even left town." He pulled out a battered pack of cigarettes and shook one out. He stuck it in his mouth and held out the pack to Clay. Clay shook his head. Monroe lit up and inhaled deeply, blowing smoke out of the side of his mouth.

"How many times do I have to tell you I don't smoke?" Clay asked him.

Clay Hargraves had been a fitness buff in the old days before the war. He was rich, didn't have to work and spent all his time having fun and working out. He and his many friends partied in the clubs at night and spent their days lounging on his dad's yacht. All his friends were rich as well, but their parents didn't have the billions that Will Hargraves had made in the defense industry. Clay was always surrounded by beautiful women... all hoping to be Mrs. Clay Hargraves.

Life was good until the fucking war! At twenty-eight he was still in great shape, if a little thin from lack of food. Yesterday was his birthday and if it hadn't been for the war his father would have given him a new car, a boat or some other expensive gift. He had lived in his dad's bomb shelter for six and a half months, and had only been forced to forage for food for the past six weeks.

Clay had been interested in one of the young women in the shelter, but his advances had been rejected. Sandy Baker was in a relationship with Pete Thompson and wanted nothing to do with Clay. He wasn't used to not getting what he wanted, and one day, coming upon Sandy in an isolated part of the shelter, he attempted to rape her. Interrupted by one of the other residents he was banished from the shelter by his own father.

He would kill him for that.

The other men in Clay's band, miners, had survived in a silver mine that had been stocked with food so they didn't have to go to town for meals. There were barrels of water but very little else. One man had been above in the work shed and heard about the war on the radio. No one believed him and they came above ground just in time to see the mushroom clouds blossoming in the south. Several of the men with families had wanted to go home, but except for one old Jeep, their cars wouldn't start. They all piled into the Jeep and headed north toward Red River where two of the men lived. The plan was to drop them off and return south to Cimarron, where the rest lived. Jinx, Monroe and the others never learned what became of them.

Those that stayed behind, scared shitless, had managed to stay underground until the food supply was exhausted and they were forced to exit the mine and return to town, just in time for winter. They had missed the worst of the radiation but some had become sick after a couple of weeks. They lost their hair in chunks and were violently ill. Most had scabrous, open wounds covering their bodies. But they eventually recovered. Of the nineteen miners that exited the mine, fourteen were still alive.

Four of the men had very strange reactions to the radiation. In varying degrees, once they were above ground and exposed, they had changed. Two had developed huge brows and foreheads and their torsos had actually lengthened, adding an inch or two to their height. Although their arms and legs had grown as well, it had been out of proportion to their torso, giving them a strange, unbalanced appearance. They also seemed to have changed mentally, were less intelligent, and were generally more aggressive. The others had known these men all their lives but were afraid and had become very uncomfortable around them. Clay would have killed them but their aggressiveness would be useful in an assault on the bomb shelter. The other two showed similar changes but to a lesser degree. They all seemed to worship Clay and did his every bidding. At least for now, he could control them.

And they all stank to high heaven!

The winter had been hell. They stayed indoors most of the time, which probably saved lives as it lessened the amount of radiation they received. The town was empty of people, except for a few bodies, and in the beginning the stores had plenty of food. They chose houses to live in, and raided the supermarket.

But it wasn't a large town and they gradually became aware that the supplies were diminishing and started to wonder what they would do when they ran out. Fortunately, there were cigarettes to last them a very long time. And alcohol. There were two liquor stores, three convenience stores, two bars and several restaurants. All had beer or hard liquor.

Then a couple of months ago, along came Clay Hargraves, riding a bicycle down from the north. He was obviously well-fed and told them of a bomb shelter with food, alcohol, and women. Clay and the leader of the group of miners, arguing about whether Clay could remain with them, got into a fight and Clay broke Hollister's neck with a twist of his powerful arms. Clay wasn't a big man, five-eleven, but was very strong. He was also arrogant and charismatic, and with Hollister gone, the others chose to follow him.

The bait and tackle shop in town sold rifles, and they were all armed and had plenty of ammo. At least they did for now... as they tended to get drunk and shoot their weapons into the air with very little provocation. Handguns were scarce, but Clay had found one in an old house on the hill behind town, along with several boxes of ammo and three full magazines. The weapon strengthened his position as leader. Although the house was old and in disrepair, it commanded a view of the entire town and he could see all the roads leading into town from every direction. It was perfect for his purpose.

If they just had more food and some women they could hold out a long time.

During the winter and early spring others had walked into town from the east; from Cimarron and beyond. All men, all rough. They told tales of living in basements or reinforced public buildings or even underground as the miners did. Most had come west due to gangs of even rougher men that had taken over towns they had come from. Their number had swollen to over forty.

No one had come from the west... from the direction of Los Alamos or Santa Fe. Two months ago a man rode into town on an old Indian motorcycle, running on fumes, its tank close to empty. Even so, Clay, who had only been their leader for one day, ordered them to ambush the rider and they shot him down in cold blood to get their hands on the bike. Without power, they hadn't figured out how to get gas from the underground tanks at the two service stations in town.

Jinx came out on the porch. "It's your turn again Clay. Jackson's finished."

Clay looked at Monroe. "Get some of the guys to form a search party. Tell them to be here at one o'clock. Let's find these SOB's before the afternoon rainstorm gets here."

The weather had been extreme ever since the war. In the beginning, the clouds had settled in, and the dust storms had lingered for months. The snow was deeper than the men had ever remembered and they almost froze to death. They chopped down trees, and even unoccupied houses to keep the fires burning. Spring was late. It was now May, and there were still patches of snow in areas protected from the unbelievable rainstorms they were having. Every day, sometimes starting in the morning, but more often in the afternoon, black clouds rolled in from the west, the skies darkened and the rains came. Occasionally it was just a drizzle, but most often it poured, along with crashing thunder and lightning that lasted for hours.

Terry regained consciousness to find himself, once more, chained to the railing of the old brass bed. The mattress was lumpy and smelled like mold. They had brought the bed from one of the bedrooms in order to keep him secured. He was having difficulty breathing and rolled onto his side to allow the blood and mucus to drain from his throat. Hanging his head over the side of the bed, he spat out huge blood clots onto the floor. Jinx jumped up from the couch and started toward him, but just then the door to the bedroom opened and one of his captors came out of the hallway, zipping his pants and grinning at Jinx.

Jinx was fifteen years older than Jackson or Monroe, his whiskers grey and white and his unruly, light brown hair was shot through with gray streaks. He was lean, with a lack of muscle tone, where Jackson, still in his mid-thirties, had jet black hair unevenly cut short, and he looked like an athlete. Monroe was average; height, weight and looks. Jinx had been their supervisor in the mine but in Clay's army they were all equal.

"She's a little tiger, that one." Jackson went through the door into the kitchen and Terry could hear the refrigerator door opening and the sound of a beer can opening.

He could also hear the sobs of his sixteen year old daughter coming from the bedroom off the hallway. Gritting his teeth, he tried to block it from his mind. But he recalled, and was tortured by, the botched episode that landed them in this house of degeneracy, prisoners to these madmen. He was terrified for the rest of his family.

After surviving the war by living in the basement of their home in Raton, New Mexico, the Holcomb family decided to get away from the town when it became progressively more dangerous. Heading south they took Interstate 25 and then headed west on Highway 64 into the mountains. They needed to find a place where they could build a cabin and hunt, fish and garden. They hoped to find a spot up around Eagle Nest Lake where Terry and the kids had gone fishing on several occasions.

Barreling through Cimarron to avoid any confrontation, they easily outdistanced a half-hearted pursuit and it was a mile later before they realized nine year old Kristen had been shot. Riding in the far back of the Jeep, a bullet had penetrated the wall and grazed her hip. She had been so excited during the she chase, she didn't notice it until the pain started.

"Mommy!" she screamed, and started to cry. "I think they shot me. There's blood all over!"

"Oh God. Terry, pull over."

He swung the Jeep onto an overgrown, side road where Izzy stripped off Kristen's pants and examined the wound. Cody, Melissa and Marci provided cover.

"How bad is it?" Terry asked anxiously.

"It looks like it grazed her hip. It didn't penetrate far." She sounded very relieved. "I'll clean it up and dress it but we don't have any antibiotics left."

It was now dark and they spent a long, cold night on the spur road, since they weren't in a location to set up a proper camp. Terry, Izzy, Marci and Cody slept on the ground, with Melissa and Kris each sleeping on one of the seats. The adults and Cody each pulled a three hour watch. They hadn't come far from Cimarron when Kristen had noticed the blood, and they worried they'd been followed.

The next morning they finished the trip to Eagle Nest and as they approached the town they went off road, drove past the north shore of the lake and continued west, hoping they hadn't been observed.

But their luck had run out. From his vantage point on the porch Clay saw them come over the hill toward town. He tried to follow their movements, but they hadn't stayed on the main road and he lost sight of them as they drove around the lake and over the hill to the west. But looking through his binoculars he had seen a woman in the front seat and one or two more people in the back. It looked like at least four and maybe five family members.

During their trip south, when they needed supplies, Terry and his oldest daughter Marci had foraged in empty, outlying houses and in tiny towns. Cody and Izzy stayed with the Jeep to protect Melissa and Kristen. It worked well and the family members were very good at moving stealthily. So far, they hadn't run into any problems.

Until now. They had hoped to find some food, ammo and medical supplies in Eagle Nest. Izzy used some disinfectant on Kristen's wound but she worried about infection and they were out of antibiotics. Terry hoped to find some in town.

Izzy held him close and whispered, "Please be careful and don't take any chances. I love you so much."

"Don't worry Iz. Remember that if we don't get back by morning, you guys head for the high country. Find a place to make a home. I love you."

"You'll be back, or else, Mister." She swatted him on the arm and smiled through tears. She turned to Marci and gave her a hug.

He and Marci waited until midnight, to allow anyone in town to go to sleep, and then left the others and hiked almost three miles to get to the outskirts of town. Terry used his binoculars to scan around and look for lights. Everything looked clear and they scampered from building to building with their handguns held ready.

But Clay was ready for them and had laid down an ambush. When Terry and Marci rounded the corner of a small market they were waylaid by twenty men. They didn't stand a chance.

"Drop the guns or we'll shoot you both," came a voice out of the darkness. Terry dropped his gun and screamed for his daughter to run.

"Marci. Go!" He threw himself into a group of men, bowling them over, trying to clear a path, but Marci was grabbed and thrown to the ground. Men surrounded Terry and he was punched and kicked until they managed to get his hands tied behind his back with a zip tie. He felt sick as he realized the enormity of what had happened. Coming into town had been a huge mistake on his part, knowing what was going to happen and being powerless to stop it. He could only hope the rest of his family would go on and find a place to survive. Cody and Izzy were tough and competent.

Now he was lying in this filth, injured and unable to help Marci.

Jinx went out the front door and a minute later Clay reentered the house. Jackson had lit a cigarette and Clay slapped it out of his hand. "Get the hell out of the house with that thing." Jackson picked up the cigarette and stepped on the ember that had fallen from it.

"Tell Jinx to get back in here and watch this asshole." He walked over to Terry and stood with his arms folded. "I really want that Jeep, buddy. Tell us where the rest of your family is and I will leave your sweet little thing alone. And I'll make sure the others don't mess with her anymore either."

Thinking of his wife and two younger daughters, Terry said, "No, you'll just rape the others instead." His voice sounded nasally through his broken nose.

"Yeah, but then there's more to go around. Right now your little girl is getting quite a workout." He jumped back as Terry tried to kick him, but Terry was hurt and Clay was quicker. He laughed at Terry. "Well then, time for some sweetness."

Terry struggled to loosen the ties that bound his wrists but they were so tight they dug into his flesh. The chain that looped through them and the bedpost cut into his side. As the bedroom door closed tears coursed down his cheeks and he closed his eyes. But he could still hear what went on in the next room.

Clay went into the bedroom and found that Marci had slunk down in the corner behind the bed. She was nude but had pulled the sheet down over her. He walked around the bed and grabbed the sheet. "Don't cover up like that, sweet thing. If you want this to be over, tell me where the others are." She looked up, glaring at him with hate in her eyes.

"Go to hell!" She snapped at him. He reached down and grabbed her by arm and lifted her to the bed. She spit at him and tried to knee him in the groin, but he turned and blocked the blow.

Then he took his turn.

Chapter 5

Earlier that morning, dawn had erupted out of the east in a brilliance of color, long shafts of pink and gold illuminating the valley and turning the lake from black to greenish-blue. Cody was on guard, rifle at the ready, eyes scanning the town from his perch on the hill. His father and sister were late. He gritted his teeth so hard his jaw ached and he was on the verge of tears. A boy and a man, eighteen years old, his emotions were all over the place as he wracked his brain trying to figure out what went wrong.

Izzy lifted the edge of the camo cover they had thrown over the jeep. She walked down the wash and into the bushes with a roll of toilet paper and an AK-47. There were only three rolls of TP left. A minute later she re-emerged, went back around their vehicle and climbed to the vantage point from which she had watched through the night, and where her son now hid behind a large, rock outcropping. She had a vicious headache from straining all night to see through the darkness. Lit only by a crescent moon, she had looked for any movement that would indicate her husband and daughter were returning. She thought she heard a shout about fifty minutes after Terry and Marci had left and was almost sick from the constant anxiety. When Cody relieved her around 4 a.m., she returned to the Jeep, but was unable to sleep.

"No sign of them?" She asked him as she raised binoculars to her eyes and scanned the town for any movement.

"No Mom, nothing. What do you think happened?"

"I think someone saw us come into town, and they caught them. I guess we should have waited 'til dark, but they would have heard our engine and known we were here anyway. Your Dad waited until midnight to go into town so he thought it would be okay. I… I guess we should have just kept going. We have enough supplies." Tears spilled over and ran down her cheeks. "We had such an easy time of it in the other places where we found supplies. This town is bigger. We should have known there might be survivors. There must be quite a few of them or they wouldn't have been able to take your Dad. We just took too many chances."

"Well, I'm going after them!" He whirled back to face the town.

"Wait a minute, Cody." She put her hand on his arm. "Let's not make any more mistakes. We need to think this over."

They heard a noise behind them and Melissa climbed up the hill to their position.

"I can watch for a while if you want. Kris is still asleep." She rubbed sleep from her dark eyes and peeked around the rocks at the town. "Why aren't they back Mom?"

"I don't know Mija. They must have run into trouble. It would be great if you could spell us, so we can talk about it. Okay?"

"Uh huh." She took the binoculars from her mother.

Izzy and Cody gingerly made their way back down the slope to their car.

They each ate a breakfast bar and a couple of pilot crackers with peanut butter, and drank a cup of water from the five gallon jug Izzy had placed on a rock by the vehicle.

"Your Dad wanted us to forget about them and go on, but I just can't do that without trying to find out what happened."

"I'll go into town and find them," Cody said. "You guys can wait until I signal you and then drive like crazy to get us. Then we head for the hills."

"Cody, I can't let you go alone. This is what we're going to do. We'll go together and reconnoiter. If we can find them we will try and get them out, but we have to wait until dark or we won't have a prayer."

"Mom, that's crazy! We don't know what they're doing to them. That's a whole day. They could be dead by then!"

Izzy had a feeling she knew what was happening to them, but she couldn't risk the rest of her family. "Look, we have no idea how many of them there are. We can't get killed or captured or the girls will be on their own. Missy can drive this thing, and they can come after us if we find Dad and Marci. We won't take any chances. We'll take our time and sneak in, and if it looks too dangerous we'll have to abandon the search and go on without them. We have to think of the young ones."

Cody knew she was right, but he stood there with a stubborn look on his face. He grabbed his rifle and stormed away, back up the hill to where his sister watched the town.

Izzy walked down the wash and around a rock where she slumped down on the ground, her back to the rock, and bawled like a baby. When she went back to the Jeep, Melissa and Kris were eating their breakfast and looking scared. Kris limped over to the bushes with the TP. "Go get Cody," she told Missy. "We need to talk."

When Missy and Cody came down the hill, and Kris had returned, they sat down on rocks that filled the wash alongside the car. They had tied the camouflage car cover down to these rocks.

"Okay, here's the deal." She looked at her children and almost couldn't go on. "I think Dad and Marci have been captured or they would have been back by now. Honey, please don't cry." She turned to Kris who had begun to sniffle. "We have to be tough. Tonight, after dark, Cody and I are going to sneak into town and see if we can find them. Now don't be scared. We absolutely won't take any chances. We will come back to you for sure. Missy, you will be on guard and if you see three flashes from the flashlight, you drive over this hill and along the left side of the town. The highway runs north. Get on the road and don't leave it."

"What if you never come back? What will me and Kris do? We'll be all alone!" Her eyes were huge and she twisted her T-shirt in her hands.

"We will come back. Don't worry. We won't get caught cause we're going to be real careful. When you see the signal, go north on the road. We'll come out to the road whether we have them or not. If we don't show up, drive a little farther north on the highway and wait until morning. Honest, honey, we'll try so hard to meet you, but if something terrible happens just go north to Red River. Find some people to stay with." Then they all broke down, including Cody, and they held on to each other in the bottom of the wash while the sun broke above the ridge and spilled over them.

Izzy rubbed the tears from her eyes and told Missy to go back up the hill. She could finish her watch and Izzy would take over for a few hours. She didn't want anyone to get too tired and let down their guard. Kris would stand guard for the dinner hour and Cody would finish up until midnight. Then they would go after her husband and child.

They were far enough from town that Izzy felt safe. She didn't think the townspeople had any vehicles and they wouldn't come way out here looking for them anyway, when they could just wait for them to come into town looking for their family. Izzy had to try and find them, but she intended to come back to the girls. She knew neither she nor Cody could live with themselves if they didn't at least try.

Around noon Cody came down the hill and ducked under the camo to lie down on the back bench of the Wrangler. She still couldn't sleep and checked on Missy periodically during the day. When Kris went up the hill, Izzy fixed some dehydrated Alfredo and peas and they tried to eat.

After cleaning up, they removed the camo, storing it in the box that was strapped to the roof rack. Cody relieved Kris and Izzy laid down in the Jeep. She honestly didn't think she would sleep but she was exhausted and soon fell into a troubled slumber.

***

Mark sat on the box in the middle of the building and watched as the residents gathered. Most came in from outside but the Thompsons had been over in the aisle that had been blocked off with sheets for Sandy and the new baby. He talked with Lori about their adventure that morning, rescuing Micah from the hellish creature. Some folks were over at the kitchen area starting to prepare dinner. He could see Rana Patel, Sarah Thompson, Helen and Ernest and several others. The kids, including Ashley and Kevin, were all back in the childcare corner. When everyone seemed to be there he stood up on the solid wooden box and waited for the room to quiet. Most of the Remnant sat cross legged on the floor, but twenty or so had found metal folding chairs and camp chairs on one of the shelving units and were sitting in a ring around the others. Quite a few stood around the edge.

"I guess it's time to meet and make some plans for the future," Mark began. "First of all, Dr. Jim thinks Micah will be fine but he's still unconscious. Jim will keep us updated on his condition. It's hard to believe, with everything going on, that we've only been out of the shelter for just over thirty hours."

"What about the monster?" Tucker asked.

"Well, we fired at it and I think we hit it, but it escaped up the hill and back onto the ridge. I'm sure it was the one that almost got me in the shelter, which means it found a way out. It seems almost indestructible. After all, I shot it with a 12 gauge shotgun, at close range, and it just kept coming."

"Yeah," Lori chimed in, "but I was able to kill two of them. So if we hit them with enough lead we can kill them."

"How many do you think there are?" Jimbo asked squinting up at Mark. He hadn't been with them in the power plant when they first came upon the creatures. When an earthquake disabled one of the elevators with Sandy Thompson in it, he had been one of the men that helped Pete get her out.

"We killed one in the power plant, and I don't know, but it looked like there were another half dozen or so. Maybe more."

"I thought it looked like more," said David. "I saw more than that when they got Lenny." During the battle with the creatures in the power plant, David's best friend Lenny, had been ripped to pieces. "But I don't care how many of them there are… I'm going to find and kill every one of the sons-of-bitches." There were murmurs from the crowd and many of them looked very frightened. Very few of the residents had actually seen the creatures; those that had battled them in the power plant and the people that had fled from them in the farm cave. But everyone had heard the stories of the battle and the flight to this valley.

"What do think those things are, Mark?" Ted asked.

"I'm not sure, but I think they were men. Somehow, the radiation affected them and they mutated into those creatures."

Ted's wife Beth asked, "Do you think everyone that was exposed has turned into a monster? That would be horrid!"

"God, I hope not," Mark said. "What do you think Terry? Is that a possibility?" Terry, a biochemist, had studied human evolution.

"I guess it's possible, but maybe there was something in their biochemistry that caused them to change, or evolve, or even devolve. Something about their DNA maybe."

"They devolved alright," Beth added. "They're Devols!" That brought a few chuckles from the crowd.

"Well," Mark said, "I really hope there are other people out there that are normal."

"We know there are normal people out there." This came from James Bascomb. He was one of the men that had been a member of the control room team, a communications expert and one of several African-Americans in the group. "We had a message from NORAD. They sounded completely normal."

"Yeah, but they were underground. These Devols may have been caught outside and became irradiated," Terry said.

"We have to assume that more of them escaped the shelter, and make sure that our security is beefed up. Especially since so many of us are sleeping outside in tents." Mark looked around as people realized the implication of that statement.

"Damn," someone called out, "I'm moving inside!" Several others echoed that sentiment and Mark held up his hands for quiet.

"I guess anyone that really feels like they need to, can move inside, but you'll have to just move your cot or sleeping bags into this open space or in the aisles. It could get pretty crowded. I think with enough sentries we should be able to keep everyone safe. The tents are all in the open meadow, away from the trees. One of the things we'll have to deal with is to get a hunting party together to try and hunt those things down. I'll never really feel safe until we get them all. "

"So what happens now?" Ted Wright asked him. "We can't live in this building forever. We need to decide whether we stay here or move on."

Lucas spoke up. "I don't think there's any question about leaving. We need to create a community so we can grow food and build places to live. What do you think you'll find out there? Civilization is gone." Discussions started up throughout the crowd and Mark had to quiet them again.

"Let me have Marilyn give us an idea of what we have here and what Will's ideas were for our next steps."

He stepped down and Marilyn Simmons stepped up on the box. Kate Barkley moved to the front and sat her chair a few feet from Marilyn. They had been two of the seven permanent staff members Hargraves had hired to manage the shelter. Marilyn was in her forties and on the slim side unlike fifty-two year old Kate, who was a little overweight even after being in the shelter for eight months. Exercise wasn't Kate's thing but Marilyn was regularly seen in the gym.

"Will had this storage building constructed to serve as a half-way house so to speak," she began. "The original plan was to live in the shelter for about a year, until the radiation diminished, and then through the nuclear winter, depending on what time of the year we had to take up residence. There was really no data to go on as to how long the radiation or the atmospheric effects would last, especially since it looks like the Chinese used weapons that created an unknown type of radiation. It looks like the radiation levels are quite safe now, at least in this valley, but the winter has continued due to the dust and clouds thrown into the atmosphere. The temperatures were well below normal throughout the winter, and although it doesn't seem too bad now, the trees are still completely bare and we may still get frost. And it's May already.

"The idea was, that the supplies in this building and in the shelter would allow us to get a good start on building our own new civilization. You've all noticed the posters on the walls. They're laminated and contain instructions for skills we're going to need. Most of you learned a lot while we were in the shelter, but we didn't get to practice much at things like candle making, tanning hides or making soap. Now we're going to have to put that knowledge to use. Will thought we would have access to the shops, supplies, electricity, books and other stuff from the shelter but that's no longer an option. The books we have here and these supplies are all we have."

Again the crowd became restless, asking questions all at once. "This place is crammed to the rafters. What is all this stuff?" someone called out.

"We tried to brainstorm about what we would need but I'm sure we forgot half of it." Marilyn told him. "Because of the type of lightweight clothing we had in the shelter, we knew we would need clothes, jackets and shoes. You've all been issued those already, as well as sleeping supplies. The lumber stacked back by the medical area is for flooring in the cabins. It's hard to cut flat pieces of wood from the trees. We can use logs to build the sides and roofs. We need to dig clay if we can find it, or mud, and make wattle and daub to fill the cracks in the cabins we make. There are cottonwoods and willows by the lake at the south end of the valley and their branches can be used for this. We have a limited number of bags of concrete and buckets of nails. There are metal joist holders and other metal parts to use in construction. In the future, we'll have to learn to build without these items but, again, the supplies here are to help us in the transition." She turned to her co-worker, "Can you explain about the food supplies, Kate?"

"Of course." She stood and addressed the crowd. "Just like in the shelter, we have the entire basement of this building stocked with five gallon buckets of dehydrated food. We have enough heirloom seeds to plant acres and acres of crops, and since they're not hybrids, we'll be able to save the seeds for next year."

"Wait!" David exclaimed. "There's a basement? Why didn't you tell us? That's important for security. Where's the entrance?"

"It's in that walled off area in the front corner. There's an outside entrance too. The outer doors have been covered over with dirt since we didn't think we needed to go in that way anymore and we wanted the doors hidden for security. Remember, we never really believed there would be a war. The basement is just a big open area with support beams and a dirt floor, and it has a lot more supplies. The food's down there because the temperature is better for food storage. It's easier to regulate the temp than in this big open building. This structure is the kind they use for horse arenas. As big as it is, we had so much stuff we wanted to stock, that we needed more room. You're right Dave, if we needed to, people could go below for safety."

She gestured to the immense storage units. "All the shelving up here has those side beams that kept the supplies from coming down in the earthquakes. Downstairs some of the stuff fell over and we'll have to clean it up. I just haven't had time. Our farming equipment is down there. One important thing is that we get our crops going as soon as possible since we may not get a very long growing season. We need to lay in food for next winter. Like we did in the shelter, we'll try and stretch our stored food by using the stuff we grow." She giggled and sat down.

"You know Kate," Mark told her, "You don't have to feel like you have to do everything yourself. We have plenty of people to help you clean the basement."

"I know, Mark. It's just that the seven of us were here by ourselves for so long that we don't think to ask."

Marilyn stood again. "The theory behind all this is to have supplies to transition us to a lifestyle using completely natural products. For example, we have the clothing you have all been issued and then we have materials to make clothing. After that, we actually have animal hides and bone needles to teach us to make clothing from animal skins." She looked over at Mark.

"Another example is our power. We have a generator and two underground gas tanks with stabilized fuel. There's another tank with diesel fuel. We have solar panels, but the storage batteries usually only last around eight years. The propane tanks run the heaters for this building and we use it for cooking. When it's gone we will use old fashioned fireplaces. We have materials to make candles, we have lanterns and oil lamps. We'll have to learn to make oil from natural materials. We can use logs for houses and God knows there are enough rocks out there to use for construction. Anyway, that's the theory behind this building."

"Marilyn, are there any more weapons?" David asked her.

"We have sheaths and knives for everyone. There's a small weapon's locker downstairs, and boxes of ammo. Will was the one that stocked the rifles and handguns so I'm not sure what's there." She looked over to Mark and he once again stood up on the box.

"Hey Mark. I know where we can get more weapons," Darryl Washington called out. "There are still quite a few left in the vault in the Crow's Nest."

The crowd quieted as they digested this information. Tom Galloway said, "Are you kidding me, Darryl? How would we get in? Those things might still be in there." Tom had never been to the control room and didn't know its layout.

"There's a tunnel that goes from the outside to the alcove just below the control room. The weapon's locker is in the alcove and since Micah got out through the tunnel, it must not have caved in. The staircase to the alcove from the shelter collapsed so the beasts can't get to the alcove."

"He's right," Mark told the crowd. "But we know the Devols are outside the shelter, on the ridge where the outside entrance to the alcove is. Let's inventory the weapons many of you brought from the shelter and see what's in the box downstairs. Then we can evaluate the need for the ones still in the shelter."

"I'm keepin' my rifle!" Jimbo said.

"We're not going to take the arms that you guys already have. We just want to know what's available, that's all." Mark reassured Jimbo and the others that still had the guns they brought from the shelter.

The building began to shake and people looked around nervously. One woman screamed and several people dropped to the floor. This aftershock seemed larger than the previous ones they'd felt since leaving the shelter.

"Hang on everybody." Greg Whitehorse, a geologist, tried to calm them. "There are bound to be more of those but they've been diminishing in frequency and intensity. They're just aftershocks."

Mark had just stood there not reacting to the quake. He thought of "L.A. Story" with Steve Martin, where the Californian's didn't notice the quake and the mid-westerners were freaking out.

He again raised his arms to quiet everyone down. "Come on guys, we need to address these issues. We need to get together some groups to accomplish specific goals. David is in charge of security and Chris will be in charge of food production, including traditional farming and any way we can use modern techniques."

"Wait a second, Mark." He was interrupted by Lucas, who jumped to his feet and looked around at the crowd. "I don't mean to be disrespectful but I'm wondering why you're in charge. Will's gone. I think some of us may have different ideas about how we should do things."

When the survivors had entered the shelter and Will had held the very first meeting in the auditorium, Lucas had questioned the benefit of modern technology and what good it had done them. He thought they should rely much less on it in their new environment. Will had pointed out that they had no choice in the matter, that their technology was already gone, destroyed in a matter of hours.

Mark stared at him in disbelief. "Seriously, Lucas? You want to do this now? We have some pretty important things to worry about. Government and 'who's in charge' nonsense can wait until we're secure and have a good start on making a safe community. Then we can elect a leader, committees, or whatever."

"You know, that's what they all say and then the elections never happen," he bristled.

Chris Hargraves had been sitting on the floor with Aaron's arm around her. She jumped to her feet and glared at Lucas. "My father owned this entire valley, this building and all these supplies! With civilization gone, the laws of property may change. But for now, as far as I'm concerned, it all belongs to me! Mark's right. We need to accomplish some important tasks first and then I'm willing to defer to the community about how we're going live and govern. At that time we can decide about those other things, like do we use barter or a medium of exchange? We need to decide whether we give away all this stuff to the residents, or make them purchase it, so we can pay for, say, our security guards or whatever. Or what form our government will take and who will be our leaders. All that stuff can wait!"

Walter Thompson stood at the back of the crowd, dressed in jeans and a denim shirt. He shouted out, "I nominate Mark Teller for our temporary CEO!"

Several others shouted out, "second!"

Walter added, "Any other nominations?" Lucas glanced at a few of the others sitting around him but they all remained silent.

"All for Mark?" Walter threw his arm in the air. Almost one hundred percent of the crowd raised their hands. Mark's eyes met Walter's and Walter smiled and gave a brief nod.

"I guess that settles it," Mark said. "I'll compile a list of people to head up groups to handle different chores and I'll meet with all of them tomorrow. Let's get some dinner." He stepped off the box and several of the others patted him on the back. He walked over to Lori and hugged her. "I didn't expect that so soon but it was bound to happen sooner or later." They started back toward the chow line when Chris and Aaron joined them.

"Thanks for that, Chris."

"Not a problem, Mark. You ran a multi-billion dollar company. I guess you can lead a rag-tag group of survivors for a while." She flashed him a smile. "You're the best man to lead us right now."

They joined the line of people getting plates that were filled with dehydrated Chicken Teriyaki and vegetables, pilot crackers and canned fruit. "Thanks Helen." Mark accepted his plate from the woman that had been a domestic worker for Will Hargraves for many years. Mark had known her since he was ten years old. "Wow," he told Chris, "You'd better get the garden going. This could get old in a hurry."

They found a place to sit and had just begun to eat when the deafening gunfire of large caliber rifles erupted from behind the building. Everyone that had a weapon grabbed it, and putting down their plates, stampeded for the door with all the others right behind them.

The gunfire continued as they rounded the building to see a half dozen men firing wildly into the forest. The cattle were bawling, rolling their eyes in fear, as they stampeded around the corral. In the second corral the sheep and goats screamed and the hogs, huddled in the corner of the third corral were making an earsplitting noise that Mark hardly recognized as being porcine. He worried the flimsy, temporary corrals would fall if they didn't get the animals under control. Mark could hardly see for the dust clouds.

"Ted! Can you try and calm them down?" he yelled to the veterinarian. Ted and Beth started talking to the animals in a crooning voice that seemed to help, but it was still too dangerous to enter the corrals. David ran up to one of the men and grabbed his rifle.

"Stop firing! You're wasting ammo."

"Oh man, it was one of those things!" The sentry cried out. "It grabbed a goat right out of the corral. We never saw or heard it coming. Man, it could have been one of us!"

"What the hell are you guys doing here?" Jimbo said to the other guards.

"We were trying to help Kyle and Al."

"Well get back to your posts! There may be more of them."

The other men ran off in the gathering darkness toward the west and north.

"Shit, David. Those guys need a lot more training and discipline or we're in trouble," Jimbo told Cunningham.

Mark looked around at the crowd hovering in the background. "Everybody that's unarmed get back into the building. The rest of you fan out around the camp and make sure it's secure."

They searched the entire forest surrounding the camp but found no further evidence of the creature. It had stolen the goat and made its escape.

By the time they'd regrouped at the corrals, the husband and wife veterinarians had calmed the animals and David was assigning additional men to patrol the perimeter. "We need to move some of the tents so they're more concentrated in front of the building and away from the edge of the woods. Mark, can you find out who's moving inside and have them take down their tents for now?"

When they had pitched the tents the previous afternoon they'd spread them out for privacy, but now for safety Mark had them move in closer. In the gathering darkness he stood under the porch and watched flashlights moving around the meadow. He'd already moved his own tent closer. With additional sentries and a smaller perimeter he felt they should be safe. They set up emergency lights behind the corrals at the forest's edge, running off storage batteries and they hoped they wouldn't need to run a generator and use their precious fuel.

Entering the building, he went to the aisle where Lori had set up cots for the kids. She had a thermal pad and sleeping bag on the floor beside them.

"Hi, Mark." She slipped her arms around him and laid her head on his shoulder. "How can we ever be safe from those things?"

"We can hunt them down and exterminate them, that's how! I just can't believe, if there are any people left out there, that they're all like that. It's way too horrible to contemplate. Tomorrow we'll have to relocate the corrals to the center of the meadow. When Will had them built and put in this building against the woods he could never have imagined those creatures."

They sat on her sleeping bag and talked like they used to in the reservoir cave, and an hour later the power to the building was shut down. Quite a few people had chosen to move indoors and they could hear other hushed conversations in the dark. Mark was content being here with Lori and the kids and when he said goodnight to head outside to his tent, Lori held him, and pulled him down on her sleeping bag to stay with them for the night.

Chapter 6

Izzy was dreaming of the day she met Terry Holcomb. He came into the dentist's office for a teeth cleaning, and kept coming back to have other work done, work that he had put off for years, just so he could see more of her. Eventually, he had asked her out and they had been inseparable ever since. Terry had been a marine and considered himself a man's man. He and his buddies backpacked and hunted and didn't have much time for women... until he met Isobel.

He was hooked for life.

She dreamed of their wedding in Albuquerque with forty members of her extended Hispanic family in attendance. They started their family right away and the kids kept coming until he panicked and had a vasectomy. Izzy's older sisters both had five kids and her brother six! The two older Holcomb kids had their father's blonde hair, although they had dark eyes. Several of Izzy's relatives had blonde hair from a Spanish heritage. The younger two girls took after their mother, with masses of dark curls and dark eyes.

Her family had survived the war by being prepared. Isobel Oliveras Holcomb and her husband Terry were "preppers." They both believed there was going to be an economic collapse that would bring civilization to its knees and create a societal nightmare. Living in Raton, New Mexico, they figured it wouldn't be as bad as in the big cities. Nevertheless, they had purchased food and supplies to last a year, for the two of them, their seventeen year old son, and their daughters, sixteen, fourteen and nine. Both parents worked hard to provide for the family, with Izzy working full-time as a dental hygienist and Terry owning a heavy construction company.

Their lives were full, with work and raising four kids. Terry coached soccer for Kristen, and Izzy hauled Missy to volleyball practice. Cody had a new car and a girlfriend, and Marci was in the drama club. They were a typical American family... except they practiced survival skills and prepared for the end-of-the-world-as-they-knew-it. They were prepared for the worst, and then went about their otherwise very normal lives.

They had a modest home with a large basement and an acre of land, and practiced gardening and survival skills in their backyard. They could start fires with a magnesium flint, sneak quietly in the dark, and all of them had attended a four day rifle course at Front Sight Firearms Training Institute in Nevada, combining it with a family vacation to Las Vegas. They went to the local firing range regularly and were proficient with rifles, shotguns and handguns. They thought they were ready for anything... anything but a nuclear war.

They heard the news on the radio last August, and following their pre-made plan, Izzy had picked up the two younger daughters, and Cody drove Marci home from their high school where he had just started his senior year and she her sophomore year. Terry arrived home to find them in the basement tacking plastic sheeting over the windows and filling the bathtub in the basement full of water. The window wells had slatted covers and Terry went up and locked them down. They all took their potassium iodide tablets and settled down to wait. Raton is halfway between Denver and Albuquerque and they never saw or heard any bombs, but when the power went out and the radio went dead, they knew it had really happened.

Part of their prepping had included plans to rely on their neighborhood and local community to set up security, share gardening and provide companionship. Now, all of that was completely out the window as they realized people who hadn't prepared would die from radiation poisoning. Surviving a nuclear war was very different than surviving other apocalyptic disasters. There was no opportunity to use their outdoor garden and Terry chafed at the thought that he couldn't keep an eye on his truck he'd stored in a grounded garage.

They had an eight square-foot, raised garden on one side of the basement where the light was best. It produced very little greens but they relished the miniscule harvest when they consumed it on several occasions.

In the beginning, people had come and knocked on their door. Operational security had been difficult with four children. Kids have trouble keeping secrets and they talked about the family's preps and told friends that they were armed and prepared for the worst.

The first time someone came they huddled together, quieting the kids and hoped the person or persons would leave. "Who is it, do you think?" Izzy whispered to Terry. He had recognized the voice calling out to them. It was the neighbors from across the street, their best friends. When he told her she moaned, "Oh God, Terry, what can we do?"

"How many times did we try to get them to prepare?" he asked angrily. "They always laughed at us."

"Terry, we know you're in there!" Max Kramer shouted down the window well at the front of the house. "Come on man, let us in! We're out of food. Think of our kids!"

They remained quiet, thinking of their own kids. Suddenly they heard the sound of breaking glass and realized Max had broken the window beside the door. They heard footsteps and the door at the top of the basement stairs was thrown back.

Terry stepped up the three steps to the landing and looked to the right, up the staircase. He pointed his shotgun at the man, woman and two children that had started down the stairs.

"Don't come any farther Max," he warned.

"What the hell, Terry. We'll die up here!"

"You know Max, we tried to get you guys to prepare but you never did. I can't risk my family. There's some food in the hall closet upstairs. Take it and get out. We had planned to help our neighbors if something happened and they weren't prepared, like you guys, but a nuclear war changes everything. So, please, take it and go. It's all we can spare." He gestured with the shotgun.

Ginny started to cry, "You can't just let us die. We're your friends!"

"I'm sorry, Ginny, but there's no more we can do." He noticed Max's hair was thinning and he and Ginny had sores on their faces. The children were hidden behind their parents, but he knew they too had been exposed. He took a risk and went part way up the stairs, whispering to Max, "Max, listen to me. You've been exposed for over a week. You guys are dead already. Take the food and go. There's some meds; anti-nausea stuff, and pain meds. Go home. Feed your family, if they can eat, and keep them comfortable." He fought back tears as he realized what he was saying.

Ginny heard what he said to Max, and was so shocked she grabbed Max's arm and pulled him back upstairs. Izzy heard hurried footsteps and a few minutes later, the hall closet door slam. Had it been just an economic collapse they had intended to take care of neighbors and establish a community for mutual protection. They stocked extra food for charity.

But not now... everything had changed.

He backed down into the basement where Izzy and Kris were crying.

"Daddy, can't they stay? Jodie's my very best friend," Kris wailed.

"Honey, they took some food and they're going home. We'll try to see them later, when it's safe." He saw the truth, though, in the eyes of the older children and his wife. They knew what he did was necessary.

They hastily tacked up more plastic over the opening to the stairs. Later, Terry rushed upstairs and closed the door.

They had cooking and heating equipment but couldn't take a chance using it with all the windows covered and no air circulation, so they ate cold rations for a while. They cracked the windows each day to allow air in and were deathly afraid they were letting in a poisonous atmosphere. But no one showed symptoms of radiation sickness. The MRE's, meals-ready-to-eat, had small individual heating packs. When they had been eaten, Izzy took a chance to heat water for their dehydrated meals using a propane stove, but she had to pull back the plastic on one of the windows when the carbon monoxide detector went off.

After a month Izzy took the propane stove to the top of the stairwell, hoping the interior of the house would help to protect her from radiation. They beat themselves up for not considering nuclear war and having a device to monitor radiation, although they thought it might be better not to know.

Staying in the basement for months had taken its toll. They cried for lost friends and family and for a world and country that would never be the same. They played family games, read books, including their survival skill's books, and watched movies on the I Pad until the storage batteries all went dead and they couldn't charge it any longer. They didn't dare run the gennie for fear of attracting more attention. They exercised and tried to stay in shape but they had all lost weight and were suffering appetite fatigue from eating such a limited diet.

There had been several shouting matches and one knock-down fight between Marci, the sixteen year old and Melissa, the fourteen year old. Terry was aware that they couldn't continue the way they had been living, so he took a chance and went upstairs to see if he could tell what was going on.

After a week, when he didn't become ill they started going upstairs more often. By staying in the basement they hadn't been bothered by others since that first week or two. Now, with activity at their house, it became known that they survived, and had supplies. They were in danger from the few people that were left alive in town.

There was no longer a question of whether these few were good or bad. Starving people would do anything to get food for themselves or their family. None even pretended to be friendly. They attacked without provocation, trying to get their hands on the food and supplies. Terry, Izzy and the children fired from the upstairs windows and drove off the intruders. They were forced to keep watch twenty-four seven.

The weather was still very brisk with frequent snow flurries. One freezing night Cody was on guard duty when three men tried to storm the house. Cody killed one and the body had remained across the street for days. It disappeared one night and they didn't know what had taken it. Cody was despondent for days, but the family prayed together and his parents tried to convince him that the world was a different place and he had saved his family. The final straw came when Terry and Izzy were in the living room, sweeping the neighborhood with binoculars. Across the street, rummaging through the ruins of the home where their kids had played since they were toddlers, they spotted an unimaginable beast. It was huge. They could tell it had once been a man but with the elongated torso, slavering jaws with razor-sharp teeth and claws in place of nails, it appeared more reptilian than human.

They all froze in place to minimize any noise. As soon as it had left the area they threw the rest of the food and supplies into the four-door Jeep and got the hell out of Dodge as fast as they could. The Jeep had been kept in a grounded, steel storage building behind the garage. Serving as a Faraday cage, it protected the Jeep from the EMP. Fortunately, no one had broken into the building. The back of the vehicle was covered with gas cans and the spare tire had been moved to the very substantial rack on the top of the vehicle. They put their remaining five gallon buckets of dehydrated foods in the rack, and tools and other supplies in a large plastic container. They strapped down a tarp over the top and tied it all down. Their personal bug-out bags were stacked in the cargo space behind the back seat, pushed to one side to allow Kris to ride back there.

In the end, the distance from the blasts, covering their windows with plastic and staying underground for months had saved them.

Izzy felt a hand on her arm, shaking her awake. She tried to shrug it off, but it persisted. "Wake up Mom, it's midnight. It's time to go."

The black "Baby" Glock went into Izzy's side holster and she slipped three ten-round magazines into separate pockets of her hunting vest. She surreptitiously watched Cody pack his weapons and was satisfied he was taking what he needed. They each had a bottle of water and ration bars that they would consume on the walk to town. The vest also contained a high intensity, LED flashlight that functioned as a stun gun, and extra ammo for her rifle. They had kept the batteries for the flashlights charged at home using a solar panel, and on the road using a DC to AC inverter. The shock from the stun gun wasn't very powerful but could possibly give them an edge in a fight.

"Here's your knife, Mom." He handed her the belt and sheath. She had already strapped on her ankle knife. She slipped on her gloves and a light jacket and shivered in the cold. She zipped it up but would unzip it when they got to town so she would have access to her vest.

"Okay guys. We'll start the car and very slowly move up this wash. The ridge to our right and the distance from town should mask the sound. When we get closer we'll have to kill the engine, and Missy? You'll go up on the ridge and watch for lights." She took a swig from her water bottle and handed it to Cody.

"I'm not thirsty, Mom."

"You know better than that, Cody. Stay hydrated. Even though it's dark and still cold, this altitude can dry you out. Once we get to town there may be no way to get more water." She handed it back and this time he took several swallows.

"When we're ready for pickup we'll flash the light three times, pause for three and then three more times. That should differentiate our signal from any other random lights. Melissa, when you see our light, get back to the car, fire it up and head north. Hopefully this gully will run out when it gets to the road. Turn right on the road until it hits the highway and then go north. If we aren't somewhere along the road just keep driving for another mile. If we don't get to you by dawn, leave us. We've only come a hundred miles from home so there's plenty of gas. Plus you have the three cans on the back."

Kris started to cry. "Mom, you said you wouldn't take any chances. You'll be at the road, right?"

"One of us will be for sure. We won't leave you. It's just that you never know what may happen and you two need to find someone that survived that will take you in. Good people."

She wondered if there were any good people left. It was her husband, her soul-mate, who was in that town. And her oldest daughter. God only knew what they were going through... if they were still alive. She was going to find out, no matter what.

If things went bad she was going to send Cody, undoubtedly against his wishes, back to the girls. He had turned eighteen a month ago and was big and strong for his age. He could take care of them. Get them into the mountains, build shelter and hunt food. Eventually she hoped civilization would return and they could leave their isolation.

She gathered both girls into her arms and hugged them fiercely. "Watch for my signal, okay?" They nodded in unison and she swung away quickly to walk up to the car. They had moved it higher on the side of the hill during the afternoon rain as the wash became a small creek, and they didn't want it to flood into the Jeep. They had all taken a last bathroom break and had stowed all their gear. She didn't have any more excuses.

It was time.

Once they were all belted in she started the car and very slowly moved forward up the wash. She figured she could go two miles before they needed to park it. It seemed as if the trip took an eternity. She could barely see, and relied on the terrain to tell her which way to go. Occasionally Cody had to get out and make sure they were still going up the wash. Anytime she had to gun the engine to get over or around rocks, she shuddered at the noise it made, and finally becoming concerned, she pulled to a stop.

She didn't want another tear-filled goodbye; it was now time for action, so she motioned Kris to stay in the back seat and for Missy and Cody to follow her to the top of the ridge. She scanned the town with her binoculars but the town was dark and she couldn't see anything. She carefully looked at the terrain between the last houses and their position checking for any lights that would indicate someone had heard the vehicle and were coming for them. Cody had his own smaller pair and was scanning the houses on the hill beyond the town.

"It's a small town and there are only two areas where there are many houses; down around the lake and on the hill behind town. I would think they'd be holed up on the hill, since it gives them a better view of the surroundings."

"Mom…" he hissed. "I thought I saw something."

She scrambled around Missy to his side. "What was it?" she whispered.

"I'm not sure, but it looked like a light that flashed and went out." He pointed to the area where he thought he saw it, on the hill behind town.

"Well, that settles it. It's the only sign of life we've seen, so let's start in that direction. It's not too far from the road either." She gave her binoculars to Melissa and whispered in her ear, "We're going up the highway and then we'll cut across to those houses on the hill. Watch for our light but don't forget to keep looking in other areas in case they try to sneak up on you. Once you see our light, you can use the headlights and come after us, hell bent for leather. Got it?"

"Yes Mommy." Izzy grinned in the dark. Fourteen year old Missy hadn't called her Mommy in years.

Cody and Izzy carefully moved back down the hill and started up the wash. It wound around a few curves and several large boulders and after they had made a couple turns Izzy took Cody's arm in the dark. She pulled him close so she could speak quietly.

"Son, I knew there was no way you would let me come alone, but we absolutely cannot let the girls be left without one of us." He started to speak but she put her hand up to his mouth. "Listen to me! We are both going on this damn fool errand but if I tell you to leave, you will, by God, leave. Do you understand me?"

He gently moved her hand down and nodded, even though it was pitch black. "I know Mom. I don't want them to be alone either. But if we get in a bind, it might have to be you that gets away. Whoever has the best chance, okay?"

She had to admit that it made sense. "Okay," she reluctantly agreed.

The moon had risen but was still too low on the horizon to shed much light. She told Cody it was time to maintain silence. The exertion had warmed them up and Izzy unzipped her jacket. She held her AK at the ready and they continued up the wash in near-total darkness. Cody, in the lead, put his hand on her arm and they halted. Izzy had noticed that the ridge to their right had almost disappeared as they progressed. Their eyes had adjusted to the faint light from the stars and the moon and he pointed to the road that crossed their path just ahead. They watched for several minutes, and finally, quickly moved forward at a trot, crouching as they crossed to the other side and entered the bushes directly across from the wash. Again they paused and listened but heard nothing to concern them.

They went east until they came to the highway, and paralleling it moving north, crossing it when they thought they had gone about a hundred yards beyond the area where Cody had seen the light. After crossing the highway, they discovered a side road that led east into low hills. A hundred yards later it came to a junction with another road that ran north and south and they went in the direction they believed would lead them toward the faint light Cody had seen, what seemed hours ago, but in reality, had been fifty minutes. The road split, one branch curving east following the contour of the hill and running behind the last row of houses that backed up to the hill. The other went straight ahead sloping downward toward the town.

Izzy motioned to him and they scooted across the road to continue east on the north side away from the houses. Moving as quietly as possible, they had gone thirty feet when Cody put his hand on her shoulder and pointed back the way they had come. South and west of their position Cody had seen the same light he had noticed from their Jeep. They backtracked, re-crossed the road, and then turned south to get a look at the side of the first house. They separated by fifteen feet, so they couldn't be surprised or taken together.

Moving off to the right side of the road, they had just begun to enter a small stand of trees they heard a noise in the trees just ahead of them. They froze, afraid to move forward. Izzy heard someone walking through the trees not making much effort at stealth. The footsteps ceased and she heard a zipping sound and someone urinating into the bushes. Using the sound as cover she signaled Cody to move forward and they saw a shadow in the dark. They could see by the faint light of a cigarette hanging from the man's mouth and they quickly dashed toward the figure while the sound of him peeing in the bushes masked their own very slight noise. She never thought she would be happy that someone was a smoker, but it was probably the light from his lighter that Cody spotted from the ridge that led them here.

Cody rose up behind the man, clamped his left hand over the man's mouth and put a knife to his throat. The man began to struggle but quieted quickly when Izzy shoved her Glock in his face. Through it all, he still had the cigarette in his mouth and even with the gun pointed at his nose, he fumbled for his zipper and zipped it up. He raised his hands in surrender. Cody pulled him backwards into the bushes at the edge of the tiny clearing where the brush was densest.

Izzy slipped a piece of nylon rope around one wrist, pulled his arm behind his back and tied it to the other wrist.

"If you make any noise, you're dead," Cody whispered in the man's ear. "You got it?"

The figure nodded vigorously in the dark and Izzy saw the cigarette bob up and down. Cody slowly released the grip over the man's mouth, alert to any sound he might try to make.

Izzy leaned in to whisper, "You have my husband and daughter. I want to know where they are."

No sound came from the figure. Cody covered the man's mouth again and pressed the knife against his throat, breaking the skin and drawing blood. The figure stiffened and made a whimpering noise, again nodding his head. Cody uncovered the mouth once again. "We want answers or I'll cut your throat," he growled softly.

"Clay has 'em. They're in that house over there." Cody felt the man move his head in the direction of the house across the street.

"Are they hurt?" Izzy whispered.

"The guy's beat up pretty bad, and they been using the girl all day, but they're alive. I swear! I never went in the house. I'm a good guy. Not like those evil bastards that turned into monsters. You can see I'm still human," His voice started to get louder as he rambled on and Cody repeated the process of shutting him up. "Keep it down or die. I won't warn you again."

Izzy stood immobile, shocked by what they'd heard. *My poor Marci.* In her fury she wanted to kill this man here and now but they needed more information.

"How many guards are there and what's the layout of the house?" She asked as Cody released his hand.

"Me and three other guys are around the house. This is my side. Clay sleeps in the bedroom over on the left. The girl's locked in the one on the right and the guy's in the living room. They put a bed in there and chained him to it. You can't get 'em out. If it gets noisy those monsters Clay keeps will hear you and come kill us all. Please, I'm just a miner. We have to do what Clay says or he'll sic those things on us." He slumped to his knees.

After they had the information, Izzy was conflicted about what to do. She had never hurt anybody even when their house was attacked. She had only fired her rifle over the attackers' heads to drive them off. It was one thing to practice maneuvers in the backyard and play at survival, but this was the real thing and she was scared. Adrenaline pounded through her body and she had to fight down the anger over what had been done to her loved ones. This man may just be a pawn of the gang leader and he was helping them by providing needed information.

Cody was looking to her for direction and their prisoner felt, rather than saw, her hesitation. Clay had relaxed his grip and the man jumped to his feet and surged forward, the nylon rope slipping off his wrists. He knocked Izzy to the ground but Cody threw his full weight on the man's back and bore him down. The man grunted and flipped over, throwing Cody off, but Cody wrapped his arms around the figure as Izzy came to her feet, drawing her knife. Just as he opened his mouth to yell a warning, she reached out without thinking and slit his throat. He gurgled and slipped to the grass, blood pulsing out of his neck. The knife stuck in the cartilage of the man's windpipe and Izzy had to jerk it loose, almost vomiting in her horror.

They stood in the dark, breathing heavily and trying to determine if anyone had heard the noise. They stood for what seemed like hours. Izzy was shaking so badly she wondered if she could go on.

"Mom, I'm sorry I let him go. I promise it won't happen again." He wiped his hands on his pants trying to rub off the sticky blood. "It's okay, Mom. You did great." He hugged her and said in her ear, "We need to decide what to do. This may be where you go back to the girls and I'll try to get Dad and Marci."

That snapped her out of it. "No! So far we've found them, taken out one bad guy and haven't been discovered. Let's keep going, but be ready to retreat and get back to the car if I say so."

They waited a few minutes longer and then approached the road through the trees. The front of the house had a fence surrounding a small yard and steep stairs that went down the hill to the street. One guard was probably at the bottom of the staircase. The back had a garage with a driveway that went a short distance up the hill to another road behind the house. Izzy figured that's where another guard would be. The third would be on the opposite side of the house from them.

She motioned to Cody and they slipped across the street and slid behind the garage on the side toward the house. The moonlight was slightly brighter and Izzy could see a clothesline between them and the back windows. She got right in Cody's ear. "Watch out for the clothesline. Duck under it. We either have to try and take out the other sentries, and somehow manage to keep quiet, or we just have to storm the place, take the leader hostage and get the hell out before those super bad guys show up. What do you think?" she whispered to Cody.

"The doors are all locked. I don't see how we can maintain silence and still get them open. So I say we just go in. We'll grab the guy and tie him up. You cut Dad loose and I'll break down the door to Marci's room."

"Okay. I'll tie the rope a lot tighter this time. It slipped off the other guy cause I was trying not to hurt him. No more Ms. Nice Guy! Let's go." She hesitated and turned to hug him. "I love you Cody. Remember, if it goes bad and I say 'retreat', you get back to the girls, get out of here and find someplace to call home."

They scooted across the lawn to the back of the house, keeping the garage between them and the back road where they assumed the sentry to be. Pressed against the house, they slid around the corner to the west side. The silence was shattered by the loud, hoarse barking of a dog as it came rushing around the front corner of the house at full tilt. They were on the darkest side of the house and Izzy couldn't see the dog until it was on her. She jumped back as she felt it bite into her leg, her pants ripping as it growled and backed off. Involuntarily she let out a loud yelp and realized their stealth was blown. The knife was still in her left hand and she started to lunge for the animal when Cody brushed past her and took a swing with his AR-15, connecting with a vicious blow to the shoulder. The dog went down but immediately jumped up and backed away around the corner, barking furiously. They followed and Cody peeked around the corner to see if he could detect anyone coming.

"Jigger, c'mere," someone called from the other side of the house. "Damn fool dog. What the hell are you barkin' at?"

"Shut him up before he wakes up Clay!" someone else yelled out in an exaggerated whisper.

Cody saw three embers from cigarettes coming across the field on the far side of the front lawn, heading for a gap in the fence that surrounded the yard. He couldn't believe their luck. All three sentries were together, probably bullshitting in the dark for companionship. No wonder the guards hadn't heard them kill the first man they had encountered.

"Mom, stay back!" He threw himself forward on the ground in a prone firing position and opened fire. Starting at the left of the cigarette lights, and moving to the right, he fired off six rounds in rapid succession. The dog, frightened by the gunfire backed further away and Cody was gratified to hear at least one scream of pain and a thud in the dark. A cigarette fell into the grass and the other two could be seen moving off into the distance. *Damn, I only got one of them.*

"Come on!"

Scrambling up onto the porch they heard a scraping sound and were startled by a dark figure that appeared at the eastern corner of the old house. Hitting the porch at the same time they fired in the direction of the muzzle flash as the other figure opened fire. They heard a grunt and the sound of running footsteps disappearing down the hill.

"We don't have much time!" Izzy yelled. "I think that was the leader." She tried the door but it was locked. Cody reared back and kicked it as hard as he could, let out a curse, and bounced back, hopping on one foot.

"Shit, that hurt!"

Izzy didn't want to fire her weapon for fear she'd hit someone but they were out of options. "Stand back!" She fired at the lock and immediately hit the door with her shoulder. She too bounced off. "This is SO much harder than it looks in the movies," she muttered. Cody fired two more rounds and this time when he slammed his body into the door it shattered and flew open. He stumbled into the room, caught his foot on a rug and sprawled headlong to the floor. He looked up to find his father staring at him in amazement.

"Dad! We're here to rescue you!"

"I can see that," he said through clenched teeth, and even that hurt.

Izzy, unable to see Terry in the dark raced over and hugged him. He screamed in agony and she quickly backed away. "God Terry, I'm so sorry! Roll onto your side so I can cut your bonds." Cody leaped up and groped his way through an opening in the wall to the right to find himself in a short hallway. He opened the door on the right and saw by the moonlight entering the open window that the room was empty. They'd made so much noise, the head of the gang had jumped out the window and fled to safety. Cody backed into the hallway and tried the door on the left.

He rattled the door handle and heard movement on the other side, and muffled sobs, "Please, just go away. Leave me alone."

"Marci, it's Cody. Get as far away from the door as you can. Off to the side. I'm going to shoot the lock." He waited for a few seconds and then fired. The flimsy interior door exploded inward. Marci flew into his arms. "Oh... thank you, Cody. Where's Mom and Dad?"

"They're here. Come on we need to hurry."

Suddenly very self-conscious with just a blanket wrapped around her, she whimpered, "I don't have any clothes."

Cody quickly shook off his jacket and put it around her shoulders, over the blanket to secure it. "Let's go! They're going to come back with help." Just then they heard the dog barking and the sound was growing closer. Another noise, a God-awful keening arose, froze them temporarily in place and sent chills up their spines.

"It must be the creature the guy we killed talked about!" Izzy pulled Terry's arm over her shoulders and helped him get to the door. "Oh no, they're coming!"

Hustling Terry down the stairs and around the corner, they crossed the yard and the street and entered the trees. Terry stumbled as Izzy tried to help him stay upright. "I can't breathe," he wheezed. "My ribs are on fire." He was much heavier than Izzy and sunk to his knees in the grass, landing in a pool of blood, as he stared at the blank face of a dead man, the open throat gaping up at him in the weak moonlight that barely penetrated through the trees.

"Ahhh, what the hell?" He scrambled back to his feet, his whole body in agonizing pain. Izzy grabbed under his arm to help him up.

"We had to kill him to keep him quiet," she explained. "Cody, help him. I have to give the signal." She ran back into the street, where she had a line of sight to the southwest of town, and using her Maglite, gave the pre-arranged signal. Rushing back into the trees, she and Cody each took a side and helped Terry through the trees and up the hill to the intersection. When they reached it and turned left toward the highway, she glanced back and saw lights on the road in front of the house. They were coming fast and the low moaning sound of the creature turned her blood cold!

By the time they reached the highway they were fully supporting Terry and half dragging him along. Izzy could hear the Jeep, but it seemed so far away, and she could hear the predators coming. They started down the highway so they could meet the Jeep, rather than waiting for it at the side road… but she feared Missy wouldn't get here in time.

She heard heavy breathing and realized the creature had broken from the pack and was almost upon them. A headlight swung around the corner onto the highway and swept past the beast coming at them from the side road. Izzy gasped as she realized it was one of the things they had seen in their neighbor's yard, and was the main reason they had left Raton to find a home in the mountains.

The Jeep was accelerating up the hill. Cody and Izzy each had ahold of Terry. She screamed at Cody to fire on the creature. He fired his weapon and got off a single shot when the thing swung a clawed hand at him, knocking the rifle aside and throwing him against the car as it screeched to a stop.

"Come on!" Kris and Missy yelled simultaneously.

The monster turned on Izzy as she leaped forward with the tiny stun gun in her hand. Marci had jumped in the vehicle, and grabbing Terry's shirt, she opened the door and pulled him onto the back seat.

As the stun gun hit the creature with a staccato firing, it shrieked and backed off a step… but it didn't go down. Cody pulled up his weapon from where he sat on the ground and fired off two shots that he knew had to have hit the thing, and it took another step back. Izzy leaped in the car and reached out her hand for Cody.

"Cody, jump in!" She heard the approaching footsteps of the rest of the gang and suddenly the beast, drool dripping from its lips, swung on the group of men and yelled out a challenge to keep them away from its prey.

She heard someone call out as Cody made it to his feet.

"Stewart! Down man. Get the truck, NOW!" The creature swung back to the Wrangler as Cody jumped in and the vehicle burned rubber, swinging around and heading south on the highway. Gunfire erupted to their rear and Izzy felt a body slam into her as the Jeep fishtailed down the road. She thought it was Missy's driving but Cody didn't move and she realized he'd been hit.

Chapter 7

"How come you aren't coming with us?" Lori asked Mark, her lower lip thrust out in a feigned pout.

"I would love to go but I have to get some work parties organized. There's so much to do, especially if we get an early fall and winter. I'd like your group to come to the meeting this morning so we all know what everybody else is doing." He rolled over and rose from the sleeping bag. It was early, and still very cold, and he quickly pulled on his clothes. Sounds of activity came to him from the back of the building where someone was starting to get breakfast ready.

The solar bathrooms were just beyond the corrals, and after he visited there, Mark went to talk to the sentries. The original group had been replaced during the night. The perimeter for the sentries was smaller than the previous one they patrolled, before the creature attacked. All the sentries were within the meadow except for two pair positioned in the forest behind the corrals.

"Everything's quiet, Mark," Ruben Ritz told him. "No sign of the Devols or any other predators. If there's big cats or coyotes out there I doubt they'll bother us with those things hangin' around."

"As quick as those creatures are, we can't let our guard down even during the day," Mark stared into the forest but everything seemed calm. Ruben and Dick Gray patrolled behind the building and Tom and Jimbo were behind the corrals over by the bathrooms. Mark walked into the meadow and sat on a rock in front of his tent. He looked at the tents in the meadow and estimated there were only about a third of what there had been the first night. They couldn't sleep inside the building for long. It was too crowded.

Lori came out a few minutes later. She was dressed in the shorts and T-shirt she had worn when they left the shelter even though the temperature was still in the forties. A holster containing a revolver was strapped around her waist and Mark had to laugh at the picture she made.

"What in the world are you doing?" he asked her.

"Let's go for our run. I don't want to get out of the habit. I don't think we have to worry if we both go, and we're armed."

"I'd love to. Let me change clothes." He crawled into the tent, found his old shelter clothes and changed into them. They were dry, but were stiff from having been wet, and he almost took them off when he saw a spot of blood on one leg. Will's blood, he guessed. They would have to set up to do laundry as soon as possible. Leaving the tent, he went to talk to Dave, who had just crawled out of his own tent, shivering in the cold.

"Hey Mark, are you crazy? What are you doing in shorts?"

"Lori and I are going for a run. Can I borrow your gun? I'll get one from the weapon's locker today, but I don't want to leave camp unarmed. I think anytime someone goes away from camp they should at least go in pairs and be armed. They should also check out with the sentries and let them know where they're going and approximately when they'll be back."

"Yeah, at least for the first few days, until we have a chance to get to know the area." Dave agreed. He reached back inside the tent and handed Mark a gun belt with a .45 caliber, semi-automatic pistol.

"Can you gather everyone together after breakfast so we can have a meeting when I get back from my run? We need to form some committees to start working on projects."

"Sure Mark. Should I have them save you some breakfast?"

"No, we'll just do cereal when we get back."

He and Lori jogged toward the path leading across the meadow and into the woods. He immediately relaxed into his stride and realized how much he missed being able to just run without being chased by something. As hard as the last few days had been, he was beginning to adjust to their new circumstances. They had exited the shelter less than two days ago and already it seemed like a lifetime. Lori led the way and was setting a brisk pace. After about ten minutes he began to warm up. He'd always heard that once a runner warms up, the temperature seems about twenty degrees warmer than ambient. They soon came to the bridge and Mark stopped in the middle, his hands on the rock railing, to look over toward the grave in the small meadow by the river. It was still in shadow from the high cliffs to the east but he could see the mound of dirt covering the man that had given him everything. He took the place of Mark's absent father, put him through college and given him a job that he loved, and flourished in.

"Mark? We're getting wet." Lori brought him back to reality and they left the mist of the waterfall behind as they headed into new territory along the base of the cliff that formed the north side of the valley. They ran below the ledge outside the opening to the cave that led back into the shelter. The outer blast door was open but the interior one had shut down, ostensibly trapping the creatures inside. But Mark was sure the creature that clawed Micah was the same one that had chased him in the last few minutes in the shelter, before he threw himself under the rapidly descending door and saved himself from the beast.

He heard Lori laugh and she picked up the pace. He couldn't help grinning as he realized she was laughing from the sheer joy of being outside and running at an unconstrained pace. Even in the larger dragon caves, where they tried to run regularly, they were unable to stretch out and run as fast as they wanted. The caves derived their name from the map of the shelter. It designated the doors that led to the unimproved areas, the caverns the shelter had been built in, as "Beyond These Doors There Be Dragons."

As they followed a barely visible trail that snaked through the rocks that had fallen from the cliff overhead, they had to slow down or risk getting injured. There were fresh rock falls, a result of the earthquakes that had destroyed the shelter. The valley seemed about two miles wide and Mark estimated they were midway along the north face when they discovered a fork in the trail with the main trail leading west and another leading to the right. This new trail entered a stand of trees and then began to switchback up the mountain.

"Wow," Lori said, staring up the cliff. "The mountain here isn't as steep as the cliff behind us, but this trail must be really difficult. I bet the view from the top is incredible."

"Yeah, but with the earthquakes, it might have been swept away in places. If we ever try to climb it we may have to take ropes to get across the slippage. After we get the valley secure we can make this a day trip."

They continued across the valley and turned south at the far side. The land was slightly higher than the meadow where their camp was located and they could see most of the way to the south end of the valley. Stopping for a brief break they stood side by side and enjoyed the view. A very light breeze had come up, ruffling his longish dark hair and blowing it into his blue eyes. The sun had topped the ridge and was warm on their faces although their camp, on the east side of the valley was still in shadow. Mark stood there a moment with a feeling that something was wrong.

Puzzled, he turned to Lori, "I have the weirdest feeling, like something's missing."

She took his hand and smiled up at him. "It's quiet. Just listen."

She was right. He stood there and listened to the sound of silence. For eight months the sounds of the shelter had been ever present; the susurration of the air filtering and conditioning system, the slight rumble and trembling of the power plant, as the rushing water flowed through the penstocks, spun the turbines and exited through the encased aqueduct, the human sounds of voices, laughter and tears. *I'd forgotten what quiet was like,* he thought. Standing there for several minutes, listening to the silence, he became aware of bees and insects buzzing through the morning chill. In the distance he heard the sound of the breeze ruffling the few leaves the aspens had sprouted and the roar of rushing water in the river. Natural sounds.

He took a deep breath and gazed out over the valley. The areas still in shade were swathed in low lying fog, the ghostly tendrils snaking through the trees. The river sprung from the mist at the base of the falls, flowing west for about one-third of the way across the valley, and then in a wide sweeping arc, it turned south and ran almost straight until he lost sight of it. The trail they were following continued south and entered a large stand of aspens that lined the west side of the valley, bulging out into the meadow a couple of miles away. The land sloped down for half a mile and then leveled out and ran fairly flat for at least a mile beyond their camp that was tucked into the pines trees, on the other side of the river. After that, the valley became a jumble of rocks. There was a pile of them surrounding the base of a tall, oval boulder, closer to the river than it was to the western hills.

The mountains on the west side of the valley were tall, but not nearly as steep as the cliffs in the northeast corner by the waterfall, or even the more sloping mountains along the east. There was still a dusting of snow along the crown. At the far end of the valley the hills pinched together, sweeping around on the left all the way to the river. The opening into the valley was about a mile wide on the right side of the river, but he couldn't see very much for the rocks and boulders that were blocking his view. The grass was still brown but in a few places he could see a faint, green tinge. The meadow was dotted with large bushes and abundant foliage that was also turning green. Just below the bend of the river was a small hill, maybe thirty feet high, with a few pine trees and rock outcroppings on the top.

"It's really beautiful, isn't it?" He smiled down at Lori and saw that she was unbuckling her gun belt. His smile widened and he unbuckled his own, sweeping the valley with his eyes to ensure, that at least for now, there wasn't any danger. He laid the holster and gun on the ground and pulled Lori into an embrace. They kissed tentatively at first, and then the long absence of physical and emotional intimacy for them both caused them to increase the urgency of their caresses. She pulled his T-shirt over his head and he, hers. Laying them on the grass they stripped the rest of the way, stretched out on the clothes and gave in to their passion.

Lori lay with Mark's arm across her stomach, his head tucked on her shoulder as she gazed up at a deep, blue sky. She couldn't remember the last time she'd had sex with someone she'd felt genuine love for. When first married she had loved her husband very much, but it had quickly died after their first child was born and he became abusive. When her father sent her the signaling device that forewarned her of the war, she took the children and abandoned the bastard to die in the inferno. She had kept her feelings bottled up, guilty for what she'd done to him. Over the months in the shelter, she had come to know, and love, this kind and understanding man lying beside her in this magnificent valley. In the glow of their love making she allowed herself to be vulnerable, opening up and telling him of the hell her life had become before the war. She told him all the details she had withheld the few times he'd tried to talk to her about the past. Of meeting her dream man, discovering his true nature and having her life dissolve into one of fear and self-loathing.

"I look back now and wonder how I could have let him hurt my children. He verbally and physically abused me and Kevin. He never hit Ashley but he verbally abused her. I would distract him from them by saying things that redirected his anger at me. In the last days before the war I became aware that he was having an affair with his personal assistant. Gives a whole new meaning to that title, huh? When the signal box went off I jumped at the chance to get away from him, even though it meant he would die. I hope Ash and Kevin can forgive me for not protecting them from the bastard." Her lips quivered and she tried to hold back the tears. "I was so weak."

He rolled onto his side and kissed away her tears. "What they will remember, is that you saved them from the creatures. You're not that woman any longer. I myself saw the change in you as you became strong. I love you so much for who you are."

She ruffled his hair. "We better get back or they'll be sending out a search party." They quickly dressed and strapped on their weapons. Deciding to cut across the meadow, they wound through the brush toward the river, where Mark stopped at the hill.

"It looks like a sentinel standing guard over the valley."

"Then Sentinel Hill it is," she agreed.

Neither of them knew anything about crops, but although there were a lot of rocks in the meadow, it looked like the soil was dark and deep. Mark took a stick, leaned down and scooped out a few chunks of dirt. He crumbled it in his hand and looked up at Lori with a shrug.

"Chris will know," she told him.

They turned back north to go around to the bridge. "It would be good if we could put in another bridge on this side of the valley," Mark said.

"Maybe when the river goes down we can cross it on foot."

"Yeah, well it's really raging now from the snow melt."

Working their way back to the bridge, they noticed a lone figure just beyond the gravesite. Mark recognized Samuel. He was picking up rocks and laying them in a line to form a rock wall. He had already made a single layer along the north side and another on the west at a distance of around twenty feet from the grave. They trotted over to him.

"Hey Sam," Mark said. "What are you doing? You shouldn't be out here alone."

Samuel pointed to a rifle leaning up against a small boulder.

"I'm okay. I'm going to turn this into a proper cemetery. I have a feeling it will have more graves here and I want Brian to bless it or consecrate it, or whatever will make it a proper resting place for people."

"Why don't you come back with us? We're going to have a meeting to hand out projects. I think that's a real good idea and I'm sure some folks would come back to help. You should have someone stand guard until we kill the rest of those things."

Samuel reluctantly agreed and grabbing his rifle, joined them when they turned toward the trail.

Reaching the camp while it was still shaded, Mark and Lori had begun to chill so they quickly changed clothes and went to the kitchen for cereal.

"You don't think you're going to eat cold cereal do you?" Kate asked them. She had saved dehydrated scrambled eggs and canned white potatoes for them, and Mark, finding that the run had stimulated his appetite, was very glad he didn't have to settle for cereal.

Chapter 8

"You incompetent, lazy, asshole FUCKS!" Clay screamed at the cowering men standing in front of him. His face was crimson as he paced back and forth on the front lawn of the house he used as headquarters. "You slackers almost got me killed, and we lost the girl. You're going to get them back, or I swear, I'll set loose Stewart and Billy on you!" Fuming, he continued pacing, staring at the group of ten or twelve men. The morning sun hit them at a low angle as it climbed into the sky.

"The Jeep turned on highway 127. Where does it go?" He swung and glared at Jinx.

Shuffling his feet, Jinx gave a sideways glance at Stewart who was standing slightly behind Clay, mucus drooling down his chest. "If you go south at the fork it heads down to the main highway to Taos. The other fork leads to Platte Ranch. It's over some hills into Paradise Valley."

"Where does it go after that?"

"It don't go nowhere. Except maybe up into Hidden Valley. That there's a box canyon. Only way out is another canyon on the west side that's kind of hard to see, and a foot trail up north."

Clay brightened. "You mean if they took the road to the ranch, they might be trapped?"

"Yeah, unless they took the other road, or found the side canyon."

"Well, that's more like it. How far to the ranch?"

Jinx shrugged and looked at Monroe.

Monroe considered a moment and said, "I guess it's about five miles. Maybe a little more." He looked at the others and several nodded.

Clay stopped moving and looked them over. "You guys, plus Jake and Herrera, are going with me. Stewart, you and Billy are going for a walk, okay?"

Stewart nodded his half shaggy, half bald head. "Yes Clay, yes Clay," he said through swollen lips.

"The rest of you hit the tackle shop. I think they have daypacks and camelbacks. Everyone needs to carry water and some snacks. Jinx, bring me a pack. Everybody meet back here at oh-nine hundred. Have five or six armed guys down at the road, in case they come back. I'm going back to bed. When you're ready to go, wake me up and call Stewart."

He turned to Stewart and said, "Go home Stewart. You and Billy come back when Jinx tells you."

"Yes Clay, yes Clay." They started off for the house at the end of the road.

Monroe told Clay, "I think they finished off that deer they killed. They're gonna get hungry."

"Give them Alan's body. He deserves to be chow, letting those bastards sneak in here like that. He's lucky they killed him or I would have let Stewart eat him alive. And bury Phillips. At least he was standing guard like he was supposed to."

Monroe nodded and sent two guys to get the body they found in the trees by the road. He wished one more time, that he could just get drunk and hang out, instead of all this nonsense. The girl was a great piece of tail, though, and he would like to get her back.

***

Marshmallow galleons floated across a sapphire sky. There was no sign of the darker clouds that would bring the afternoon storm; the thunder, lightning and driving rain. Matthew Pennington III laid back in the grass, his arm behind his head, long black hair draped over the arm. He was chewing on the stem of a licorice weed, his battered cowboy hat pushed forward, shading his dark eyes. He scratched his scruffy beard and dreamily watched the clouds drift by while he tried to decide where to go next. *No hurry,* he thought. He had left the old mine shaft around two months ago and had wandered aimlessly ever since, trying to find some new meaning to a life devoid of feeling. He heard a nicker from one of the mares tethered to the only tree on the hill. He knew it wasn't Chief. His Appaloosa stallion was trained to silence.

The four horses had regained most of the weight they lost while living in a mine shaft through the long, freezing winter. Matthew had closed up the entrance to the mine with bales of hay just before his grandfather's new pickup truck suddenly quit working. He had already moved Grandpa's disaster supplies from the basement to the mine shaft. Matthew might have been able to survive in the basement, but the horses would have perished. The mine went into the mountain for two hundred feet and then forked. The side tunnel widened out into a cavern that accommodated the horses and most of the water barrels. He created a living space out of the other fork and stored his food there.

It was an unbelievable nightmare. The second day the ground shook and the bales of hay actually jumped inward a foot. He suspected another bomb had gone off. The horses didn't appreciate being underground even though they had enough head room. Chief was just about the best trained horse he had ever known, but the months of confinement combined with proximity to the mares drove him wild. It was all Matthew could do to control him. He covered one of the mares that had come in heat and smashed his head against a jagged rock in the ceiling, gashing it from his poll to his forehead. Matthew had worried about infection but it had eventually healed with no treatment, leaving a long scar between his ears.

As time went on, the stench became unbearable. Each day Matthew shoveled the manure to the front of the shaft. After a couple of months, when he just couldn't take it anymore, he took a chance and moved a bale of hay to allow him to throw it outside. But there was nothing he could do about the urine. The floor of the mine became saturated and eventually the smell of ammonia penetrated to his living space. His own latrine in the back corner of his space was disgusting. He had no supplies for bathing and couldn't spare the water. The horses drank too much.

He was sick for two weeks, with vomiting and diarrhea and was sure he had radiation sickness, and was dying… but even though he no longer cared at that point, he recovered. He'd lost considerable weight, leaving him weak and fatigued.

The first aid kit contained only a few medicines, the dehydrated food lacked variety and there weren't any books or games. He cut up the cardboard from boxes that held provisions and fashioned a deck of cards, playing solitaire until he thought he would go insane... and maybe he did a little. He cried and screamed and slept as much as possible. He thought of his grandfather, and wondered what had happened to his parents... and he thought about Sophie and his unborn son, blasted away in the inferno that had taken Albuquerque, New Mexico.

Don Pedro Hernandez, Matthew's grandfather owned thirty-two hundred acres in the mountains north of Santa Fe and just southeast of Taos. The ranch had been handed down since the family had received a land grant from the provincial government before the territory became a state. The Don had wed an Indian woman and the younger of their two daughters, Shona, became Matthew's mother. His father, Matthew Pennington II, had come from England to study Southwestern American archeology and fell in love with Shona when they studied together at University of New Mexico at the Santa Fe campus. He was an excellent researcher, had a knack for finding or trading artifacts and he and Shona opened a highly regarded antiquities store in the best part of Santa Fe. Matthew's mother was tall, thin and beautiful and he'd always thought of his father as a British Indiana Jones. They were prominent members of the Santa Fe community until the day they died on the I-25 Freeway trying to get home before the bombs came.

Matthew grew up in Santa Fe but spent weekends, long summers and holidays at Grandpa's ranch. He loved archeology, like his parents, but he loved geology more and earned his degree from Southwestern Technical College in Socorro. It was still in his beloved New Mexico but gave him a break from his parents, something every young man needs. He met Sophie there and his parents didn't even know of the relationship until they announced they were getting married. Grad school at New Mexico Tech qualified him as a research assistant for the New

Mexico Bureau of Geology and Mineral Resources. Most days would find him at eight or nine thousand feet in the Sandia Mountains, collecting samples for research. He was amazed that he could do what he loved best... and even get paid for it.

He and Sophie had been married a year when she became pregnant, and their families were thrilled when the ultrasound indicated he and Sophie were going to have a son. They were both just twenty-six years old and the future looked bright ahead.

Matthew spent much of his childhood and teen years at Don Pedro's ranch, learning to ride and train horses, hunting, fishing and helping out with the many chores that always needed done, even with a crew of working hands. His grandmother died when Matthew was eleven and as his grandfather aged, Matthew helped him run the ranch, spending one or two weekends a month in the mountains he loved. Sophie was quite a horsewoman herself and traveled north to the ranch whenever she could. At eight months pregnant, though, she stayed home on August 21... the day his world ended.

Riding Chief through thick brush he'd examined the fences for breaks in the barbed wire. A long-sleeved white shirt helped to protect him from the brilliant sunshine, his jeans covered by chaps that protected his legs, and his hat was pulled low over his eyes to shade them from the intense afternoon heat and light. The only departure from the typical southwestern cowboy attire was his work boots. He found cowboy boots insufferable.

When the sky lit up, he grabbed his hat and pulled it lower, not knowing what had caused the brilliant illumination. When he looked up his jaw dropped and he immediately recognized the malignant mushroom cloud growing in the distance. Matthew just sat on his horse, as it skittered sideways, with an increasing sense of emptiness. He didn't try to ride in the direction of his wrenching loss or believe that, by some miracle, she had been spared. The cloud was directly over his home and the love of his life. He screamed at the heavens, shouting out his grief, and then whirled Chief and galloped at full speed in the direction of the ranch. He had to contact his parents, take care of his grandfather, do anything to take his mind off Sophie.

Twenty minutes later he rode into the yard in front of the barn, and jumped from Chief even as the horse skidded to a stop. The heavily lathered horse immediately stopped as his rider dismounted and wouldn't move again until Matthew returned. His eyes rolled in the direction of the mushroom cloud, by now turning to a dirty gray, but he didn't move.

Matthew slammed through the backdoor of the ranch house and raced into the Spanish style, stucco living room where his grandfather always sat in his leather chair, looking out the picture window to the south where he could see out across the hills of his domain. Don Pedro sat in his chair, a cellphone in his lap. A high pitched sound was coming from the phone but it ceased when Matthew entered the room. He crossed to his grandfather's side and immediately knew something was wrong.

"Nooo...!" He screamed and picked up the phone, throwing it across the room. Don Pedro's view from the front window had an unobstructed view of the cloud that was now anvil shaped and flowing southward. His grandfather had one hand clutching at his chest.

It was obvious to Matthew that Don Pedro was dead.

He cried then. He slid down onto the floor, holding Grandpa's hand, and cried for Don Pedro, for his Sophie and his Mom and Dad. He didn't know how long he stayed there but the will to survive asserted itself and he went into action. The wind was blowing out of the north and he thought that might buy him some time. Running out to the barn, he saw no sign of the ranch hands. He assumed they had tried to get home or back to town which probably meant their deaths. The old mine was about a mile north in the side of Robber's Hill. Matthew had played there repeatedly as a child, imagining it to be a pirate hangout or a shelter for outlaws.

Leading the three mares out of the barn, and riding Chief, he led them to the mine. He spent several precious minutes getting the horses into the mine, as they were already spooked by the light from the bombs and they weren't used to being in a confined space. He could now see there was more than one cloud and he re-doubled his efforts. Working as fast as he could, with sweat pouring down his cheeks, he used Don Pedro's truck to move the supplies to the mine and then used the ranch's flatbed to haul bales of hay to the entrance. He was in excellent shape but hours had passed since he first saw the mushroom cloud and he had been working hard the entire time. Just as he finished with the hay, and started back for the house, the truck died. It just quit. When he turned the key, absolutely nothing happened, not even a click. He didn't know how long he would have to hold out or how long his supplies would last so he just crawled through the tiny opening he'd left in the hay, closed it up and settled down for the duration.

He didn't even get to bury his grandfather.

Chapter 9

Cody was bleeding badly. The bullet had gone through the right side of his back and blown out through his chest almost under his right arm. They had driven for a mile along County Rd. 127 and then pulled over so Izzy could examine him. She bound his chest with a dressing and took over the driving.

They had hoped to find a temporary home somewhere around Eagle Nest Lake, but that was now out of the question. During their disaster preparations they had decided to shelter-in-place, and had failed to have a backup location. Now the improvised location they had chosen when they fled Raton was unavailable. Terry was unconscious and he was the only one that really knew the area. He mentioned once that if they traveled west from Eagle Nest, there was a way to get to the high country.

Dawn was breaking, and she was shocked that the night had fled so quickly. The paved road morphed into dirt and a fork in the road appeared ahead. The road to the right seemed the larger of the two so she swung the Jeep onto it and continued to travel at a dangerous speed. The Wrangler topped a slight hill and a valley opened up in front of them with a large ranch house in the distance. White fences now lined the road, and up ahead Izzy could see it dead-ended in a large, cleared area in front of the house. She slowed and considered returning the way they had come, but she needed to find someplace to shelter her family while she treated their wounds.

Pulling the car to the side of the road, she coasted to a stop. "I need to check it out," she told the girls. "You stay here and keep an eye out for anything that moves. I'll be back in a few minutes."

She exited the car and climbed through the white fence to the left. Brush and bushes had grown up in the fields between her and the house, providing fairly good cover as she made her way along the base of a hill trying to circle around to the back. There were horse shelters in each of the fenced pastures and she used them to hide behind as she kept her eyes on the ranch. When she had circled to the back she noticed a herd of some kind of animals, maybe cattle, about a mile away in the back pasture. That seemed odd, but if they had shelter, water and food they probably survived without human assistance.

In thirty minutes, she finally came up behind the house, flattening herself against the back wall. A screen door stood open, banging against the wall with every gust of wind. *They wouldn't put up with that if anyone was here,* she thought. Ducking into a covered porch, she quickly crossed to the back door that led into the house. It was unlocked. Holding her 9mm in front of her she stepped inside, swinging the gun left and right as her eyes swept the room.

It was empty.

The house appeared to be deserted as she went from room to room… until she came to the master bedroom. She smelled the sickly, sweet odor of death as she entered the hallway and when she opened the door to the bedroom she gagged at the strength of it. Someone was in the bed and another body stretched out from the bathroom into the carpeted bedroom.

Izzy quickly slammed the door and backed down the hall into the living room, gulping great lungsful of air and trying to settle her stomach. Still gagging, she opened the front door, went out to the yard and waved at the girls to come forward. She was relieved to see the Jeep moving slowly down the driveway. Missy pulled it up beside her.

"Missy, drive it around back so it'll be hidden from view." She ran around the side of the house with the car following her.

"Let's get Dad first. He'll be easier if we can wake him. Terry!" She gently slapped his face. "Terry, wake up. We need to get you in the house." He groaned and opened one eye.

"Wha…Where are we?"

"We're at a deserted ranch. Cody's been shot! We need to get you guys in the house. Can you stand?"

He nodded his head. "How's Cody? How bad?" he moaned loudly as she helped him out of the car with Missy helping from his other side.

"I don't know. We need to get him inside."

Holding the door open with her butt, they managed to get Terry into the porch, and from there, through a kitchen and dining room, into the living room.

"Missy, there are dead people in the bedroom, stay in this part of the house, okay?"

Missy looked shocked, but quickly agreed.

After laying Terry on the couch, they returned to get Cody. He was completely out.

"Marci, honey, I know you've had a terrible experience but we need you to help. Please, get his feet, okay?"

Marci slowly looked over as if in a dream, but grabbed the roof and climbed over the half door to come around the car and help them. Izzy took him under the shoulders and the girls got his feet. They struggled until Izzy felt someone brush past her and she saw Terry, fire in his eyes, take Cody's feet and they carried him into the house. As soon as they had him on the sofa, Terry slumped to his knees in pain. "Oh God, Iz! My ribs hurt so bad, I can barely breathe."

She had him stretch out on the floor with one of the couch pillows under his head. Then she turned to examine Cody. Still bleeding, he was pale and clammy. She held pressure on the exit wound until the bleeding finally slowed to an ooze. Bandaging both the entrance and exit wounds, she looked up to see him gazing at her. She lit up with a smile, took his face in her hands and started to cry.

"Mom, am I going to die?" he whispered.

"No Cody! You'll be alright. I got the bleeding stopped. Mostly."

"What about infection?" She could barely hear him as he rasped out the question.

"We'll think about that later."

"Dad? Marci?"

"They're fine. Be quiet now."

She stood up and looked around at the girls. "This was such a beautiful home. Who started this Goddam war!" She sank down on her knees beside her husband and wept.

"Mom says there are dead people in the back. But I bet I can find you some clothes." Missy started down the hall and Izzy was too tired to stop her. "The bodies are in the first room on the left!" she yelled after her.

After she got herself under control, Izzy bound Terry's ribs. She got a shiner for her trouble when, half out of his mind with pain, he reached out and hit her in the eye with the back of his hand.

Missy came back with a pair of jeans, a T-shirt and some shoes and socks. "Found them in a drawer in one of the bedrooms. They look too big. A fat girl musta owned them."

Marci stepped into the hallway and put the clothes on, returning with a stronger step, no longer being naked.

"Girls, see if there's any food in the kitchen. Kris, keep an eye out the front window. We need to lay low until everyone gets some rest. Maybe your Dad will be able to help us decide what to do."

They found some canned fruit and beans and supplemented it with dehydrated beef from their own stores.

"Mommy, there's two mules out back. Who feeds 'em?" Kris asked her.

"I don't know, honey. I think they just live on their own." She fervently hoped there wasn't anyone around to care for the animals, and with the bodies in the bedroom she couldn't imagine anyone staying here.

Checking Cody's wounds, she was relieved to find the bleeding had stopped. She sat on the floor and leaned back against the couch, closing her eyes and trying to calm down after all they had been through since midnight. Would she do it again? In retrospect she wasn't sure, with Cody wounded so badly. Jerking awake, she realized she had dozed off and wondered how long she'd been asleep. Cody was asleep or unconscious and Terry was trying to sit up.

"Terry, just stay down and get some rest."

"What happened to your eye?"

"You slugged me, you bastard."

"Ow! It hurts when I laugh."

"Then shut up and get some more rest. It doesn't even look like it's noon yet. I can't believe everything that's happened in only a few hours."

He looked at her and smiled through the pain. "Izzy, thank you for coming for us. It was probably stupid, but thank you."

"I had no choice. Your son was going after you, no matter what, so we just had to do it."

"How is he?"

"I think he's hurt real bad. If it had hit something vital I think he'd be dead by now, but even so, it's a pretty big hole and he bled a lot."

"Is it stopped?"

"Yeah, and he woke up once."

"How far are we from town?"

"A few miles. I don't think they have any transportation."

He grimaced and laid back down. "Just a little sleep, and then we'll decide what we're going to do. Talk to Marci, Iz." With that he fell back asleep.

***

Clay awoke with a start. Jinx said they had the men gathered together and were ready to start for the ranch. Clay had been dreaming of his father's yacht, and sailing to Catalina or the Channel Islands with a bevy of beautiful women and all his friends. They were drinking and partying and living the good life. He woke to a world far different than the one he was dreaming about and his mood soured. Now he only cared about revenge.

He went out to the front porch and found the men gathered with Stewart and Billy.

"Listen up! We're going to take a little hike. The ranch is only a few miles, so we're going to walk out there. If they went in that direction I expect we'll have them trapped. When they went through town, I saw at least three women. We'll get back the little cunt we had before and the rest of you can have the others."

The men looked around at each other, smiled and nodded. They figured it was worth a little hike to get ahold of the women. They had their backpacks and supplies and actually looked forward to getting out of town for a few hours. Walking down the main street, Therma, they headed west with Clay Hargraves in the lead, making their way through the town and along the county road. When they reached the fork in the road Clay looked at the tracks and became excited. It looked like the Jeep had taken the right fork.

They made good time and covered the first few miles in an hour and a half. As they topped the hill that gave them a view of the Platte Ranch, Clay had them fan out and take cover behind rocks and bushes. Stewart didn't understand the order and continued down the road in full view of the house.

"Stewart! Get back here!" Clay screamed at him.

Stewart looked hurt and returned to Clay's side. "Yes Clay. Yes Clay." He squatted behind the bush with Clay. He watched the house, trying to figure out if the Jeep had come this way. Waving his hand at the men, they all moved forward, staying behind cover as they snuck down the road.

***

"Mom! Someone's coming," Missy yelled.

Izzy jumped over to the window where Missy was pointing down the road. She took the binoculars and spotted a group of men coming over the hill. As soon as they crested it, they spread out behind boulders and all were hidden except two. They looked odd, and she was dismayed to realize they were two of those things that had almost gotten them a few short hours ago.

"Oh God, Missy. We have to get going. I really don't want to move Cody. He might start bleeding again but we have no choice." She started gathering their things, shoving the medical supplies into the backpack.

"They can't see the Jeep where we left it in back. Kris, take this backpack and get in the car. Missy and Marci, let's help your Dad."

Terry grimaced and tried to speak through his battered lips. "Get Cody first," he whispered in a raspy voice. "It will take you longer, and if you have to leave me, just go."

"Not a chance, buddy. Not after what we went through to rescue you. But, you're right, he will take longer. Come on girls."

Hoisting Cody to his feet, Izzy once again grasped him around the chest, under his arms, and the girls got his feet. Blood soaked through the bandages and stained her shirt. Terry watched but was unable to assist. Worried that he'd punctured a lung when he tried to man up and help them bring Cody into the house, all he could do was lie on the floor and watch them struggle to carry Cody out to the car. Izzy returned with Marci to help him up. When he tried to rise, he caught his breath with a sharp intake of air as they hoisted him to his feet. It took forever to get to the car, as each step brought a fiery stab of pain. Cody was lying on the back seat and Marci climbed over the side and raised him up to rest his head in her lap with Missy slipping in under his legs and Terry sitting on the passenger side of the vehicle. Kris was in her usual cubby hole behind the back seat.

Izzy ran around to the driver's side, climbed in and started the Jeep, taking off toward the north. As she rounded the back corner of the house she glanced back at the drive where it crested the hill, and saw two figures standing in the road. She accelerated and sped along the dirt road that led to a notch in the hills a couple of miles ahead of her. *Thank God Missy kept her eyes peeled!* She thought. *They would have caught us.*

***

Before Clay's band reached the halfway point between the hill and the ranch house, the Jeep screamed from behind the structure, heading north toward the next valley.

"Fuck!" he yelled. "Damn it Stewart, they saw you!" He kicked a rock that flew toward Stewart, barely missing him. Stewart looked crushed, and lowering his head, slunk to the back of the group of men that had come out of hiding and were gathered around Clay.

"Jinx. You said that the valley north of here is a dead end, right?"

"Yeah. There's a way out on the west side, but if they stay on the road they'll miss it and head into the valley where there's no way out."

"Let's get down to the house. We'll just wait for them to come back this way." They continued down the road to the ranch house and as they neared the house, Stewart became agitated.

"What the hell's wrong with him?" Jinx asked Clay.

Stewart was looking beyond the house to the back pasture where Clay could see a herd of animals. "Shit, look at that, will you? It looks like cattle. Go get 'em Stewart! Bring us one for dinner."

He clapped his hands and Stewart and Billy took off at a trot, heading for the distant cattle. Clay and the others continued on to the house. They didn't worry about stealth after seeing the Jeep take off from the back of the ranch house.

Clay tried the front door. It wasn't locked and all fifteen of the men followed him into the dark interior.

"Wow, this was a real nice place," Monroe said.

"Yeah, look at that gigantic fireplace."

"This is nothing. You should have seen the mansion I grew up in. Big, white, Spanish-looking place overlooking the Pacific Ocean. My Dad's a billionaire, remember? I can't wait to see the look on his face when I look him right in the eyes and pull the trigger, with him knowing what's going to happen. I hope he begs!" He was staring into space as he spoke.

The living room was dominated by a huge fireplace that took up half the south wall of the room. The area was carpeted with a plush carpet and an expensive sectional framed a stone and glass coffee table in front of the fireplace. Paintings covered the walls and there were tasteful objet d'art on the cherry wood accent tables.

Clay went through the dining room into a modern kitchen with a huge island. He opened the refrigerator and found several cans of warm beer. "Well, hell," he said. "It beats nothing." He popped the top of a can and drained half of it in one swallow.

"Hey Clay, check it out," Monroe called to him. He went back into the living room and Monroe pointed out bloodstains on the sofa.

"One of them is hurt."

Jackson said, "Yeah, it's probably the dude we messed up."

"I don't think so," Clay told him. "There's too much blood. Maybe we hit one of them when they got away. That puts them at a disadvantage if we have to fight them."

Clay plopped himself down on the couch. "I like this place, I think we'll move our headquarters here. All you guys get out of here. Set up sentries at the road and up at the north end of the valley."

There was a clatter in the back yard and Stewart broke in through the back door. He had a huge grin on his Neanderthal-like face and was breathing heavily. "Brought food!" he told Clay between gasps of air. Cows run fast!"

"Sweet! Good boy Stewart. Some of you guys gut that cow and let's have lunch!"

One of the men came up and whispered in his ear, "Uh, Clay? There's some dead folks back in the bedroom. It smells somethin' terrible."

"Well, get them out of there and open the windows. We need to use this place for a while. Monroe, go with the guys out to the road and be sure no one can get back from that valley. I want a blockade."

"You got it Boss."

By midafternoon they had disposed of the bodies in a bonfire and had steaks on a propane grill they found on the back patio. "This is more like it!" Clay said. "Give Stewart and Billy the rest of the cow."

The two changelings grabbed the carcass and moved off toward the barn. Clay finished his steak and went out front where he had a view of the northern hills and the dirt road that paralleled the river as it flowed toward Eagle Nest Lake.

"Just let them try to get past us." He pulled out his gun and checked the magazine.

Chapter 10

"We need to set up committees to get started on some projects." Mark stood on the rock in the center of the meadow looking out on the crowd of people. Almost everyone was in attendance, since the meeting would determine what they would be working on in the months ahead.

"First thing, of course, is security. Dave has that under control for now but we need a more permanent solution. I think we need to move the corrals to the center of the meadow, with tents around them so the creatures won't even try to get at them. What do you guys think?"

"Why don't we put them in the basement at night?" Trish Evans asked. She had been one of those working with the animals in the shelter and had a name for every one of them. "We can keep them out here during the day and let them into the basement at night. We can move the supplies together and wall off one end."

Al Spears said, "I don't like the idea of them being down there with the food. And it means we'd have to remove the waste. And those Billy goats smell something awful."

"He's right. But we can keep that in mind for emergencies if we can't secure the camp from the Devols," Mark said. "Hey Ted, or Beth. Have you made any plans for using the animals for food, or for a breeding program?"

"Well, not really," Ted answered. "It's only been two days, but if you want, we can get all the animal handlers together after the meeting and start discussing it."

"That would be great. Get a team together and decide how to manage the stock. Check with Marilyn and see what animal feed we have and how we can feed them with the natural resources we have in the valley."

He glanced over at Chris. "Chris, get your farmers together and start planning for the growing of crops."

"Actually, we've already done an inventory of the seeds and equipment," she said. "The weather seems a little better today so Samuel, Rana and some others of my team are going to 'walk the land' and see where the best areas are for planting. We need to feed over two hundred people so we need some fairly extensive acreage."

"Okay, select your team after this meeting. Does anyone know exactly how many people we have?"

Dr. Jim stood up. "Yeah, we have two-hundred and five adults and forty-seven kids under the age of eighteen. There are ninety-six men and one-hundred and nine women."

There were several hoots from the men in the crowd and Mark laughed. "Some of the women are pretty good with their weapons and can help out with guard duty if they want. All the men can take their turn."

"Wait a minute," Danny Fielder said. "You can't make us stay out at night with those things out there. I can do something else." He had been one of Clay's friends in the shelter.

"You know Danny, you never did any work in the shelter nor did you or your friends contribute in any way. It wasn't a big factor since there were plenty of supplies and no one had to go hungry. It's going to be different out here. Everyone's going to have to do their share, even you."

"Well, I can do something else."

"Make him one of the babysitters," Jimbo said sarcastically. Others in the crowd laughed, and someone else called out, "He can do the laundry!"

Dave said, "The problem is, that since we need so many sentries, we need every able- bodied man to help us out. And some of the women that are willing. Otherwise, guys will get tired from pulling duty too often."

"Okay, let's identify all our needs and then we can see what we'll do about the guard duty. Lori and some of the others are going to explore the valley this morning, and I suggested that her group form a hunting party. We don't want to eat our domestic animals unless we have to. If we can bring in game, we can just breed the domestic stock until we have sustainable herds. So Lori, can you lead that group?"

She nodded at him and beamed with pride at his confidence in her.

"Other things we need are 'sanitation engineers', a construction crew, a committee to decide how we're going to govern ourselves, someone to schedule childcare and education, food preparation, a laundry service and a tech group to set up the solar panels and communications."

Lucas James stood up and Mark sighed, knowing Lucas would try to throw a wrench in the works. "I think we need to decide if we want to have a 'tech' group as you call it. Why don't we just learn to live like they did in the nineteenth century? We don't need all that crap. Look where it got us."

He started to go on but was interrupted by Dr. Herbert Laskey, Ph.D. and formerly a college professor. "Mr. James, you would not be living like they did in the nineteenth century but more like the eighteenth. The nineteenth century had a burgeoning technology sector with telegraph communications, railroads, photography, and toward the end of the century even automobiles and electricity. People in the seventeen hundreds were cold and hungry. Their only firearms were muskets and they were scarce. Hunting was difficult. Medicine was almost non-existent. Ask any of THEM if they would choose to live like that if they had a way to make it better."

"Yeah Lucas," Walter continued. "You know, this isn't some kind of a camping trip. Why should we purposely be uncomfortable when we have the means to do better? There's a small tractor in the basement. Should we furrow the fields by hand if we can use the tractor instead? That's crazy and I think you're the only one who feels that way. I've got kids and a new granddaughter and I want to make their lives as comfortable as possible." There were murmurs of assent in the crowd and almost everyone was nodding.

"Lucas, you dick. What do you think it would be like if we came out of the shelter and this building wasn't here?" Jimbo asked him. "We'd be standing around in our skimpy T-shirts and shorts, freezing our asses off with nothing to eat, and turning into dinner for those things out there."

"Remember," Chris put in, "there's still a world beyond this valley. We don't know if there are many others still alive, but at some point they will impact our lives. We need to establish a community and get a thriving civilization going, so if there are others out there we can meet them on our own terms. If we go back to the Dark Ages they may just beat the shit out of us."

Mark held up his hands for quiet. These meetings always seemed to disintegrate into dozens of separate conversations. "Listen, the committee on governance can address your concerns, Lucas, but I believe the majority of us would like to use everything at our disposal to get us ready for next winter. Am I right? How many of you want to forgo using the tools Will left for us and live Lucas's primitive lifestyle?"

Lucas and his wife, and one other couple raised their hands. "You know Lucas, when we get the community going, you and Stephen can build your cabins without modern tools or conveniences. That's up to you." He turned away from Lucas and told the others, "It's too hard to conduct business with the full population in attendance, so in the future I'll meet with the committee heads and they can keep their teams informed. Everyone can serve on a working team and still rotate on guard duty. Lori, get your group together and head out on your exploration. You probably won't find game today, but if you go early enough tomorrow morning it'll be better."

At this point Glen, Marilyn and Kate all stood up. Glen said, "Down at the south end of the valley, just before it narrows, there's a break in the hills on the west side. The hills coming down from the north turn inward and the southern cliff turns west. In between them is what we call 'the ramp.' It's about a quarter of a mile wide and the land climbs upward toward the northwest into the high country. It's covered in pine trees and a lot of game comes down out of the mountains to graze and get water from the spring at Platte Rock. The rocks hide the entrance to the ramp so it's hard to see. Anyway, that's a good place for hunting. We saw a herd of some kind of animal grazing down that way when we exited the cave so I know some of the game animals survived."

"Thanks Glen, can you meet with Lori and give them a better description of the valley so they know what to expect?" Glen nodded and started over toward Lori.

"Dave, pick a cadre of lead security guys and set up a rotation using all the men. Any of you women that feel you can help, talk to Dave. Chris, get your farmers together. Lucas, you were a carpenter, right?"

"I was a framer."

"Okay, would you be willing to head the building team?" He wanted to get Lucas involved, hoping it would stop his complaining.

"Okay."

"Marilyn, please meet with each team and let them know what tools they have to accomplish their goals. Kate, please assign someone for food prep, laundry and sanitation. Ted, get the animal handlers together. Dr. Laskey set up a governance group, and Barbara Thompson? Can you start planning for education?" He ticked them off on his fingers.

"Lucas, the first thing we need is a bachelor's building, a log cabin that can house twenty or so guys so we can get everyone into a building. We won't need as many sentries that way. Figure out a good location and we'll meet this afternoon. I will meet individually with this leadership group this afternoon after lunch. That gives everyone a chance to put together their teams and have a planning session. Team leaders spread out in the meadow and all you others go to the team you want to work in. We will reassign as necessary if, for example, no one wants the shit detail. Any comments?"

The leaders began to spread out and gather their helpers.

"Hey Marilyn," Mark asked. "Can you show me the basement?"

***

Matthew heard the horse whinny again, louder this time. He rolled over and saw all four horses looking southeast from the ridge Matthew had camped on the night before. Coming over the western hills late last night, he was unable to see much detail in the fading twilight. He and the horses were tired after a longer than usual ride the day before. Spotting a small band of survivors several miles to the west, he had wanted to put as much distance as possible between him and them before dark. Over the past two months, since he had emerged from the mine, he had seen several groups of people, but his attempts to make contact had always ended in bloodshed. Fortunately, theirs. The groups were never large and the people looked half-starved and wild-eyed. Only one group had children... two emaciated looking boys.

When dawn had broken that morning, he had checked out his surroundings. In the light of day, he could see that this ridge overlooked two valleys below. The one to the north was completely surrounded by mountains with the exception of the opening at the south end. The other was larger, pretty flat, and had mountains on the north side that separated it from the first valley and there were more mountains to the west. Low hills formed a barrier to the south but to the east the terrain looked open. In the distance was a large modern-looking ranch house with a big, beautiful barn and several out-buildings.

He glanced in the direction the horses were looking and the first thing he noticed was the large ranch he'd seen that morning. With its corrals and shelters for horses, he felt a pang of homesickness for his grandfather's place.

When he'd finally had enough of subterranean living, he'd left the mine shaft, not caring whether the radiation was gone or not. He never fully recovered from the intestinal upset he'd suffered and his weight had fallen to one hundred and sixty pounds. As he moved aside the last few remaining bales of hay, the horses had brushed past him into the freedom of the open countryside. Chief pounded beyond the mares and rounded them up, circling and nipping at them until they settled down a hundred yards from the entrance to the mine and began to eat at the brown grass that was partially covered with snow. The bright sunlight was almost too much and Matthew walked over and sat down on a rock to allow his eyes to adjust to the brilliance. His mood lifted, as if being out of the mine released some of his torment. He was weak, actually winded from moving a few hay bales. He considered returning to the mine shaft to see if there was anything he could use, but couldn't bring himself to go back in there even one more time.

Whistling for Chief, he started off in the direction of the ranch, dreading, yet anticipating the chance to lay his Grandfather to rest. The big appaloosa trotted up to him with the mares following behind. He crossed a meadow onto an overgrown service road that led through a stand of Pinyon pines toward the ranch. Just walking the mile down the road to the ranch left him exhausted. When the road left the trees and the barn was visible the mares took off and even Chief couldn't stop them as they galloped into the barn, as if they hadn't been gone for months.

Matthew slowed his steps as he approached the rear of the ranch house. He hesitated, and then with a firmness he didn't really feel, he opened the door and entered the kitchen of the hacienda. The smell of death still lingered in the house and he silently made his way to the living room where his Grandfather's body reposed in his chair, his hand still over his chest. Matthew stood looking at his Grandfather for an eternity, remembering all the great times during his journey from childhood to man. Don Pedro had taught him to ride and train horses, to rope calves, track and hunt game and make bows and arrows. His father had taught him about women but Don Pedro had been the one that helped him get beyond the breakup with his first girlfriend. They had ridden through the hills until the pain had slipped away and his heart began to heal.

He went into the bedroom and brought out the large comforter, laying it on the floor next to Don Pedro's chair. Very carefully, as the body was deteriorating, he lowered his grandfather onto the bedspread. Wrapping the body, he left enough cloth left to drag him through the door and into the front yard that overlooked the valley. Retrieving a shovel from the barn, he spent hours digging a hole. After laying Don Pedro in the shallow grave, he refilled it and spent another hour bringing large rocks from the wall that lined one side of the yard. He piled the rocks on the fresh earth to ensure no animals would dig into the grave. Getting down on his knees beside the grave, he prayed for his grandfather's soul, then sat cross legged in front of it, gazing over the valley and watching as the sun set through a reddish haze that cast an ominous pall over the area.

When it was dark, and he was freezing, Matthew climbed stiffly to his feet and went back to the house. He searched the cupboards and found some canned goods. Preparing a meal of Spam and chili he ate more than he had eaten at one sitting in the last six months. Going to the barn he saw that the mares had all entered stalls and he even managed a chuckle at that. Chief stood in the corridor looking at him as if to wonder, "What's next?"

He didn't know what was next. He pulled some hay from the back room of the barn and fed the mares, closing the stall doors to ensure they wouldn't leave. He left Chief free. The horse would act as a watchdog and alert him if there was trouble. The barn had snow blowing in through the door and the temperature was dropping quickly. The old mine shaft was cold, but had maintained a fairly constant temperature for all those months. He pulled the door almost closed but left room for Chief to exit if he needed to and he went back to the house, crawled into his bed and fell asleep

The next day, after more cold spam, he saddled Chief and rode the property. Fences were falling apart and he saw no sign of the cattle or the herd of horses that had roamed freely on the land. He considered staying here. It was now his ranch and he had nowhere else to go. There were seeds in the basement that his grandfather had squirreled away with the other supplies, and he could hunt game for food. He knew he could survive and be fairly comfortable but he knew the ghosts of the past, his memories of Don Pedro, his grandmother and his parents, and especially of Sophie would never let him rest. He would have to leave.

That afternoon a storm moved in and pummeled the house and barn. Already the barn had leaks, though the house itself seemed secure. Matthew organized the gear he'd left in the basement when he moved to the mine shaft and brought in additional supplies from the barn. He tried to think about what he would do or where he would go but found it impossible to make concrete plans. He had seen the bombs to the south and knew they were pretty far away but the one he felt on the second day in the mine had shaken the ground severely. It had to have been closer but there didn't seem to be any damage other than stuff that had been thrown around in the basement and the barn

It wouldn't be wise to head south for Santa Fe. In his heart he knew his parents were gone. That last bomb had been too close to there. He made a decision to go to Taos and see if others still lived besides himself. If the town hadn't suffered damage he could probably pick up all the supplies he needed. With the decision made, he slept the last night in his home.

Matthew squinted into the early afternoon sun and the second thing he saw was something he wasn't sure he would ever see again. A plume of dust from a vehicle. It was moving at a very high speed up the valley toward the notch in the hills leading into the valley to the north.

The third thing, in the valley on the left, was smoke rising in a column as if from a controlled source. It was around two-thirds of the way to the northern cliffs where he could just make out a waterfall cascading downward until he lost it behind the forest.

Matthew crossed to the line where the horses were tethered and the saddlebags were stacked on the ground. He saddled Daisy with the bag for his gear and Rose with the bags for his weapons. The pregnant mare, Tulip, carried no load. His bedroll was still next to the cold remnants of his campfire and he quickly rolled the bag, and packed it and his other gear into the saddlebags on Daisy. Grabbing his rifle from the scabbard, he moved like a wraith to the rocks at the edge of the drop-off just as the car, a Jeep, drove through the opening into the second valley. On the west side of the valley, there was a break in the hills with the land gradually sloping up into the mountains, but the Jeep stayed by the river flowing through the meadow and their view of this escape route was blocked by piles of large boulders, some bigger than houses. They slowed when they entered the valley, probably out of caution. Moving forward they came alongside a huge oval monolith when their vehicle was suddenly surrounded by armed men. The vehicle accelerated, and pulled a one-eighty, dust flying high behind it, but other men stepped forward with rifles aimed at the occupants of the car and it slammed to a stop. Matthew bent low and went back to the horses to finish packing his gear.

Chapter 11

A group of hunters that included Lori, big Tom Galloway, Al Spears, Sheri Summerland and five others headed out to explore the valley and see if they could hunt any game. They thought Greg Whitehorse, being an American Indian, would be the best hunter, but he laughed and told them, "I'm a geology professor, not a hunter. I've never been hunting in my life."

"I don't suppose you can track animals?" Lori asked him.

"Sorry, no," he said with a sheepish grin.

Pete Thompson laughed and told him, "Some Indian you are! Well, me and Jerry have hunted lots of times so let's hit the road." He and his brother Jerry went to the head of the group as they all took the trail leading north out of camp.

They stopped on the bridge to admire the falls. The water cascaded down the cliff with at least seven actual falls that spilled over rocks, each plummeting anywhere from six to sixty feet.

The pool at the base of the falls was large, with a flat boulder in the middle.

"That would be a great place to swim and sunbathe," Pete remarked. "At least after the water warms up later in the summer. Right now I bet it's colder than a witch's tit." Even the mist from the falls was freezing cold.

"C'mon guys we need to get to the south end of the valley. Let's cross over to the west side and go through the trees. If there's any game, maybe that will mask our approach. As silently as they could they moved across the brush covered meadow almost a mile and a half to the aspen groves to the west. There were some pines sprinkled in amongst the aspens that gave better cover than the almost leafless aspens. An animal trail wound through the trees and encouraged them to believe there might be game farther south.

The trees petered out and the trail ended in a jumble of rocks at the base of the hills to the west. Jerry jumped up on a boulder to get a better look. After a minute he rejoined the group and said, "I can see a herd of some kind of deer about a mile south. There's no cover between here and there. We can try and sneak as close as we can get, take a long shot and hope we hit something. Tomorrow we need to get out here before dawn and set up a hide before they come down out of the high country."

"Do we stand a chance?" Lori asked him.

"I doubt it, but we came out to explore the valley. I didn't really think we would get any game this late in the day. It's past noon."

"Well everyone try and keep quiet. If we can't get close enough, don't waste any ammo."

Working their way down the valley, staying in the cover of the rocks they eventually spotted the herd grazing close to a break in the hills on their right.

Everyone threw their rifles to their shoulders. "Everyone take one shot, no more!" But before they fired a single shot the herd spooked and disappeared up the ramp to the west. Lowering their weapons they all muttered curses and looked over at Lori, who just shrugged and motioned them forward.

They came to the ramp where the deer had disappeared. The hills abruptly ended and the land gradually rose up into the high country to the west. The ramp was covered with rocks and pine trees and the undergrowth was so thick it hid most of the ground. To their left and ahead a quarter of a mile was a pile of boulders surrounding a large, weathered rock that shot straight up above them.

"Glen said that was called 'Platte Rock'," Jerry told them. "There's supposed to be a spring there."

"Let's check it out."

A short hike brought them to the base of the granite giant and they circled the entire jumble of rocks. When they reached the west side they spied a trickle of water that came from under the rocks and created a small pool. The water then ran over a rock berm and formed a tiny stream that ran south.

"Not much of a spring," Jerry said.

"No. But there's probably not much water at the top of that ramp and there's the river down here, too. That's why the animals all come down here to graze." Pete looked up the ramp and then suddenly said, "What the hell's that sound?"

Quieting down, they all listened for whatever Pete had heard. Lori waved her arm at them. "It sounds like a car! It's coming up the valley." They scurried toward the rocks, keeping the boulders between them and the sound of the vehicle. Lori pointed to Jerry, Pete and Greg to go around to the north side of the rocks that extended into the meadow and the others went with her, sneaking past the rock pile and coming up behind the car.

Jerry and Pete jumped from behind a rock and rushed over in front of the Jeep, yelling, "Halt! Drop your weapons!"

Jerry had noticed that a girl in the back seat held a rifle.

The car accelerated and swung away from them toward the river, the driver cranking the wheel hard, with the back of the car sliding around and throwing up dirt and rocks into their faces. As the car came about facing south Tom and Al stepped up on either side of the front seat and thrust their rifles into the faces of the driver and young women in the back.

"Stop the car or I'll shoot!" Boomed out Tom's voice. The girl in back with the rifle had dropped it and the vehicle came to a sudden halt.

Lori saw that the driver was a woman, and there were four others in the car. As she approached she could hear a teenaged girl in the backseat crying and saying something to the driver. There appeared to be two males, both unconscious, and another younger girl in the back seat.

The driver looked stricken, as though her worst nightmare was about to become true.

***

Mark was flabbergasted at the amount of supplies in the basement, and once again, at Will's foresight. The basement wasn't quite as large as the structure above, which allowed the building to rest on solid ground. There were rows of supplies filling most of the areas between the stairs and the back wall. On the left, in front of the stairs, was a clear area extending all the way to the back. A ramp could be seen on the left that Mark assumed led up to the outside. The place was a mess, with supplies tumbled about like they had been tossed by a tornado. Upstairs, they had been more secured.

"Marilyn, we'll get a work crew down here to clean this up."

"Thanks. We could use the help." Marilyn looked over at Kate, who giggled and bobbed her head.

Walter Thompson stood with his hands on his hips, shaking his head at the mess. "Mark, you're going to need someone to manage the resources. Everybody is going to want to use the tractor and fuel. I volunteer for the job."

"I didn't think of that. Thanks for offering. The job's yours." They walked down the first aisle and saw that most of the supplies down there were foodstuffs. There were fifty-five gallon drums of wheat and rice, and five gallon plastic containers with freeze dried food of every description.

Walter laughed and pointed at a several pallets stacked high with #10 cans. "Oh my God, enough freeze-dried potatoes to last a lifetime. Someone really likes potatoes!"

Walking up and down the narrow alleyways, and stepping over and around the fallen containers, they discovered, in addition to food, cooking utensils, propane stoves, and cast iron pots. Marilyn hefted several boxes back onto a stack of cartons that had fallen over.

"Once people begin to build their own cabins," Marilyn explained, "they will need to stock their kitchens with supplies. I think there's enough to furnish about thirty households, more if they spread the supplies out. After that folks will have to make their own."

In the back corner they located two tractors sitting alongside various attachments. There were three portables generators, a utility ATV with front and rear racks and a trailer that could be pulled with the ATV.

"Seems almost a waste to have all this stuff that runs on gas. There's a couple of underground gas tanks but the supply is limited, and then these things will make great planter boxes and decorations," Walter told the others.

"The idea," Marilyn said, "was to get a good start on planting crops and building a town. These tools will allow that to go faster and then we can learn to do all the work manually. But at least we'll get a jump on next winter."

Someone shouted from the top of the stairs, "Hey Mark! Doc wants to see you."

"I'll be right there," he called back. "Walter, will you get some folks to help the ladies clean this up? Get those guys that used to hang around with Clay. I didn't see any of them joining any of the other work groups."

"Yeah. I'll kick some ass if need be," Walter said with relish.

Mark went upstairs and headed back to the medical area. Before he arrived he could hear a high-pitched moaning. It rose and fell, like an animal caught in a trap and in severe pain. When he went around the screen he saw Jim and Aaron holding Micah down on the bed. He strained against them alternately going rigid and limp, in what appeared to be some kind of seizure.

"What the hell's going on with him?" He rushed over to help.

"Don't know. He suddenly came out of his coma and started thrashing around. Then he went into a sort of tetany with his entire body stiffening up, and then he just went limp. He keeps repeating that cycle. He's gritting his teeth so hard I'm afraid he's going to break 'em." Micah thrashed about and Jim grabbed his arms to keep him still. "Carmen! See if there's any restraints in those drawers. If not, get me some bandannas and parachute cord."

As Mark neared the bed Micah flipped on his side as though to get out of bed.

His nightshirt was soaked through with sweat, and even though it was white it appeared green.

"Wha…Aaron grab him!" Micah surged to his feet and they all latched on to a body part as they wrestled him back onto the bed. His shirt ripped and Aaron jumped back.

"Shit! What's happening to his back?" Aaron had green slime all over his arm.

Holding him face down, Doctor Jim examined the inflamed, weeping wounds on his back. "It looks infected but not like anything I've ever seen. His skin looks like those monsters out there."

Mark looked troubled and blurted out, "You don't think he's turning into one?" Mark had worked very closely with Micah over the past eight months and really cared about him.

"I haven't a clue." All of a sudden Micah quit struggling and collapsed back on the bed, becoming quiet and returning to his almost catatonic state. Aaron got some saline and bandages and began to clean up and dress Micah's back.

Carmen hurried over with the bandannas and rope but Jim waved her away. "Don't think we'll need those now. He seems to be falling back into his coma."

"What would cause his back to look like those things?"

"I don't know, Mark. Aaron said the creature slobbered all over the cuts on his back. It could be infected but we're filling him full of antibiotics and his skin looks like it's morphing into something alien. He seems to be quiet now. We'll keep a close eye on him. I hope to hell he wakes up, we're using up a lot of our I.V. fluids and if we run out we have no way to hydrate him."

"Okay." He was breathing hard. "Well, I'll be back in the basement."

***

Leaving the first valley, and the graded road behind, Izzy had slowed and moved forward past the river on her right. There was a ghost of a two-track road almost completely overgrown, that she was trying to follow. There were masses of rocks on the left and she was uncertain about where to go, when suddenly, in the road ahead, she saw a figure rise up from behind a rock and shout for them to stop.

She glanced in the rearview mirror and saw Marci's terrified look. That decided her and she hit the accelerator while cranking the wheel all the way to the right. The tires spit up dirt and rocks and the men threw their arms over their faces to protect them. As the car came about she started to hit the gas again when men stepped up on either side of the Jeep and stuck their rifles in the faces of her and the girls. Terry had moaned and come awake at the abrupt movement of the car but seemed disoriented. Another figure stepped in front of the car down the road, but far enough away to dodge, if necessary. Without conscious thought she slammed on the brakes and skidded to a stop.

"Oh no, Mom. Please, please don't stop! Oh God, don't let them get me!" Marci whimpered over and over and Izzy almost hit the gas again but there were too many men.

"Drop your weapons! Don't be stupid lady!"

"She frantically looked around for a way out, but the big man on her side of the car reached back and grabbed the rifle Missy had dropped. Terry was more awake now, but when he tried to sit up the man on his side of the car shoved a pistol in his face and said, "Stay real still Mister." Cody was lying across Marci's legs and Missy was frozen in place. She knew what had happened to Marci and was terrified of these men.

Izzy threw her hands in the air. "Please, we haven't done anything to you. Please, let us go!"

"We're not going to hurt you."

Shocked, Izzy glanced quickly toward the sound of a female voice and saw two armed women walking toward the Jeep. She was stunned into silence, her mind trying to process the implications of these women being equal to, rather than slaves, of these men.

"I'm Lori. Where'd you get a working vehicle?" A movement caught Lori's eye and she threw up her weapon, as a little girl came up out of the space behind the back seat with a handgun.

"Duck!" Lori screamed, and they all hit the dirt just as the gun went off. The round went high due to the recoil and Jimbo jumped up just as the girl tried to fire again. He grabbed the gun out of her hand as her mother screamed at her.

"Kris, stop!" Intuition warned her that these people may not be like the animals they had encountered in town.

Lori's head came back above the half-door of the Jeep. "You have any more surprises for us? You need to settle down. I said we wouldn't hurt you. Get out of the car so we can find all the guns you've got."

Terry tried to speak but Jerry pushed his gun against his temple. "Just stay out of it, Bud."

Lori waved her rifle at the woman, to exit the car, but she didn't move.

"Please, you have to let us go. I have to find help! My son's been shot. He's going to die! I have to find help."

Greg looked at the boy lying across the girl's lap. "He's bleeding Lori."

Marci had thrown her arm up when the man approached and he gave her a puzzled look. "This guy over here's not in real good shape either," Jerry told her.

"We have a doctor. Come with us and we'll see what he can do."

"You have a doctor?" Izzy couldn't believe her ears. "You have a doctor? Please hurry!"

The Jeep had running boards so Lori jumped onto the one by the driver and grabbed onto the roof. "Let's go."

"You're not going off with these guys by yourself, Lori." Jimbo climbed on the running board opposite her. "Don't try any funny business," he told Terry, still leveling his pistol at the man's temple.

"Alright, the rest of you get back to camp. We'll see you there," Lori called out as the car moved off toward the north.

The vehicle had to go slowly due to the uneven terrain. Lori thought she was going to be thrown from it on several occasions.

When it came opposite the camp, she saw Chris and several others checking out the land on the opposite side of the river. They had heard the car coming and were grabbing their weapons even as Lori called out to them.

"Chris, It's me. It's okay. We have some injured people. Can you get two stretchers and come to the bridge in case the car can't fit?"

"We'll be right there." Chris took off running toward camp with the others trying to keep up.

***

Mark went back to the basement with Walter, to check out the weapon's locker. There were quite a few boxes of 9mm, Springfield 30-06 and .223 ammo. Each box had one thousand rounds. After moving aside some of the other supplies he discovered shotgun shells and even some ammo for the Uzi, the only fully automatic weapon they possessed. He selected a Smith and Wesson .45 caliber for himself, and immediately felt better. There were fifty various handguns and rifles in the locker. They still didn't have enough for everyone to have one, and he again thought about the guns that remained in the shelter. The residents, including all the men and most of the women, wore belts with sheaths for knives. Dave and some of the other men that were skilled with knives were holding classes to familiarize folks with their use. Maybe at some point they could organize a party to enter the "Crow's Nest" to retrieve the handguns and rifles.

"We need to issue these to some of the guys so they can help out with guard duty."

"I'll get together a list and get the men down here so they can get their ammo." Walter turned and started toward the stairs. He glanced up quickly as someone screamed down from above, "Hey Mark. There's a car coming! Lori says it's got injured folks. C'mon. They need you."

***

Lori directed Izzy to parallel the river and when they got to the bend they followed the curve around to the bridge. When they came to it, it was just as she suspected, the Jeep was too wide to cross over. She looked up to see Chris, Mark, Aaron and, what appeared to be the entire population of the camp, coming out of the forest.

The Jeep halted just north of the bridge and Lori jumped off to meet Chris and the others as they came across the meadow with the stretchers.

"What do you have there?" Mark called out as he trotted across the bridge and up to the car. Aaron leaned over the door to check out Terry and Jimbo backed off to keep the occupants of the car covered. Izzy had run around the front of the Jeep.

"Please. Are you the doctor? My son's been shot."

"Can some of you guys pull the boy out of the car?" Aaron directed as he opened the front door and gently lifted Terry out and down onto a stretcher.

"Broken ribs?"

Terry nodded. "Get my son. He's hurt worse than me." Grimacing in pain he pointed back to where three men were sliding Cody out of the car and onto the second stretcher.

"I can't do much here," Aaron told them. "Let's get them back to camp."

The crowd parted to let them through with the stretchers, and Lori walked up to Izzy who was motioning for the girls to follow them. She put her arm over Izzy's shoulder. "Jim and Aaron are great doctors. If anyone can help them, they can. The camp is a half mile. You'll have to leave the Jeep here."

Crowding around their mother, the girls and Izzy hurried after the men that carried her loved ones, the rest of the residents of the survival camp trailing behind.

Dr. Jim had pulled two of the beds out of the area where Micah was sleeping and put a partition between the two areas. Both of the injured men were slipped onto beds and Jim had everyone leave except he and Aaron, Izzy and the girls, and Lori and Mark.

"Kris, my youngest, has been wounded, too. It was just a graze, but could you look at it?"

"Of course. We'll check it soon as we take care of these two. What are their names?" Jim asked her.

"My husband is Terry and my son is Cody."

While Jim examined Cody, Aaron took a look at Terry.

"You might want to send the girls out to get cleaned up and get some food. You just go over there to the left and ask for Helen."

"I'll take them," Lori told him. "Come on girls, let them do their work."

"Mom, I want to stay with you! Please don't make me go," the older girl begged.

"I think it's okay Marci." She pulled Marci close and whispered in her ear, "These people seem to be okay and I don't think they're going to hurt us." She looked over at Missy and Kris and told them all to go with Lori.

Aaron removed the bandages Izzy had used to bind Terry's ribs and after examining them he rebound them tighter than she had originally. "You need to be still and stop moving around so much."

"You're not spitting up blood so I don't think you punctured a lung but more than one rib is broken. The pleura, the lining of the lung, is extremely sensitive. One of the broken ribs may be poking it and that's why you're in so much pain."

He moved over to assist Jim and found that Jim had cleaned up the wound and was assessing the damage.

Carmen had started an I.V., checked Cody's hemoglobin with a handheld device and was administering antibiotics.

Jim turned to Terry and Izzy. "He's lost a lot of blood but his hemoglobin is still 7.5 grams. That's pretty low but if it doesn't go much lower he should be okay. We're giving him antibiotics and Aaron can do some surgery to clean it up. He may lose some use of his right arm but will probably still be able to use it for most things.

"Whoa!" He jumped forward as Izzy slumped and eased her to the ground. She had passed out cold.

Later that evening, after a good meal, Izzy and the girls sat in the couches at the front of the building and carried on a conversation with a small portion of the Remnant, as they had come to think of themselves.

Izzy's normally bronzed skin was pale, a result of the non-ending danger they had encountered since passing through Cimarron; the hair-raising rescue of her family, the unimaginable treatment of her daughter and the flight to this valley. She gave them a brief accounting of how they had survived the war and how they had come to Eagle Nest. When she tried to tell of Terry and Marci's capture, she broke down and had to be comforted by Lori and Chris.

"You don't have to relive it at this moment, Isobel."

"My nickname's Izzy. I prefer it," she told Lori. "How is it all of you are here? It looks like you just got here rather than living here the whole time. You must have been protected for the past few months."

"Well, that's an interesting story," said Chris, but before she began they looked up to see Terry making a very slow approach with Aaron at this elbow.

"This guy's pretty stubborn. Wants to be out here with his family." Aaron eased Terry down next to Izzy as Lori moved over to give him room. Izzy smiled at him and took his hand.

Lori, Chris and several others took turns telling the story of the few days before the war and how most of them had received devices that warned them of the coming conflict. They chimed in with their personal stories and after a couple of hours had brought the Holcomb family up-to-date with the tale of how Will had built an underground shelter that protected them all from the radiation and nurtured them through the past eight months . They explained how they had lived underground, studying and learning skills to help them survive, how the earthquakes had led up to the "big one" and about the horrifying creatures they had encountered.

Terry's eyes widened. "Geez, we saw some of those! There was one in Raton that caused us to leave. I'd never seen anything like it before. Then, when we were being held by those animals in town there were more of them. At least two or three. Funny though. They didn't seem to be as bad as the first one we saw. What are they?"

"We aren't sure," Mark said. "We've speculated that they were once men, and I guess women, although we haven't seen any, that were somehow changed by the radiation. Someone suggested they came from underground after the earthquakes but most of us think that's unlikely."

"There was a man we talked to in Eagle Nest," Izzy said, "that claimed he was still human, and that meant he wasn't evil. Like somehow it was the evil guys that changed. He said the ones that look like Neanderthals were really evil men before the war. Is that possible?"

Herbert Laskey said, "There's been a debate for decades about whether evil people, like serial killers, are born that way or are shaped by their environment. I have always felt it was a combination of the two. There's no denying that some people with a good upbringing just seem rotten to the core and turn out bad. Maybe there's an 'evil gene' that was changed by the radiation."

"Yeah, and the more evil, the more they changed," Chris said. "That would be a good way to tell who was bad, except that the evil guys that weren't exposed to radiation didn't change. That could be misleading. We still can't tell if they're bad guys."

"No," said Terry. "Like the leader of the band. He looked perfectly normal but was about the most evil asshole I've ever encountered."

"Would you recognize him if you saw him again? We might need to know," Mark asked.

"Are you kidding? I'll never forget that face." He was staring at his daughter. "If I ever run into him again, I'll kill him.

"The guy's name is Clay Hargraves."

Chapter 12

"You know," Clay said, "this place isn't half bad. It beats the shit out of my old place on the hill."

"Yeah, but it's kind of out o' the way and the town has all the supplies."

Clay was stretched out on the long couch and Monroe lay on the short sofa with his legs hanging over the arm.

"After we get that fucking Jeep, we can move a ton of stuff out here. It looks like we have a whole herd of cattle. And there's a couple of mules, too. If we can catch them." Clay slung his feet around and stood looking down at Monroe. "We're going to spend the night, and then tomorrow I'm going to leave a bunch of guys to keep up the blockade, and the rest of us are going back to town. I'm sick of waiting around. It's time to go teach the old man a lesson."

Clay, becoming agitated by thinking of his father and how he had treated him stalked to the kitchen for another warm beer. Monroe watched him leave the room and wished again that he could just walk away from town and never look back. One of the guys had tried to sneak away at night and Clay had sent the changelings after him. They must have a great sense of smell, which was weird since they smelled so bad themselves, because they tracked the guy down and killed him. Stewart came back chewing on a leg bone.

Walking into the covered porch, Clay gazed out the window at Stewart and Billy as they came out of the barn. Their faces, arms and hands were covered with blood.

"Look at those assholes," Jinx said from behind him. "They changed so much they's just like a couple of animals. I wonder if they ate that whole cow."

"Yeah, well, they're very useful animals. They do exactly what I say and as long as we can feed them, I think they'll be okay. If they outlive their usefulness, we'll kill them."

He went back through the house to check out the bedrooms. The first room, where they found the bodies, still stank. He continued down the hallway and went in the first room to the right. It was painted a light blue with wallpaper on one wall depicting flying unicorns. The furniture was white with gold trim and there were stuffed animals on the dresser and the neatly made bed. Posters of Justin Bieber and Taylor Lautner adorned the walls.

"I wonder what happened to the kid that had this room. Reminds me of the sweet thing you let escape." He scowled at the men that followed him into the room. "The bed's big enough, I'll sleep here. You guys find somewhere else to crash."

He went back to the living room and instructed Jinx to get some wood to start a fire in the fireplace. Reclining on the couch, he told the men stories of his glory days, living in his father's mansion and spending his days in idyllic idleness, with unlimited booze, women and money.

***

Chief picked his way down the hill and around the thick, gray-green brush that spread between the trees and rocks. Matthew gave him his head and let him choose his own path. The mares followed, connected together by a long tether. The day was warm and most of the snow at the top of the ramp had melted with only a few patches under the bushes. When they neared the bottom of the ramp where it flattened out into the valley, Matthew left the horses and proceeded on foot. The mares were tied off but Chief was free. He would remain with the mares until Matthew came for him. As he moved away, Chief watched him with ears forward and the mares grazed peacefully.

Moving quickly and silently, he slipped behind a large boulder that offered a view of Platte Rock and the surrounding area. There was no one in the meadow. Matthew assumed the others had taken their prisoners to their camp, so he slipped around the boulders and turned north into the trees that lined the west side of the valley. He had no idea who he was dealing with or their skills, or even what kind of sentries they had posted, so he very carefully made his way through the trees until they petered out almost to the north side of the valley. It was now late afternoon and he settled down to wait until darkness fell.

Now that his life was over he had unlimited patience.

***

The creature that had been Benji Cuttler sat on his haunches and watched the car approach from the south. He licked his pendulous lips, but he wasn't hungry. The feelings that overcame him when he saw the people in the car were longing and loneliness. The Benji-thing stood and started to pick his way down the overgrown trail, cautiously moving down the slope. The trail was faint and overgrown but there was a trace of where it had once switch-backed down the hill. Coming to an area where a rock fall had occurred, and the trail crossed loose, dangerous scree he stopped and looked across to the other side. He knew he couldn't get safely across so he carefully headed straight down the slope hanging on to the bushes and tree branches until he eventually reached the bottom of the hill. Sitting behind a boulder, he waited for darkness to cover his movements.

A violent temper had been Benji's worst characteristic. Convicted of domestic violence he'd served three years. When released, his wife had welcomed him back home, but the cycle had soon started again. He hit her, hard, and she had fallen and struck her head on the corner of the fireplace, killing her instantly. This time he got life. But he was sorry, and hated himself for what he'd done. He didn't believe he belonged with the gang of prisoners that had morphed into the creatures of the dark. Benji might have died during the transformation if not for his great strength.

When nightfall arrived, he rose and started along the trail to the south, raising his head and sniffing the twilight air. Sensing the approach of another being, he stared into the valley and saw an apparition that quietly slipped from boulder to boulder, disappearing toward the waterfall. Had he been the creature that once had been Arby Clarke, he would have pursued and killed the man, but what he really longed for was to see what the people in the camp were doing, observe them interacting and share their companionship.

**

As good as Matthew was at moving stealthily in the dark, he never realized he had been spotted by something he couldn't even imagine existed. Slipping over to the Jeep, he quickly checked it over and then silently moved across the bridge. He expected to find sentries guarding this entry point to the area where the camp was located, and where he had seen smoke earlier in the day, but there were none. He made his way south along the cliffs, winding his way along and around large rocks until he was opposite the camp on the east. He then continued on for another half-mile and then turned west to approach the camp from the south.

It was totally dark when he finally spotted guards in the woods directly south of the camp. *Why are they so close to their camp?* He wondered. Either they felt relatively secure or there was something in these woods that they were afraid of... very afraid. He stood silently and listened to the natural sounds around him. The light breeze whispered through the trees and there were small sounds of the night creatures coming out to hunt their prey. But he didn't hear anything that concerned him. He eluded the watchers and found a vantage point from which he could observe the goings on of the camp. These people would not be safe until they became better at security.

Although he could hear the guards talking, he wanted to stay away from them, inching along the ground until he could slip alongside the building. From this vantage point he could hear a group of women sitting in front of the building discussing the newcomers to their camp. Although Matthew couldn't hear everything they said, he gleaned from the conversation that the newcomers had not been harmed or badly treated. From what he was hearing, he became convinced that this group of survivors weren't the like desperate beings he had met up until now;

people that had lost everything and didn't have shelter, or enough to eat. He had tried to tell one group he'd met to go to Taos, that there were food and supplies there. But they were too far gone and wanting what he had, at any cost, they had fired upon him. He had ridden away with a heavy heart as they screamed at him for help. As he lay alongside the building listening to the women share stories, and plan for tomorrow's work, an overwhelming sense of loneliness engulfed him. Did he really need to be alone? He could approach these people, join them... but he wasn't ready to open himself up to others, to make friends, to be heartbroken.

Crouching low he backtracked along the building and made his way through the forest, heading back to his own camp and the companionship of his horses.

***

The creature had waited until the man-thing had passed beyond him, and then followed. When Benji had cleared the bridge he turned to the right. A light breeze uncharacteristically blew from the south and he stayed downwind of the men. He sniffed at a newly dug mound of dirt and then entered the forest and moved south toward the camp, where even at this distance he could hear voices and laughter. He could hear the guards at the edge of the forest but easily snuck between them and in seconds had quietly scrambled up an aspen to huddle on a branch, observing the camp from on high.

He saw a campfire with the man-things and females sitting around it talking and sharing stories. Another fire further across the meadow, surrounded by several females, had a large pot that straddled rocks, holding it above the low flames. The people continually scanned the forest with their gazes even as they talked and laughed. Young ones, surrounded a third campfire, took turns singing in a strange, singsong way that sounded more like talking than singing. In the center of the meadow there were enclosures with animals. Bright colored dens surrounded these enclosures and there were guards keeping them safe.

But Benji wasn't hungry. Each day, up on the plateau, he caught deer by hiding downwind of his prey and leaping out as the animals came to the lake for water. Retaining more of his human abilities to think and reason, than the others of his kind did, he wouldn't go hungry.

He'd split off from the other creatures when they entered the shelter from the farm cave. They were slaughtering the humans, but he just wanted to get out of the place where the ground shook and the roof was falling down around them. He no longer shared anything with these others of his kind but he was lonely… so lonely.

Benji remembered some of the things the humans were doing. Sharing, talking, singing and being together. As he watched, a small whimpering sound escaped him but he suppressed it immediately, knowing these humans would never, ever, accept him into their midst.

The meadow had cleared as the people entered the dens or went into the huge building. Coils of mist swirled between the trees, bringing with them a bone chilling cold. Benji slid down from the tree and passed through the line of sentries. As he reached the trail and began to ascend he stopped and looked back toward the camp. Raising his head, he let out a loud, anguished howl that reverberated down the valley.

"What the hell was that?" Mark whispered to Lori.

"It sounded like an injured animal. Go back to sleep. I have a hunting party in the morning."

"Damn! Dehydrated beef for dinner again."

She grinned and elbowed him gently in the ribs.

***

Chris lay in the darkness, wide awake. Aaron snored softly beside her, snorted and turned over, flopping his arm across her body. When Terry had spoken the name of his torturer she felt as if someone had punched her in the gut. Mark had quickly turned and looked at her as had most of the others.

"Clay Hargraves? Are you sure?"

"Yeah, the guy told me himself. Why?"

Her face had turned white as a ghost and she had trouble breathing. "He's my brother." She said almost too low to hear.

"Your brother! Why isn't he here?"

There had been parts of the story the Remnant had left out when they told it to these strangers and Clay's banishment had been one of them. Chris couldn't speak of it so Mark filled them in about the attempted rape and subsequent punishment.

"The last we saw of him, he was heading across the parking lot toward the road."

As they told the story, Marci had started to cry. She was next to her father and he put his arm around her and pulled her close, even though it shot red hot pain through his chest.

They were all looking at Marci and she looked up defiantly, blurting out, "This time it wasn't 'attempted'." She jumped up and ran toward the aisle that held the cots they had been assigned.

***

In the darkness of the back corner, Dr. Jim lay half asleep on his narrow cot, thinking about the newcomers and praying they had done all they could to save the young man. Cody's parents seemed like good people and they had been through hell. He hoped the boy wouldn't lose too much use of his arm. It depended on the muscles affected by the gunshot.

He heard a noise, a soft sound, as if it were right beside his bed. His heart rate increased as a blast of adrenaline surged through his body. He held his breath, afraid to move and wondering why he was so frightened. Sweat broke out on his forehead.

Silence. He became aware that he was holding his breath, and realized he couldn't hold it any longer. As quietly as possible, he exhaled... and heard it again. A soft, hoarse breathing. He smelled a very faint odor of decay. He couldn't tell where it was in the room but was convinced it stood directly over him. Holding his breath again, he could now clearly hear it. Very slowly, he began to sit up, when he felt a tiny movement of the covers at the foot of his bed... and panicked.

"Get away! Help!" he screamed. Snatching his feet back, he shimmied up into the corner of his bed where the head met the wall. "Somebody, help!"

He pulled the covers up to his chin, as if for protection, and continued to scream until a flashlight swung around the partition into the room and he saw Micah standing over him, not moving.

"What the hell's goin' on?" Aaron, who slept next to the medical area, came to a sudden stop. "Jim! Stop bellowing. It's just Micah."

But Micah had begun to shake, and a quavering, high-pitched sound began to issue from between his lips as he clamped his teeth together. His hands were clenched in fists, his eyes wide.

Mark slipped up beside Aaron and they stared in amazement as Micah backed away. The noise had brought men in from the yard and several people had come up behind Mark.

"Let's get him!" Jimbo yelled as he started forward.

"No! Leave him be." Jim had jumped up and moved over to where Mark and the others stood. Shaking as badly as Micah, he held Jimbo back.

Mark watched Micah back away to the center of the room, where he still stood as if he were having a seizure. The whine had become louder and Mark was struck by the look in Micah's eyes; pleading, struggling for control, as though a battle raged within.

"Micah, come on man. Fight it. You're a good man. Don't let it get you!" Mark begged as he took a step toward the tortured figure.

Micah looked at Mark, his eyes full of pain. They were bloodshot. His eyes widened further, his screaming was deafening and the shaking was consuming him. He shook his head, leaned back, looking at the ceiling as his mouth opened as wide as it could and he screamed, "Noooooo..." Long and drawn out and ululating, until his breath was gone.

Then he collapsed into a heap on the floor. The others jumped forward and Jim pushed them back as he grabbed Micah's wrist. He raised an eyelid as Aaron thrust a stethoscope into his hands. Jim listened to Micah's chest and then said over his shoulder, "Let's get him onto his bed. This time I'm restraining him!"

Chapter 13

In the pre-dawn darkness, seven hunters set out to try, once again, to bag some game to feed the community of over two hundred people. They had eaten an early breakfast and noticed others moving around in the meadow, also trying to get an early start. Several men and two women were gathering supplies to begin laying out the foundation for the bachelors' cabin. Lori saw Chris and Samuel heading back toward the river to the west to take up where they'd left off yesterday when the Jeep had appeared in the valley. It amazed her that they all were about their business so early after the night they had experienced. She shivered thinking of the tortured, alien look on Micah's face.

Everyone had been slow to get back to bed. Jordy Haines, another of Clay's young friends grumbled to Danny Fielder, "We're usin' up our medical supplies trying to keep that joker alive."

Jim had jumped at him and Mark and Aaron had to hold him back. "You stupid, useless S.O.B.! You and your friends contribute nothing. And you complain about using our supplies for someone who worked his butt off in the shelter? Get out of here!"

The hunting party started out, and today they didn't bother to try and stay in the trees, but went straight down the valley, winding through brown bushes to the rocky area before the ramp. Jerry and Pete had them spread out and take hidden positions where they would wait for the game to approach. Lori was with Greg and they sat with their backs against the rocks, relaxing and hoping to get a good shot if the deer got close enough. Most of them hadn't hunted before the war and weren't skilled with rifles. Pete and Jerry were their best bets to bring down a deer. The young men had hunted for years as teens in Los Alamos and as adults in these very mountains.

A soft rustling sound alerted them to the presence of large bodies moving through the brush. Lori peeked around the rock and saw several deer moving past them to the spring. But they were still two hundred yards away. Greg put his hand on her shoulder to signal her to wait until they were closer when someone suddenly jumped up and opened fire. There were several shots fired as the rest of the group followed suit. The deer sprang back toward the ramp scattering into the brush as bullets flew everywhere.

"I got one!" Jimbo yelled as he leaped forward from his position and ran to the brush, the others in hot pursuit.

"Jimbo, you ass! We weren't supposed to fire until they were closer."

"Yeah, well I got me one!"

They broke through the tall bushes into a tiny clearing and stood staring with their mouths open. Lori started to chuckle, and then to laugh, Pete guffawed and all the others clutched their stomachs as they doubled over in stitches.

Lying on the ground was a dead rabbit, completely decapitated by the Springfield 30-06 caliber round from Jimbo's Winchester Model 70.

When Lori could breathe she said, "You know guys, this really isn't funny," as everyone collapsed into another round of hysterics. Jimbo's face was red from embarrassment and when they had finally gained control Lori scolded them.

"Everyone is counting on us for venison. We've lost our chance for the day so we'll have to try again tomorrow. Jerry, what do you think? Are there too many of us?"

"Well, for sure there's one too many."

Jimbo tackled him. His pony tail flying loose, and they fell to the ground, laughing their asses off.

***

Scratching his beard, Mark looked around the meadow. He held a steaming cup of coffee. The sun was up and work had already started on the cabin. Lucas had selected a building site diagonally across the meadow from the steel building, in the northwest corner. This way, the meadow, with the corrals and tents, was between the two buildings affording them better protection. The door would face south and the orientation would allow them to mount solar panels on the roof. The plan was to wall off one end of the cabin to create a room for the controller and the communication equipment. The storage batteries would be on the outside of the east wall in an enclosure.

Meetings would be going on all morning, delayed from yesterday due to the arrival of the outsiders. They had stayed up late, trying to get as much information about the world outside of the valley as they possibly could. Mark was surprised at how eager he and the others were to hear what was going on. Until now, he'd tried not to think about it too much. Then these strangers appeared and reminded them that life still existed outside their tiny realm. Especially encouraging was the fact that people had survived and were normal.

He scratched again and went back inside to get rid of that damnably uncomfortable hair on his face. Every time he thought about growing it out, the itching drove him back to his razor. His hair was long and hung below his ears. If he didn't get Gail to cut it before long, it would be down to his shoulders. He looked like a teenager, Lori had told him.

As people gathered around him in the meadow, the sun shot golden arrows through the trees along the ridge and the mist began to lift. The leaders of the work groups sat in the chairs in front of the rock Mark liked to sit on. Other curious residents stood around the periphery and Mark didn't have the heart to chase them away. They all wore jackets and hats or caps against the bitter cold.

"Mornin' everyone. Quite a night, huh?" He took a swig from his coffee cup.

"How's Micah?" Walter asked.

"He's back in his coma. He pulled the I.V. loose before he scared the living shit out of Doc, but they got it restarted and restrained him."

A hand went up. "Yeah Dave?"

"I've been thinking. We need to be able to get across that river. We have two enemies now, the Devols, and the guys that chased the Holcombs. We need to be able to muster our forces on the other side a lot faster than going across the falls bridge."

"Those guys don't know we're here," Tom said. "They probably know the Jeep came into this valley but I'll bet they didn't see any of us. Maybe Clay thinks we're still in the shelter. Did he know about the exit before we exiled him?" He looked at Chris.

"I don't think so. I didn't know about it until Clay was gone. I'm sure Dad wouldn't have told him before me."

Marilyn stood up. "There's already one bridge, but you need to build another one. If you go south about two hundred yards the river splits around an island. A suspension bridge goes to the island, but you need to build one from the island to the other side. The river's anywhere from sixty to a hundred feet wide. In the wider spots it flows more smoothly and slowly, especially down south. Where it splits around the island it's only about thirty feet on each side. Will had the first bridge built as a guide for you to be able to build the second one. Supplies are in the building."

"Well, what are we waiting for?" Dave stood up. "Let's get it built."

"I want to meet with the other group leaders and then we'll let Thornton take charge. He's an engineer."

The leaders of the other groups all gave their reports and left the meeting to get started with their tasks.

They heard an almost forgotten noise, a loud, rumbling sound, as Samuel came roaring up the ramp on the green John Deere. Crossing the meadow, he passed through the thin line of trees into the prairie between the trees and the river. The tractor was pulling a trailer with implements for plowing the fields.

Chris approached Mark. "I've checked out the soil on the other side of the river and it's actually better than the closer fields. There's a problem with security, though. I'm thinking we need to start planting over here when we get rid of the Devols and guarantee the safety of the folks working there."

"Maybe we can eventually build a walled enclosure like the forts in the old west," Mark said.

Dr. Laskey was listening to their conversation and added, "The walls of the forts protected the living spaces and shops. The crops were grown outside the walls but there were guards on the ramparts of the forts."

"Well, we need food sooner than later so the closer area will have to do for now."

***

So they wouldn't waste the morning, the hunting party continued the exploration that had been interrupted the day before.

"We don't know where the guys are that were after the Holcombs, so keep a close eye out."

About a half mile south of Platte Rock the valley narrowed. They stood at the river's edge looking across at the cliff that came within a few yards of the river on the east bank.

"Would you look at that?" Greg said. About twenty feet in the air they spotted a small granary. "The Anasazi Indians were in this area several hundred years ago. That shelf up there would make an excellent guard post. The Indians usually had a crude ladder built into the cliff, in the form of hand and toe holds dug into the rock. We could put a sentry up there and they would command a view of this whole entrance to the valley."

A faint trail passed through the gap between the river and the cliff. "I think that's the trail we followed south of the camp when we went after Micah," Lori said.

The hills to the west also curved in and the actual pass was less than a mile wide. A log fence crossed most of the width. The fence had posts shaped like "X's" with the crossbars resting in the notch formed by the intersections and secondary posts resting on blocks nailed to the posts about halfway down. The two-lane track passed through a gap in the fence, and about a quarter mile along the fence, Lori could see it was blackened and missing for several yards. It looked as if it had been struck by lightning and considering the almost daily freakish storms she wouldn't be surprised if that's what had happened.

"I bet there's a lot we could be doing back at camp, since we scared all the deer away. Let's get back and help out."

Turning north they followed the river as it meandered up the valley. At this south end it was wider and calmer than up north. There were far fewer rocks and the banks were only a couple feet above the level of the water. "In the summer I bet the river's a lot lower," Jerry pointed out.

On the other side they saw a small lake bulging out from the river. His younger brother Pete said, "We could put in a dock. I bet we could catch some delicious fish in that lake. That little meadow behind the lake would be a great spot for a cabin."

"Yeah. If we can kill all those damn monsters," Jimbo added.

The group quickened their steps at the thought of the creatures and they headed north, a headless rabbit hanging by its feet from Jimbo's belt.

***

Annie approached Dr. Jim timidly. She desperately wanted to help the medical team but was afraid that, at seventeen, the doctor would think she was too young. She brushed her long dark brown hair back from her face, tucking the right side behind her ear, and took a deep breath. Jim was sitting at a folding table in the dining area, chewing on a peanut butter sandwich.

"Hi Dr. Jim." She pulled up a chair opposite him, sat down and lowered her eyes.

"What's up, Annie?"

"I…well I was wondering if you could use some help in the clinic? I could help you and Dr. Brown and it would be sweet if you could teach me some medicine." She looked up at him, hoping to tell from his expression what he thought of the idea.

"Well, sure Annie. You could help Carmen out."

Her hopeful look faded but she was emboldened by his answer. "What I meant, what I really want, is to be a doctor. You could teach me! I read everything I could find in the shelter about medicine. I'd work hard."

Considering her request for a minute, he said, "Tell you what. Be in the clinic after breakfast tomorrow and we'll see what you know and how you work, and then we'll decide. You don't get queasy, do you?"

"Oh no. Blood and guts don't bother me at all! Thank you. I'll be there." She jumped up with a big grin on her face and left him sitting there with just as big a smile.

His next visitor was Izzy.

He'd examined and redressed Kristen's wound after he and Aaron had finished with Terry and Cody.

"It's already scabbed over. I don't see any sign of infection. How's your dog bite?"

"It's good, thanks."

He briefed her on her son's condition. He'd briefly regained consciousness that morning, but had almost immediately fallen back asleep.

"We just need him to heal, now. He asked about his family, but I didn't call you since he fell asleep as soon as I assured him you were all okay. Is there something else, Izzy? You look troubled."

Tears slipped from her eyes and ran down her cheeks. She looked down at her hands. "When Terry and Marci were held captive, Marci was repeatedly raped by several men. She won't talk about it but I thought you could talk to her and get her to let you examine her." She looked up at him. "What if she's pregnant?"

He took her hands in his. "We'll cross that bridge when we come to it. I'll talk to her today," he promised.

***

"You assholes stay here and make sure that Jeep doesn't get past you." Clay wanted to get back to town. Now that he'd worked himself up over his father's treatment of him, he was anxious to get his revenge. Of the dozen men that had accompanied him to the ranch, he left half of them to guard the road, and he and the rest hiked back to town, Stewart and Billy following behind them.

When Clay reached his old house on the hill he sent Jinx and Monroe into town to gather the other men. They returned an hour later with twenty two. "Here's the plan," he told them. "We're going to the bomb shelter where my Dad and the others are staying. If the earthquakes haven't killed them, then we're going to. They are basically unarmed, have lots of women, and enough food to last a long time. They even have animals we can take out to the ranch. That ranch out west is real nice and we can make homes and use the women to even have families. You guys want real lives right?" Most of the men nodded. Even men that had lived through what they had, wanted life to go back to normal.

The earthquake had been a big one, but Clay figured if the shelter was strong enough to survive a nuclear war, it must be strong enough to get through an earthquake. "When I left, the front door was open. If they closed it, we're going to have Andy walk right up and get them to open it. The radiation seems to be gone and they won't refuse him. They're a bunch of pansies. We'll sneak up on either side of the door, and when they open it, we'll swarm in. I lived in that rat hole for a few weeks so I know there's a stairway that goes down to the shelter. They put it in, in case the elevator was out of commission. We'll use it, since they can stop the elevator if they want and we'd be stuck. Kill all the men and round up the women. Just one thing though. There's a man with grey hair and eyes. He'll be shouting out orders. That's my asshole father and I'm the only one that gets to kill him. Got it?" More nods.

"If you're in doubt, just capture the guy and I'll let you know which one is him. We're going to go in the morning. Get up here around sun up and we'll head out. It shouldn't take more than two or three hours to get there."

After the others had left, he tried to explain it to Stewart and Billy. Billy continually nodded his head and Stewart just kept repeating, "Yes Clay. Yes Clay." He finally waved them away, back to their lair where he knew they had hunks of disgusting meat stashed away. He'd like to kill the creatures, and would if they became unmanageable, but they were his guarantee that the men would follow him.

He sat on the porch, drinking a beer and imagining what tomorrow would be like when he had his father at his mercy. He might even threaten him with Stewart. But in the end, with men holding his father's arms, he would put the gun to his forehead, look him right in the eyes, say "Goodbye, you fucking asshole," and pull the trigger.

He hadn't decided yet what he would do with his sister. And with Mark. He hated Mark Teller for taking his family from him. He would probably feed him to Stewart. His sister, though, was different. He had been jealous of her and their father's relationship, but she'd never been unkind. He would give her to the men. Or maybe to Stewart.

***

Mark and Lori explored the small island that sat in the middle of the river about two hundred yards south of the camp. As Marilyn had said, there was a suspension bridge that spanned the east side of the river. Two posts were sunk into the earth six feet back from the bank. Ropes were stretched from stakes in the ground behind the posts, wrapped around and through a hole in the top of the post and then across the river to a similar setup on the other side. Additional ropes went from the bottom of the posts across the river and had wooden slats connected to these bottom ropes. There were stabilizers that wound around the top and bottom ropes all the way over to the far bank. They had all crossed the river and were checking out the island.

"I know we have too many things to do this year," Lucas said, "but this would be a great place to put a grain mill. I studied them in the shelter and we could build one to span the river between here and the west bank."

Walter grinned, "That's a great idea, Lucas. Eventually we will need to build a whole village."

"Yeah, I been thinking about that. We need to dig a well, and put in irrigation."

"I saw a lake down south where a cabin could be built," Pete said. "I'll bet Sandy would love it there."

"Okay you guys, the first thing we need to do is get the other bridge built," Dave said. "Thornton is in the basement looking for supplies. Let's get back and help him."

They met Thornton and several others coming from camp all carrying rope, post-hole diggers and wood. "There's not enough wood," Thornton told Mark. "We need to start cutting some."

"I've been thinking about that Mark," Walter said. "We need to be careful of our resources. I think we should do all our wood cutting in the stand of trees across the valley and leave our forest on this side of the river alone. We need to send a wood cutting group over there every day and start felling trees for our cabins."

"Wow, there's just so much to do. That's another thing we hadn't thought about." Mark had run a multi-billion dollar business but didn't have any idea of all the things they needed to do to build lives in this valley.

***

After dinner, the usual group sat in chairs under the portico in front of the building. Some were drinking beers they had found in the basement and others just had water or iced tea. They talked of the future and tried to make plans for the overwhelming tasks ahead of them. In the waning light of late evening Mark could see that the walls of the bachelor's cabin were already shoulder height. With twenty or so people working on it they were making quick progress. The weather had warmed up significantly and the evening was balmy, most of the group not even wearing jackets.

"You can't beat this weather," Walter said. "I thought the cold would last a lot longer."

"We could still have some cold snaps," Samuel told him. "It never just warms up without reverting to some frost conditions."

"Mr. Thompson," Tucker said. "I was reading about this whole 'nuclear winter' thing. Nobody really knew if it existed or not. It was just a theory by Carl Sagan and a lot of others. They used computers to model the weather in the event of a nuclear war. After all, we didn't have anything to base it on until now. It seems to me, that even though it was a very cold winter and there was a lot of crap in the air, that it doesn't seem much worse here than a regular winter would be."

"That seems right Tucker, and watch your language." Walter responded.

The others chuckled and Tucker's ears turned red.

"I lived over in Las Vegas... the New Mexico one," Walter added, "and I think the boy's right. This time of year, without the war, we would have just been getting the trees to bloom."

"Speaking of the weather, how's your planting coming, Chris?"

"The first field is plowed already. We need a work crew to dig an irrigation canal from the river above the field to a sluice gate. We can open the gate to water the crops."

Mark groaned, "We need about five hundred more residents to do all the work that needs done."

"Speaking of that," Stephen said, "how many new people are we going to allow to come here? These new folks, sorry ma'am," he looked at Izzy, "came with some supplies, but what if folks show up with nothing? How many can we take in without hurting us?"

The others all looked around at each other. Some shrugged. "I don't know how many people the resources in this valley can support," Walter said, "but we need hands to do all the work. Is it fair to ask newcomers to work without supporting them? I guess he's right, though. It's something we need to think about."

"Well, right now everyone is still living off the stuff in the building. Later, though, we need to come up with a money system. That way people can trade labor for money and then buy what they need. Lazy people, like Danny Fielder, will have to work for his food."

Mark added, "Dr. Laskey's group is trying to come up with a governance model and that will include barter and how we pay for things. I realize we have to get some things accomplished pretty quickly if we're going to make it through next winter."

Marilyn cleared her throat. "I guess it's time to tell you about the gold."

Several people raised their eyebrows. "What gold?"

"There's a vault in the ground down in the basement next to the weapon's locker. The locker and the vault were locked since the building itself wasn't. Will bought gold back when it was around five hundred dollars an ounce. There are two thousand, one-ounce gold pieces and ten thousand, one ounce silver rounds. Over a million dollars in gold and silver at the price he paid. Way more by the time of the war. In a post-war world, he thought gold and silver would be the only currency with any value. We can use the coins as a medium of exchange. After barter, of course. I guess Dr. Laskey and his group can place an arbitrary value on the coins and a ratio of gold to silver so we can pay for things."

None of them had thought about money for many months and they all sat there thinking about the possibilities when Izzy interrupted their thoughts. "After my family's well, we may be leaving," Izzy said. "I haven't had a chance to discuss it with my husband."

"That's crazy," Lori told her. "Where else would you go?"

"I don't know. We are so grateful to you and so thankful that the Lord led us to you when we needed help. We don't want to be a burden."

"Believe me, there is plenty of work to do to ensure you pay your way."

"How's your boy?" Samuel asked. "I heard he's awake."

"Yes. He's conscious and Dr. Brown said the surgery to clean out the wound went well. We'll just have to wait and see. What's wrong with the other man in the infirmary?"

No one answered until Mark said, "We really don't know. He was attacked by one of those monsters. We call them Devols because someone hypothesized that they were humans that were devolving into pre-humans. Anyway, he hasn't come out of the coma yet except for a couple of times when he seemed to be struggling against something. Micah's a really good guy, so we're hoping he'll be okay."

Darkness had fallen and folks began to wander to their tents or to enter the building. The evening campfires had been lit and it seemed such a peaceful scene. Mark had been sitting with Kevin asleep in his lap and his butt was half asleep. He rose and took the sleeping boy into the building and put him on his cot.

"I'll put his shorts and T-shirt on him," Lori said. "Can you get Ashley from Barbara and we'll put her to bed too?"

"Sure, then I'll be over talking to Dr. Jim."

"Okay, but don't be too long or I might be asleep when you get back."

"Hmmm. Maybe I'll just stay right here until both kids are asleep."

Chapter 14

"I need to take a leak." Jason started to head off into the woods. He and Tony were patrolling the north end of the meadow where the woods ran behind the new bachelors' cabin.

"Just pee right here. You modest or somethin'?"

"No, dude, but a man needs a little privacy. I'm only goin' in a few feet. Keep your eyes open."

Jason walked into the woods and turned to see that he could still see Tony through the trees. He moved further into the dense forest until Tony was no longer visible and then reached into his pocket for the pill bottle he had stolen from the infirmary that morning. He pulled it out and it caught on the edge of his pocket, causing it to fly a few feet into the brush. "Well fuck!" He got down on his hands and knees and felt around for the bottle not wanting to use his flashlight for fear Tony would come after him. "This is ridiculous," he muttered. He would have let it go but it was Oxycodone. He hadn't had a good high since he came to this place. His wife's parents had received a signal box, but when the alarm had gone off they were in South America and He and Amy had used it to lead them to the shelter.

He thought he had the bottle when he heard Tony come up behind him. He jumped up and whirled around... but no one was there.

"Shit!" his heart was racing. He dropped to his knees and moved forward as he searched for the pills. A couple more feet and he felt the bottle. Snatching it up he rose and twisted the bottle cap, spilling four of the pills into his hand. "That ought to do it!" He pulled his water bottle from his waist pack and washed down the pills. He had kept his rifle with him but had laid down the flashlight a few feet back and didn't know where it was.

Once again he heard a noise, a slight rustling of the leaves on the forest floor. He turned in a circle looking for Tony but now he wasn't sure which way he faced. Starting off for camp he wound in and around the trees trying to see the lights from the campfires in the clearing, but it only seemed darker.

Another rustling, and he increased his speed through the woods and away from the sound. Beginning to panic, he stopped and looked around wildly, trying to hear the sounds of the people in the camp but he heard nothing but the breeze blowing through the trees. His chest was heaving but he held as still as possible and listened intently. It was coming closer!

He took off running away from the sound, tripping over the brush and falling to the ground. The sound was to his right so he jumped up and ran left. It had been downwind but now he could smell it! He hid behind a tree gasping for breath but trying to breathe silently. He waited and didn't hear it any longer. He relaxed slightly just as the smell became overpowering and he heard it breathing on the other side of the tree.

"Oh God, no. Fuck, it's one of them." Suddenly finding himself out of the trees and in the small meadow that held the graveyard, he screamed for Tony, but knew he was too far away. Whirling around, he saw a darkness in the night, blacker than the woods. It stood there unmoving, toying with him. He backed away and raised the rifle, somehow knowing it was useless. The thing was so big!

He opened fire, getting off only a few shots before he was lifted completely off the ground, as fangs tore into him… ripping his throat out.

***

Gunshots rang out through the forest where Doug and Larry were patrolling. Doug was the lead guard for the night and took off at a run toward the shots just as Tony came out of the woods.

"Tony, what's going on! Where's Jason?"

"I don't know man. He had to take a leak and went into the woods." Tony came up to Doug, breathing heavily and when Doug flashed his light on Tony's face, he could see the fear in his wide eyes.

People were pouring out of the building and crawling from tents. Dave asked Doug, "Where's the fourth guy?"

"We don't know. It's Jason. He went into the forest to pee. We just heard shots but haven't checked 'em out yet."

"Well, let's go! Tony and Larry, patrol west, and for God's sake, stay together! Jimbo, get some extra men to secure the perimeter." Jimbo appointed some guys to spread out around the edge of the meadow and then, not one to be left out of the action, he followed Dave and the others into the woods. Mark ran across the field and caught up to the group just as they crossed into the trees.

They stayed in a tight group, flashlights illuminating the woods around them. There were no more shots or noises of any kind. It was over a half mile to the northern edge of the forest and it took them fifteen minutes to traverse it, searching the woods on either side of them as they moved forward calling out Jason's name.

"I don't hear anything at all," Jimbo told Dave. "Doug, how far away were the shots?"

"They sounded pretty far. Why would he head away from camp like that?"

"He may have been chased. It was freakin' stupid to go off on his own like that."

Leaving the forest, they entered the meadow to the south of the cemetery. One of the lights flashed across a lump farther out in the field. The men ran over, and saw what was left of Jason's body lying in a pool of black blood. Most of the men held back, fanning out in a circle facing the darkness, as Jimbo, Mark and Dave approached the gory mess. Jason's neck had been torn open and his head lolled sideways at an unnatural angle. His shoulder was completely missing and the right arm was torn off and lying on the ground four feet away. "God, he's been partially eaten," Dave said. "It was one of those things. This is it! We can't let this go on any longer!"

He stomped back to the others. "We need a stretcher to get his remains back to camp. Pete, Jerry, can you guys take care of that? Mark, what do you want to do? I say we go after them."

Mark had been standing, staring down at Jason's body. Jason had a young wife and Mark would have to tell her what happened. "You're right Dave. Enough is enough. We can't live in fear of these things anymore. First light we get a party after them. I don't know how many there are but we need to take out as many as we can. Let's get back to camp. I need to tell Amy."

As they entered the camp a hysterical Amy Knight ran up to them. "Tony said Jason's gone. Did you find him? Please, where is he?"

Mark put his arms around her. "Amy, I'm so sorry. Jason was killed by one of the Devols."

"Nooo…" She jerked away but Chris took her by the arms and led her away.

"Listen up everyone!" Mark called out. He glanced to the east and saw a faint lightening of the sky. "We're going after those things as soon as it's light. We need a group of, I would say, fifteen guys. Make sure you have a rifle and a handgun. Plenty of magazines and ammo."

"I'm going too," Lori called out.

"And me," Sheri said. "Do you think we'll get near the front entrance? I want to get my bike. We could use some faster transportation around here than walking."

"I don't know, Sheri. I think we'll be up on the ridge overlooking the place we left the cars and chopper, but I don't know if we can get down there. It's pretty steep," Mark told her.

Pete said, "I'm going too, and I agree that it would be nice to have that bike. If we're going toward the Crow's Nest, we could hunt those things, and also get the weapons out of the armory. Me and Sheri could go around to the northwest, past the lake and get to the entrance that way. It's the same trail Sandy and I took when we went backpacking just before the war. From the Crow's Nest you can get down by going around to the south east, but it's really far. There are some hunter's cabins down that way and maybe they have some supplies."

"I'm going with you guys. Can't let my little brother get eaten," Jerry chimed in.

"Okay," Mark said. "I think it's a good idea to have more than one objective, so if we don't find any creatures, we can still get the guns and the bike. We'll check out the cabins at a later time. Get some breakfast and meet back here in an hour." He and Lori went into the building and could hear Amy's sobs from the far side of the building where the young couple had made their beds. Grabbing a quick breakfast, they checked with Barbara to once again watch the children who were still sleeping soundly.

Mark's fifteen guys turned into twenty as they traveled south to get to the point where the Devol almost got Micah. Here the ridge met the floor of the valley and they were able to climb onto the hill above the camp. When they reached the barrier formed by the rock wall that had almost proved Micah's undoing, they turned east to go around the barrier rather than try to climb it. Coming back to the cliff, north of the rock wall one of the men tripped over something and when he looked to see what snagged him, he jumped up and backed away.

"Hey guys! Look at this?" It was a large bone.

Gathering around the remains of one of the creatures they speculated about what had happened. It had been stripped clean of all meat even though it had only been a couple of days since it had been killed.

"Something ate every speck of meat off those bones. You can see where the bones have been gnawed."

Greg squatted alongside it. "Look at the spine. See how long it is? I think it's one of the Devols. It sure smells like one. I wonder what could have killed it?"

"A bigger Devol, that's what killed it. I think the big one did it." Mark was thinking of the size of the creature that almost killed him in the shelter. "I don't think they're all buddies anymore."

"Hey Mark, How many of them do you think there are?"

"I know there must have been eight or nine of them when we saw them in the power plant. We killed one there and Lori killed two. This one makes four down. I'd say there's still a half a dozen."

Continuing along the ridge for another mile they came to a point opposite the camp but thick trees growing on the side of the hill prevented them from looking down on their friends. They eventually heard the roar of the falls as they progressed northward and the cliff became steeper as they approached the top where the water cascaded over the edge. They turned inland, east, to head in the direction of the tunnel entrance leading to the Crow's Nest.

***

Clay turned over in his bed and looked toward the window. He could see through the pulled blinds that the early morning had slipped away. This really wasn't all that different then before the war. He usually slept until around noon and stayed up half the night partying. His father complained incessantly about it and Clay added that to the list of reasons to kill him.

He climbed out of bed, and after a trip to the bathroom, went in search of Jinx to get him some breakfast.

"Hey Jinx, fix me some eggs, huh?"

"Yeah, Clay. But it's almost lunchtime. You want a steak instead? We got some left from that cow we butchered, before we gave the rest to Stewart, and it'll go bad if we don't eat it."

"Make it steak and eggs then."

There were only a few chickens left after Billy had broken into the roost and killed most of the hens one night. The roosters too, were dead, so in a few months there wouldn't be any more eggs. Another reason to take care of business at the shelter and then get the hell out of this dump. Clay had no idea how much radiation lingered or where the hotspots were, but he needed to leave this place. The town was old and the men who followed Clay were rough and uncultured. And there were no women. He planned on killing Pete Thompson, along with the other men, and taking Sandy Barber with him when he left this place for good. He would take his creatures, if he could still control them, for protection, and try to make his way back to the west coast. He had no idea what he would find, but the ocean was his life and the only thing he ever really cared about. Maybe there was someplace left where he could make a new life.

He walked out on the porch and saw the men beginning to gather. The people in the shelter were unarmed and most of them were weak, not soldiers, unused to confrontation. They didn't have the ability to defend themselves. It would be a slaughter. They just needed an opening to get in and it would all be over in a short amount of time. The youngest man in town was Andy Milkins. Fairly good looking when cleaned up, Clay planned on using him to get the inhabitants of the shelter to open the door. While staying in the entrance cave Clay had discovered a staircase that could be used in the event of a power failure. If they could get through the blast door they had a way into the shelter with no resistance. The door wasn't locked.

Twenty guys had gathered in the yard, checking their guns and petting the mangy dog.

"Here's the plan," Clay announced. "We hike up to the shelter in around three or four hours. The road's six or seven miles up the highway and then we have to hike a few miles in to the cave entrance. Shut the fuck up!" Several of the men were grumbling about the distance. "If you were in better shape, it would be easy. If the blast door isn't open, Andy's going to walk up and beg them to let him in. He'll pretend he doesn't know they're there but just yell out something about all the cars and that 'there must be someone around.' My Dad's such a pushover, he'll open the door. We line up ten guys on a side and when the door opens, we rush in, take the stairs and storm the shelter. Kill the men and capture the women. No dicking around with them until we secure the place. There are probably a hundred women, so we need to lock them up and you can pick the ones you want after we kill the men. We'll keep some old ones for servants. After you fuck yourselves silly, we'll kill the ones we don't want, and get back to town. Just one thing. Don't kill the old guy with the silver hair. He'll be giving orders and the other assholes will be jumping to do his bidding. He's all mine. If you're not sure it's him, take him captive and after I ID my old man we can kill the others. Everybody got it?"

Although Clay could bet Stewart hadn't understood half of what he said, the creature said, "yes Clay. Yes Clay." And nodded its massive head.

"Alright. Do you all have water?" Not waiting to see whether or not they did, Clay said, "Let's split." He went around the house and started northward, his small army following reluctantly.

After two and a half hours, they came to an intersection of the highway and a dirt road that led into the trees on the left. Two cars had collided and spilled bodies onto the pavement. There wasn't any flesh left on the scattered bones and some of Clay's men looked a little green.

"Come on you pussy's. They're just bones. Let's keep moving. The shelter's at the end of this road."

They strode along the dirt road, picking up the pace when they realized they were close to the women and a night of sexual frenzy.

***

Leaving the thundering sound of the falls behind, the hunting party went east until Pete called out to Mark.

"This is where we need to split up. From here your group will climb up the mountain that covered the Crow's Nest. We'll need to go north and stay at this altitude while we swing around the ridge for a couple miles and then descend to the parking area where we all left our cars. We'll be at the foot of the cliff a few hundred feet below you."

"Okay. Who's going with you?"

"Sheri, me and Jerry, and Darryl and Bruce. That should be enough of us to stay safe. We'll get the bike, check all the vehicles and come back to take the trail down the north end of the valley. If we run into any Devols, you'll hear our gunfire. I hope we get a chance at one or two of 'em."

"There's a lot more of us," Mark told him. "Don't do anything risky."

"Oh, we won't. We'll probably beat you back to camp. Happy monster hunting."

The smaller group shook hands all around amidst muttered tidings of "Good luck" from Mark's band and a hug for Sheri by Lori.

Mark watched them for a minute as they went north through the trees and then led the remainder of the group east as it started to climb gently up the forested and rocky mountain side.

Gradually becoming steeper the hill left some of the men panting, and once again Mark wished they had worked out more often like most of the residents had. Beautiful wildflowers were sprinkled throughout the vegetation. As they neared the area where the trees thinned out he called a halt for a break to allow them a chance to have a snack and drink from their water packs. The day had warmed and even though mid-morning the men were sweating.

Mark handed Lori a pack of dried apricots. "It's a beautiful day. Look at those fluffy clouds. Hard to believe that those evil things are out there."

"Look at the horizon, though. The darker rain clouds are already gathering. I hope it holds off until we get the guns and start back. I'm glad to be out of the shelter, even with the harsher conditions. I didn't realize how much I missed the outdoors."

Just then they heard a crashing in the trees and a tremendous scream as two of the immense creatures attacked from behind the boulders they had stopped to rest against. The three men standing guard had their rifles at the ready and opened fire even as the others brought their weapons to bear.

Chapter 15

"Hey Doc. How come my hands are tied to the bed?"
Doctor Jim whirled around and hurried to Micah's side.
"Well, young man. Am I glad to see you awake! How do
you feel?" He checked Micah's pulse. Out of long habit Jim
looked down at his own wrist, but of course, there was no watch.
No matter. He could tell that the pulse rate was normal.
"I'm starving. How long have I been out? Last thing I
remember was that creature going after me in the rocks." Micah
sat up in bed and looked at the I.V. in his arm.
"You were out of it for a while so we had to restrain you.
It's been four days." As Jim untied the rope from Micah's wrists,
he watched the young man for any sign of violence. But Micah
seemed like his old self, smiling up at the doctor.
"Wow. No wonder I'm hungry. What is this place?"
"It's a storage building in the forest. Hargraves stocked it
with the supplies he thought we'd need to start building a
community out here in the woods. Let me check your wounds."
He was shocked to see that Micah's back, although still healing,
now looked normal. The skin no longer had a wet, green look,
and his eyes, still bloodshot, were much less so than the night
before last when he scared Jim half to death in the middle of the
night.
The doctor removed the I.V. and put pressure on it for a
minute before binding it with tape. "Let's get you something to
eat." He helped Micah to his feet and held on as he staggered
slightly.
"Give me a minute, Doc. Just a little dizzy." After allowing
Micah to regain his balance they left the medical area and slowly
walked toward the kitchen, Jim holding up his hand to forestall
several people from questioning Micah before he could get
seated. Helen, a big smile on her face, came over to see what she
could get him and others gathered around to inquire about his
health.
"I feel fine," he lied. "I'll be better, though, after I eat."

Little Kevin came over and put his hand on Micah's knee. "We thought you wuz turning into a monster!" Micah patted his hand and said, "No, really, I'm fine." He looked up at Jim with a questioning look.

"I'll tell you about all that later. Here, eat." Helen brought over a sandwich made with newly baked bread and stuffed with tuna. There were chips and a bottle of water. It seemed like a gourmet feast to Micah.

***

As they came down the dirt track toward the shelter, Clay had his men move off into the trees on the north side of the road.

"They have cameras that show the parking area. We can get pretty close in the trees until I can see if they left the blast door up when I split. If they didn't we'll have to use Andy." He glanced over at Andy, who had shaved and cleaned up and looked reasonably presentable.

Approximately a half mile from the entrance cave, they slowed their approach and checked their weapons. Stewart and Billy seemed nervous, glancing around at the trees and sniffing the air as though there was something they were afraid of. Clay couldn't imagine what could scare those two but he scanned the forest with his eyes until satisfied they were alone.

"Move out." He motioned for them to go deeper into the woods and they moved silently toward the west, slowing down as they finally saw the rock wall ahead.

"Stay here," Clay ordered them. He wound his way through the trees until the parking lot was right in front of him. He felt a pang of homesickness as he looked at the cars, symbols of his lost civilization. Across the clearing, he could see his father's chopper where they had left it after flying in from the Albuquerque airport. They almost died waiting for Mark's sister to arrive from Texas.

The reasons were piling up to kill his father.

From his vantage point he could see the blast door was open. The idiots hadn't bothered to close it after he left. He had no way to know the earthquakes had triggered it open before the power died in the shelter. They weren't going to have to use Andy after all. He went back to the men and gave final instructions.

"We'll stay in the woods until we get to the cliff. There's a blind spot where the camera can't see along the wall. Stretch out behind me in single file. We'll go through the cave and down the stairs into the shelter. Man, are they going to be fucking surprised! Remember, do not kill any older men. If someone blows away my old man I will feed him to Stewart. Capture all the old guys until I find dear old Dad. There's an auditorium on the top floor. Herd all the chicks into it and post guards. After we have the situation under control we'll deal with them." He thrust his hips forward and the men laughed, several licking their lips or thrusting in return.

"Let's go get some pussy. Stewart, stay with me when we go in. Okay?"

"Yes Clay."

He started through the trees with the men in single file behind him. Stewart and Billy lagged behind the others, warily checking out the surroundings. They approached the rock wall but before they could exit the trees Clay heard a noise to his right. It was the sound of human voices. He threw up his hand and motioned the men back a few yards. "Shhh...don't move," he whispered.

***

"Look!" Pete pointed out, as his group approached the edge of a lake. They'd hiked for twenty minutes alongside the river where it poured out of the spillway of a small dam. The dam had partially collapsed from the earthquakes that had destroyed the shelter, but was sufficiently intact to maintain the lake behind it. "This is the lake that fed the penstocks to the power plant. Sandy and I camped on the other side and we didn't have any idea why they'd built the dam. Remember Jerry? This lake wasn't here the last time you and me camped here."

They continued around the lake and past the spot where he and Sandy had camped the night before the bombs came and changed their world. They had run back along the trail to get to their car. They intended to get home to find out if Pete's family survived the blasts. When they arrived at the parking area they were shocked to find a hundred vehicles in the lot. Hearing a voice, they had been invited to enter the shelter where, to Pete's great relief, they found his family was already there.

They were all ecstatic about being out of the underground shelter and just sauntered along the path enjoying the beautiful spring day. Sheri ran up the trail, ran back, ran behind them a ways and then returned to the group. She punched Darryl Washington in the arm and took off again.

"Sheri!" Jerry yelled. "You better stay with us. Those things are still out there somewhere."

"They wouldn't dare ruin this day for me."

The trail wound north through the pines and across a meadow filled with wildflowers and rocks. The flowers had come back after the radiation had soaked this area and Pete recognized the familiar purple Columbine, the orange Indian Paintbrush and a yellow flower he didn't recognize. He wondered if it had mutated.

Sweating, Pete's group switched back up a gentle hill and crested the top of the ridge. They could see over the trees to the gigantic canyon to the north and the path went along the ridge a hundred yards before descending the other side. Once they came to the edge of the canyon the path forked and Pete led them to the right. This trail would go over a low pass and curve back south to end up at the parking area before the entrance to the shelter.

"When we get to the parking area, let's try to start every single car. It's been eight months, so even if the power system wasn't knocked out by the EMP, the batteries are probably dead but it's worth a try."

"Yeah," Bruce said. "The Holcomb's Jeep works so maybe we'll get lucky."

"Any of you guys know how to fly a chopper? That would be sweet if we flew into camp with that sucker!" Jerry laughed.

Sheri skipped along the trail. "When we get my bike, I think I need to ride it down the highway and back into the valley from the south. Taking it along this trail would be a nightmare."

"That's not a very good idea." Darryl frowned at her. "According to Izzy, there are quite a few of Clay's guys in town and they may even be at that ranch. You might not get past them."

"Yeah, maybe you're right."

"When you try to start the cars check the seats for anything someone may have left behind. Might be something useful. Hey, we're here!" They left the trail where it entered the parking area. Pete had a flashback of him and Sandy coming out of this same trail to this lot full of cars.

"What the hell! My bike's gone." Sheri ran forward to where she had dropped the bike with her still fully loaded panniers over the rear wheel. She had supplies in those bags that she had counted on.

"You sure you didn't leave it over by the entrance?"

"No, it was by that BMW."

Pete looked over to the blast doors. "Hey! The door's open. That's weird."

"Yeah, I thought it was weird too. Hello Petey Boy."

Chapter 16

"Get back!" Mark reached out and grabbed Lori's arm, pulling her behind him as they backed away. The others were firing rapidly and the creatures reared up and screamed. They had come upon the group from downwind, which was why they hadn't been detected while approaching the unsuspecting humans, but in these close quarters the stench was unbearable. One of the Devols turned to run, but the other rushed forward and grabbed Tom by the head. Before he could react, the thing violently twisted and Tom's neck snapped with a loud crack. Before the creature could drop the body, the gunfire drove it back against the rock where it was unable to avoid the assault.

"Don't let the other one get away!" Mark chased it, firing as he ran. "Come back here you mother fucker!" He couldn't let it escape.

It veered off to the right, where Mark wasn't in the line of fire, and the staccato clatter of the Uzi automatic shattered the air as the bullets flew by him, cutting the legs out from under the fleeing Devol. Then it was at their mercy, as they fired dozens of rounds into the downed monster until it lay still in a pool of vile-smelling brown blood.

Mark's heart was bursting from the chase, and the anger of yet another of the Remnant going down to these creatures. He and Lori sprinted back to the others and found the second creature on the ground unmoving. The other men were surrounding Tom, cursing and angrily pacing. "Fuckers came out of nowhere!"

Lori turned away and Mark held her as tears flowed down her cheeks. Jimbo went over and kicked the creature lying on the ground. It didn't move. He went on to the one that tried to run and repeated the gesture to make sure it was dead. "Well, we wanted to get them and we did, but dammit, they just keep taking a toll."

The stunned group of humans sat around on rocks or on the ground for a full half hour, not speaking or moving. Finally Mark rose. "I need some of you guys to go back to camp and get a stretcher. Bring a blanket or something to cover him with." Four of the men picked up their weapons and headed back the way they came. "Mike and Al, stay with the body. Let's find the tunnel and get the rest of the guns." They slowly started back up the slope, their spirits crushed but still having a job to do.

The trees thinned out and in another fifty yards they were in an area devoid of vegetation. There were piles of rocks. Glen led them south, around an outcropping, and they stood before the opening of the tunnel that led to the "Crow's Nest," the control room of the shelter.

"God, it smells like those things," Jimbo said, wrinkling his nose.

"It looks like they were using the tunnel for a lair. Look over there." Al pointed to a ledge slightly below where they stood. It was covered with excrement. Bones of smaller animals littered the ground around the tunnel entrance.

"Be careful. If they're living here, there may be more of them inside." Mark moved forward into the dark entrance, turning on his LED flashlight to illuminate the way. As he crept down the slightly descending tunnel, he occasionally kicked aside more bones. The tunnel led straight ahead for the length of a football field and when they arrived at the alcove they found the door wide open. Leaves and tree limbs, with branches still attached, littered the floor. More bones were scattered everywhere.

"Assholes tried to make a nest," Jimbo muttered. "Real fucking domestic."

Mark quickly crossed the room, afraid the creatures had broken into the weapon's vault but the door was still secured and he breathed a sigh of relief as he swung it open and found the contents unharmed.

During the battle with the Devols in the shelter, they had issued many of the guns to the residents but Will had stocked this room with what looked like two hundred handguns and rifles. The Uzi had been for fun, the only fully automatic weapon in the vault. Lori had grabbed it when they first opened this vault, thinking it was "cute."

It had saved her.

And now there was nobody that seriously considered taking it from her.

"Everyone grab at least one rifle." He rummaged around the ten foot by sixteen foot vault and found a cache of canvas bags. They put handguns and magazines in each of six bags and passed them out.

"The ammo is really heavy. Break open the one thousand round boxes and put the smaller fifty round boxes in your pockets." Additionally, there were ammo cans with handles on each end. Two men could carry each can. "Jimbo, Dave and Al, you three guys will cover us so don't weigh yourselves down. Let's go. We can always come back for more until we've transferred it all to the camp."

Weighted down by the guns and ammo, they returned through the tunnel to the light of day. The guards went first and when they signaled the others it was safe, the group exited and started back down the mountain. Arriving at the point where the creatures had attacked, they saw that the sentries were spread out and alert. As Mark's group approached, rifles swung in their direction but were quickly lowered when the men saw who it was.

"Hi guys. We'll leave these two ammo boxes for you to take back with you after the others return with the stretcher. Stay alert." The group moved off and descended into the thicker trees.

As they circumnavigated the rock outcropping, they met a group coming from the camp. In addition to the men that had gone for help, there were two additional guys including Aaron.

"Sorry Aaron, he won't be needing you," Mark said.

"No, I just wanted to help. Tom was a good man."

The groups passed and continued on their way. They had started out several hours ago with high expectations but it was a solemn, heavily-laden group that straggled into camp.

***

"Fuck, nooo..." Pete whirled and saw his greatest nightmare, Clay Hargraves, standing at the edge of the trees only a few feet away, with a gun held in both hands and pointed directly at Pete's head.

Without even thinking, Pete screamed, "Sheri! Run!" simultaneously ducking under Clay's aim and throwing himself against Clay's legs. Action is faster than reaction. A shot rang out, temporarily freezing everyone and he and Clay went down in a heap. Sheri took off like a scared rabbit toward the trail they had just exited and the other three men rushed Clay's guys. It happened so fast no one had time to think. Pete just knew he couldn't let Sheri fall into their clutches. Not after what happened to Marci.

"Stewart! Billy! Get the girl!" Clay and Pete were struggling for the gun, when someone kicked Clay in the teeth and Pete felt himself lifted bodily off the ground. Pete saw the creatures and almost had a fatal moment of terror, but realized as the beasts took off after Sheri, they were with Clay.

He was shoved toward the cave as Jerry screamed at him, "Guys! Get in the cave!"

Pete heard the crack of another shot as he and Jerry zig-zagged toward the cave entrance. Then heavy gunfire erupted as they made their mad dash toward safety. He glanced over his shoulder and saw Darryl, who had been right behind him, go down with a gunshot to the back. Pete whirled about to help Darryl but Jerry hit him hard, lifting him from the ground and carrying him a few feet.

"You can't help him!" Jerry put Pete down in front of him, shielding Pete's body from the gunfire, and gave him another shove toward the cave. They flew around the corner and were finally able to pull their own guns, firing back toward their attackers.

Clay and his men faded back into the trees and Pete saw Darryl on the ground, halfway between the cave and the area where Clay had ambushed them. He started firing randomly into the trees but Jerry laid his hand on Pete's shoulder.

"Pete, save your ammo. You don't know where they are. We'll wait and see if they leave, then we can check on him. I think they killed Bruce, or else they took him with them. I don't see him anywhere."

"That Devol was with them. It went after Sheri. We've got to help her!"

"We can't do anything! I couldn't tell how many there are but it looked like quite a few, and they were all armed. She's the fastest runner I've ever seen. Hopefully she'll outrun it."

"We have to help them. We have to get Bruce back! God, I hate that fucker. I thought we were through with him."

"Well, we knew he was alive and in town. We should have known he'd come for us."

A shot rang out and ricocheted off the rock in front of Pete's face. He shouted and jumped back. They could hear someone yelling instructions from the trees.

"We're sitting ducks here. If they move over behind the cars in front of the cave we won't have any cover. Come on, Pete! We have to go."

More shots came from the direction of the cars and they squeezed back as far as they could to the side of the cave, but the shots were uncomfortably close.

"Now!" Jerry grabbed the sleeve of Pete's shirt and tugged. They ran for the door that led to the stairs, their arms thrown over their heads. Jerry grabbed the door as shots hit all around them, throwing up dirt from the floor and chips of rock from the back of the cave. He threw it open and ducked behind it as Pete dodged through. Jerry stepped around it, but as he slipped through into the darkness he was knocked forward by a shot striking his left tricep. He fell forward into Pete and they scrambled down the stairs into the darkness of the lifeless shelter, Jerry holding onto the wound to try and staunch the flow of blood.

***

"We killed two of them. But it wasn't worth Tom's life," Mark told the group that met them when they entered the camp. "We got a dozen more rifles and several sacks full of handguns and magazines." They handed out the weapons to people who'd gathered around. With the guns they'd brought from the shelter, the ones they found in the weapon's locker in the building's basement and the new cache they had just delivered, almost every man in camp, and fourteen of the women were armed. All the residents, with the exception of those who didn't want them, had knives strapped to their waist.

"Hey, Mark," Tucker called out. "Micah woke up!"

"Again? How is he?"

"I'm feeling pretty good!" The crowd parted and Micah squeezed through, coming up to Mark and throwing his arms around him.

"Micah, you had us worried, man." He started to pat Micah on the back but thought better of it, with the wounds he knew Micah had suffered. Instead, he put his hands on Micah's shoulders and examined him at arm's length. His eyes were still bloodshot but not nearly as bad as they had been. He looked pale and gaunt but there was no sign of the yellowish-green caste of his skin.

"I'm still a little dizzy and tired, but Doc says I'll be fine."

Mark reached out and handed Micah the last handgun. "Hang onto this. At least you won't be helpless next time."

"Don't know that this peashooter will stop one of those things." Micah laughed.

"There's two less than before," Mark told him. "There can't be too many more."

He turned to Dave. "Any word from the other group?"

"No, they have to walk the bike back along that trail so it's probably pretty slow going."

Dr. Jim pushed his way through. "Come on, break it up. I need Micah back in bed and the rest of you need some food and rest."

The crowd split up and Mark and his group went into the building, Lori immediately going to check on her kids.

When she located Barbara and the children, she gave them a big hug. "Thanks Barbara. I owe you another one."

"You're welcome. You know Lori, I love watching the kids, but do you think you should keep putting yourself in harm's way? What if it was you that was killed by the Devols. What would they do without you?"

"I know Barb. I might be over-reacting to the fact that I let my husband harm them, and I was too weak to resist. I say I'm doing this for them, to prove I'm strong, but to tell you the truth, I love going out there with Mark. I love having my Uzi and fighting against those things. I think when the danger's over I'll settle down. And I know you will see that they're okay if anything happens to me. I just need some time, okay?"

"Of course. You know I'm always here for them... and you."

Lori smiled at her, genuinely thankful for all that Barbara had done.

"Lori, have you heard anything about Jerry?"

"They went with Sheri to get the bike. It's a few miles farther than what we did and they have to push the bike back along a fairly rough, overgrown trail. They were going to check all the cars, as well. They will probably be another two or three hours." Barbara didn't look any more relieved.

Lori carried Kevin with her to their area of the building, Ashley holding on to Lori's shirttail. She settled down with them, until Mark found her reading them a story, her head nodding as she struggled to stay awake. Sitting down beside her and taking the book from her hand, Mark took over the reading chores. With Lori's head on his shoulder, and even though it was only midafternoon, she fell fast asleep.

***

"What are you asswipes doing out of the shelter?" Bruce was on his knees, hands tied behind his back. Clay paced before him, alternately kicking and backhanding him across the face.

"We were trying to get Sheri's bike." He was trying to talk through tears, realizing he was probably going to die.

"Yeah, well you came from the wrong direction, north. You were outside. What the hell happened?"

Bruce lowered his head, saying nothing. Clay reached out, grasped Bruce's hair and jerked his head up. "I asked you a question! I want to know what's happening. Why is the blast door open? Why were you outside? Why hasn't my old man come to investigate, now that Jerry and his useless brother have gone back inside?" He gave Bruce's hair a jerk.

Bruce looked into Clay's angrily insane eyes. "Hargraves is dead. The earthquakes destroyed the shelter and we had to leave. Your father was killed during our escape. Those creatures, like the one you have with you, came and forced us out."

But Clay was no longer listening. He was shocked clear through to his marrow.

"My Dad is dead?" he whispered, trying to assimilate what he'd heard. He'd been robbed of his chance to kill his father himself, but instead of being upset over that fact, he was profoundly hurt. He turned and staggered over to a fallen log and sat down heavily. The other men shuffled about, fearful of Clay's legendary temper.

"Stay here." He turned suddenly and walked off into the woods, tears running down his cheeks, and when beyond the hearing of the men, his shoulders shook as he remembered his father's eyes and his strength. Trying to think about the past, before they had descended into this hell, he knew that even though he had acted distant toward his father he had loved him and craved his attention and approval. He had tried to build up hatred towards Will, but knew in truth, that Will Hargraves was the most important man in his life.

He still would have killed him.

He thought of his mother and his sister. For the first time since the war, he allowed himself to think about his parents and his childhood. Oh, he'd told the men tales of his lifestyle, to impress them, but hadn't really thought about anything personal or the people in his life.

Then he thought about Mark and how he had come between him and his father. And at last, he thought about his father's final betrayal, when he'd banished his only son from the shelter over a woman. Pete's woman.

And he had just allowed Pete to escape him! They had him covered with at least a dozen guns, and they let him get away. This bunch of incompetents was all he had, but he would use them to get Pete back if they all died in the attempt. He was sure Stewart would catch the girl, and he knew Bruce would give him all the answers he needed. All emotion but rage drained from him, and storming back to where they held the unfortunate man he coldly questioned him.

"You said you were forced out of the shelter. Where is everyone?"

Bruce realized he had said too much and pressed his lips together in silence.

"Where the hell did they go?" He backhanded the man across the face again and kicked him in the ribs for good measure. Bruce grunted and fell to his side in the dirt and pine needles that covered the forest floor.

"Jinx, Monroe, try that door in the cave. I don't think it locks. Check it out. The rest of you bring this Son-of-a-bitch with us. He's going to talk, one way or the other. Why isn't Stewart back with that girl?"

"I don't know Clay. She took off pretty fast. It took a minute before Stewart got it in his fat head what you wanted him to do."

Jinx came trotting back into the clearing. "The door is unlocked, just like you said, Boss."

"The residents aren't in the shelter anymore. Pete will go back to wherever they are. They must be living around here somewhere or Petey Boy wouldn't still be in the vicinity." He pointed out four men. "You guys stay here and wait for Stewart and make sure those assholes don't come back out that door. Bring him." He gestured to Bruce. "Drag him if you have to."

He strode off onto the road that led back to the highway, with a frightened bunch of men following him. They would shoot him if Stewart and Billy weren't out there behind them somewhere.

Chapter 17

Sheri ran like she'd never run before, as she flew along the trail. She leaped rocks and roots and dodged around new-growth trees sprouting in the middle of the trail. If those things hadn't been behind her, she would have been having the time of her life. The underground existence didn't sit well with her, and no one was happier to be out of the shelter than she was. But those things were after her and she didn't know what to do besides keep on running. Her Glock was in her hand, but what good would it be against those monsters? If she had to, she would shoot them and hope to at least slow them down.

She reached the point where the trail led over a low pass to the west and she took a quick look over her shoulder. From her elevated vantage point, she saw one of the creatures below her, just as it looked up and spotted her and stopped in the trail. It started to leave the trail to head straight up the hill after her, when a second, smaller Devol crashed into it from behind. They went down and started rolling about on the ground, their pursuit momentarily forgotten as their animalistic nature asserted itself. Sheri took advantage of their fight to sprint further up the trail.

The two Devols bit and scratched at each other until they were both covered in blood. As the fight turned in favor of the larger, more changed creature, the smaller one became frightened and tried to escape. Jumping on his back the large one bit deep into the side of the other's neck. The smaller creature screamed and struggled only to find its strength waning as its lifeblood pumped out through the jagged gash. Sheri, tired from the climb, looked down once more and saw the surviving creature climb to its feet. It looked up at her again but this time, glancing back along the trail, it looked frightened and unsure of its course of action. It stared up at her again and then back along the trail toward the parking area where she heard a horrible scream, louder, more primal.

The creature below her sprinted along the trail in her direction. Just before she crested the ridge she looked back and saw a gigantic creature leap from the brush between the trees and fall on the carcass of the smaller, dead Devol.

Oh God, one down and now an even bigger one on my trail. Now that she was running down the backside of the hill, she regained her breath and her speed. She hoped that the creature behind her was too concerned about the new, giant Devol and would forget about her. Coming to the fork at the edge of the canyon she bore left, but she was beginning to flag. She had to slow her pace, but kept going at a steady clip that ate up the distance. She ascended the switchbacks to the wildflower-covered meadow that had earlier filled her with such wonder. Now she ran through it without even seeing it.

She was breathing heavily now and needed to rest. Past the meadow, the trail snaked down to the creek that ran southeast to the lake. She ran into the creek and splashed downstream to try and mask her scent. After a quarter of a mile, she left the stream on the opposite side from where she entered and ran directly south away from the trail and the stream. With no trail to follow she had to slow to a walk, giving her some much needed rest but filling her with anxiety about the creature behind her. She continually looked over her shoulder, expecting at any minute to see it right behind her. Cutting across the plateau would enable her to cut off some distance, since the trail that descended to the valley was further along the cliff to the west. She had never been here but Pete had told her that the trail crossed the river below the dam and then worked its way back west. It spilled over the cliff and descended through dense trees and down a very steep decline to the valley floor.

She heard someone or something behind her and quickly ducked behind a small cluster of rocks. Peering carefully around the edge she saw the Devol across the plateau, still following the trail. It had its head in the air, sniffing as it went, but seemed unable to pick up her scent. She grinned.

The water trick had worked! At least for now. When the creature had disappeared down the trail toward the lake she quietly continued toward the cliffs at the south side of the plateau.

Reaching the edge, she was slightly confused. She hadn't crossed any trails so she had to assume she was too far to the west. The last thing she wanted was to go back east toward the creature but she needed to find where the trail went over the edge. She knew she should hurry, but was terrified of running into the Devol and crept along at a snail's pace. Due to the overgrowth and the fact that she couldn't see over the edge she almost missed the trail. When she spotted it, she leaped ahead to the right. It went through a stand of trees and as she reached the edge, she heard a whining from behind her. Her heart in her throat she took off running again, burst through the bushes and almost flew off the cliff before she was able to put on the brakes and slide forward into bushes that lined the edge.

She heard crashing in the brush behind her and started down the cliff. The trail was dug into the side of the hill and in many places was almost missing. It traversed back and forth, switch backing ever downward. She had to slow down or risk a fatal fall. Now she was on autopilot. One foot in front of the other. She was sniffling now and so tired. She made a turn and headed back west. And stopped. The trail was gone, the steep hill covered with a rock fall that she thought would be impossible for her to cross without sliding down the slope to her death.

She turned around and saw the creature standing at the last turn in the trail. It stood and looked at her, not moving. It knew it had her. Suddenly, a look of alarm crossed its face and it took a step backward.

Then the beast quickly started forward as she heard, "Grab my hand!" from behind her. Whirling around, she saw a man swinging toward her, grasping a rope. She was so shocked that she didn't realize what he wanted. Then she saw his outstretched hand and simultaneously heard the creature racing toward her from the back. The rope was tied off above and the man ran across the scree slope, one hand grasping the rope and the other beckoning to her. Making a quick decision, she reached out and grabbed his hand in both of hers just as he reached the end of his swing. She felt the creature skid to a stop behind her, as it let out a tremendous scream of frustration, and she was jerked forward, running along the scree slope, hanging on to the man's hand with all her remaining strength. When she reached the trail on the other side of the rock fall, she felt the man's hand jerk free and she ran along the trail a few steps to catch her balance. When she looked back, her rescuer was climbing hand over hand up the rope and the creature was gingerly trying to cross the rocks. It slipped, wind milling its arms, and managing to get back to the solid purchase of the trail. It stood and stared at her.

She stared back.

When she looked up, the man was gone.

Glancing once more across the abyss, she saw the creature turn and start back along the trail, disappointment obvious in its posture. She continued down the mountain at the best pace she could manage. The hill was becoming less steep, the switchbacks longer. What little she could see of the trail, it began to go straight down the hill now, through brush and trees. She breathed a sigh of relief and sped up. Seeing something flash at the side of the trail she tried to leap over it, tripped over an obstacle that moved into her path and flew headlong for several feet. She slammed into the ground, completely knocking her breath out, and lay still for a moment, stunned. A wave of nausea washed over her and she rolled onto her side. Her vision blurred, she had trouble making out the obstacle… and then it moved again. She threw up her arm and rubbed her eyes to try and clear her vision. Coming to her knees, her eyesight cleared… and she looked straight into the face of Bud Nagle.

**

Clay was so infuriated, he outpaced the men and made it back to town in three hours. The rest came straggling back in groups of two or three until the final four guys came into the yard, with Bruce barely able to stand between two of them. Many of the men slunk away to their own houses to escape Clay's fury. Jinx and Monroe went into Clay's house and grabbed beers from the refrigerator. They were as angry as Clay, their plans for a quick takeover of the shelter laid to rest. Monroe didn't question that the shelter was real. He saw the blast door for himself, and the people that had escaped had to come from somewhere, but he questioned whether the large number of people, especially women, had been a figment of Clay's imagination.

Clay had gone to his room, and the men dragging Bruce brought him into the living room and chained him to the same bed they had used for Holcomb.

"Hey Clay," Monroe shouted through the bedroom door. "He's here. What do you want to do?"

"Call me when Stewart gets back with the girl." He didn't want to do anything until he had violent sex to take the edge off.

They waited the rest of the afternoon, and Stewart and Billy hadn't returned. Clay finally came out of room, his eyes red and swollen. Jinx, Monroe and Jackson pretended not to notice. They had been drinking for three hours, ever since they'd returned and all were wasted.

Hearing voices on the porch, he went to the screen door and saw that the four men he had left behind had returned.

"What the hell are you doing back?"

"Stewart didn't come back with the girl, and it's getting dark so we hightailed it back."

"Get out of here then. Be ready to go back to the ranch tomorrow."

Clay walked over to Bruce and stared down at him until Bruce began to squirm. "C'mon, Clay. I never did anything to you in the shelter. Hell, I liked your boys. I didn't vote to put you out." He looked up at Clay hoping for some mercy.

"You were as fucked up as the rest of them. I want some answers. Where are the others?"

"Bruce Gechter. Sergeant Major. Service number RA 8-225-555." He laughed. "Just kidding Clay."

Clay reached out and punched him in the face.

"Shit, Clay! C'mon man. I don't know nuthin," he started to whimper. "Please, they just brought me along to help get the bike."

"You are a lying piece of shit. Tell me where they are." He turned to Monroe. "Get me some pliers." Bruce's eyes got real wide and he started to cry.

Monroe was emboldened by the fact that Stewart and Billy hadn't returned. This slimeball was nothing without the threat of his two creatures.

"Come on Clay. How far can they be if they left the shelter. There's nowhere for them to go on this side of the mountains. We would have seen some evidence of them. These guys came along the trail from the north, but it just goes around the ridge, and climbs over Hunter's Meadow to get behind the line of mountains that your shelter was in. They must be behind that ridge."

Clay thought about that for a moment. "Okay, where else could they be?"

Jinx said, "They could be on the plateau by the river or maybe they got down the trail to Hidden valley."

"Hidden Valley? Isn't that where you said the Jeep went?"

"Yeah, Clay. Maybe they're all together. Wouldn't that be sweet? We could fuckin' hose 'em all at the same time."

"Didn't I tell you to get me some pliers?" Clay asked Monroe.

"Hey man, you don't need 'em now. We know where they gotta be."

Clay stepped over to Monroe, faked a gut punch and when the slower man went for it Clay hit him with a roundhouse punch alongside the head. Monroe went down but rolled over and came to his feet. He gestured to Clay to come at him again.

"You fuckin' asshole. You're real brave, but your freaks don't seem to be here. So come on, let's finish this." He swung at Clay, throwing his whole body forward and bearing Clay to the floor. Clay rolled out from under Monroe and came to his feet. As Monroe tried to rise, Clay leveled a vicious kick at his head slamming him back to the floor. Clay now faced the door. He stepped back and grinned looking over Monroe's head. Sitting on his butt on the floor, Monroe looked back over his shoulder, and grew very pale.

Clay pointed at Monroe. "Kill him Stewart. Eat."

***

It was so dark that neither Jerry, nor Pete, could see his hand in front of his face. They had reached the bottom of the stairs, pushed open the door and slipped inside the shelter.

"Pete, I'm hit."

"What? Where? How bad is it?"

"I don't know. Hit me in the back of the arm when we went through the door. I don't think it's real bad but it's bleeding a lot."

Pete felt Jerry's arm and concurred, "Yeah, it feels like it's really bleeding." He pulled off his shirt and after several attempts, was finally able to tear off some strips of cloth.

"Take off your shirt." Jerry stripped it off and Pete wrapped the strips around Jerry's arm as tight as he dared. "Let me know if your hand or your arm starts to get numb. Can you walk okay?"

"Yeah, I don't feel dizzy or anything. I think I would if I lost too much blood. Don't you think?"

"I guess so," Pete agreed. "Here. Put your shirt back on but leave your arm out of the sleeve."

"Do you remember where this door comes out?"

"It's pretty close to the big elevator but how do you think we can find our way to an exit in this dark?"

"We just have to try." They found they were whispering. "Do you think there are any more of those things in here?"

Pete had been wondering the same thing. "I don't think even they can see in this absolute darkness. Reminds me of that cave, Grand Canyon Caverns, where they turned off the lights while we were at the bottom. Remember how dark it was?"

"Yeah, Mom freaked out. Let's try to remember how to get to the exit."

"The blast door's closed. How can we get out?"

"I have no idea, but the Devols got in here somehow, so there must be another way out. I just don't know where. So our only choice is the exit cave."

They slid down to the floor and tried to reconstruct the route. Once they thought they had it, they stood and started along the wall to the left. They kept their hands on the wall which was difficult for Jerry. After what seemed like forever, they came to a perpendicular wall and continued along it to the right. The going was hard, due to piles of debris that littered the hallway. In several places the wall was pushed in by tons of rock that had collapsed behind it.

They arrived at a small alcove.

"This is the stairway that comes out by Will's quarters. Remember?"

Jerry nodded, and realizing Pete couldn't see him, said, "We'll go down and stay against this wall on the next level. There was another stairwell farther down that corridor."

They pushed open the door, relieved that it wasn't stuck. Very slowly they descended to the next level where all the living quarters had been. At the bottom, they pushed against the door but it took all their strength to get it far enough open for them to squeeze through.

"I just need a little break," Jerry whispered. They slid to the floor again and Pete could hear Jerry breathing heavily. He felt the bandage but so far it hadn't bled through.

"Let's go. The sooner we get out of here, the sooner we can get you to Dr. Jim." Helping Jerry to his feet, they again followed the wall on the left toward the rear of the shelter. Locating the next door, they descended to the bottom level only to be unable to open the door. Pete was so disappointed, that if his brother's life wasn't at stake, he could have sat down and cried. They climbed back up the stairs, exited the stairwell and decided to try for the one around the next corner. They reached another intersection and followed the wall around the corner. Pete could hear Jerry's labored breathing again… and then froze as he realized it wasn't his brother's.

He leaned toward him and whispered in his ear, "There's someone else in here besides us. It's close. Listen, you can hear it." They both held their breath and could clearly hear something breathing. "I think it's asleep or it would know we're here."

"What are we going to do?" Jerry was wavering on his feet although he didn't tell Pete he was in trouble.

"We have to go to the other side and descend to the bottom from there." They moved back, making as little noise as possible, but not knowing when they might run into debris.

It became a waking nightmare for Jerry as he became nauseated and dizzy. If he retched, he knew it was over. The dark journey across the second floor was surreal; the unbelievable quiet and darkness, stepping over fallen rocks and pieces of wooden framing, while holding Pete's hand and following mindlessly as he became progressively more dizzy. They made it across the second floor by going back the way they had come, holding onto the right wall. Finally arriving at the stairwell leading down to just outside the farm cave, they again descended into the darkness, praying the door would open.

Both doors opened, but the one at the bottom of the stairwell groaned loudly as they pushed it inward.

"Man, we're toast if that thing heard us. Let's go." Pete pulled Jerry into the hallway and tripped over something. He jumped up, rubbing his hands on his pants as he realized it was the remains of people or creatures. He didn't wait to find out, but grabbed Jerry's hand again and started along the right hand wall, coming to yet another intersection and turning toward the rear of the shelter.

They heard a thumping from above.

The creature was awake!

***

An exhausted Sheri Summerland crossed the bridge with Bud's arm across her shoulder.

"Samuel!" She yelled with her last remaining strength. He was working in the graveyard, placing stone upon stone to build a wall around the cemetery. He dropped the rock he was about to place on the wall and ran to the bridge, relieving Sheri of her burden. She collapsed to the ground.

"Bud Nagle? Where in the world did you find him?" Bud had been their power man, in charge of the power plant in the shelter. They had thought him dead when he went missing soon after the creatures had entered the shelter.

"On the north trail." She was breathing hard but climbed to her feet. "There may be a Devol behind me and Clay Hargraves and his bunch ambushed us. I need to get to camp. Can you bring him?"

"Yeah, hand me my rifle. Get goin'."

Mark was feeling guilty. He was sitting on his sleeping bag, leaning up against the wall of the building with Lori's head in his lap. The kids had gone off to play, and their little corner of the world was dim and cool. He thought about the fight with the Devols, trying to think of how they could have done things differently. Three guards had watched while they took a short break. Mark thought it was enough. The damn things move so fast. The others had fallen back at the first indication of trouble but Big Tom had stood his ground. It cost him his life. The men still hadn't returned with Tom's body.

Chris, Samuel, Rana and the rest of the farmers were plowing the field to plant their first crop. Farnsworth and a couple of other guys had already built the sluice gate that would allow them to flood the fields with water once the irrigation ditch was dug, and a group of at least twenty men and women were working on that ditch. Using the smaller of the two tractors, they were digging the ditch from the center of the north edge of the field, diagonally northwest where it would connect with the river fifty yards upstream. Farnsworth's guys were building another gate at the north end of the ditch.

Thornton and several others were working on the bridge, and Lucas had a crew of two dozen people working on the cabin. The walls were now head height and going up fast. With three more of the creatures dead, he hoped the bachelor's cabin was more for comfort than safety. Dr. Laskey and his team were discussing how they would govern themselves and what medium of exchange they would use.

And he sat there doing absolutely nothing.

He felt Lori stir and looked down to see her eyes open.

"Hey sleepy head. You sleep well?"

Sitting up, she swung her legs around and leaned against the wall, laying her head against his shoulder. "I've slept better. Can't keep from seeing those monsters murder Tom. I didn't react quickly enough."

"It happened so fast I don't think there was anything any of us could do. We killed two of the bastards, found evidence a third is dead and supplied two score more people with weapons and ammo. Hopefully the other team will find some useful stuff in the parking lot."

"Yeah, like a working vehicle. That would be a miracle. We could use one. Where are the kids?"

"They're all out playing in the meadow. Everybody's working but us."

"I have a feeling we'll put in our share of the work in the future." She yawned and stretched loudly, reaching her arms toward the ceiling. He leaned over and kissed her, a lingering "the kids aren't here" kiss, but she pushed him away. "We should see how everything's going. How long did I sleep?"

"About an hour. The other team should be getting back before long. I hope they're alright. When we came out of the tunnel I could have sworn I heard a gunshot."

"Really? Cause I thought I heard one too."

"That's not good. Geez…what else can go wrong?"

She gave him a scathing look and punched his arm. "Oh no, you did NOT just say that!"

"Why, what's wrong?" He rubbed his arm vigorously.

"Last time I heard you say that we got earthquakes and monsters."

He climbed to his feet and extended his hand to help her up when they heard, "Mark! Mark, come quick!"

Lori popped up and gave him her very best, "I told you so look" as they hurried to the door.

The sun was low and cast long shadows across the meadow from the trees at the west end. There was already a nip in the air as they ran to a crowd where the trail entered the meadow. Mark followed Tucker through the crowd and saw Sheri standing with her hands on her knees trying to catch her breath.

"Sheri! Where are the others?"

"They…they're back at the cars. Got ambushed by Clay. Found… I found Bud Nagle and a strange Indian helped me escape from the monster! We need…"

"Wait. What did you say? Bud Nagle?"

"Samuel's helping him. Send some guys."

"Come on!" Lori grabbed Craig's arm and they took off to the trail.

Just then Walter pushed through the people surrounding Sheri. "Where's my boys. Where's Pete and Jerry?"

Sheri put her hands on Walter's big chest. "When Clay jumped us Pete yelled at me to take off and he threw himself at Clay. I heard a gunshot and the last thing I saw was Pete and Clay go down. They were fighting. I don't think anyone was hit."

"How long ago?" Walter asked her.

"I don't know. I was being chased by a Devol, actually two of them. They got in a fight and the big one killed the little one, then a bigger one jumped out of the woods. I just took off again but a Devol followed me. Must have been at least an hour. It's a few miles."

"What did you say about an Indian?" Greg put in.

"I never saw him before. I couldn't get across where the trail comes to a rock fall. The Devol was right behind me. I thought I was a goner. Next thing I knew somebody yells at me to take his hand and I turned around just as this guy reaches for me. He was tied to a rope from above. I just grabbed his hand and we ran across the slope in a big arc. He let me go at the continuation of the trail and when I turned around he was scrambling up the rope and just disappeared." She was regaining her breath and stood looking at the others. "We need to go after them but we can't go back up that trail cause of the rock fall. We need to go the way we went this morning. The way Micah came down. We all need lights. It's going to get dark."

"Jimbo! Get fifteen armed guys. Ten minutes. Let's go!" Mark started toward the trail when Lori and the others came out of the forest. Dave and Samuel carried Bud between them. They laid him on the grass where Jim quickly looked him over.

"He's in bad shape. Extremely dehydrated. Let's get him to the clinic."

They lifted him and started for the building with Jim leading the way. Men had come from the other side of the meadow where they had been working on the cabin and in ten minutes a group was ready to leave. "Walter, I don't think you should go. There's a pretty steep climb up the hill. No offense man, but I think you'd just slow us down." Mark checked his weapons and slammed home his magazine.

"Just try and stop me!"

"Walter!" Sarah came through the crowd. "You just let them go. They need to get there as fast as they can. I need you to stay here!" She grabbed his arm with sudden strength.

Walter looked at her and then swung around to Mark. "Don't just stand there. GO!"

With Sheri leading the way, they once again took off toward the trail heading south.

Chapter 18

The hill seemed steeper and the way longer this time around. Lori could see Sheri was exhausted but she kept up with the others as they climbed the long ridge to the top of the waterfall. Once again, they went inland a ways and then headed north until they came to the lake. At this point Sheri took the lead again, as none of them had been this way before.

"Keep your eyes peeled. That Devol had to come back this way. I forgot to tell you the thing was with Clay's group. It seemed more human than the ones from the shelter. Clay actually sent it after me."

"Well, that proves they came from the outside and not from inside the earth after the quakes," Greg said.

The evening wore on and the temperature dropped. The rescue party became spooked as shadows lengthened and created dark recesses in the forest. By the time they reached the fork at the edge of the canyon it was dark. Everyone had their lights on and three of the group wore headlamps. Progressing fearfully, they continually shined their lights into the trees around them. The quiet and the darkness combined to make Lori feel as though she were in a fantasy world, time moving forward at a snail's pace. Sheri explained to them that the pass they were in descended to where the Devols fought. She had told them of the giant she had seen that devoured the little Devol and Mark was convinced it was his nemesis. They shut off all but one light and descended the hill as quietly as possible. Every few minutes they would stop and listen. A light breeze soughed through the trees but they didn't hear anything that sounded like a living being.

After reaching the ground level, Sheri led them forward to the point where the Devols fought. There were bones and large chunks of tissue strewn around and the stench lingered after death. The remains were unrecognizable as a humanoid. Sheri shined the light over the mess and then into the trees at the side of the trail. She stifled a scream as red eyes stared back out of the forest at them and she jumped back into Jimbo's arms. Fifteen rifles came up simultaneously but the light shown on the severed head of the thing that had been Billy Judd.

Sheri turned and buried her head in Jimbo's chest, and if the moment hadn't been so somber Lori would have been amused at the look on his face.

"There, there little lady. Come on, let's keep going. How far do we have to go?"

Self-consciously, she backed away and started forward down the trail. "It's only about a half mile to the parking lot. Ten minutes at the most."

The men in the rear of the column kept alert for any sign of life behind them and the group stretched out along the trail. When they reached the open ground of the parking lot they switched their lights back on, and at the extreme edge of illumination, Mark immediately spotted a body lying half way to the open door of the shelter. He ran over, knelt down and groaned as he turned the corpse over and saw his friend, Darryl Washington.

"Damn it!" He jumped to his feet and quickly looked around for signs of the others. Standing in a circle around him the rescue party was staring into the darkness at high alert. "His body's cold," Mark said. "They must have killed him right after Sheri took off. Spread out in groups of three. See if you can find any sign of the others."

"Hey, Mark. Over here." One of the groups was at the open entrance to the shelter. "There're footprints. At least two guys, maybe all three."

Jimbo walked into the cave, flashing his light into the corners and along the back wall.

"Uh oh. There's some blood here." He was standing at the door leading to the stairwell. The other two guys in his group stood back, their rifles pointed at the door as Jimbo put his hand on the door knob. Mark nodded at him and Jimbo quickly jerked the door back. All of them jumped, but grinned self-consciously as the stairwell behind the door was empty.

"Look here! There's more blood."

"It looks like they all tried to make it into the shelter when Clay's guys fired on them. Darryl was killed and one of the others were hit." Mark looked down the stairs. "I doubt if Clay went after them. I don't see more footprints. It looks like just two or three guys. And they could hold the staircase against Clay's guys forever."

The other groups returned from searching the parking lot. "No sign of the bastards, Mark. They probably went back to town."

Mark stepped to the top of the stairs and yelled for Pete and Jerry but there was no response. He looked to the others and shrugged.

"What do we do now, Boss?"

"One of them is hurt, Mark," Lori said. "We have to go after them."

"Bring Darryl's body in here. I won't leave it where the animals or Devols can get it. We'll put it inside the door. Our lights should last for a few hours yet and we have plenty of ammo in case there are any of those things left in there. We'll come back for the body later. Let's move."

"Hey Mark," Al said. "I don't know if I can go in there. The blast door at the back's closed. What if we're trapped and can't get out? I...I can't." He was visibly trembling and Mark knew what he was feeling. The thought of re-entering the collapsed shelter didn't appeal to him either. Al's son had broken his leg in a rock fall in one of the Dragon caves, and his wife, her arm, as they escaped the shelter in the last terrifying moments of the earthquake.

"Look, there may be another way out. Somehow Bud Nagle escaped the creatures. He was last seen in the power plant. Al, Mike and Stephen, stay here and guard our flank. If we aren't back by daybreak, get yourselves back to camp. Everyone else okay to go after the boys?"

"Yeah Mark, let's boogie." Jimbo leaped down the stairs.

***

"Hurry, it heard us!" Pete and Jerry came upon an alcove and Pete became disoriented.

"This is a Dragon door. Just go across to the other side and keep going," Jerry told him.

"You're right. Come on." Pete held Jerry's hand but he released the wall and strode across the alcove. Tripping over something he jumped back to his feet but continued a little left of the line he needed to reach the opposite side of the alcove. Not immediately finding the opposite wall, he panicked. He started to turn back but Jerry grabbed and hugged him tight. "Easy little brother, I need you to keep it together. Okay?"

"Yeah, I'm sorry. I... I can't find the wall. We could be turned around."

"No you're going right. Just keep on."

Pete took a deep breath and took three more steps where his hand touched the wall.

"I got it! Come on."

They heard the creaking of the door to the third level, and throwing caution to the winds, hustled along the wall to the next intersection and then left to the opening that led to the escape tunnel. The door was open and they quickly rounded the corner into the tunnel. Once they reached and went around the ninety-degree turn into the quarter-mile long escape tunnel they saw a very faint light ahead. Pete grabbed Jerry and they half ran, half stumbled forward. The blast door was closed but Pete saw the door to the utility closet was open. That's where the light was coming from. Most of the water had drained from the tunnel, but a few inches remained. When they had escaped a few days before, the tunnel had been flooding and Pete fled with Sandy, who was in the final stages of labor. He could barely recall that flight.

They looked behind them and saw a Devol enter the tunnel.

Pete fired a shot in that direction and the creature stepped back around the corner. Pete figured it must know the power of weapons and had possibly been hit before. Shuffling down the wet tunnel, they thought the quarter mile would take forever but they finally came to the closet and hustled inside. The emergency light had been on almost a week and was so faint it was almost out. Only the contrast with the utter dark made it visible.

"Jerry, I have to work on this door control. You're going to have to be in the corridor and keep firing at that thing to keep it back. Can you do that?"

"Yeah, keep it back."

"Come on bro. Man, I love you big brother. You just keep it back and I'll get the damn door open!"

Pete helped him to sit in the tunnel and then immediately returned to the controls. He pulled off the cover and stared at the multitude of wires and gauges. "I'd love it if there was just a control marked "open the door," right?" he muttered. Gunfire caused him to jump a foot off the ground. He looked around the door and saw Jerry with both hands on his gun pointing down the tunnel. The creature was out of sight.

He went back to work trying to figure out the wiring. He flipped a couple of switches and nothing happened. There wasn't enough power. Frustrated, he smashed his fist against the panel. He looked wildly around and saw another cover. This one was hinged. He lifted it and almost fainted when he saw a large wheel inside the compartment. Grabbing it he began to turn it when he heard a grunt, looked at the doorway and up into the beady eyes of the Devol staring right down at him. His gun was on a ledge and he grabbed it without thinking.

"Jerry!" He opened fire as the creature reached for him. He heard Jerry fire off a shot and the Devol backed away to look down at Pete's helpless brother.

"Get away from him!" Pete began to fire repeatedly and the creature backed further away, its arms across its ugly face. Then Jerry opened fire and they pumped every round in their magazines into the face and body of the creature. With each shot it jerked back until it hit the opposite wall. Pete was reminded of the game where you swing a flashlight rapidly back and forth to create a strobe effect. The muzzle flashes caused the entire scene to play out like an old fashioned black and white movie.

He'd heard once, that someone who knew what they were doing could change a magazine in seconds. It took him much longer than that but he got it swapped out just as the monster was coming back at him. He continued to fire but could no longer hear Jerry's gun. The creature went down against the far wall. Pete jumped out into the hallway and saw Jerry lying on the floor, his hand outstretched. Grabbing Jerry's rifle, he emptied it too, but it was over. He stood there breathing hard, then swung around to check on Jerry. His brother was unconscious, but still alive. He kept glancing at the creature as he turned the wheel of the door control. A faint line of light appeared beneath the door and slowly widened as he continued to turn the wheel. The door was massive and he must have made a million turns of the wheel before the space was high enough to drag his brother through. He pulled Jerry into the back cave of the shelter and hoisted him over his shoulder. He exited down the ramp and staggered to the bridge. Resting a few minutes, he knew if he didn't keep going Jerry could bleed out. He half carried and half dragged him to the camp. Someone lifted Jerry from his shoulder and he collapsed onto the field.

"If anyone needs to get in the shelter," he said to no one in particular, "we left the door open for ya."

***

They split up while making their way through the silent corridors of the shelter so they could cover the area more quickly. There were three groups of three. Lori felt another aftershock just as they finished searching the first floor. She threw herself against the wall, crouching down until it stopped. This time, Mark felt a moment of panic, as the small quake brought back the memories of the nightmare as they searched for the children during their panic-stricken escape from the creatures. They quickly resumed their exploration.

Mark, Lori and Dave were on the second floor where the quarters of the residents had been, when Mark realized they were right outside his room. "Lori, hang on. I need to get something."

"You know this place could fall down around our ears any minute, right?"

"I know. It's important." He disappeared into the room and she waited until she lost her patience.

"What the hell are you doing?" She stepped into the room and found him shimmying under the timbers of a fallen wall. He was dragging a duffle bag behind him.

"I got it. Let's go." The room was filled with dust and one of the timbers shifted and fell.

She shook her head as they reentered the hallway and continued the search. As they finished each level the groups came together to report their findings.

"We found a lair in the far corner of this level," Jimbo said. "Looks like one of the things has been living there. Shit's everywhere, and bones. I think it ate some of the people that were killed when we escaped."

Mark felt his stomach turn. "Let's get to the last level. I want out of here."

They descended to the third level and did a thorough search, not finding any evidence of the Thompsons or Bruce. "The only way out might be through the power plant. The water's drained out of this level. That means that somehow the penstocks got plugged up and no more flooding has occurred. Let's see if we can get in there." Mark led the way to the doors that led to the power plant but when they arrived it was obvious that no one got out that way. The area behind the door was filled with rock and debris. It appeared the entire ceiling of the cave had collapsed into the room. "That explains why the water has drained. There's no more coming in from the lake above. Well, they must be holed up in the escape tunnel. Let's keep a watch for the creature that lived upstairs. It has to be down here somewhere."

"Hey Mark! Over there." Dave pointed to a mass partially covered by rocks.

"It's a Devol. There's another one over there." Jimbo pointed out. "That one looks like toast. Got himself electrocuted I'd say. Fucking idiot."

As they made their way back through the shelter and entered the tunnel that led to the blast doors, Mark remembered the nightmare he'd had before they came to this place. A premonition that had come true. He re-lived the feelings of panic he'd felt as he was chased by the gigantic creature of his dream, the anxiety concerning the fate of Lori and the kids, and his intense fear for Will, knowing the head injury was probably fatal. Lori sensed his hesitation, took his arm and squeezed it gently.

They rounded the turn and saw the tunnel before them. Their lights only reached a couple hundred feet and they slowly moved forward, their rifles leveled at the darkness before them.

"What's that?" Jimbo was ahead of the others and they saw him quickly move forward. The rest ran after him, afraid of the worst. When they reached the body of the creature Pete and Jerry had killed, they felt relief that it wasn't another body of a friend.

"Mark look! The door is up."

The door had been raised about three feet. They looked around and found the small control closet with the manual wheel for raising the door.

"Well, I'll be damned," Jimbo drawled. "They're probably back at camp wondering where the hell we are."

"Come on guys, let's go." They all scooted under the door, exited the cave and headed back to camp.

When they arrived, they were challenged by three guards who materialized out of nowhere. Mark hadn't heard them approaching. They were finally getting better at protecting the camp. Hurrying to the building, they found a very busy medical clinic.

Mark and Lori found Pete sitting on the sofa with Sandy. Pete filled them in on him and Jerry's flight through the shelter and Mark shuddered at the thought of going through there with no lights. It was hard enough to do it with flashlights and headlamps and Mark was impressed they had managed to kill another of the creatures.

"Dr. Jim says Jerry's wound isn't all that bad," Pete told them. "He lost a lot of blood but he'll be okay. Did you find Darryl and Bruce?"

"Bruce? You mean he's not with you guys? We found Darryl's body. He'd been shot in the back."

"Damn! I was afraid of that."

"What happened to Bruce?" Lori asked.

"Oh, God. I bet Clay has him. They were waiting for us at the parking lot. Probably coincidental since there was no way for them to know we were coming. We yelled at Sheri to run, and I jumped Clay. Then me, Jerry and Darryl took off for the cave. I thought Bruce was right behind us."

"We didn't see any sign of him. We're going to have to try and rescue him." Mark stood up. "It's the middle of the night and everyone needs rest. We can't do anything for him right now. The guys we left behind will be back in the morning and we'll decide what to do then."

Lori left to check on the kids and Mark went to the medical clinic. Walter, Sarah and Barbara were sitting beside Jerry's bed and Dr. Jim met Mark at the partition that separated off the area from the rest of the building.

"Hi Mark. You think all this crap is ever going to end? It would be good if we could just concentrate on building a civilization."

"How's Bud?"

"I have no idea how he survived. He's unconscious and we're giving him I.V. fluids for the dehydration. I can't find any serious injuries, so I think he'll be okay. I can't wait to hear his tale. Mary's in shock after thinking him dead these few days. She's with him now."

"Well, we killed two of those things and the Thompson boys killed a third. We found the remains of another one on the ridge and two more bodies in the power cave, and Sheri says she saw Clay's pet creature kill one. We lost two good men and we think Clay captured another, so I'm not sure it was worth it, but we have to be a lot safer from those things."

"You're right. Not a good trade off. Well, let's all get some sleep."

"Okay, nite Jim."

Mark started back toward the hallway he and Lori called home. He clutched the duffle bag that carried the mementos of his former life. He didn't realized how much they meant to him until he had a chance to retrieve them. When he got to his sleeping bag he saw that Lori had already fallen asleep. He sat down with his back against the wall and pulled out the photos. By the light of a flashlight, he gazed at them one by one, tears beginning to flow down his cheeks as he let his mind drift back to his life before the senseless war. He thought about his childhood, his life as the CEO of a multi-billion dollar aerospace company, his running friends, and most of all, the man that had been a father to him, and whom he had lost only a short week ago. It seemed like a lifetime since they had left the shelter.

He was sure they would be safer now, glad they had eliminated several of the mutated creatures…but he knew the big one was still out there.

And it would be coming for him.

***

After a very short night, Mark stepped off the platform that housed the shower stalls and sinks that the residents used for shaving and washing up, and looked up to see men entering the meadow from the trail to the north. He realized it was Al and the others he had left behind to guard the entrance to the shelter. Good, everyone was home.

He had put a notice on the bulletin board just inside the door of the building for a general forum at 0900.

He was sick to death of burying good people and wanted nothing more than to get on with their lives. He thought about what Samuel had told him, that they would be needing a cemetery. Every day, Samuel had continued to pile up rocks to make a wall around the graveyard. Now they had three more bodies. Men were digging the graves this morning and Brian would preside over the funerals in the early afternoon.

Work needed to go on, however, and the people were working on the cabin and at the field where crops had already been planted. Mark met Al and the others as they crossed the field.

"Hi Mark. We waited until daybreak and figured you'd found a way through the shelter. We brought Darryl's body back with us. We made a gurney with aspen trunks and branches. We left him at the cemetery."

"Thanks guys. Get some breakfast and some rest. I'll see you this afternoon." He crossed the field to the cabin and asked Lucas when he thought it would be finished.

"We need another week. The walls are going up quick but the roof will take longer. We have some lumber in the building that we can use for this roof but for future cabins we'll have to cut lumber."

"You guys are doing a great job. I'll see you at the funerals."

Mark walked into the woods north of the cabin and stood for several minutes, trying to make sense of it all. He would miss Darryl a lot. They had become good friends over the past months. Tired of losing friends, he was well aware that Clay and his group were still out there, a problem that would have to be dealt with.

He went back to headquarters to start the forum and as he entered the building he found a group of people standing around drinking coffee and waiting for the meeting to start. Fifty or sixty people were out on work details but it seemed most of the rest of the residents were gathering for information. Mark stood on the box he used for these meetings and held up his hands for quiet.

"To begin with, we found Bud Nagle alive. He escaped from the shelter and crawled most of the way here. Sheri found him on her way back and he's with Doc right now. Mary's with him. You all know we lost Tom Galloway and Darryl Washington. Tom was killed by a Devol and Darryl by Clay Hargraves and his group. Bruce is still missing and we're pretty sure he's been taken prisoner by Clay."

"Well, let's go get him!" someone called out.

"That's a possibility. But we need to plan our next moves carefully. We don't know how many people he has, how well armed they are or very many other details. We know he has one or two Devols in his group that do his bidding." That seemed to shock quite a few people.

"You're kidding, right?"

"No. He's telling the truth." Izzy and Terry had been with Cody but now joined the group. "It's weird," Terry said. "A couple of them are pretty bad and they're the ones that follow Clay. I saw one or two others that you could tell had changed but they still looked mostly human. They kept to themselves and I didn't see them again after they helped to capture me and Marci. They have a lot of guys. I hate to tell you this but your friend is a goner. If Clay hasn't already tortured him to death, it won't be long. I heard Clay talk about killing all the men in the shelter, especially his father. He wanted to keep the women. I bet your friend has already told him Hargraves is dead and that you are in this valley. His men chased us to the entrance so they know we're up here. I guarantee you he's going to come for you."

"Well, let him come! We'll be ready," Jimbo called out.

"That's just it!" Terry said, his voice rising as he grimaced with the pain of yelling. "You aren't ready. You're a bunch of cream puffs. You've been sheltered for the past eight months while the rest of the survivors have been out here living in the real world. You had barn dances and sock hops while my family had to turn away our neighbors to die, and we ate the same damn thing for months. My son was almost killed and will lose some of the use of his arm. I was beaten to within an inch of my life and my daughter was repeatedly raped by Clay and his followers. Damn it, even my nine year old was shot! You people are all scientists, teachers and businessmen. Hell, you don't know the difference between a clip and a magazine. You don't have a prayer against these guys unless you toughen up. Even your military guy was a martial arts instructor!"

Dave got in Terry's face. "If you weren't busted up, buddy, I'd show you who's a cream puff."

Izzy stepped between the men and pleaded with Mark to calm things down.

"Listen," Mark said. "I know we had it made in the shelter. But we're all healthy and most of us are fit. We have that advantage over those that have been struggling to survive on the outside. Dave's training the men. We just need more time. You were military. You could help us get ready. We have weapons, but you're right, most of us aren't trained in their use. We've been winging it. I know there are a few of the Devols left out there including the big one that chased me out of the shelter but we killed several yesterday. What do you think we should do?"

Terry was caught off guard. He didn't expect them to be reasonable and ask for his help. "I, uh, think you should beef up your security. I'll be better in a few days and can help Dave train the men. It's hard to say whether you should wait for them to come for you or you should take the fight to them."

"Why don't we just mind our own business and leave them alone?" Jenkins asked.

"Sooner or later you're going to have to fight them. Clay won't let you just hang out here and play 'Little House on the Prairie.' He hates you guys."

"How about Bruce?" Jimbo asked.

"Bruce is dead. Or he will be before you can get to him," Terry told him.

"Alright, listen," Mark asked for quiet. "Terry's right. We have a lot of work to do to get ready to defend ourselves. We need to practice skills we couldn't practice in the shelter. We'll set up a firing range and learn to use the knives we all carry. Let's get back to work."

As people left the building Mark approached Terry and Izzy.

"Hey Mark, I didn't mean you guys aren't doin' good here. You just don't have any fighting skills, you know?"

"I know, Terry. We need you guys to help us. Izzy said you might be leaving but I sure would like you to stay. We could use your expertise."

"We can't go anywhere until we're healed up. We can help out until then. We'll make a decision about leaving after we're better. Deal?"

"Deal. You talked about sending someone to spy on them. Do you think they're still at the ranch?"

Izzy said, "They may have left some guys there. I'm sure Clay wants to keep us bottled up here. It's a nice place, other than the dead bodies, and there's a herd of cattle off to the west."

"Cattle? How many?"

"Looked like about thirty or forty."

"You're kidding. We need to get our hands on them. We have a few, but a herd like that could go a long way toward ensuring our survival. I'll see you later."

Excited about the cattle, Mark found Dave and Jimbo and told them he wanted to make a raid to round them up and bring them back to the valley. The rest of the morning was spent getting a group together and having Izzy describe the terrain, and the ranch, to the raiding party. That afternoon they laid Jason, Darryl and Tom to rest. The afternoon rains came in on schedule and further depressed the moods of the Remnant. By the time they returned to headquarters they were soaked through to the skin. The weather had taken a turn for the worse, the temperature dropping into the forties as they sought warmth in the building and in each other. Marilyn, Kate and Helen had dinner ready when they returned and all but the sentries joined together for dinner in the big building. Mark heard the baby crying until Sandy picked her up and began to breast feed.

They talked of their experiences since leaving the shelter less than a week before and Mark realized that while he was busy with the Devols, the work crews had made significant progress. Chris expected they would finish the canal the next day, and the cabin was ready for the crossbeams that would support the roof. The solar panels were assembled and ready to mount on the roof as soon as it was built.

Mark was dead tired and left the congregation right after dinner. He and Lori put the kids to bed and laid in each other's arms until they fell asleep. It was the first night since leaving the shelter that they slept through the night without an emergency.

Chapter 19

"Happy hunting!" Mark waved to Lori, Greg, Ron and Pete as his raiding party split off just north of Platte Rock.

"You too, Mark. Be careful and don't take any chances." She waved and watched as the men headed south, keeping the rock pile between them and the valley's entrance. It was still dark, the sky in the east just beginning to glow. Lori and her hunters went west, crossing the half mile to the rocks they had used for cover two mornings ago when Jimbo had bagged his rabbit. They hadn't brought him on this trip, convincing him that he would be better suited to the cattle raid.

"What the hell is that?" Pete asked as they approached the ramp and spotted something atop one of the rocks.

"It's a deer," Greg said. The carcass was laid across a rock as if it were an offering.

"Whose deer is it?" They had all dropped to their knees and pointed their rifles up the ramp wondering who might have left it there.

"Damned if I know," Pete said. They crept forward until they stood beside the animal.

Ron reached over and stuck his finger in a hole in the deer's side. "This is really weird. I think it was Sheri's Indian. Look at that. It was killed with an arrow. I think he meant it for us. If he's been watching us he knows we can't hunt for shit."

"Well then, let's take it back. Even if we were able to shoot another one, we can't carry them both. Let's string him up," Lori told them.

Ron was carrying the aspen trunk they brought to carry their kill. They tied the legs of the deer over the trunk and two of the men hoisted the ends onto their shoulders with the deer hanging upside down. The sun was just beginning to peek above the horizon when they started their journey back to camp.

***

Creeping forward on their bellies, Mark's raiding party slithered under the old wooden fence. They had sent two scouts forward and they had reported back that there didn't seem to be any sentries watching the entrance to the valley. They shifted their position to the right side of the gap and stayed along the cliff as they moved through the rocks at the base of the hill. Vegetation was sparse and they kept to the rocks for cover. The hill made a wide sweep to the west and as they came over a rise Mark could see the ranch in the open valley a few miles to the south.

"No wonder they don't have any sentries. The ranch is a long way from here." Now that the sun was up, he could see black dots in the distance that were probably the cattle they sought.

Terry had shown them some hand signals so they could maintain silence and Mark gestured to the others to move forward. They slipped through the rocks, keeping low. It was at least two miles until they were even with the cattle. They could see the ranch beyond the herd which meant that anyone at the ranch would be able to see them if they tried to cross the field in the open. The fields weren't perfectly flat and there was a small creek with brackish water in the bottom.

He motioned Mike, Jimbo and Dave into the creek and then he followed. Two guys had been stationed back up at the fence line and three men were left behind to guard their rear as they slipped into the ditch. They tried to stay out of the water but found that to be impossible. Within a hundred feet all four men were drenched and covered with mud. Mark could feel something biting him but he brushed the mud off his leg and kept going. Meandering through the field, the creek gradually became larger as it flowed toward the river, until it passed under a chain link fence.

The cattle became restless as they passed them in the field. Once they were beyond the herd they crawled out of the creek, two going north and two south making a line between the cattle and the ranch. Lying as flat to the ground as possible, they moved forward, driving the cows before them and moving in the direction of their rear guard. Jimbo had his rope out and came alongside of one of the heifers. She shied away but he made a cooing sound and approached her again. Slipping the rope around her neck, he kept her between him and the ranch and quickly led her westward. The rest of the herd followed. They had gone over a mile when Mark heard a pounding behind him. He rose up and looked back, shocked to see a bull thundering across the field right at them. They threw caution to the wind, jumped to their feet and waved their arms to speed up the cattle. Jimbo had gone on ahead with his heifer in tow and now he sprinted forward to the fence, throwing open the gate.

The opening in the gate was only six feet, creating a bottleneck that caused the cows to bunch up. The men tried to encircle the rear and keep them moving through the gap. Two of the cattle swung around and they couldn't get them back in line. Mark could hear the bull snorting and grunting as it approached their rear.

"Hurry, hurry you guys!" Jimbo screamed, all thoughts of maintaining silence gone.

The last of the cattle were through the breach, with and Dave and Mike following them through. Mark heard the bull and juked to the right. He whirled around to find it standing between him and the gate!

"Don't let it through the gate!" Mark yelled. He was ten yards north of the furious beast, and hoping he could reach it before the bull got to him he took off for the fence.

The bull leaped after him.

He heard the gate slam as he hit the fence. He didn't remember climbing over, just hitting the ground hard on the far side. Jimbo was rolling on the ground laughing as Dave and Mike grabbed Mark by the arms and hoisted him up. The bull was running back and forth along the fence snorting and pawing the ground. The dust he threw up obscured the ranch from view but they started off running across the field chasing after the herd. They all took out their ropes and as the herd slowed they were able to get the ropes around the necks of three of the cows.

Jimbo picked up the end of his rope that trailed his heifer and they all led the cattle toward the hills.

Reaching the rear guard they turned north, the docile cattle following the few they led with ropes. They reached the fence line and paralleled it until they came to the downed section. There Mark waved his arms to the men that had stayed behind to defend against pursuit and they all caught their breaths while they waited for them to catch up.

"Man that was close. You know Mark, you literally hurdled that fence."

"I don't remember anything after I took off for the fence until you guys lifted me up." He had a huge grin on his mud-covered face, grateful he hadn't been gored like a runner in Pamplona. They kept their guard up, watching the ranch in the valley below, but the only people they saw were their own guards as they made their way through the rocks and headed in their direction.

***

Standing behind a large clump of greasewood, Matthew looked down at the two groups of people in the valley below. The smaller bunch waved at the others and went west toward the ramp leading up into the hills, while the larger group went south around the giant rock that reached toward the sky. These people were so inept. They never looked up at the rim of the cliffs that surrounded their valley and even though they were sneaking, Matthew was sure they would be visible if there were any sentries posted outside the entrance of the valley. Fortunately for them, it didn't appear there were any. The men quartered in the ranch house appeared to be just as inept and had drawn their defensive perimeter back to within shouting distance of the ranch house. He had to wonder where these folks came from. They looked healthy and well fed but they were terrible hunters. They had to have been holed up somewhere with a cache of food and supplies.

He reflected on the fact that he'd had a lifetime of experience hunting, fishing and surviving in the wilderness. His father and grandfather had taught him these skills from the time he was four years old. When he turned twelve they started sending him into wild areas in the mountains to make his own shelter and secure his food. He loved those tests and never wanted to go back home when they ended. He chuckled at the memory of the time when he was fourteen, and a monstrous storm had come in unexpectedly, tearing apart his poorly made lean-to. By the time he had reconstructed his shelter in almost tornado-like winds he was soaked to the bone, wind lashed and freezing. He spent an endless night shivering in the darkness. He never settled for less than perfect work after that bitter lesson. He knew his father was never far away, however, and wouldn't have allowed him to come to serious harm. As a geologist, he often stayed in the field, camping out for days at a time.

He had been observing the two very different groups of survivors. From their different treatment of the family in the Jeep, he assumed the valley people were good people, and the ones at the ranch were not. There had to be a reason the family was fleeing the group at the ranch. Even though the family had been initially captured at gunpoint, when Matthew had spied on their camp that night, he saw that they were being treated well. He could tell they were being watched carefully but didn't seem to be prisoners.

Most of the men at the ranch had gone back toward town, and the others had formed a loose cordon around the valley entrance. Over the past couple of days they had relaxed that defensive line and fallen back toward the ranch, until this morning there were only a few men stretched out between the ranch and the river. Had the Jeep come down the road traveling even twenty or thirty miles per hour, they could have easily avoided the cordon and escaped.

As he watched the men heading south, he nodded in approval as they snuck over to the western hills and took cover in the rocks. Maybe they were learning.

He heard the horses stomping their hooves and crossed the plateau to where they were tethered. Matthew could hear voices approaching from the west, north of his position. Dodging from one bush or tree to another he stealthily made his way along the cliff's edge until he could see the two men on horseback as one dismounted and tied his horse to the branches of a downed tree. They looked around his age, one slightly younger than the other. Both men had short, unkempt beards.

"Oh man! Look at that drop-off. How we supposed to get around that? This sucks, Bro."

"Heck yeah. Let's eat some breakfast and then we'll figure out what to do."

"I tol' you before. We ain't got enough food to eat breakfast. Quit askin' me."

"I'd rather have breakfast than save it for later. My stomach thinks my throat's been cut. Come on Sam, let's eat some of it."

The younger of the two walked over to the bag on the withers of the older man's horse. They looked like cowboys. Both had on jeans and long sleeved shirts and the younger man wore a leather vest. They both had battered cowboy hats and bandannas. Their clothes were ripped and worn.

"Don't touch that bag Willy! I'll kick your head off." He swung his boot back, connecting with Willy's hand.

"Damn you Sam!" Willy jerked his hand back and grasped Sam's leg, attempting to drag him off his horse. Sam leaped down on him from above.

Matthew watched in amazement as the two men wrestled on the ground, throwing up dust until he couldn't see them. Then he was even more amazed as he heard laughter coming from the dust cloud. "Damn it kid, you broke my finger!"

"Did not. I just bent it a little. Can we eat?"

"Just a piece of jerky, you jerk."

They emerged from the dust cloud, hatless and laughing. The younger man went to the saddlebag and rummaged inside coming up with two large pieces of some kind of jerky. "We need to shoot another deer. There's only a couple pieces of this jerky left."

"You know, we're almost out of ammo." He stopped laughing and looked over at Willy. "I don't know what the hell we'll do after that, Bro. Starve, I guess." He walked over to the edge of the ridge and looked down into the valley below. He suddenly crouched down.

"Hey little brother, c'mere quick."

"What'cha see?"

"There's smoke comin' from over there in them trees. Shoot, it must be people!"

Willy shook his head. "Yeah, well you seen the kind of people that's out here now. They'll kill us as well as look at us."

"Maybe these guys are better. Maybe they're normal."

"Yeah, the last ones seemed normal too until they tried to kill Jasper. They were so hungry they were willing to eat horsemeat."

The brothers walked over to their horses and sat down in the grass. "Damn it Sam. We need to find someone to throw in with. I'm sick of riding day after day, running from the wanderer's."

"Me too little brother. I miss people. Even our rodeo buddies that we only saw once or twice a year. They were like family when we got together in Cheyenne or Amarillo. I'm tired of riding too. You really think those might be real people down there?" He bit off a small piece of the jerky and swallowed it without chewing.

"Our luck, it's a forest fire." He climbed to his feet and retrieved his canteen from the side of his saddle. He tossed it to Willy who wasn't looking, the canteen smacking him on the shoulder. He jumped to his feet and pushed Sam, who plunked down in the grass on his butt. Both men laughed and Matthew just shook his head. They seemed like twelve year olds but he sensed they were good men.

Debating whether to make himself known to these likeable buffoons, he heard Tulip whinny. The brothers heard it too and both men jumped to their horses, snatching the reins from the tree limbs. "Who do you think it is? You think he's dangerous?" Willy asked as he swung up into his saddle.

"Shhh… He might hear us. Let's just ride north and get away from him."

That decided Matthew, as their first response was to run and they hadn't reached for the hunting rifles in the scabbards attached to their saddles.

"Hold on boys." He walked out from behind the bush with his hands in the air.

One of the horses spooked and skittered sideways causing Willy to slip to his side. He lost his hold and slammed to the ground as Sam burst out laughing even as he jumped from his horse and hefted Willy to his feet.

"Hey man. We don't want no trouble. We'll just be on our way."

"It's okay. I just want to talk to you. That's my horse you hear. Let's sit and have a powwow."

"You an Indian? You talk like you're from England."

Matthew chuckled. "I'm an American. Dad was British so I have a teeny bit of an English accent. Mom was half Indian. That's where I got my looks." He walked out with his hand outstretched and the boys shook it warily.

Matthew pulled three energy bars out of his vest pocket and offered two of them to the cowboys who accepted greedily.

Sitting in a circle on the grass, they talked for an hour. Matthew didn't understand why he felt so protective of the small community in the valley but he wanted to be sure these strangers meant them no harm.

"You guys seem like you're okay. I think you would be welcomed into their group if you wanted to join them. They're going to be wary of you for a while but you have horses and you're young and strong. They need you."

"You think they have any single women?" Willy asked, reaching out and poking his brother in the ribs.

"They probably do."

"How come you don't know any more? Aren't you part of 'em?"

Matthew climbed to his feet and gazed across the valley at the smoke. He yearned to be a part of them, but just wasn't ready. "No. I've been here a few days but I don't know if I want to stay or move on."

"Stay safe." He disappeared behind the bush he had materialized from.

They watched him go and stood up to get the horses.

"C'mon Bro, let's get down that ramp he told us about."

***

Mark saw a look of alarm on Mike's face and swung around to see two men on horseback with a white bandanna tied to a tree branch riding in their direction. He and the others immediately raised their rifles and the men came to an abrupt halt.

"Hey, hey you guys. We got us a white flag here. Don't shoot."

"What do you want?" Mark yelled. "Don't come any closer."

"The Indian said you was good guys and we might find a place with y'all. You know, these horses are rodeo and cattle horses. Looks like you could use some help."

Mark looked at the others and shrugged. "What Indian?"

"He's up on the ridge. Said you folks were normal."

Jimbo lowered his rifle. "Could be Sheri's Indian."

"You boys dismount and move away from your horses. You can have 'em back soon as we take your rifles." Mark motioned with his rifle for them to move away from their mounts. Jimbo grabbed the rifles out of the scabbards and the boys were allowed to remount the horses.

"What's your names?"

"I'm Sam and this here's my brother Willy. We've ridden a long way and we're just looking for someone to hook up with. We got skills and these here horses. We can be a big help to y'all."

"That may be. You boys would have to prove yourselves."

Suddenly the boys took off in opposite directions giving the horses their heads. They dipped and bobbed, came up behind the cattle and herded them first toward the river and then north.

"Hey! Get back here," Jimbo shouted after them.

Mark laughed. "Let them go Jimbo. They're going in the right direction. They can't get out of the valley. Let's go. I'm just glad we finally accomplished something without losing anybody." They passed Platte Rock and continued up the valley following their new herd of cattle and their newfound friends.

***

"He's half dead. Maybe we should let him be." Jinx splashed water over Bruce's head causing him to sit back up and splutter. He opened his swollen eyes and looked up at Clay.

"Well, hello sunshine. Back in the realm of the conscious?"

Clay lifted Bruce's chin. "Okay, you told me about the quakes and Stewart's relatives chasing all you guys out the back door. My dear ol' dad never told me about that door. Nice of him, huh? I saw that Petey Boy had a rifle. Where did he get it?"

Bruce could barely talk. He had been broken by Clay when his fingers had been crushed with pliers. He had only made it to one. Bruce wasn't strong enough to resist any kind of torture. Most people weren't. He told Clay everything.

"There was a weapon's locker up in the Crow's Nest." His head drooped and Clay motioned to Jinx to drench him again. Jinx had come from the kitchen with a full, plastic, five-gallon bucket and he upended it over Bruce's head. "Stop, please, I'll tell you. Just let me get my breath."

"Go on, enlighten me."

"There's a big storage building in a meadow in the valley. It's got more guns and all kinds of supplies. There's gas, diesel and propane. A couple tractors and even solar panels and radios. There's more guns and ammo in the basement. I think almost everyone is armed." Bruce had convinced himself that this information wouldn't help Clay. He thought the valley was impregnable. "Your dad even left them a box of gold and silver coins."

"Hmm…" Clay turned and walked away deep in thought. "Looks like they are in better shape than I thought. Gold and silver? That kind of supplies could really set us up."

"Yeah, can you imagine? If we could get that Jeep and we had that gas?" Even Jinx and the other men were getting excited about the prospect of leading a more normal life.

Jackson said "Supplies, food, women, gold. We could keep the old men for slaves and make 'em grow crops and things. We could live high on the hog. Have families and a real life."

Clay didn't care about families or a return to a normal life. He wanted to kill Mark Teller and most of the others. He wanted the supplies and the gas so he could outfit an expedition to the west coast. He wanted to go home.

"Tell me about their defenses, Bruce."

"Come on Clay. I told you enough. You said you'd let me go if I told you where they were and about the valley. Please, man. Let me go?"

Clay's face darkened. "You bastard! Tell me everything about their defenses or I'll put a bullet right between your eyes."

Bruce knew he'd said too much and shook his head.

Clay pulled out his gun and fired, blood and brain matter splattering on the wall behind Bruce's head.

"I always keep my word. Get him out of here. We need to get back to the ranch."

"Hey Clay!" Andy ran up the front steps and burst through the door. "Guess wha…What the fuck?" He stopped dead in his tracks at the sight of Bruce and the gore splattered on the wall.

"What's up, Andy?" Clay snapped his fingers in front of Andy's face to get his attention.

"We got you some gas. One of the guys found a hand pump with a long hose and we dropped it down the tank at the old station." He looked back at the bed, turned and ran back out the door.

"That's great!" Clay called after him. He grinned at Jinx. "Kid can't take it. Let's go see what gas they've got.

Andy stood with two other guys on the front lawn. They had two five gallon gas cans and a funnel. "Where's that bike you took off the old guy?" Hank asked him. "Or we could gas up one of the cars down on Therma Street."

"No, let's do the bike because I know the battery's good. It's in the garage. This is great. You guys did good. Was there much gas in the tank?"

"Seemed almost full. They musta had it filled just before the war hit. We can get lots more."

"Cool. I'm going to ride the bike out to the ranch. I want all the guys to follow me. We're moving headquarters to the ranch so we can keep an eye out to make sure no one leaves that valley. Get all the men in town over here in thirty minutes, including the guys living down by the lake and the other mutants."

Jinx and the others went down to the town and brought back all the scruffy men that inhabited Eagle Nest. Clay explained his strategy. Jinx and Jackson were to go to Cimarron with a flag of truce and convince anyone living there that they should join with Clay to form an army big enough to crush the residents of Hidden Valley. They were to promise them women, liquor, supplies, gas and even gold and silver, anything that would get them to join forces with Clay's group.

"See if the station or the mercantile has any new batteries. Put one in any car that was kept in a garage and gas it up. There's plenty to choose from. That way you can drive down to Cimarron. The car will impress them so they'll want to come back here. If you guys have any thoughts of keeping on down that highway, just remember that the world out there is worse than we have it here. Those people have been holed up in comfort and safety all this time and those women are healthy and clean. You could have a real good life here compared to what you'd find out there. Just get me an army and you'll live like kings."

He turned to the others. "We're in no hurry. It might take several trips, but I want you to go through town and pull everything that's left out of all the buildings. We don't want to waste gas, so use that old wagon at the feed store to bring the stuff out to the ranch. Take turns pulling it. There's a herd of cattle out there so we'll have plenty of meat. They had a barn and a bunkhouse so there's room for all you guys."

By the following day, after trying the battery in seven different cars, they had managed to get one started. Jinx and Jackson drove up the road that climbed over the hill heading south to Cimarron. Clay was sure, if they weren't shot on sight, that the residents would be ready to do something besides eek out a meager existence in their tiny town.

He was elated to be riding a motorized vehicle. Even an old motorcycle made him feel like civilization was within his grasp. Coming over the last hill, with the ranch visible off in the distance below him, he gunned it and flew down the road into the driveway. The men he'd left behind to guard the valley were streaming out the door, rifles at the ready, shocked to hear the sound of an engine.

Clay slammed the cycle sideways, kicking up dirt as he came to an abrupt stop. Laughing, he jumped off the bike. "Here, take my horse and put it in the barn," he ordered one of the men.

"We're all moving out here, boys. We have a way to get gas out of the service station tanks and Jinx and Jackson have gone to Cimarron to bring reinforcements." He led them back into the house and explained about the ill-fated trip to the shelter and the man they had captured and tortured. "Can you believe that? The survivors are in this same fucking valley as the Jeep people. It might take us a while to get it all together but we're going to steamroll over these guys. It'll be like shooting fish in a barrel." He didn't tell them that the shelter refugees were armed.

"Let's celebrate and have steaks for dinner. Butcher one of those cows and let's eat, boys."

The men looked at one another and Lincoln finally stepped forward. "Uh Clay. We went out back this morning and it looks like the cattle got away. The bull's still out there and a few of the cows but the others are missin'."

Clay jumped off the sofa and struck the man across the face. He was livid. "I left you assholes here to take care of things! How did they get out of the fenced area?"

"I don't know Clay, honest. Someone had to open the gate. We been guardin' the road out of the valley. We didn't know we was to guard the cattle too." He wiped blood from the corner of his mouth.

"I'm surrounded by incompetents! All of you. Get out of my sight!"

Every last man ran from the room and Clay flopped back on the couch. "Bring me a beer!"

Chapter 20

Mark and his cattle raiders followed the river back up the valley and when they came opposite the island in the river, he was hailed by Thornton. "Hey Mark! Take a look. It's finished." Mark looked right and to his surprise he saw a group of people standing on the island examining the brand new suspension bridge that spanned the west fork of the river.

"Wow, you guys got that up fast. Has anyone crossed it?"

"No. We were waiting for you. Chris is going to have the honors." Mark saw Chris standing at the east end of the bridge, a look of trepidation on her face.

"Come on Chris. It looks sturdy." The bridge looked exactly like the one on the other side of the island. Chris walked onto the first planks that actually rested on the ground and then moved forward until her foot rested on a plank suspended over the water. She tested her weight on it and glanced over at Mark.

He motioned for her to proceed. "Don't be a chicken!"

She scowled at him and moved farther onto the bridge. It swung slightly under her weight but seemed steady enough, so taking a deep breath, she quickly moved across the span. Almost to the other side she let out a whoop and ran the rest of the way.

"Hey, way to go Miss Hargraves." Mark started to hug her but she shied away.

"Don't touch me! You're covered with mud and you stink to high heaven!"

"That may be, but we got the cattle." He pointed across the valley where the boys had driven the cattle.

"Who the hell is that? Hey, they have horses!"

"They came down the ramp just as we got back with the cattle. They seem friendly enough and we've disarmed them. Beats having to lead those cows around by ropes."

They all crossed over both bridges, walked north a couple hundred yards and went east right into camp.

"That bridge will make it so much easier than going around by the falls. Thornton, can you have Dave send some men to bring back the cowboys? Maybe they'll let us use the horses to keep the herd at the upper end of the valley. I'm going to take a shower."

After getting clean clothes from his duffle bag, he quickly showered, changed and went looking for Lori. He dropped off his dirty clothing at the laundry pot. The woman stirring the clothing with a broom handle was Rachel Morrison, a stunningly beautiful woman that had come to the shelter on her own and who had never told anyone about her past. Dr. Jim had tried to encourage her to tell him what had happened to her, but she chose to remain a mystery. She pulled a bunch of clothes out of the pot with the handle and dropped them into the second cauldron of plain hot water for rinsing and added Mark's dirty clothes to the first soapy pot. She told Mark that Lori was in the forest to the south with a group of people. They had killed a deer and were setting up an area where they would dress their game and tan the hides. *This should be interesting,* he thought as he headed south to find them.

A couple hundred yards south he came to a clearing. About a dozen individuals stood around a large buck, stretched out on the ground. As Mark came up to them, Terry was instructing in how to string it up to a tree limb of a large aspen growing in the meadow.

"Hi Mark." Lori came over and hugged him. "How'd it go?"

"We got twenty four cows and two cowboys."

"Huh? What's that mean?"

"The raid was successful and nobody got hurt. Even me and I got chased by a bull." He chuckled. "I'm glad we have two bulls cause I don't want to have to go back for that one. On the way back we met a couple of guys on horseback. They're youngsters, early twenties I'd say, and they have two horses. We brought them back with us. I think we can use them."

"Cool. Well, as you can see, we have a deer. Terry and Pete have both dressed deer before so they're going to butcher it and tan the hide."

Terry said, "Yeah, this clearing is perfect for our purposes. We need to build some drying and stretching racks for the hides. We need some tools. Do you know if you have a fleshing blade and a skin scraper?"

"We'll have to ask Glen or Marilyn."

"After we skin the deer, we'll need the hide to dry for a few days so we have plenty of time to build the racks."

"And we need to make a fire ring so we can smoke the hides and cook the brains," Pete said.

"Uh, what do you mean?" Jimbo looked a little green.

"The animal's brain has oils that the hides need to stay supple. Each type of animal has the right size of brain to tan its own hide."

"Alrighty then, you boys just go ahead and set up your mad scientist laboratory here. I'm gonna go help someone else do something. Anything else." He quickly strode north toward camp.

"Who shot the deer?" Mark asked Lori.

"Funny thing about that. We found it hung over a rock at the area we've been hiding in. Like someone knew we would be there and left it for us. It was still warm so it was fresh kill. Looks like it was killed with an arrow."

"Hmm… I think it may have been our friendly ghost. The guy that helped Sheri. Willy and Sam said they met him and he told them about us. I get the impression he wants to join us but has some reason he's reluctant. Let's go check the building for whatever you guys need to set up your abattoir."

***

Beth didn't think she would ever again see or ride another horse, and she was thrilled when the Yancey boys had come trotting up the valley, driving a herd of cattle before them. The cattle were in the upper, northern area of the valley grazing on the new spring grass. The rodeo boys were anxious to be accepted and readily agreed to allow their mounts to be used by the community. Ted and Beth, sitting astride Jasper and Patches, rode across the open meadow to keep the cattle corralled.

"Too bad Jasper's a gelding," Beth told Ted.

"Yeah, we could use a stallion or two. We'll need to build another corral to keep the cattle in at night or else post additional guards. In addition to the Devols, we need to worry about Clay's guys coming after them. They must know by now that we stole them."

"Serves them right. You know Ted, I like it out here in the open. I feel safer than being in the forest where I can't see what's creeping up on me. I think we should build a fence across this part of the valley. The cliffs to the north and west serve as a barrier. We would need about a half mile of fence and the cattle and horses would have a good place to graze."

"That's a great idea. Lucas and Stephen are pretty fast at cutting down trees for lumber. Look at how fast the cabin's going up. Maybe when they finish it they could start cutting lumber for the fence."

"Speak of the devil." She was looking south. "Is that Lucas?"

Ted turned and looked where she was pointing. "Looks like him What's he doing?"

"Let's find out." They rode the half mile to where Lucas was pacing the ground in measured steps.

"What'cha doin' Lucas?" Ted pulled up Jasper alongside him.

"I'm thinking of putting up a cabin here." He took off his baseball cap, wiped his forehead with his sleeve and reseated the cap. "I like it in the open. Stephen's gonna help me build my cabin and I'll help him build his. He wants to move down there where the aspens grow out into the meadow. We figure we'll claim about ten acres apiece. That way we can grow our own crops."

"Well, maybe you should wait and see what everybody wants to do. Dr. Laskey is going to report on what his committee is thinking about. If we each go off and do our own thing it might not be the best thing."

"I'm a little tired of doing things their way. I don't want their technology but no one's listening to me."

"You're using the tools from the building to cut your lumber and build the cabin. How primitive do you want to be? Why don't you just wait a couple days. I think Dr. Laskey's going to present something to the leadership tonight. Then they'll let us know what they're thinking."

"I'm just scoping out this area. I can't do anything til the cabin's finished."

"Okay, see ya later."

He and Beth rode back north. Two of the cows had broken from the herd and were walking toward the east. Beth clicked her heels against Patches side and the pony took off toward the errant cattle, rounding them up and sending them trotting back to the others. Beth laughed with glee at the wonderfully trained animal.

***

Another week had passed and there had been no additional attacks from the Devols. Mark knew they weren't all dead but maybe they'd killed enough that the others were wary of the camp. After dinner, Chris and Aaron sat in the front row waiting for the forum to begin. Chris held Aaron's arm and leaned her head against his shoulder. Tonight's meeting was especially important. After being out of the shelter for two weeks, Dr. Laskey was going to tell them what his committee thought they should do about governance.

Mark and Dr. Laskey went to the center of the building and Mark stood on the platform Farnsworth had built for meetings. He wasn't surprised at the size of the crowd. It looked like most of the residents were here with the exception of the guards posted around the compound.

"Before Dr. Laskey gives his report, I'd like to bring you all up to speed with the progress of the work. It's only been two weeks and over two acres of land have been tilled and planted." There was applause around the room and someone patted Chris on the back. Mark smiled and said, "Please, I know we're all thrilled with the progress but if you applaud every announcement, we'll never get to Herbert's report. The irrigation ditch is finished. You've all seen it. The first sluice gate is at the river and the second is at the north end of the fields. Farnsworth opens the one until the ditch is full. Then he closes it and opens the other to allow a controlled amount of water into the furrows. Chris tells me that's so they don't wash away the soil or the seeds. The afternoon rains make it so they don't have to irrigate very much for now. Today was the first day I can remember that we didn't get our afternoon storm. First plants will be sprouting in a couple of weeks and we'll have some edible veggies in about sixty days."

Ariana, a pretty, petite, black woman held up her hand. "Mark, I would like to start an herb garden. Do we have seeds for that?"

Chris sat up straighter and turned around. "Yeah, we have seeds for everything. Unfortunately some of the stuff won't grow here real well but the herbs should do fine." She turned back to face Farnsworth. "Can you build us a raised bed? We have some bags of potting soil we can mix with the native soil. Next winter, if we empty out this building we can use it for a greenhouse and grow lots of things we would never be able to grow outside."

"What do you mean empty this building?" Ruben asked her. "Where we gonna live?"

"I'd hope by winter, we have cabins built for everyone."

Once again everyone in the room started talking and Mark had to call for silence.

"She's right. There's over a hundred adults and almost fifty kids living in this building and in the basement. We can't continue to live like this." About twenty of the men that had moved into the building had moved back into their tents when the Devols quit attacking but there were still way too many occupying the space inside. There were blankets and sheets hanging everywhere to separate off the living quarters of the families.

Mark looked at Walter. "Have you figured out the resources needed to build the cabins? How many families do we have?"

"I've talked to Lucas about this. It took two weeks to finish the big cabin. He thinks we can build one regular cabin a week with the current guys working on them. But we have about fifty couples and families. That would take a year and we only have, maybe five months until the weather gets cold. I, for one, don't want to spend a winter in this building. And like Chris says, we need this building for a greenhouse this winter. If we use more guys, and especially as they learn to build cabins from Lucas, we can double up."

"Okay. I agree that building the cabins is a priority."

Lucas came to his feet. "Me and Stephen are going to move out into the valley. Over on the other side next to the aspen forest where we've been cutting trees. We've both picked out sites where we want to build cabins for our families. I can't live in this forest. I like the open fields. We want about ten acres apiece so we can grow our own food. Does that mesh with Dr. Laskey's plan?"

"You can't move over there with those Devols out there," Ruben told him. "You can't put your kids at risk like that!"

"My kids are my responsibility, not yours Ruben. I'll take care of my family. We're free men and you can't tell us what to do."

Everyone started in again and an exasperated Mark yelled, "Shut up, all of you! I guess we better let Herbert give his report before we go much farther then."

He yielded the floor to Dr. Laskey, who stepped up on the platform and looked at the strangest collection of students he had ever seen in his thirty years of teaching. "My fellow citizens," he began. "I would appreciate it if you could remain quiet while I give my report. Mr. James is correct. There isn't enough space in this meadow to build the homes that we need to live. You all know my committee members; James Bascomb, Jean Carlin, Barbara Thompson, Greg Whitehorse, Freddie Ramirez and

Sheridan Black." He asked them to stand and they all gave bows to the assemblage.

"We would like to recommend, that instead of building in this forest, we build across the river." Loud murmurs interrupted him but he used the evil eye on them. The same evil eye that had quieted his students over an entire career of teaching.

"We believe we should construct a town on the flat area, about half way between the river and the western forest. We need to start with a village square and a well should be dug in front of the town hall. Two rows of businesses would run east and west on either side of the street, with the town square in the center. Some of the businesses could have residences attached to the rear so the proprietor could live on site. These would be entrepreneurs who have no interest in farming. History shows us that having a central meeting area brings people together."

The crowd had become still, considering the proposal and imagining this ambitious development scheme. They yearned for a return to normalcy after the traumatic events of the past two weeks but none had thought that far into the future.

"Many of the other residents would have individual cabins spread throughout the valley with acreage for farming. This, I believe is your plan, Mr. James. We recommend fifteen to twenty acres per homestead. The valley is approximately two miles wide by four long. That's eight square miles at 640 acres per square mile, or around five thousand acres. Of course, the forested areas, the river and along the base of the mountains cannot be counted but there is still at least four thousand acres for homesteading. We recommend that the area between Platte Rock and the valley entrance, and a half mile north of the rock be left as is. The deer come down out of the mountains to use the spring and the elk migrate through that same corridor and to the south."

"What about the Devols and Clay Hargraves?" Micah asked.

"We can't live our lives in fear. We must plan our future regardless of these dangers. David Cunningham, the Holcombs and others can have the responsibility for our defenses while the rest of us build our community."

"What kind of businesses?"

"Well, Marilyn tells me there is a printing press in the basement. Someone could start a newspaper and someone could start a restaurant for the folks that don't have families. We need a blacksmith and maybe a boarding house or Bed and Breakfast for those who prefer a simple room to living alone in a cabin. We need a building to conduct trade out of the weather."

Beth said, "Could we get a barn and stables built for the animals? We need to get our breeding program going." The residents were getting excited about their individual and collective futures. None of them had thought this far ahead. They were just trying to stay alive and get things going.

"The next item is commerce. We recommend that everyone be given five gold pieces and two hundred pieces of silver and that the ratio be set at one gold piece equals twenty pieces of silver. Historically the ratio has been sixteen to one but in recent years that changed dramatically. By fixing the price of precious metals we prevent inflation and manipulation of the currency. The remainder of the treasury is to be held in a vault in the town hall and used for paying for certain community obligations."

"What kind of obligations?"

"We may choose to eventually pay our educators or hire a sheriff."

"A sheriff? We haven't had that much trouble!" Ruben said. Once again, the evil eye was employed by Herbert Laskey and the crowd quieted quickly.

"I am suggesting that we plan for the future. Most transactions would be settled by barter. Prices could be set low enough that there would be a free exchange of money without people going broke."

"Herbert? How about people that won't work?"

"If certain individuals choose not to work, they could buy food and shelter for a time, but would eventually end up sleeping in the snow." He glanced over the edge of his glasses in the direction of Danny and Clay's other friends. "Everyone will need to figure out for themselves what they can do to earn a living.

We feel that the community growing of crops and distribution of the remainder of the food stores Mr. Hargraves left for us should continue until spring, a year from now. By then, the economy should be up and running. Supplies for businesses shall be provided to those who wish them from the stores in the building. Please begin immediately to plan your future. Walter will be in charge of the supplies and other resources as he is now."

Everyone sat, stunned by the immensity of the job ahead. "Another topic we discussed is a name for our community and town. We believe we need to look to the future, when the rest of the country emerges from this disaster we have all experienced. In time, we will be contacted by others and need to demonstrate that we are a viable community. I believe that the resources we have here, for example the towns outside these valleys, and the lake, will provide a location for many refugees that have survived outside our area. I think the New Mexico Colony will be a major location for the population of the southwest. We already have eight new residents and there will undoubtedly be many more."

"What if we don't want more?"

"We can't live in a vacuum, Stephen. People will come and we need to assimilate them or end up fighting them."

"Yeah, we might need that sheriff after all," Jimbo said wryly.

"The last item is governance. I recommend that we have unpaid, elected, citizen leaders. We will have a town hall with monthly or quarterly meetings. Most agenda items can be decided by a simple majority vote. But there is always a need for a leader and a group to chair the meetings and settle disputes. We believe a mayor, elected every other year, and three council members who serve for three years, with one swapped out each year should be sufficient. The council would serve as arbitrators with the mayor not participating. He or she would chair the meetings and act as the treasurer. The final fifth member of the governing body would be the historian. Any thoughts?"

He probably shouldn't have said that as the room erupted with everyone having comments, and the evil eye was insufficient to stop it. Mark again shouted for quiet.

"This is a lot to think about. Let's adjourn and everyone can discuss this. We'll meet again tomorrow after dinner. Be ready to discuss it, and to agree, amend or disagree."

"When do we get the gold?" Danny asked.

"When we decide if that's what we want to do. Goodnight folks."

Mark, Lori, Chris and Aaron and several others remained behind to talk as the others filed out of the area. They moved to the couches up front and Helen and Ernest brought them all decaf. "Wow," Walter said. "That was a lot of info. Those guys really put a lot of thought into it."

"Dad. How will they decide where each person's land is? Do we have any way to survey it?" Pete sat with his arm around Sandy who was cuddling her two week old baby.

"I suspect it will be by pacing off the dimensions and painting a big rock to mark the corners. I don't think it needs to be complicated. We have plenty of paper. We can draw up a map of the valley with Laskey's help. He's the obvious choice for this historian position. He could also be the New Mexico Colony's recorder."

"I like that name," Chris said. "Is that the whole area, like a county or state? I think we need a separate name for the town."

"I agree," Aaron put in. How about New Hope?"

"Kind of corny. How about Independence?"

"There's been too many by that name. I like New Hope."

"Give it a rest baby."

Mark grinned at them. They were so comfortable together. He had loved Chris once, in a former lifetime it seemed, but he had to admit she and Aaron belonged together. He now loved Lori with all his heart. Life has a funny way of working out.

"We should have a community contest. Whoever picks the name gets their cabin built first."

"That's a great idea, Mark. I'll put up a notice."

"What do you guys think about our mystery man?" Aaron asked.

"I don't know," Walter said. "He seems harmless."

"Yeah, he's actually helped us a few times. I'm sure it was him that left us the deer," Pete added.

"He certainly helped Sheri get away from the Devol."

"I guess he must think we can't take care of ourselves," Walter chuckled. "He's having to help us out. Why doesn't he just come join us?"

"The rodeo boys said he told them he wasn't sure if he was going to stick around."

"Let's all keep a lookout for him. If anyone sees him, ask him to come and have a chat."

"Not likely we'll see him unless he wants us to," Walter said.

Chapter 21

"You got him!"

"Hey dude, your Daddy would be proud!"

"Good shot, Greg. That's at least a hundred yards. Let's make sure he's down. C'mon guys."

The hunting party crossed the lower slope of the ramp and found the buck lying behind a greasewood bush. He'd hit it directly behind the front leg and it looked like it died instantly. Greg was glad of that and had a slightly queasy feeling in his gut. It was the first time he's killed anything in his life. They had pared the number of hunters down to four, to keep down the noise and keep Jimbo from ruining their chances to make a kill. Ron was again carrying the branch and they strung up the deer for transport to the camp. Ron and Greg left with the deer and Lori and Pete went further up the ramp to check the trap they set out two days before. It had been tripped, but was empty.

"Let's go see how the construction is going on the sentry tower."

Pete reset the trap and followed Lori. "I am in no hurry to get back to camp. I love being out here in the outdoors. On the way back I'd like to check out the meadow on the other side of the lake. It looks like a great site for a cabin once all this drama is over. I'd love to surprise Sandy."

"The only way to get across the river is to go back to the bridge. Unless we go into Platte valley a ways and use the bridge down there where the road crosses the river."

"Whoa, I don't know. That could be pretty dangerous. How far down is it to the bridge?"

"Izzy says there's a main bridge in front of the house but that she saw one closer to this end of the valley." They had been hiking toward the river, past Platte Rock and came opposite the Anasazi site, where four guys were building a rock wall at the edge of the plateau where the granary was located. It was about twenty feet above ground and as Greg had predicted, they'd found niches cut into the rock to provide hand and toeholds to the top. The men had used this primitive ladder to gain the ledge, but their man of all trades, Clarence Farnsworth, was building a more conventional ladder they would use in the future.

Lori waved at the men on the cliff and they waved back at her. She and Pete went south to the wooden fence and found the sentries, Marv, Bob and Skillet. The latter had received his nickname while a cook in the Army. He helped Helen and the others with cooking chores and had a knack with making the dehydrated food taste palatable. For a cook, he was a skinny man.

"You guys been down that way at all?" she pointed downriver.

"Just to pee."

"Okay, way too much information." She laughed. "Could you see the bridge that crosses the river?"

"Yeah. Soon as you go over that little hill you can see it about half a mile away. Why?" Marv looked at her suspiciously.

"We need to get to the other side of the river and don't want to go all the way back to the bridge. We'll be real careful." She started off and Pete had no choice but to follow.

"You want one of us to go with you?" Marv called after them, but she just waved.

"We'll be fine."

Just before crossing over the small hill, she and Pete slid down into the brush. They crawled over the hill and paused for several minutes to scope out the view.

"There's where the road splits." Pete pointed to their right. "Izzy came on straight ahead and the side road goes over the bridge. I think it's more than a half a mile. Where do you think they have their guards?"

"They're probably closer to the ranch. C'mon, let's move real slow."

They crept through the brush and hid behind some small cottonwood trees that grew along the river banks. As they neared the bridge, they used the hand signals Terry had shown them and no longer communicated verbally. Lori was having so much fun.

Her life had been so boring in Denver and for the first time in her life she felt really alive.

The washboard, dirt road was rutted from the daily storms and weeds had begun to come up through the dirt. Pete held up his hand and pointed to the right where Lori could see two armed men standing at the intersection of the roads. That made sense as they were only trying to ensure the Jeep didn't leave the valley.

They crept to the bridge, and staying below the level of the railing, they scuttled across and dived into the bushes at the far side. Quickly looking back, they could see that the guards were unaware of their presence. Lori and Pete grinned at each other and Pete flashed a thumbs up… when they heard a low growling on the other side of the road.

***

Rolling to a stop west of the town of Cimarron, Jinx turned off the ignition of the old Camaro. They had tried seven vehicles before they found one that would start with the new battery. It was in a battered, metal garage and they had to tear off the side to get to it. The door was locked with a massive padlock.

"You think that's a good idea? Maybe we should leave it running in case we get attacked."

"It's overheating a little. I can't leave it runnin'."

"I don't see nobody. You think anyone's left?"

Jackson picked up the branch with the bandanna tied to it, got out of the car and stepped forward. "C'mon Jinx. Let's get this over with. If I'm gonna die I'd just as soon not drag it out."

The two men examined the dusty little town ahead of them. There were a few buildings along the main highway but another intersecting, paved road headed south into town.

"If there's anyone still alive, they know we're here. Let's just stand here til they come to us. That way we can jump in the car and hightail it if they start shooting."

The wait seemed interminable. Five… ten minutes passed and no one came.

"We have three choices, Jinx. We can drive the car closer, walk closer, or get the fuck outta here!"

"Shh… I see someone. Look over there at the side of that building. There's a head sticking around the corner."

"Fuck yeah, and I can see a rifle barrel too. Back up slow toward the car."

"No need to be scared boys. Where'd you get this vehicle?"

Swinging around in a panic, they threw their hands in the air as a dozen men came around their car with rifles pointed at their hearts.

"Please dude. We came in peace. See? White flag." Jackson waved the ridiculous bandanna at the man.

"Don't do anything stupid and you'll be okay. Name's Einstein. Who're you?"

"We came to see if anybody was still living here."

"You mean you came to steal anything that wasn't nailed down!" came a raspy voice from the man behind Einstein. He had a beard down his chest and his face was deformed and burned. Einstein held up his hand.

"Jake. Put a sock in it. Frisk em' boys."

Two men approached Jinx and Jackson and ran their hands down their bodies finding ankle knives on each man.

"Not very trucelike to come armed." Einstein smiled wickedly, his right side of his mouth not curling up like the left. Jinx saw a scar across Einstein's lip.

"We don't have no guns, man! I'm so used to the knife I didn't even think to take it off!"

"Well now. You just start this car and you and me can drive right into town for a little parlay. Kapeesh?"

"Yeah Einstein. That sounds good." Jinx gave Jackson a shove toward the car and they walked back to the Camaro where the men stood aside to let them in. Einstein climbed in the back, behind the driver, and Jake went around the car and slid onto the backseat behind Jackson.

Driving slowly, they examined the town as they traveled up the main street. It looked worse than Eagle Nest, dustier and more overgrown. Men came out to watch as they passed. The car was a curiosity. Apparently they hadn't had any luck getting vehicles to work.

"Pull over at that bar on the right and follow me."

They entered the dark bar and Jinx saw the first woman he'd seen since the Jeep family, over two weeks ago. She was dressed like a whore, a wine glass in her hand, and smirked at him as one of the Cimarron men shoved him into a round, upholstered chair at a small table. Einstein turned a wooden chair backward and sat on it facing Jinx and Jackson.

"Jennie, bring these guys a drink. We don't have any more beer but there's plenty of whiskey. That okay?"

"That's great, man." The woman went behind the bar and took out two glasses that didn't look very clean to Jinx. Pouring two fingers of whisky, she came over and plunked the glasses in front of Jinx and Jackson. As their eyes adjusted to the dimness, Jinx saw four more men at a booth in the corner.

"Okay gents. Tell us where you came from, how you got that car to work and what the hell you want from us."

***

"It's a dog," Lori whispered. The mangy animal slunk forward out of the bushes and stood in the road, a low growl issuing from its throat.

Pete snapped his fingers. "C'mere boy. Come on. It's okay."

Lori looked over at the sentries. They were smoking and laughing.

"Nice fella. C'mon."

The dog stepped forward and quit growling. It cocked its head and took another step. Pete saw that it was limping on its hind leg but it took another step in their direction. It stood six feet away and it let out a soft whine. Pete kept his hand outstretched while Lori kept an eye on the guards. The dog sniffed Pete's hand and he moved his hand up to scratch it behind the ears. "Nice doggy. Good doggy. I think it's okay." He motioned to move back into the bushes. They turned and started to sneak away when they heard another, louder whine from the dog.

"Hey Jigger, you mangy mut! Where the hell are you?"

Hunched over, they quickly turned north and took off for the cliffs that separated the two valleys. Pete heard a noise and glanced over his shoulder to see the dog following them.

"Shit. Go back, shoo." Pete tried to make the dog stop.

"C'mon Pete. Don't worry about it."

They hiked the rest of the way and waved at the guards on the other side of the river.

"Whatcha got there?"

"It's a dog. Can't seem to get rid of him."

They took the trail where it traversed the narrow path between the river and the cliff.

"Look out below!" Pete jumped back as a rock fell from above, one of the men placing it too far forward as they built the rock wall.

Laughing, Lori and Pete took off running into the trees north of the cliff, the dog happily leaping about behind them. Pete stopped to pet the dog. "I heard the guard calling him. Names Jigger. C'mere Jigger!"

The dog lowered his head, tail between his legs and scooted up to Pete. "Looks like he's been abused." He petted the dog, then turned and strode along the trail after Lori with Jigger following obediently.

"Looks like you got yourself a dog, Pete."

The day had warmed up and there were insects buzzing around the meadow when they arrived ten minutes later. In just over two weeks since leaving the shelter, the foliage and grass had turned completely green. The meadow was lush, filled with bushes covered with yellow blossoms. A few downed logs and large rocks were scattered about.

"I'd have to clear away some of the bushes and rocks but this would be a perfect place for a cabin. I could build it secretly and then bring Sandy and the baby here when it's done." He walked around the clearing looking at it from different angles.

"Look. This is where I'd build the house. There's a perfect view of the lake from the front porch." They walked down to the water's edge where a few trees created a small copse. "This would be a perfect spot for a dock. I'd build a little boat and go fishing every day." Lori felt his happiness and went back into the meadow to stretch out on the grass. Pete came back and sat down by her side. "You know, I often wonder what's going on out there in the rest of the world but for the time being this is a great place to be. I think we could all have a pretty good life here after we get used to the slower pace."

***

"So you're telling me, you want me and my men to join up with this Clay Hargraves to kill some dudes for him?"

"Not just for him man. For all of us. They had this bomb shelter and they have a hundred women. They've got gold and silver, gas and diesel. It's a fucking treasure, man. They have food, supplies, guns and ammo. We just need a hundred guys to go after them. We have around forty. Can you raise sixty or seventy?"

"Maybe. So we'd all share in the loot?"

"Yeah. Clay says we'll split it up between all of us."

Two other women came out of the back room behind the bar. One came over and sat on Einstein's knee and he buried his face in her neck, kissed her soundly and then pushed her away. "We've got business here, sweetie."

"We don't need no more women, honey. I can take care of you." She gave Jinx a dirty look and went back behind the bar.

"You do fine, honey. But there's guys in this town that don't have a woman. We'll just think about this, but in the meantime, let's party!"

He stood and held his drink up high. "Go get some of the guys. Pull out a few more bottles and let's get shit-faced."

Jinx looked over at Jackson and shrugged. "What the fuck. Sounds good to me. Hey Einstein, any chance I can get one of your women?"

"That's up to them. I don't own them, you know."

The third woman, a small gal dressed in Levi's and a tank top came around the bar and said, "We can have some fun later, buddy. After we drink our brains out." She sat in his lap and swung her leg over the arm of the chair. Jinx grinned over at Jackson.

"How about my friend?"

"Threesome's are always a blast." She wriggled on his lab seductively and raised her eyebrow at Jackson.

He licked his lips, raised his glass and up-ended the contents straight down his throat.

Hours later, men were sprawled on the tables and floor. Einstein was still drinking trying to erase the memories of the past that haunted how he got here. At thirty-one, he was a highly intelligent businessman on his way up in Albuquerque, New Mexico. Derek Thorson, owner of a development company that specialized in commercial property, he was quickly amassing a fortune. He had a beautiful, Southwestern style home on the lower slopes of Sandia Mountain.

All the others were passed out, so he let himself feel the pain as he remembered the drag race and the red Corvette that squealed around the corner and smashed into Becky and the kids. Sara, holding Becky's hand and his six week old son, were thrown twenty feet by the impact. He had stepped off the curb first and the car barely brushed him, knocking him to the ground. In a red haze, he jumped to his feet, saw the broken bodies of his precious family and ran to where the Corvette had come to a halt. He didn't remember anything after he saw the bodies, but at his trial they said he had pulled the driver from the car and pummeled the nineteen year old so badly that the face was unrecognizable and his neck was broken.

He was convicted of manslaughter and sent to the state prison at Springer for two years. At the time the bombs rained down, he was in the sickbay having his lip sewn up after being sliced with a shiv by another inmate. As guards and medical personnel heard the news and ran home to their families, he just walked out a free man.

Unable to find a working vehicle, and hoping to hole up in the mountains to the west, he walked the twenty five miles to Cimarron in a day and a half. Water was plentiful. Food was scarce.

In Cimarron, several families had gone to ground in the basement of a local church. The Pastor welcomed anyone who asked for shelter. There were supplies squirreled away in a store room for emergencies. They had planned for blizzards and tornadoes. Taping plastic over the windows and setting up a latrine in one of the tiny rooms, they hunkered down and spent their time talking, reading, playing games and sleeping. He became sick a few days after arriving at the church and in the next week lost some of his hair. He thought he was a goner, but he recovered.

As the weeks passed, food ran out and tempers flared. People began to leave, some too early, and they sickened and died as the radiation passed through their bodies, destroying organs and DNA. Nightmares of his family haunted him as he saw children starving and dying. He made a bed in the back of the store room and spent his time almost comatose, eating rarely and drinking only enough of the water to stay alive. If not for the Pastor he would have died.

It didn't help. All but four of the children perished.

Cimarron lies at sixty four hundred feet. The worst of the winter was behind them in March, although still freezing at night, and the rest of the survivors left the church. Most stayed together and took up residence in a cluster of houses at the south end of the main street. They scavenged groceries from the local markets and were still living there today. Einstein hadn't joined the Pastor's people in their little community, unable to live with the children and the other survivors, watching them struggle to survive… and sometimes die. He fell in with men that had managed to live through the winter on their own by staying in the St. James Hotel and raiding the stores in town. Many didn't survive and many more were burned or damaged but there were around thirty or forty men and women that had made it.

When he joined them, they were disorganized, hostile to one another and using up their supplies at an alarming rate. They immediately realized he was the man to lead them, to ration their dwindling supplies and to pull them together. He organized a search of outlying homes for supplies, and set up sentries to protect them from the few vagrants that came to town looking for trouble.

They dubbed him Einstein

When one of Einstein's men had assaulted one of the Pastor's flock, to steal his box of crackers, Einstein had shot him. He'd forbidden his men from harming them in any way.

***

"Okay folks. Settle down. Let's just get right into it with Dr. Laskey's plan being discussed and voted on." Mark stepped off the platform and Herbert took his place.

"I would like to consider each item individually. First of all, how about the idea of building a town across the river? The committee thought this would be fairly self-evident, that we don't have room in this meadow, and that we need more than just living quarters if we're going to have a viable community. If anyone has any discussion about this item please raise your hand."

No one raised their hand and everyone tried to talk at once.

"That's enough!" Mark stepped up alongside Herbert. "We're going to run this like a town meeting. If you want to speak, raise your hand. If you're in favor of the proposal, keep your mouth shut. We want to hear any questions or concerns before we vote. Got it?"

One hand shot up. *Oh no,* Mark thought. *Lucas already?*

"Yes Mr. James."

"How will we decide who gets what supplies and does what job?"

"Let's vote on the village first. All in favor of constructing a town?"

Every hand in the room shot up.

"Excellent. Is across the river approved?" Again, they all voted yes.

It went on in that manner until they had decided to begin immediately on the town hall, and a group of men, along with Sheri, had volunteered to begin digging a well.

"There are only so many people that can work effectively without getting in one another's way. Mr. James, please choose your workgroup and add additional men if necessary. I believe everyone wants to accomplish this task as soon as possible."

"I'm willing to do that," Lucas said, "but we need to make a list of priorities. After the town hall I want to build my own cabin. Some others with the skill may want to do the same. After that we can get back to more buildings in town."

That elicited a lot of discussion and arguments. They made a list of their priorities and Mark was surprised they agreed fairly quickly. Ted and Beth wanted a corral constructed at the north end of the valley for the cattle and horses. It was decided to move the existing corrals for the sheep, goats and hogs to the town site once the town hall was finished and people lived across the river to provide protection.

Tucker raised his hand. "Why can't we use the Jeep or tractor to move the old fence at the south end of the valley for Beth's corral. We wouldn't need to cut lumber for it that way."

"Wow, Tucker. That's a great idea. Can you organize that?" Mark asked him. One of Mark's strong points as a manager was to make the most of other peoples' talent. Tucker looked panicked but nodded his head.

The meeting went late and they all got to bed much later than usual but with the amazing feeling that progress was being made toward creating their new community.

It was decided to make a list of the type of work everyone wanted to do and after cabins were up and stores were built, supplies would be distributed. Mark had announced the contest to name the town and everyone had agreed on the New Mexico Colony for the name of the territory comprising their valley, the valley south, the town of Eagle Nest and the lake.

"Someday this may be the hub of the Southwestern part of the United States. We have two hundred fifty residents now but we may grow to thousands in the future. Tomorrow we begin building that new country."

***

Benji sat in his usual tree and watched as the humans left the building and went to their lairs. Even a few women had moved back outside to get out of the crowded conditions in the building now that the Devols seemed to be leaving them alone. Benji was having more trouble getting to the tree each night as the guards became more skilled. He was almost seen the night before and he knew he wouldn't be able to spy on them much longer.

The pain was palpable as he thought of spending his life alone. Slipping down from the tree he slunk off into the forest, crossed the bridge at the falls and circled the valley. It took him an hour to make his way to the southern entrance of the valley, where he went west to the hills and then made his way south. There were animals in the fields but he let them be. He was looking for people. Across the field he could see a light in a building. He'd seen this light the night before, when after watching the humans until they'd retired for the night, he'd skirted the cliff to the west of their camp, going south. Past a jumble of rocks at the base of the hill, he went up onto the ridge and, again going south, he climbed to the highest spot on the mountain that separated the two valleys. He raised his misshapen head and cried out the long, undulating howl that expressed his utter loneliness. Tears flowed down his clammy face and he howled again and again until drained, he glanced south and spotted a light in the pool of darkness below. Cocking his head, he listened for any sound that might indicate what created the light. He settled down on his haunches and gazed longingly into the night for over an hour. Unable to determine the source of the light he had returned to his den in the tunnel leading to the control room of the shelter. Even there he was alone. He had found the bodies of the other two creatures he had shared the lair with, in the rocks below.

He made his way toward the light and eventually, in the moonlight, was able to see it was in the window of a large human habitat. Carefully approaching the window in the darkness he heard the sound of human voices, talking and laughing. As he watched, a large shadow passed before the back window.

It was one of his kind!

***

Clay was tossing a knife, catching it by the handle and tossing it again. He was telling the men about the women in the shelter, describing them in detail and explaining to each man which woman would be right for him. They had butchered another cow and had a barbeque on the back patio. Since Billy had disappeared, Stewart spent more time in the presence of the humans and had stayed in the house after they'd eaten. He ate twice what the other men had, consuming his portion raw.

"How long do you think it'll take Jinx and Jackson?" Andy asked Clay.

"If they didn't get shot, they'll probably be back tomorrow or the next day. Unless, the good folks of Cimarron take the car, in which case it could take them quite a while to hoof it back here."

"What if they don't come back? They might just stay there."

Clay sat up and gave Andy his worst frown.

"They'll be back. If they stay, they know I'll send Stewart to kill them." He stretched back out. "Besides. They want their share of the booty. This is absolutely our best chance to have a decent life. We just have to take it."

Stewart had been sitting in the corner, staring off into space. Now he began to fidget and emitted a low whining sound. He stood up and walked to the kitchen side of the living room, staring toward the back of the house. Then he paced back to his corner.

"Stewart, what the fuck's wrong with you?" Clay asked.

"Check and see what's going on out back." Clay waved at Jackson, who picked up his rifle and went out through the kitchen. He swept his flashlight in an arc past the patio and then jerked it back.

"Boss! Come here. It's one of those things! Like Stewart and Billy."

"Is it Billy?" Clay yelled as the men that had been lounging in the living room ran through the kitchen.

"No man. It's way bigger... and uglier. Worse than Stewart."

The men spilled out the back door into the yard, weapons trained on the creature who stood at the extreme range of their flashlights. Clay moved forward a step and Stewart came up behind him. He seemed cowed, as if afraid of the larger creature in front of them. The beast stood for a moment longer and then to their amazement it raised a hand in greeting, flashing them a little wave like the Queen of England.

"What the hell?" Clay waved back.

"If that thing moves in my direction, you guys shoot the shit out of it." Slowly, one step at a time, while watching for any sign of aggressiveness, he approached the creature. "Come on Stewart," he said. "Stay with me."

When still ten feet away, he stopped and asked it, "Can you understand me?"

It nodded its head.

"What's your name?"

The Benji-thing tried to answer but it hadn't spoken in months and its swollen lips only produced a similarly sounding name.

"B.J.?" It nodded again.

"What do you want?" Clay was relaxing a little, and becoming excited as he realized this gigantic creature seemed more intelligent than Stewart.

"Freeend." Clay had been increasingly worried since Billy had disappeared. With this monster by his side he would once again be secure around the men. And what a fighter it must be!

"Do you want to join us? Will you do what I say?" Benji nodded again.

"Tell you what, B.J. you and Stewart need to get along. If anyone hurts me, you kill them, okay?" He made sure the men could here that last order. "You too, Stewart?"

"Yes Clay, yes Clay."

"Then you two go spend the night in the barn. Don't hurt each other and you can be my friends."

Simultaneously, the two mutants nodded and said, "Yes Clay."

Clay pointed at the barn and the creatures slunk away. Clay smirked as Stewart stayed six feet away from the larger creature.

"I've got me a new friend," he said as he walked back to the men.

"Fuck, dude. Do you think it's safe?" Jackson asked.

"I'll bet that thing can kill half the assholes in that valley all by himself. I don't know why, but they seem to like me." They all filed back inside, Jackson casting a frightened glance over his shoulder as he passed through the door.

Evil was attracted to evil and they would follow Clay to the bitter end.

Chapter 22

The sun had topped the western rampart and it was getting hot. Mark wiped his brow and tucked his long hair behind his ear. He was helping build the second structure on Hargraves Street, the ribbon of scraped off area that ran between the two rows of what would be the businesses of Willsburg, their fledgling town. Samuel won the naming contest and had given up his prize, of the first cabin built, to allow them to construct the medical building on the north side of the street. The structure had a covered porch, a small waiting area, two back rooms that served as exam rooms with a hallway between them that led to a larger room that would be a treatment/operating room. They brought the instruments and supplies from the steel building and had set up shop. Aaron, Jim, Carmen and Annie still slept across the river but eventually Jim would have a cabin directly behind the clinic.

Aaron was waiting for the building crew to be available to build a home for him and Chris. They too, still slept in the building, but the evenings were warm and the building was becoming uncomfortable. One evening in late June, Aaron had asked Chris if she wanted to move into a tent in the meadow.

"The night would be a lot cooler and we'd have a ton more privacy."

"I don't think so Aaron. I really don't want to be sleeping on the ground."

"There are thermal pads. I don't think they're all being used. Come on, where's your sense of adventure?"

"What I really want is a cabin of our very own."

"Yeah, me too, but we need to wait our turn."

"I think they're giving priority to families where the woman is pregnant." She grinned at him, waiting for that announcement to sink in.

It took a few seconds and then he grabbed her up in his arms and swung her around. He was going to be a father!

The month of June had flown by as the Town Hall and medical office had gone up on schedule. The men were gaining experience and worked better as a team. Jim and Aaron held a clinic each morning and residents presented with summer colds, minor scrapes and bruises, and various aches and pains. After almost eight months in the shelter they were having to get used to hard physical labor and a new set of germs their immune systems weren't accustomed to. Jim and Aaron fretted over the lack of medical supplies.

"Once the antibiotics and other medications are gone, we will be limited in what we can do," Jim had reported to Mark soon after they opened the clinic.

"What's happening with Jack Iverson?" The only diabetic in the Remnant, he had used the last of the insulin.

"All we can do is keep an eye on his diet. He's so afraid of his blood sugar going up that he's not eating enough. I'm worried about him Mark. He's eating almost no carbs. That's fine for the short term but long term we're in trouble. So far his sugar is only slightly elevated. Once it starts to climb, there's not much we can do to bring it down."

"Damn, do you have any good news?"

"Actually, I do. We have seven prenatal patients! Six weeks to seven months along. And Terry Berkowitz has taken over the area in the Greenhouse where the clinic was, to grow some medicinal herbs. He'll move them outside as soon as they're big enough. There are some white willows down by the lake and he already has plans to make aspirin from the bark."

"How about the seeds Chris has? What are they for?"

"Terry's growing Aloe Vera for skin problems and moisturizing. There's Ginseng, Black Cherry for coughs, Echinacea for colds, and Chamomile for tea. There must be seeds for a hundred herbs. I'm afraid as a modern doctor I don't know much about them but Terry, Annie and I are studying the books we have on their uses. He's experimenting with growing mold to make Penicillin. After the antibiotics run out his natural remedies will be all we have."

Now they were working on a boarding house where the single women would live. It was directly across the street from the clinic, fifty yards east of the front of the Town Hall. They had become ambitious and had decided on a two story structure. Lucas told Mark it would save material.

Some of the other men were gaining experience in construction, so Lucas and Stephen spent most of their time at their "lumber mill." It consisted of a cutting bench and an area where they ripped the tree trunks to produce boards, instead of using whole logs for everything. Gasoline powered chains saws and an electric table saw had been brought over on the trailer, pulled by the Jeep, and one of their three portable generators sat in a small enclosure beside the cutting area. The hope was that the gas would hold out long enough to get the town and cabins built before they had to resort to more primitive methods. Lucas did all his cutting with an ax and an assortment of hand saws, wanting to be experienced with them when the gas ran out. As a framer, he'd always had access to power tools but loved the old ways.

"When do you think they're coming?" Jimbo asked Mark. He walked over to where Mark stood gazing toward the south.

Terry Holcomb joined them. "I think he's trying to raise an army. I don't think they'll come while it's so damn hot. If he waits until the weather cools off in the fall, we'll have crops and meat preserved for the winter, and he needs that food for his men. But we need to keep up our defenses just in case."

Terry and Dave had reworked the sentry rotation. They completed the guard tower on the ledge that held the Anasazi granary and had built another high up in the rocks surrounding Platte Rock. A platform and walls had been constructed across the tops of two large boulders. They put a cover over it to keep the sentries comfortable in the afternoon rainstorms and to keep it warmer at night. A ladder leaning up against one of the rocks led to a trapdoor in the floor of the platform. These two guard posts gave them a strategic advantage in covering the entrance to the valley.

Another guard post was located at the bottom of the ramp where Lori's hunters had hidden. It was now used for both deer hunting and as a guard house for the ramp. An additional post was located against the cliff where Micah had been attacked by the creature, where the ridge met the valley floor, and the last one was at the base of the trail down from the high plateau. Bud had told them how he'd come to the rockslide and had backtracked to the switchback, where he'd slid down the hill on his butt, lost his balance and fell to the lower portion of the trail. This is where Sheri had stumbled upon him... literally.

By guarding all the possible entry points into the valley, they were able to use fewer men each night and they felt fairly secure from man and beast.

No one had had a day off since they'd left the shelter and Helen, Marilyn, Kate and several others were planning a Fourth of July barbeque for tomorrow. Many of the cows were pregnant, but one that wasn't was chosen to be slaughtered for the feast. Few of the crops would be ready by then, as most would take sixty days or more before harvest. They had to wait until the danger of frost had passed before the beans had even been planted. Chris told Helen there would be some early mustard greens, radishes and spinach. All the other side dishes would be from their dehydrated stores.

"Well, I'm sure it's good that we have more time to train but I'm getting antsy being bottled up in this valley and not knowing when they're coming. I'm heading over to the range for some practice. You coming Terry?"

"I'll be along shortly. I'm going over to check on Jerry and Pete to see how the butchering is coming. Jerry's arm isn't a hundred percent and Pete's got a lot of work to do. Mark, why don't you come see what we've done?"

"I have a few more logs to place and I'll be over. Give me thirty minutes."

The bottleneck for the construction was not the cutting of the trees for lumber, but transporting them to the cabins. They had the jeep and the ATV trailer. Balancing the logs across the Jeep required them to drive slowly as someone walked alongside and kept them steady. One of the happy finds in the Greenhouse was a shelf with a score of pre-hung windows. The first twenty cabins would have a window cut out of the side and the windows installed. They would be the only ones, unless they could find more in one of the towns, or learn to make glass.

Mark and Ryan finished the current job, and until Lucas sent over the next batch of lumber there wasn't much more he could do. He put on his shirt and walked the mile across the fields toward the river. Due to heavy use, a trail had been naturally formed, winding around a few piles of rocks as it climbed over low mounds and between large bushes. The vegetation was lush and green and there were thick stands of foliage as high as his head. Since the new bridge had been finished, they seldom used the rock bridge over by the falls and the cemetery lay in solitude.

Crossing over the two suspension bridges, he skirted the fields with their growing bounty. He was plant retarded but had been told by Chris that they had several varieties of greens, radishes, squash, broccoli, cauliflower, beans, potatoes and tomatoes. She said she'd started asparagus in the storage building and would put it in the ground next year.

With the afternoon rainstorms, they'd seldom had to use the irrigation system put in by Farnsworth. Two-foot high corn was growing on the west side of the river. They had built a cabin for Teresa West and Candy Pitowski to share and they had chosen to plant their acreage in corn.

The tractor was kept busy everyday plowing all the fields that needed it. The crops would be harvested for summer eating and replanted to have late vegetables and other produce to put up for the winter.

Mark followed the trail into the woods and came out into the clearing where the deer and domestic animals were killed and dressed. There was a small group of three pine trees in the center of the meadow with a fire pit in front of them. One of the tripod-shaped, drying racks was suspended above the small fire and the smoke was blowing over the hide. Beyond the trees, at the far side of the clearing was the area reserved for butchering the animals.

"Hey Mark." Terry and Izzy waved and came over from the drying racks that stood on the right side of the meadow.

"Wow, Guys. What is all this stuff?"

"The shed behind the drying racks is so we can move them out of the rain. The fire pit is where we cook the brains to tan the hides and we also use it to smoke them."

Mark noticed all but one of the sheds were three sided structures.

"The first shed over here is for our tools." He gestured to one of the two sheds on the left. We built in shelving to hold our knives and skin scrapers and we're putting the finished hides on that table in there until we decide who's going to be using them to make clothing and shoes. The second shed is our rendering shed."

"Rendering? What's that?"

"It's the process where the animal fats are extracted for use in making tallow. We have pots to keep the tallow in until Savannah is ready to make her soap and candles. It can even be used for lubricating Freddie's printing press and added to soot, makes ink."

"This is amazing. I had no idea you could use so many parts of the animal. What's the enclosed shed for?"

"It's the smoking shed. We smoke or dehydrate all the meat, mostly venison, we don't use right away. That box over there with the little drawers and the glass top is the dehydrator. Izzy made it," he said proudly. "She makes some tasty jerky."

Izzy said. "We can use some of the plants too. We'll be experimenting with making oil for the lamps. When we were at home, we practiced tanning hides and rendering the fat but we never got around to using the plant materials. There are so many things we'll need to do and we know some of them, but we don't know everything."

"Jerry and Pete have some experience with dressing animals, and the Yancey boys know how to make ropes and string from natural materials. Greg Whitehorse knows how to mine and extract iron and other minerals and he knows where the iron mines are. We have a lot of folks with knowledge and expertise. And now that the solar panels are in operation, we've got the laptops with instructions for doing just about everything. Glen is the one who selected the videos and manuals. He really researched what we'd need and the database is very complete," Mark told them.

"Well, everyone had better learn it before the batteries go bad. Solar batteries usually last about eight to ten years," Terry said.

Mark saw the cow grazing on the other side of the meadow, tied to a tree by a long rope. Pete was there, doing something at a table with his dog lying in the shade behind him, and Jerry sitting on the ground scratching the dog behind the ears. "When will you kill the cow?"

"In the morning."

"Well, I don't want to be there."

***

Just for a day, the Remnant kicked back and enjoyed a rare break from the brutal schedule they had set for themselves. The Town Hall sat toward the western end of the street, with its porch and door in the end of the building, facing east. The well was being dug about fifty feet in front of it, and in the space between them, a long fire pit had been constructed, using rocks from the fields north of town. Marilyn had shown them where several metal grates were stored and these rested on the rocks. The cow had yielded one hundred and twenty five pounds of meat, which had marinated for a couple hours and was now sizzling on the grill. A long table held bowls filled with the early produce from the garden and... dehydrated potatoes.

"I can't believe it," Mark said to Chris. "I didn't think you'd ever have a kid."

"Life is just a little different now." Chris laughed. "In the old days I was too busy running around the world with Dr. Tanner and his team."

"How far along are you?" Lori wanted to know.

"Almost two months."

"That's just about how long we've been out of the shelter."

"Yeah, it was a lot colder out here!"

Kate yelled out that the steaks were ready and everyone filed past the table. As in the shelter, they were used to much smaller portions than they ate before the war and everyone took small amounts to ensure they all shared in the bounty. Mark was reminded of the barbeque they had held in the shelter, when they were mercifully unaware of what awaited them in the coming months. He had been strangely happy then. But he was glad to be out of the shelter, where life seemed more real.

Candy Pitowski and several others came over to the grassy area where Mark was eating. "You know, we've been thinking. There are a lot of things in the shelter that we could use. This party today would be a lot better with some music. My fiddle is in the music room with a lot of other instruments."

"Yeah, Mark, and I have some personal items I'd like to retrieve," Doug said. "I have pictures of my wife. It's all I have left of her."

"Uh, you guys know we're still getting aftershocks. It could be dangerous and we don't know if some of the monsters survived the floods." Mark stood up.

"We're prepared to take that risk. We could all wait in the exit cave and go in five at a time. That way if there's a cave-in, we don't lose everyone. You were able to get your stuff out of your room. We just want to do the same."

"I'm not your boss. If you want to do that it's up to you."

Dr. Jim had heard the conversation. "I'd sure like to get the medical supplies we had to leave behind."

"Okay, let's get it done. First thing in the morning, anybody who wants to go back in can meet at the cave. But I think when we're done we should close it up so no one ever goes in there again."

They all looked around and nodded at each other.

***

"What the hell took you so long, Jinx? You've been gone a month!" Clay walked out the front door when he heard the car coming down the road and into the yard. His anger was building quickly and he was looking for an explanation. Several times he'd thought of going to Cimarron, but when his men attempted to get another car working they had failed. Over the past month, they'd tried a battery in every car they could find but none worked. Deciding to take the motorcycle, he was just waiting for the right time.

"I'm real sorry Clay, but Einstein kept us there while he decided what to do. He wanted to meet you, though, so here he is." Einstein climbed out of the back seat on the opposite side of the car from Clay, to keep the car between them until he determined his host's intentions.

"Hey man. You armed? Jackson, frisk him."

Einstein was looking behind Clay at two of the largest, ugliest men he'd ever seen in his life. Jinx had told him about the creatures but he didn't believe it until this very moment. As Jackson got out of the car he checked Einstein for weapons.

"Come on in and we can chat."

Einstein took an instant dislike to this young man. It was obvious to him that the men only followed Clay because of his inhuman enforcers.

"You want a beer?" Clay offered.

"You got any whisky?"

"Jinx. Get the man a bottle of whiskey. So why'd you keep my guys so long? I was about to come get them."

Sure you were. Einstein thought. "We were discussing your problem. And your boys were gettin' drunk and gettin' laid."

Clay waited to answer, furious that Jinx and Jackson kept him waiting while they were partying. But he realized this man in front of him had been calling the shots. Einstein wasn't impressive. Average height, slim, with shoulder-length, greasy brown hair and sporting an unkempt mustache and beard. But there was something in his eyes. A haunted, but intelligent look. Clay could see why his men would follow him.

"So Jinx explained our little issue we have here?"

"He did. Why should I help you?" He threw back a jigger of the whiskey.

Clay leaned forward, his need for revenge causing a gleam in his eyes. "Because these assholes have everything we need. They have women, fuel, gold, crops. We can have it all!"

Einstein could see a madness in Clay's face. He knew there was more to this than survival. "What's your angle? Why don't you ally with them? Maybe they'll share or set up trade with you."

Clay shot to his feet. "Because they're mother-fuckers! They deserve to die. They had their chance to be friends with me and they fucked it up. Now I'll kill every last one of the men, except for old farts that can slave for us, and we'll take all the women! And I mean take them. Over and over. Including my high and mighty sister." He stood, breathing hard and glaring at Einstein.

Revenge then. That's what this man wanted. "Well, I think I can help you." He sat calmly, not reacting to Clay's outburst.

Clay sat down heavily, embarrassed that he lost it. "Well, that's a good thing. Let's drink to it." He raised his glass and downed his whiskey, trying not to choke on the burning liquid.

"I can raise about forty guys, but I think I can get some more in Red River. I need a complete accounting of your weapons and ammo. After we get our guys together we need to come up with a plan. I'll move my force up here to Eagle Nest. We'll settle in the town."

"Hey, hold on. I make the rules. You need to remember that this is my operation and I'm in charge."

"Sure buddy. I remember. Is it okay with you if I move my guys to Eagle Nest? We need to start training with your guys and it's closer to Red River. I'll send a couple of men to see if we can recruit some guys. If it's okay with you to use your car, of course." He tilted his head in deference to Clay as Jinx refilled their glasses.

"Yeah... yeah. That sounds good. Please accept my hospitality. We have some steaks left. You hungry?"

Einstein didn't remember what a steak tasted like. "Yes, please. That would be great. I'll head back to Cimarron in the morning and get my guys rounded up. To a successful campaign!" He raised his glass and they downed their drinks.

***

Over half the residents of Willsburg met at the shelter's back door just after dawn. Earlier, they had felt the tremble of a small aftershock but they didn't seem deterred. The first group of five, along with Mark, rolled under the door and while the others headed to the second level to retrieve their belongings, he went to the closet and began to turn the wheel. The door slowly raised, until when at head height, he stopped turning it. Aaron appeared in the doorway, a headlamp shining from his forehead.

"Let's go Mark." He made his way up the tunnel, Mark walking behind. He had wonderful memories of this place, like the times he spent talking with Lori, but the nightmare of the ending overshadowed them, and he was increasingly reluctant to continue. Around the corner and into the shelter proper, they hurried to the one staircase that Mark knew would be open. They had given instructions to all the residents so they could quickly get to their rooms and get their belongings.

Mark and Aaron continued up to the top floor, gagging on the odors of death and destruction, the creature's lair and the damp, musty smell left from the flood waters that had since drained from the lower level. A faint trace of dust lingered in the air from the temblors. They arrived at the clinic and Mark almost lost it when they came across Rick's body, lying on a treatment table where they had left it when they fled the shelter.

"God, Aaron, I forgot we left him here."

"I thought the creatures had taken his body but I guess they couldn't get in."

"We can't leave him here. I'll find a gurney while you start grabbing supplies."

During the war Aaron had arrived at the shelter with nothing, so he had no need to go to his quarters. They carried the body into the corridor and down the stairs with great difficulty. The smell was horrible and Mark gagged repeatedly. Eventually reaching the cave, they turned it over to others with assurances that they would transport Rick to the cemetery.

They went back in. Six trips… six worsening, hellish trips. They loaded up another gurney with everything they could find, leaving the medical suite empty with the exception of some larger equipment. None of it worked any longer anyway, even had they been able to move it. On the final trip, some of the folks that had already fetched their personal belongings gave them a hand. When Mark passed under the door for the last time, he knew there was nothing on earth that could ever make him go in again. Going down the ramp that led into the valley, he breathed in the fresh air, trying to cleanse the foul odors that clung to his clothes.

People streamed by him carrying duffle bags, musical instruments, books and stuffed animals. Some people had been unable to reach their quarters due to cave-ins so they pitched in to help the others get items from the common areas and everyone made several trips. The Jeep made numerous trips to deliver the medical supplies to the clinic.

Pete, Doug and Dave, wearing their headlamps and fully armed, went back in and Mark heard the blast door being lowered. The three men would go back through the shelter, exit out the front and seal the door to the stairs with a small explosive device Terry had rigged for them. They couldn't lower the front blast door, as it only operated off electricity but Mark needn't have worried. When they set off the device, it caused a major collapse of the cave and the three men barely escaped with their lives. Many hours later, they limped into camp from the south, having come down the eastern ridge.

Ferried to the clinic in the Jeep, they were soon patched up by Dr. Jim and that evening all agreed the effort was worth it. The clinic had several new pieces of equipment, dressings, medications, I.V. solutions and other supplies. Most of the residents had retrieved precious belongings and other irreplaceable items. The next day a team went back and emptied out the weapon's locker. Then they blew the tunnel.

Another chapter in their lives had closed.

Chapter 23

Another month passed, and as Terry predicted, there was no sign of an attack by Clay's gang. There was a major shift, however, in residency. Dr. Jim's cabin, and Chris and Aaron's, had been completed a week before and they had moved across the river. Lucas' and Stephen's families had relocated to their homes by the aspen forest and a dozen single women, including Carmen, now occupied the Claret Hotel. Two more businesses had been completed, one west of the hotel and the other next to the clinic. They would build west until the buildings extended just past the Town Hall and then would start adding more in the other direction.

The election had been held and Mark declined the nomination for Mayor. They elected James Bascomb, and chose Walter, Terry Berkowitz, and Greg Whitehorse as the council. Dr. Laskey was made Historian and Town Recorder. Mark was finally free of the responsibility for the Remnant.

They distributed the gold and silver coins, but most trade would still be conducted using barter. Before the war no one any longer personally produced anything. People worked in the service industry or sat in front of computers all day. With the exception of tradesmen, there were few things or skills to barter. Now, as the survivors learned skills and made clothing, quilts, candles and iron goods, they could trade their skills or products with others for the items they needed.

With the occupancy of Willsburg, security was beefed up around the town with more night patrols, but there were no guards during the day with the exception of the outpost guard stations. The weather was still beastly hot and the work on the cabins was slowed down by the workers having to take a mid-day break. No sunscreen had been stocked and everyone had a deep tan.

By mid-August, with over three months gone by, seventeen structures dotted the landscape. Willsburg had a Town Hall, The Claret Hotel which was their only two story structure, the medical clinic, a mercantile and the newspaper office. Herbert Laskey had an office in the latter building and Freddie Martinez was doing his best to learn how to use the small printing press that had been stored in the basement and now sat in the back room of the store. They had found a supply of ink and a large number of reams of paper, but would have to learn how to manufacturer both items in the future. Terry told Freddie he could make ink out of animal fat and soot. He wasn't looking forward to that!

A dozen cabins had been completed. Twenty men worked on the common buildings and teams of five each constructed cabins. The homes were bare bones, each having a floor, walls, a roof and a fireplace in the front room, and two small bedrooms off the back end. The window was located in whichever wall the occupants wanted. It took five men eight days to put up a cabin and another day for the men that constructed the fireplace. Using the ATV and trailer a group of ten guys collected rocks for the fireplaces, and the big, storage building they called the Greenhouse had rebar and concrete.

They were quickly running out of these supplies. Using only what they needed to ensure stability of the chimneys, they needed to quickly learn how to build with just natural materials. A swinging, iron arm for holding pots was installed in each fireplace. Cooking would be primitive and there were no separate kitchens, counters or cabinets. Each resident would need to build their own furniture or barter for the pieces that Clarence Farnsworth was making in his spare time. In the meantime, for sleeping, they would use the cots and sleeping bags from the tents and storage building.

Dr. Jim's house was behind the clinic on a side street they named Washington Street, with Chris and Aaron's house directly across from it. Each of the cabins on the side street sat on a half an acre. This allowed each home to have a small vegetable garden and a corral or two when there was enough livestock for personal purchase.

During a town meeting Lucas explained to everyone that these cabins needed to be built very quickly to house as many residents as possible before winter.

"Maybe next year we can expand them with additional rooms. We might even pull some down and just build larger ones for families that need them. It's going to be real crowded this winter."

"Hey Lucas, what about bathrooms? We're gonna freeze our tushes off in those outhouses," Jimbo said.

"We'll have to wait until next year. Maybe we can eventually cut up the Greenhouse to make septic tanks and have indoor plumbing. But that's a long way off. We're not going to have enough houses by winter, as it is, so some folks are going to have to double up. Pick people you really like cause it's gonna be cozy!"

Dr. Laskey said, "During Medieval times, and up until indoor plumbing came along they used chamber pots. It's just a pot you keep in the house to urinate in and then it's dumped in the morning. That way you don't have to go out at night. It creates odor problems, though."

"I'm thinking I'll use the outhouse," Jimbo said.

The well had hit the static water level at twenty two feet. Digging another six feet down, working in water, they then lined the bottom and built sides with rocks. There were gaps where the rocks touched, allowing water to seep into the well. They brought it three feet above ground level and covered it with a small pitched roof. A handle, attached to a rope, allowed them to pull up the bucket. Glen and Marilyn had included a hand pump when they planned supplies for the survivors and they planned to put in another, more modern well, the next year.

As buildings were completed and occupied, supplies were moved across the river and the Greenhouse was beginning to empty out. What had seemed like an inexhaustible supply of materials, was found to be much less when spread out in the various new buildings.

As the men labored on a particularly hot day, Danny whined about the work and confronted Mark. "Why didn't we just move into Eagle Nest or head for some other town like Taos or Las Vegas? There's hundreds of places already built that would be a lot more comfortable."

"Well, for one thing, There are some serious bad guys out there that pretty much have us bottled up here for now. And you want to walk thirty or forty miles?"

"Why don't we go kick their asses?"

Mark and the other men all laughed. Jimbo said, "You're kidding, right? You were the chicken that wouldn't even stand guard duty until we killed most of the Devols."

"The houses are more modern and you might think they're more comfortable, but remember, with no electricity there's no air conditioning or heat. These cabins are probably just as comfortable. Now if the power ever comes back on it would probably make sense to move on."

Glen wandered over. "There's another very good reason. Will wasn't kidding when he said this valley had special characteristics. I think we'll find that there's more radiation outside this valley, or at the very least, fewer animals. Just as the shelter was intended to get us through the worst of the fallout, this valley is a place to live until it's safe to leave."

"If anyone wants to leave, that is. We're making a pretty good place to live here," Doug said. He had lost his wife in the war, and had nowhere else to go.

"Let's get back to work. This building won't go up by itself."

Later that day Mark walked a mile to the north end of the valley. Ted and Beth had a house next to the barn they had finished last week. He waved at several people that stood in front of the corral. The Yancey boys were there, helping the Wrights take care of the livestock and working around the ranch.

"Hi guys, what's going on?"

As the group turned to him he could see into the corral. The piglets were running around playing with each other as the sow lay in the corner trying to keep cool.

"Hi Mark. We we're talking about the animals. Some of the pigs and sheep are getting up there in age. We want to keep the livestock healthy, so we were thinking about using some of them for food."

Sixteen year old Megan stuck out her lip. "We have deer for food. I'll take care of them!"

Ted smiled at her. "I know you love these animals Megan. You've helped us with them for months but we need to be practical. As the animals age they become more susceptible to disease. We want to grow our herds, so we won't be using the others regularly for food until a year or two from now. But there's one or two that need to be culled."

"Whatever! Come on Cody." Megan pulled Cody's along by his good arm and they headed off down the valley toward town, holding hands.

"She's right." Beth said. "We don't need them for food except to add a little variety. The hunters have to go farther to find game, but their marksmanship is improving, and Big Terry's been busy prepping the meat and tanning the hides."

"How many animals do we have?"

Ted ticked off the numbers on his fingers. "The two bulls, and thirty six cattle. That includes nine calves. We have seven goats, although we had eight before the Devol stole one. Two are kids. Five sheep with two lambs, and nine pigs. Two of the sows have a litter of piglets."

"Unfortunately," Beth added, "there are only eleven chickens. The turkeys and game birds were killed in the shelter by the Devols. The chickens were traumatized and quit laying, but two of them have produced eggs in the past couple of weeks. We only have one rooster and we won't know whether he's fertile until we can check the eggs for viable embryos. We're in a precarious situation with them."

"I wonder if there are any chickens at Platte Ranch or in town. I'd hate to face a life without eggs."

"Yeah, Mark. Me too."

"Our goal is to allow people to buy livestock as they become available, until all the farms and families in town have their own stock. That's going to take a while and we're worried about the small gene pool. But there's nothing we can do about that unless we can find additional stock somewhere else."

Once again the specter of the looming war with Clay worried him. A lot depended on them being able to expand their boundaries to look for additional livestock, travel outside the valley or trade with others that had survived the war. Mark knew others had to be out there. The Yancey boys made it, and the Holcombs. He wondered what had become of their mystery man. There hadn't been any more evidence that he remained in the area.

Needing a break from the on-going work, he took a side trip to Sentinel Hill. A few days before, he had borrowed the Jeep and brought some lumber to the hill. Driving as far up the side as he could, he hauled each piece up individually and spent a couple of hours building a bench. He sat and looked out over the valley marveling at the view and enjoying a few minutes of peace before heading for home. Only Lori knew of his special place.

Winding along the trail to the Greenhouse, he came around a large bush and found Tucker and Marci standing in the trail kissing. They jumped apart when they heard him, Tucker turning a bright red and Marci stammering, "You...you won't tell my dad will you?"

"Look kids. This is your business, and your parents. Marci, you've been through some pretty nasty stuff and I know Tucker's been helping you through that." Where are your weapons?"

"We left them on Marci's porch."

"That's pretty serious Tucker. That big Devol's still out there. You want to make out like adults but aren't being adult about Marci's safety. You two get back to Marci's and get your guns."

"Yeah, Mark. Please don't tell. We'll never go unarmed again. I promise."

Going ahead of him, they ran back toward the river. Mark got home just in time for dinner as Helen served venison stew, vegetables from the garden and fresh baked bread. It had taken him a while to become accustomed to the taste of venison, but now he liked it.

"This is confidential but I just caught Tucker and Marci making out on the trail between here and town."

"Don't know why you think it's confidential," Lori said around a mouthful of stew. "Everyone knows they're together. Izzy's happy that Marci has Tucker. He seems to be helping her where her folks haven't been able to."

"They were out there without their guns."

"Uh oh. Now that's serious. What were they thinking?"

"That's the thing. I wonder if people are becoming complacent."

"We haven't seen a Devol all summer so that may be true but I hope not. The men are training every day and are becoming good soldiers. We'll be ready when Clay comes."

***

Mark and Lori still slept in the Greenhouse. There were a few other families that hadn't selected the location of their land or made a decision about what jobs they wanted to perform. By early September the meadow in front of the building was empty of the multi-colored tents. Helen still cooked for those living in the building but she and Ernest worked during the day in the hotel with Rana, cooking breakfast and lunch. They had a tiny room at the hotel, saying they didn't need anything larger.

Skillet was building a rock, barbeque pit and smoker out behind the hotel whenever he could spare time from cooking, and helping out the cabin crews. Rana was in charge of the restaurant and partners with Ariana Fisher who also cooked, and grew herbs in a raised garden in the back. Helen and Ernest, Rana, Skillet, and Ariana were all learning to cook using just a fireplace and a Dutch oven, and the hotel residents raved about their food.

After dinner, Mark made his way over to the bachelor's quarters to check in on the radiomen. Micah, James, Robert Crowder and Johnny Jay rotated shifts, listening for any communications from the outside. Micah had fully recovered from his ordeal with the creature and sat with his feet up on the table with the radio. James was monitoring the solar equipment since the controllers were on the back wall of the small room that had been walled off from the barracks. The storage batteries were on the outside wall, protected by a wooden enclosure with holes in the wood, just under the overhang, so they were protected from the elements. The holes provided ventilation for the batteries, since they gave off hydrogen and even though the risk was miniscule, no one wanted an explosion.

"Any word from the rest of the world?"

"Naw, there never is. I wonder if they're all dead," James said.

"More likely," Micah said, "this valley, with the surrounding cliffs is a dead zone. Like back when we had cell phones. I knew this little bar where you couldn't get a signal. Not a single bar on the phone. Walk out the front door and, Boom, four bars!" Micah slammed one fist into the other to emphasize the "boom."

"There's only four guys left in the barracks. Mr. Laskey wants to use it as a high school since the solar is here. He wants to make as much use of the laptops as he can before they're gone forever," Crowder told him. "What do you say we build another, large cabin to house the single men. Then this clearing will just be the school, the Greenhouse and storage for the tractor, ATV and other equipment for the winter."

Mark scratched at the beard he was finally able to grow. "That's a good idea. The kids will have to meet in town, though, and come over here together. They can't come individually. But I hear two of the families want to build their cabins over here. They like the forest."

Suddenly, the radio burst to life with a loud burst of static. They all jumped up except Micah whose chair fell over backward.

"Ow! Damn." He jumped up with the others as they gathered around the radio. It continued to crackle and they could hear very faint voices trying to penetrate the static. But they never heard anything clearly. The disappointment in the room was palpable.

"What's happening with the shortwave radio?" Mark broke the silence.

James cleared his throat. "The parts were broken in the box. I'm trying to rebuild them but I have to build the parts to rebuild the other parts. I'm not giving up, but it may never happen. The antenna is okay if we ever get the radio rebuilt."

"Well, at least I think we can assume that somebody is still out there."

***

Lori and Mark lay in bed and Mark thought she was asleep when she whispered, "Mark, I want a cabin. I know we said we would wait until everyone was settled but we need to think of the kids. Almost everyone else with children are living across the river and there's more activity going on in this building as Chris and her team start gearing up for winter food production. Pete and Jerry have already finished their cabins down by the lake."

"Yes, but they aren't moving in until Terry finishes his. That way the three of them can provide protection for each other since they're so close to the forest."

"We haven't so much as caught a glimpse of the creature all summer. I wonder if it moved on. After all, I think we killed all the others. Maybe it was lonely."

"Not likely. It probably killed and ate any of the others that were left." He grinned but was half serious.

"So, do I get my cabin?"

"One of the work groups is finishing with Jeanna and Karen's place tomorrow. I'll see if they can work on ours after that. You're right. They have been giving priority to families with kids."

They had selected a location on the residential side street where the other "townies" would live. There were twenty four families spread throughout the valley that had or were planning on planting crops, trying to get in one more batch before the weather turned cold. Chris had taught them to save the seeds for next year's planting by having them participate in the mid-summer's harvest. The seeds that Marilyn had stocked were Heirloom seeds rather than hybrids and the seeds could be saved from one season to the next.

Neither Lori nor Mark were farmers, or even ranchers. They had yet to decide what kind of work they would do when they were no longer at war. As for now, they were still eating out of the stored foods and Lori's share of the venison from her hunting trips.

The Yancey boys had gone up the ramp one day, and were gone for three weeks. When they returned, they were driving a small herd of hardy mustangs they had spotted during their trek from Farmington in western New Mexico, where they were competing in a rodeo. Mark had tried to ride one of the mares and been thrown to the ground, bruising his shoulder and his pride. So working with the horses was out of the question... unless someone else broke them first.

Until now, he'd been working as part of the work crews, but last week he helped Jimbo, Mike and Craig in the new blacksmith shop. A forge, anvil, hammers and other equipment had been stored in the basement of the Greenhouse. It was hard, hot, dirty work but he found he enjoyed it more than any of the other jobs he had tried. So far they were only doing simple work, learning as they went. Mike had worked his way through college as a farrier and had a basic idea of what was involved in keeping the fire hot and forging iron implements. They had instructions in books and on the laptop, but blacksmithing was an art, learned through experience.

There were plans to melt down some of the shelving from the Greenhouse to make pots, horseshoes and swords. Their ammunition would run out someday. As they practiced at the firing range they collected the shell casings and Terry had shown them how to reload, using supplies that had been stocked by Glen. Much of their practice was "dry firing" where they didn't use ammo but still practiced positioning and firing. Unless they found a source of materials, they would only be able to reload for about a year. When the ammo ran out, they would be reduced to using more primitive weapons. They had set aside five thousand rounds of various calibers that would never be used except in an emergency. He curled around Lori, and found that she had gone to sleep.

The next morning he found her in the Mercantile, looking at some of the sorriest looking candles he had ever seen.

"Decorating the house already? Wow, those are really sad looking."

"I know they don't look so good but Savannah says they work just fine. She's getting better already, though. See these over here?"

"At least they don't lean over."

"Mark, stop. We're all still learning."

"Well, most of us are. I can't seem to do anything. There aren't any planes for me to fly. Why doesn't she use some of the paraffin we have?"

"It's being used for canning fruits and vegetables. That's more important, and she wants to learn to do it with the animal by-products."

The Mercantile was a good-sized, square building where sellers could lay out their produce and other items for barter. Farnsworth had thrown together three tables they could use to display their goods. When the weather was nice they set up in the street, but moved indoors during the afternoon drizzle. During the summer they had actually had several days when they didn't get rain, but then it always seemed to be heavier the next day.

One of the tables had quilts and another had some deerskin moccasins.

"I'm going to see Dr. Jim. I'll ask the work crew about our cabin."

When Mark entered the clinic, Jim was showing Annie how to bandage eleven year old Austen James' hand.

"What happened to him?"

"He burned his hand. Savannah hired him to help make soap and he dipped the bag of ashes too far down into the lye solution. It's not too bad, though. The solution wasn't very strong yet. Run along Austin." After the boy had left Jim pulled Mark into the treatment room in the back. A body was wrapped and lying on the table.

"Damn, Jim. Who is it?"

"Jack Iverson. He stumbled in here in severe D.K.A., Diabetic Ketoacidosis. There wasn't anything we could have done but he still waited too long. He was gone in fifteen minutes."

Mark thought of the little cemetery in the northern meadow and how the number of graves was growing.

***

Dirty and half dead, a second group of men had arrived from Red River. Clay counted them in his head, secretly thrilled that their army now numbered one hundred and seven... plus Stewart and B.J. of course. They were worth ten men apiece.

Jinx and Jackson had made two trips north. The first trip netted twenty three men that had readily agreed to come because they had families that were getting very hungry... and winter was approaching. The second trip was to convince those that had stayed behind, that a better life awaited them if they joined Clay's army. Only a small number of the older men, and women and children remained in Red River.

They still had some cattle, and two of Clay's men had become successful hunters. With additional foodstuffs still available in town they were feeding the newcomers who were rapidly regaining their strength. Einstein's group had three military veterans that were training the motley group from Cimarron, Eagle Nest and Red River. In another month his force would be in decent fighting condition.

Clay tried to get Einstein to conscript the people he had been sequestered with in the Cimarron church but he was adamant they be left alone.

"They're not fighters," Einstein told him. "They just want to be left alone and since they saved my ass I'm going to honor that. Anybody messes with them answers to me." He stared Clay down, but Clay would never forget it. He needed this man now, but after they rolled over his dad's people he would take care of him. Or rather, B.J. would. The creature turned out to be every bit as obedient as Stewart. He kept them closer than he had before.

Lloyd Harrison, the leader of the Red River bunch, and Einstein were seen in each other's company more often than Clay liked. He was becoming paranoid, worried that there were factions in the ranks of his soldiers and that they didn't all completely accept his authority. But they accepted the fact that B.J. and Stewart would devour them in an instant if he asked them to.

Chapter 24

Autumn's cold breath blew through the valley, chilling the inhabitants and causing the farmers to bring in the last of the harvest sooner than they'd planned. Chris knew they would get some warmer weather later in the month, and maybe even into early November, when the "Indian Summer" would fool them into thinking they were in for a mild winter... just before the real winter arrived and kicked them in the teeth.

There weren't nearly enough cabins and Mark was afraid some folks would have to stay in the Greenhouse during the winter or move back into the bachelor cabin that was being used for a classroom. Much of the storage building had been cleared out and was being used to start plants that would provide food during the winter and others that would be planted in the spring. The apple and pear trees would stand a better chance of surviving if they were started indoors before being planted down by Platte Rock in the Spring. Chris, Samuel and Rana were trying to get a hydroponic garden going, similar to the one they experimented with in the shelter.

The kitchen had been moved out of the back and the people that still lived in the building had formed cubicles there, to provide them with a modicum of privacy. Marilyn and Kate still slept in the Greenhouse. They had set aside a space in the basement and made it into a moderately comfortable apartment. The communal showers had been moved across the river and were housed in a building behind the hotel. Over the five months they had been living in the valley, most of the men had grown beards or goatees and hygiene was not nearly as good as it had been in the shelter.

They had been building as fast as they could but two hundred people could only do so much. Work would proceed during the winter but there would need to be long breaks for bad weather.

Mark, Lori and the kids had moved into their little cabin a week before. Both adults practiced their cooking skills, using the pot in the fireplace and a solar oven, improving a little each day. Mark had always enjoyed doing his own cooking and Lori had been forced to become a good cook by her abusive husband.

**

The creature that had been Arby Clarke, poked its head out of the cave and looked at the dark, lowering sky. It was very hungry. Rather than hibernating in the winter, this monster holed up for the summer, deep in the warren of tunnels. Having transformed into a reptile-like animal, it had trouble regulating its temperature and during the heat of the summer had suffered heat exhaustion. Crawling into its lair, it lay almost comatose for months, emerging only to hunt on the plateau above the entrance to its cave and to relieve itself.

A large ledge extended in front of the cave but wasn't visible from the valley below, due to a line of rocks along the rim and a backward slope to the ledge. Looking down into the valley from behind the rocks it saw houses scattered throughout the meadow and smoke rising from several chimneys. It emitted a low growl, turned away and crossed to the road that led upward toward the meadow.

This cave had been used in the construction of the shelter. A helicopter pad on the plateau above was used to land large pieces of the turbines that would generate power for the inhabitants. The road gave access to the cave, and tunnels lead to the cavern containing the power plant. It was much more practical than trying to take these large parts through the shelter. When construction was complete, the cave had been closed off. Arby and the other mutants had broken down the wooden door and gained access to the shelter, wreaking havoc, destroying the power plant and killing a dozen of the residents before the others escaped to the valley.

Now that the weather was cooler, and once it had eaten its fill, it could hunt the one human that it wanted to kill above all others.

***

Gazing down on Taos, New Mexico from high in the pass, Matthew felt a tug of his heartstrings. The town had been home for months, but he needed to leave before winter set in. Even as he'd tried to forget the people in the valley at Eagle Nest, he worried about them, and wondered if the men at the ranch had attacked them. Chief stood calmly, as the mares grazed and the two month old foal pranced around his mother. It was only early October but he could feel the cold and damp of early winter blowing up from the canyons.

Taos was deserted, although there were bodies in most of the homes he had explored. Either no one had survived, or less likely, they had left for greener pastures. He'd stayed in the Kachina Lodge; sleeping, scrounging for food in town and reading. He spent many days in the Taos Public Library. In preparation for leaving, he searched through the stores in town looking for items he might need. Visiting Dick's Sporting Goods he had taken several compound bows, crossbows, and arrows, strapping them onto his packs.

He could survive here for years, but eventually the food remaining on the shelves would go bad and he would have to live by hunting and gathering. After spending the summer alone, he longed for company even as he shunned it. Tying the mares out back at night, with Chief watching over them, had kept them safe, but Matthew had seen some wanderers the day before and knew he couldn't stay here forever.

Of all the places he had been since leaving his grandfather's ranch, the valley north of Eagle's Nest seemed the best. Matthew dismounted and checked the gear packed on the horses. The other two mares, Daisy and Rose, had come into heat after being outside the mine for a couple of months and both were about four months pregnant. They would foal in the early spring. Matthew had lightly packed their load, while Tulip carried a heavier load including the weapons. Everything was secure and as he swung onto Chief, he turned away from the town without a backward glance. He couldn't take the loneliness any longer. He'd made up his mind.

It was thirty five miles to Eagle Nest. He already felt better knowing he would be sleeping with the horses at night, his rifle at the ready. Neither he nor the horses had had much exercise while hiding out so he set a leisurely pace. Riding only ten miles per day, it would take three or four days to make the trip. Then he would hang out up on the ridge and decide what his next step would be.

***

"Good morning Lori." Doug was at the front door, dressed in a warm jacket with his rifle slung across his back. "Al needs to take a day off to take care of Janet. She has a bad cold or the flu. Do you think you could do some guard duty with me instead of your regular day tomorrow? We'll be at the rock."

"Sure. You go on and relieve the night guys and I'll be along in an hour or so. I'll need to find Mark and tell him and arrange for the kids."

"OK. See ya soon." He strode away for the trail that wound south to Platte Rock.

Fetching her rifle she gathered up Kevin and Ashley, bundled them in warm jackets, and went to find Mark. He didn't seem to be in town but Doc said he thought he saw him go by his cabin that morning, heading north toward the ranch. She and the kids walked the half mile to Ted and Beth's place and Lori noticed two huge rolls of alfalfa in the field with the cattle. There were four, three-sided shelters they'd built to protect the animals in the winter.

She found Mark and the Wrights digging a root cellar behind their house.

"Hi Honey. Al can't do guard duty today so I'm helping out down at the rock. I'll drop the kids at Barbara's. How's the cellar coming?"

As cold as it was, Mark didn't have a jacket on. He was generating a large amount of heat with his digging. "It's going really well. This will be the fourth one in town. Terry says that should be enough. Izzy has been dehydrating vegetables and making jerky for a couple of months. Each of the root cellars will have potatoes and onions, dehydrated food and jerky, some of the canned foods and smoked meats. That way if anything happens, like an animal gets in, the other cellars will still have plenty of food."

"Rana brought quite a lot of canned foods to the cabin this morning. It's in the cupboard. She's delivering some to all the homes in the valley."

"Cool. From what Terry and the others tell me we should make it through the winter with enough food. And of course, we still have some of the dehydrated stuff from the Greenhouse, including many year's worth of potatoes." They all chuckled at that.

Beth said, "Next year we'll have a much better idea of how much food we need to preserve to get us all through the next winter. I feel more secure knowing we have the backup stuff and Chris's winter crops in the Greenhouse."

"Me too. Well, I'll see you tonight Mark." She kissed him on the cheek and she and the kids made their way across the bridge and down the valley. The level and velocity of the river had dropped significantly but, due to the constant rain in the mountains, it still had plenty of water. Lori loved the river, the wildness of it. They talked about building a more substantial bridge, maybe of rock, the following year. More workers would be good.

Two weeks ago another family had walked down the ramp into the valley. They had been held captive by wanderers that had taken everything they owned and they had barely escaped with their lives. A couple and two young sons, eight and eleven. They were skinny, hungry and scared. The townsfolk had welcomed them, knowing that they had so many plans for next year that they needed all the help they could get. This was one family that would survive the winter, when they thought their lives were over.

Lori went past the fields with the remains of the late-season crops and the clearing where Terry, Izzy and the Thompson boys processed the meat and animal by-products. The group of three cabins by the lake came into view after another mile. Barbara was thrilled to have the kids for Jeremy to play with. Jerry waved as she left. One of the men always stayed at the cabins during the day to provide protection.

"I'll pick them up before dark. Bye." She thought about taking the shorter route out of the valley and across the bridge to the south, but it was just too dangerous so she backtracked and crossed the suspension bridges and made her way to the Platte Rock guard station.

"Do you think they're ever going to attack?" Doug asked Lori late that afternoon as they hunkered down in the sentry shack, trying to stay warm and sheltered from the uncharacteristic wind. It felt like it was blowing in a storm.

"Terry says that Clay's probably getting more men. Raising an army, if there's anyone left out there. Now that the weather's cooled off I think they'll be coming soon. Dave and Terry said that if they don't attack before the snow comes we might have to go on the offensive. We can't stay bottled up in this valley forever."

"I think they're right. If we're going to get more settlers they need to have safe access."

"I need to pick up the kids from Barbara's and get home before dark. Do you think it'd be okay if I left a few minutes early? Ruben and Pete should be here soon."

"Yeah, Lori. I'll be right behind you."

She climbed down the ladder and exited between the leaning rocks that formed the alcove containing the ladder. Glancing up at the sky she could see angry, dark clouds moving in. The afternoon rains had apparently been delayed, but it looked like a doozy of a storm brewing. She went around the cluster of rocks and hesitated. It was a lot shorter to go south over the bridge. She and Pete had done it before and if she was careful, she could get the kids home before the rain. Not wanting Doug to see her, she hiked half way to the river and snuck south until she passed the entrance to the valley. She could see that the men in the Anasazi tower were distracted, as they changed guards, so heading south toward the bridge she bent low and crept amongst the rocks and bushes. She congratulated herself on cutting thirty minutes off her trip to pick up the kids. The bridge was just ahead.

She almost made it.

***

Mark had come home from a hard day's work, cleaned up and was preparing dinner. They had fresh carrots, onions and potatoes and he was adding chopped venison, and a little flour to the stew pot. He unwrapped a loaf of bread, sliced it and rewrapped it to stay fresh. Swinging the pot into the fireplace, he sat in the only chair they owned and opened a book about root cellars and food preservation. Engrossed in his reading he only noticed the time when it became too dark to see. The fire cast a warm glow throughout the main room of the little cabin. He pulled the pot to the side where the food would stay warm but wouldn't burn.

Lori should have been home by now. Putting on a heavy jacket and a baseball cap, he left the house to see if she may have stopped by Town Hall or the mercantile. All the barterers had packed up and gone home and she wasn't in the small, first floor restaurant in the hotel. No one had seen her. As he arrived at the Town Hall, he saw Doug entering town from the direction of Platte rock.

"Hey, Doug. Where's Lori?"

"She left a little early to pick up the kids. She should be back soon. She took them to Barb and Jerry's."

"Well, I guess that means I'll be forced to have a drink and wait for her." Mark slapped Doug on the shoulder. "Join me?"

They went into the Town Hall, which at this time, contained two wooden tables and many of the canvas and webbed chairs from the Greenhouse. The small cache of liquor that had been stored in the basement of the storage building had all been moved over, and bottles were sitting on the floor in the back room. Farnsworth was building furniture as fast as Lucas could supply lumber but the town buildings and cabins were very sparsely furnished. He was training Tucker Smith and Eric Howard, two teens, as his apprentices.

A table held bottles of Bourbon and Vodka. Doug and Mark poured a third of a glass apiece and found chairs. Dave and Sheri were sitting in camp chairs, the other table between them holding a chess board.

"Any sign of the enemy?" Dave asked Doug.

"Actually, I spotted a couple of them this morning. They slipped up through the brush and then skedaddled back south. Looked like they were scouting. I'm wondering if they're getting ready to come."

"Maybe we should add a man to each guard shack. If they're waiting for us to put up our food for the winter, then they'll probably be attacking sometime in the next month," Dave said.

"It's your move Dave," Sheri suggested. "It's mate in three."

Dave looked at the board for a few moments and reached out to tip over his king.

"Damn, she beats me every time." He glanced at the door as Barbara came in with Ashley and Kevin.

"Hi Mark, Jeremy cut his hand and I dropped him off at the clinic. Lori hasn't picked up the kids yet so I brought them with me. She wasn't home. Is she here?"

Mark looked alarmed. "Doug said she left early to pick them up. You sure you didn't pass her on your way here?"

"No. I followed the main trail along the river and over the bridge. I would have seen her."

"Doug, I'm going to Platte Rock to ask the guards if they saw her as they came to relieve you. Can you check up at Ted's and at the other places in town?"

Dave and Sheri stood up and headed toward the door. "I'll go to the Greenhouse. Maybe she stopped to talk to Chris," Sheri said as she left.

"I'll get some guys to scour the town and the area between here and the ramp," Dave said, as they all ran down Hargraves Street and split in different directions. Mark ran the two miles south to the rock. He arrived out of breath but flew up the ladder into the shack.

"Ruben," he began without preamble, "did you see Lori when you guys were on your way here?"

"No. Doug said she left early. Why?"

"She never made it to Barbara's to pick up the kids. She's not in town and nobody's seen her."

Pete looked thoughtful and then told Mark, "The day we found Jigger we had gone down to the bridge a half mile south of the valley entrance. It's a lot shorter than going back to the suspension bridge to get to Barbara's."

"She never told me that, Pete. That was reckless."

"There were two of us and we were armed. We could see their sentries so it was a piece of cake. But if she tried it on her own it would be a lot more dangerous. You don't think she did, do you?"

"Yeah, It's something she would do. She's gained so much confidence over the past few months, I think she believes she's invincible. I need to get back to town and get a rescue party. God, If Clay has her, no telling what will happen."

***

"Well, look what the cat drug in." Clay stood with his arms crossed, looking down at Lori lying on the floor where the sentries had thrown her. Arms tied behind her back, she was curled in a ball to protect her stomach, afraid he might kick her. Clay leaned down and took her arm, pulling her into a sitting position.

"The last time I saw you, you were watching them put me in that elevator. You were standing with Mark Teller. Are you still his girlfriend? As soon as my sister dumped him he jumped on you."

She looked sideways up at him but didn't say a word.

"Well, no matter. Where'd you guys get her?"

"She was trying to sneak to the bridge that goes over the river up north. We had a couple guys posted at the bridge and she didn't see 'em. Her jacket and her rifle's on the back porch. It's a nice gun."

"You guys know what this means? They'll be coming for her. Jinx, get B.J. from the barn and have him join the guards at the south stable. Stewart can hang with the boys in the east field, and add a couple of other guys to each group including the west hay barn. They think they're smarter than us, so instead of a direct attack from the north I think they'll come from the east or even the south."

He smiled an evil smile down at Lori. "Now what are we going to do with you? I think maybe I'll have a little fun with you." As he spoke, he grabbed her arm and lifted her to her feet. "What a way to get back at my faux bro, by fucking his woman."

Lori looked up at him and spit directly in his face. He reached out and slapped her hard across the face, splitting her lip, and he grabbed her as she stumbled back.

"You bitch!" He spun her around, wrapping his arms around her so she couldn't move. Holding her struggling body against his, he reached around in front of her and started trying to undo the button on her pants. With his arms wrapped around the fighting woman, he was becoming excited.

"Hey Boss, can I have her too?" Jackson asked, licking his lips. His pants were bulging in front and Clay realized his weren't. He didn't know why he wasn't responding but it scared him to be unable to perform in front of his men. He thrust against her but he still wasn't responding. He started to pull her toward the bedroom when she suddenly stopped struggling.

"You know Clay? You can't hurt me. I've been abused by a master abuser. My husband beat me and took me against my will. I have a safe place inside my head where I go and I won't even know what's happening outside it."

This infuriated him and he shoved her forward where she hit and bounced off the wall. She spun around to face him... his face was purple with rage.

Stepping forward, he slammed his fist into her abdomen with all the force he could muster. Her breath whooshed out and she collapsed to the floor, gasping, able to suck in air but unable to expel it. She thought her lungs would burst when he kicked her and forced the air out in a gust. She curled into a ball, gasping and crying.

"See if your safe place can protect you from THAT you cunt!" He swung on Jackson. "Throw the bitch in the barn. Tie her to one of the posts. If she wants to be cold, she can freeze her ass off." His eyes were wide and spittle flew from his mouth when he yelled.

"Boss, it's forty degrees out there. Shall I put her jacket back on her?"

"No! If she lives through the night, I'm going to give her to B.J. and Stewart. They can have her before they eat her. I'll tell Mark what happened to her before I kill him. Let's get ready to ambush those fuckers!" He strode into the kitchen and looked out the window to the setting sun in the west. As Jackson went by him, pulling a stumbling Lori, Clay told him, "Have Andy ride the bike into town and get Einstein and his boys out here." He glared at Lori.

"It's time to go to war."

Chapter 25

Fog rolled across the fields, stirred by a howling wind and obscuring the ranch house and outbuildings. Mark could see a vague outline of the barn but the house beyond was invisible. He peered through his binoculars but they didn't help in the darkness. The moon was blocked by the clouds that had been gathering all afternoon and now threatened to release torrents of rain. Even as Mark hung his binoculars around his neck, he felt the beginning pinpricks of sleet.

"We know they're out there. They have to be expecting us," Dave whispered in Mark's ear. "Did you see anything?"

"No, and it'll be full dark in fifteen minutes. Remember when we stole their cattle? There's a trench a hundred yards from here that leads south of the house until it hits the river. Take Terry, Pete, and Mike and follow the trench. I'll take Jimbo, Ron and Greg and go through the gate. Watch out for the bull. We'll hit them from the north and you guys from the south. Sneak around the outbuilding on the west side of the house."

"Do you think he has her in the house?"

"Where else would he keep her? I can't believe he would treat her badly. She was always good to him in the shelter, even when others weren't. Man, it's freezing out here. She damn well better be in the house." But if she was... he worried what was happening to her. He would strangle Clay with his own two hands if he'd touched her.

Dave moved forward and tapped each of his team on the shoulder, and they moved off through the wet grass toward the ditch. Mark motioned for his guys to follow him as they belly crawled across the field, trying to reach the gate unseen.

He knew there would be an ambush. He just didn't know where or when.

Dave's guys went over the edge of the ditch and disappeared. The gate in the chain link fence was a hundred yards north of the creek. When he found it, he reached up a hand to release the latch. Only opening the gate eighteen inches, he slipped through, followed by his team. Once on the other side and after re-latching the gate, he brought his binoculars up to his eyes.

"I can't see shit through this fog. But they can't see in the dark either. Silence from here on." They crawled toward the house using the bushes scattered throughout the meadow as cover. Motioning for the men to spread out, he swung north toward the barn. It was completely dark now and he could no longer see the men.

There was a sudden flash of light through the fog south of his position. He heard a yell and gunfire.

The ambush was on!

From the direction of the muzzle flashes, he figured it was Dave's group being fired upon. He had no idea what happened to his men. He jumped up and took off for the side of the barn, tripped over the uneven ground and went down hard. His breath whooshed out of his lungs and he lay stunned for a moment.

More gunfire, and the scream of a beast, split the night and he feared for Dave's team as more flashes lit up the skirmish, from the fire of semi-automatic weapons. He slowly rose to his knees but didn't think he'd injured himself, so he continued to the side of the barn. Rushing around the corner, he saw that the barn door was closed but the "man" door stood wide open. He ducked inside and immediately threw himself to the side so as not to present himself as a target. He crouched in the corner of the barn, not moving, listening for sounds in the blackness. His sweat was freezing on his forehead and his exposed flesh felt numb.

He heard someone breathing.

Aiming his rifle toward the sound, he raised his foot and carefully advanced a step. He waited, and listened for movement in the inky interior of the barn. Taking another step, he paused again to listen when the breathing suddenly ceased.

He'd been discovered! The being in the dark was holding its breath, listening for him. He froze in place, hoping he could hold out longer than the other. The person in the dark suddenly sobbed, and Mark, completely stunned, leaped forward and dropped to his knees, throwing his arms around Lori.

"Lori, it's me! Are you okay?" God, she was so cold!

"Mark, Mark…" she just kept repeating, shivering so hard he could barely understand her as she clung to him in the dark. He fumbled with the rope securing her wrists behind her back. He was trembling with fury. What was Clay thinking leaving her out here like this? Pulling out his knife he sawed on the cord until it parted and she was free. He cut the second rope that secured her to the post and as he pulled her arms from behind her, she cried out in pain. She didn't even have a jacket on.

"How long have you been out here?"

"Don't… don't know. He was so angry! He's crazy Mark. Really crazy." She collapsed against him.

"We need to get you out of here. I'm going to get you up on your feet." He reached under her arms and tried to raise her up but her legs were stiff and he had to let her slide back down. The gunfire continued and suddenly he heard noise outside the barn. There was a scuffling and someone grunted. Mark rushed to the door and through the darkness he saw two men rolling on the ground.

"Jimbo?" He moved toward the fight.

"Mark! It's Ron. Help me!" Mark drew his ankle knife. "Ron." He danced around trying to figure out which man was his. One of the men screamed and Mark stabbed at the figure. It hadn't been Ron's voice.

"I bit his ear off!" Ron cried.

Thrusting the knife outward, Mark felt it hit yielding flesh and the man went down. He twisted and pushed the knife hard, and the body relaxed.

"Get him off me." Ron pushed and Mark helped drag the body off of him.

"Where're the others?"

"Jimbo had to retreat to the gate. There's just too many of them. I slipped around behind them and I'm trying to get to the house. Greg went to help Dave's guys. They're pinned down in the ditch. Let's go!"

"Ron wait. I found Lori. She's in the barn! Get to the others and signal retreat. I'll get Lori away from here."

"Okay. That's great. Go! We'll be fine." He took off in the direction of the ditch where the other men were held down.

Mark ran back into the barn and found Lori trying to stand. He grabbed her under the arms and hoisted her up, hugging her and holding her until her legs were steady. Leaning down, he picked up his rifle and they very slowly made their way to the door. He stuck his head out to check for enemies... and was slammed back into the barn.

Lori went down, and as Mark jumped up he was struck a vicious blow across the head. He spun to the side and fell to his knees. Disoriented, but knowing a kick was coming, he grabbed the man's ankle and threw his full weight against it, just as Terry had taught him. The man screamed in excruciating pain as his knee snapped.

"C'mon Lori!" Mark pulled her back to her feet and they started back for the door. They were almost blind in the dark and as they passed the fallen man, he rose up and swung a blade in their direction. It was dumb luck that the blade found its mark. Lori gasped and Mark reached out, throwing his body onto his assailant and clamping his fingers around the man's throat. He squeezed with all his might and shoved his thumbs into the windpipe until he crushed the larynx and the man went limp.

Mark pulled off his jacket and put it on Lori, and with her arm draped around his shoulder, they left the barn behind them and made their way toward the fence. It was sleeting hard now and in a few minutes they were soaked to the skin. Mark had his left arm around Lori's side and he could feel something warm in contrast to the freezing rain. They stumbled across the field, falling several times as his foot struck a rock or Lori collapsed at his side. He would haul her back up and they kept going. After an eternity Mark, walked smack into the fence. He didn't know which way to go to get to the gate. Turning left they followed the chain link until they came to a corner.

"Damn! We went the wrong way."

They slid down into the muddy grass and Mark pulled up Lori's shirt. He felt for the cut. It seemed clean, slicing through the tissue between two ribs on her left side. It was bleeding but he couldn't tell if it was superficial or had penetrated the lung. He thought that if the lung were cut, she'd have trouble breathing. The freezing rain mixed with the blood and washed it down her side. He stood and pulled her back to her feet.

"I'm so sorry, but we need to go back. I can't climb the fence and get you over." Halfway back to the gate he realized he didn't hear any more gunfire. Reaching out every few steps, he touched the fence, trying to ensure he didn't miss the gate. His hand contacted the latch of the gate and his heart leaped!

"Finally!" he murmured. Passing through the gate, they stumbled westward through the pouring rain, and had just made it to the hills when Lori slipped from his grasp and fell heavily to the ground.

"No Lori, c'mon honey. Get up." He tried to raise her but she was dead weight. The rain was now coming down in sheets and the wind blew even harder. As he leaned down and slipped his arms under her knees and neck, and lifted her up, lightning lit up the sky and a tremendous thunderclap sounded four or five seconds later, almost causing him to drop her. From then on, the sheet lightning was almost continuous, lighting his way as he stumbled around the rocks and boulders that lay all around. With each flash of lightning he could see the angry thunderclouds lowering over the valley until he felt claustrophobic as though sealed in a darkened room.

He struggled forward, tripping and almost falling a dozen times. His pants were heavy from the mud that coated his legs. Twice, he went to his knees and had to lower Lori to the ground while he grabbed a few minutes of rest, the rain pounding his head and shoulders. For a few minutes, hail the size of marbles stung his back as he laid Lori on the ground and leaned over her to protect her face.

The hills gave way to sheer cliffs, fractured and pitted from eons of weather. Picking her up again, he had made it halfway to the entrance of Hidden Valley when a bolt of lightning hit the top of the precipice above, and broken, jagged rocks plummeted down upon them. Bending over Lori to shield her from the rock fall, he rushed to the side of the cliff and hunkered down behind a boulder. Covering Lori's body with his own, he felt pieces of rock hit his back and all around him. As he pressed back toward the cliff, trying to burrow under and behind a large bush that shared the space with them, he realized there was an opening behind the bush. His adrenaline surging, he swung around Lori, grabbed her beneath the arms and pulled her along the ground into the space.

They were mercifully out of the rain. Mark sat on the ground, breathing hard. He reached out a hand toward the back of the cave and encountered only air. It was bigger than he had originally thought. *What if it's an animal lair?* He figured if they shared it with an animal, they would know about it by now. The back wall was only a couple of feet further on and it was low enough that he couldn't stand fully upright. The rain was so loud it echoed off the walls and the lightning continued to flash. Thunderclaps followed almost immediately, leading Mark to believe the storm was almost stationary over the valley. Feeling his way in the dark he pulled Lori to the rear of the cave. He went back to the entrance and found part of the bush growing into the space at the front entrance. Taking out his knife, he cut off all the branches that extended inside the cave and were relatively dry. Mark made it a habit to carry his magnesium fire starter with him at all times, again at Terry's insistence, and had practiced making a fire on many occasions. He scraped his knife on the magnesium to produce sparks, and when they ignited his kindling he blew gently to encourage the fledgling flames. He was able to keep it going on the third try, as the dry leaves and tiny branches caught fire and ignited the larger branches that he fed to the flames. In a few minutes, he had a small fire burning to the side of the cave's entrance, and he was happy to see the smoke being sucked out into the maelstrom.

Crawling over to Lori, he pulled her into a sitting position and pulled back the drenched jacket. There was blood soaking her shirt and more blood on her pants. He checked for a second wound but there was none. Removing his shirt, he used his knife to cut it into strips, tying them together and wrapping them around Lori's chest under her breasts. The bleeding had stopped and he was relieved, thinking the cut wasn't deep.

Shirtless, he was shivering, with goose bumps on his exposed flesh even though the small fire had warmed the space a few degrees. More lightning brightened the sky, penetrating into their sanctuary. There must have been fissures in the rock above their head as the wind created a low, moaning sound that echoed through the rock. The cave was damp as gusts of wind blew rain into the opening. Fortunately, he had built the fire to the side, away from the opening which prevented it from being extinguished.

They wouldn't have it for long. The wood from the bush burned quickly and there were only a few of the larger branches that he was slowly feeding to the fire. He didn't think Clay's men would follow them in this storm. If they did, Mark and Lori would be easy prey, with the light from the fire acting as a beacon to lead them to their location.

He sat with his back against the side of the cave, closest to the entrance, and pulled Lori onto his lap holding her against his chest. She curled her legs up against him, seeking warmth. He was able to cover them both with the wool jacket, which was warm even though soaked, and he hoped they wouldn't freeze to death during the night.

"Mark. Are we home?" she whispered faintly.

"No Honey, we're okay though. I found a cave and we have a little fire. They won't come after us in this storm." He looked into her eyes and was almost overcome at the love he saw there; the trust. She smiled and closed her eyes. Frightened, he held his breath and listened, but he heard normal breathing. Picking up her wrist, he felt for her pulse. It seemed strong and regular.

Mark knew he should be scared and worried, but somehow he wasn't. Looking down at Lori's face he knew he would never be alone. He brushed back the wet hair from her brow and caressed her cheek as the tiny fire flickered, and threw friendly, dancing sprites on the wall.

The cave lit up like daylight and the thunder hit almost simultaneously, the crack of the thunder so loud Mark ducked his head.

He had never known such a storm!

A monsoon of biblical proportions, buffeted and blown into the cave entrance by gusts of wind, with lightning flashing and thunder that crashed almost continuously. The wind moaned through the cave and the drumming of sheets of rain produced a staccato reverberation through the walls.

How many thousands of years had mankind huddled in caves, surviving horrendous weather and dangerous predators? Primitive humans had faced hunger, thirst and disease but lived through it all, and even prospered, to spread across the face of the earth.

Alone, an individual is weak… but man is a social animal. With another; a loved one, a friend, a mate, a brother or sister, they were never alone. Two people could face anything together and come out stronger.

Over millennia, human beings learned to care for themselves and each other. They took a primeval world and extracted what they needed to build vast civilizations, while surviving tyrants, plagues and pestilence. To this very day, they live through floods and tsunamis, volcanos and earthquakes; cataclysms that rend the very foundations of the earth. From frozen tundra, to sweltering jungles, to scorching deserts, they endure. Through inquisitions and mans' inhumanity to man. Forming families, communities and friendships. Through storms and solar flares, fire, famine and uncountable, devastating wars…… humanity abides.

Chapter 26

Through a gray, drizzly morning, Clay stared continually toward the north from his vantage point in the covered porch out back. Waiting all night for the reinforcements from Eagle Nest, he became increasingly angry and anxious. The Remnant had stolen the woman right from under their noses, even though Clay's men had expected the attack and had lain in readiness. They lost four men. One had been found in front of the barn, a knife wound that penetrated his rib cage. One of the men guarding the west approach was shot through the chest, and surprisingly, two others had died from crossbow arrows.

He wondered if these fools would be competent enough to prevail in the coming battle. It didn't matter anymore. They just needed to get him close enough to kill Mark Teller. If he lived through the encounter he would leave the hapless bastards here and head for California, back to the ocean.

Today would be the day he got his revenge!

The storm had pounded them, until close to morning, when the lightning moved on to the east and clashed with the light of the rising sun. A steady drizzle was all that remained of the epic storm. Shortly after dawn, the rest of his forces came down the dirt road from the low pass separating Platte Ranch from County Road 127. They were a disheveled bunch, clothed in winter jackets, hats with ear muffs, shooter's gloves and each carrying a rifle. They had emptied sporting goods stores in Red River and Eagle Nest. None of the bunch had bathed or shaved in weeks, their faces covered with scraggly beards.

Einstein and Lloyd Harrison led the group down the hill and up to the front door. They entered the house while the rest of the men went around the corner to join Clay's other forces in back.

"So you're thinking today's the day, eh Clay?" Einstein settled onto the couch.

"The weather's turned. They have as much stuff put up for the winter as they're ever going to have. The men can rest up during the day and tonight. We'll hit them in the morning before first light. I read somewhere, that's the best time because everyone is sound asleep."

"Yeah, I heard that too. We'll run over the plan with the guys one more time. You got any more booze?"

"Man, it's morning. You want to drink now?"

Einstein grinned. "I'm going to get shit faced early so I can sleep it off before the battle. I might get killed and never get another chance."

***

Barely able to move, Mark shifted Lori's position so he could slip out from under her. He laid her gently on the ground, covering her with the jacket. Sunlight flowed into the cave and he could see the cold remains of their fire. The chill penetrated his body as he rubbed his bare arms to warm them up.

"Mark?" She stirred and tried to sit up. He jumped to her side. "Where are we. It's so cold."

"I know honey. We're in a cave, but we're safe. Can you sit up? You'll be warmer if you can move."

Suddenly the cave darkened and Mark swung about to see a shadow bent over in the entrance to the cave. He had no weapon, not even aware when he dropped it during the fight to get Lori free, and the interminable journey to this refuge.

"Don't think about doing anything stupid, friend. It looks like you could use some help."

"Who are you?"

The shadow moved forward and thrust out his hand. "Matthew Pennington. I'm not going to hurt you. I want to help. Is she okay?"

"She's been cut in the ribs. I'm worried she's lost a lot of blood."

"Okay if I take a look?"

Mark trusted this man for some reason. He could very easily have shot them. The man slipped off his jacket and handed it to Mark as he slid by him in the narrow confines of the cave.

"You better put that on."

They helped Lori sit up and Matthew felt under her shirt for the wound. Lori sucked in her breath as he probed but didn't pull away.

"I think it's pretty shallow. I have horses outside so let's get her back to your camp."

"Are you the man that saved Sheri from the Devol?" Mark asked, as they helped Lori out of the cave. She was able to stand and they each took an arm as they walked through the morning rain to the horses.

"That what you call them? I was going up the trail to see what was on the plateau. I was looking for a campsite that had a better water source. After I tied off my rope to get across the rockslide, I heard noises coming from above." He laughed. "Suddenly she came flying around the switchback and slid to a halt, that thing right behind her. I didn't even think, just ran across the slide and stuck out my hand."

It took them both to boost her up on the mare after Matthew removed a few items from the horse's back. "This mare's about four month's pregnant so I don't want to overload her."

He went to a large bundle tied to another mare and pulled out and donned a jacket. He grabbed a hat for Lori to try and keep the rain from her face. The young man walked over to a magnificent, Appaloosa stallion, climbed into the saddle and stuck a hand out to Mark. The other two mares were loaded with supplies so Mark stepped up on a rock as the stallion came aside it and he was able to mount behind Matthew.

As they rode north toward the town the colt romped through the grass, never straying far from his mother. They rode right next to Lori, but she seemed more alert and was able to hang onto the mare's mane and stay upright.

Reaching the entrance to Hidden Valley, they continued toward the Platte Rock guardhouse that was just visible through the rain and fog. He waved, hoping the guards wouldn't shoot first and ask questions later. He slid from the horse and went forward with his hands in the air.

"Hey guys! It's Mark Teller."

Al Spears came out of the hole in the rocks and ran to Mark, keeping a close eye on Matthew. "Man, am I glad to see you!"

"This is Matthew. He's okay. We need to get Lori to town." He turned to Matthew. "I'm going to walk beside Lori's horse."

Continuing up the valley, Matthew asked Mark about where they had been during the aftermath of the war and by the time they reached town, Matthew had been filled in.

"Wow, I'm impressed with your town," he said when Willsburg came into view. "When I left here a few months ago you were living across the river in that indoor arena."

"We've been working our asses off. Where did you go?"

"Been holding up in Taos. The towns deserted. I got bored and decided this place, and you folks, were the best things I've seen since the war. Do you think I could join you?"

"You kidding me? You are most welcome."

The town sentry had been apprised of their coming using a heliograph. It consisted of a box with a slatted cover that could be opened and closed with a handle, and powered by a candle. A reflective piece of metal behind the candle served to make the light more visible. This was another of the things Terry had taught them. He didn't try and teach them Morse Code, just a few simple signals. The Platte Rock heliograph couldn't be seen in Willsburg due to the mass of rocks blocking the view to the north, so they signaled the Anasazi Tower and they relayed the message to town.

Most of the townsfolk came to meet them as they rode into Willsburg and stopped in front of the clinic. Mark helped Lori, as she almost fell off the horse and into his arms. He picked her up and carried her into the back room, setting her gently on the wooden table that Carmen had spread with a sheet.

Dr. Jim and Carmen slipped off the jacket and Jim examined the wound.

"It's a nice clean slice and it didn't go deep. She's very lucky. Mark, there's some coffee in the front room. Why don't you go get some and I'll check her out. These bruises on her face look like someone hit her. I'll be out in a few minutes."

He found a pot of coffee on the propane stove in the front room, and waited with several others. He told them about the raid and how he'd found Lori in the barn, half frozen.

"That bastard," Jimbo growled. "We should capture him and stake him out for the winter. Naked!" That elicited a few chuckles but there were some folks that thought it was fitting punishment.

Dave came in and gave Mark a hug, clapping him on the back.

"We didn't know what happened to you but Ron said you told him to sound the retreat, that you had Lori. We were going to keep looking but there were two Devols and we sort of panicked. When we got back we were surprised you weren't here. Some of us tried to go back out, but lightning was hitting the ground and all we could do was hope you holed up somewhere in that storm. We didn't lose anybody in the fight." He looked over at Matthew. "I suppose we have you to thank for that? I saw two of their guys go down with arrows in their chests and that sort of took the wind out of their sails and they retreated."

Mark asked Matthew, "How did you find us this morning?"

"Like your friend said, I was at the fight. Thought you could use some help since you were outnumbered and they had those things helping them. By the time the fight was over, you had gone on and I just tracked you to the cave. I could see the light of your fire so I figured you were okay for the night and I had to get my horses under cover. I found a deep overhang and spent the night trying to keep the horses calm. That was some storm!"

"You must be exhausted then. You can stay at my place and tie the horses out back. They'll be safe. The kids have been at Barbara's since Lori disappeared. We'll pick them up tomorrow and you can stay at the hotel or across the river. We'll figure something out."

Just then Dr. Jim came out and motioned Mark into one of the small rooms that opened off the hallway.

"She's okay Mark. Clay didn't assault her but he punched her in the face and abdomen."

Jim saw Mark's face darken with anger and he knew if Mark ever got his hands on Clay he would kill him.

"And Mark, I... well, I'm real sorry, but she lost the baby."

Chapter 27

"Here they come!" Tyler Forbes yelled, pointing toward movement in the bushes that could only be an advancing group of men. They were visible only because of a waning moon. "Send the signal!" Sheri grabbed the control of the heliograph and started signaling toward the Anasazi Tower. The signaling device was shielded so Clay's men weren't aware they'd been discovered. Tyler had his binoculars and was trying to get a count of the enemy, but in the dark and with them hiding in the bushes, it was impossible.

"Looks like at least ninety or a hundred guys."

"If you count the women that fight for us, we might have them outnumbered and I'm sure they thought they could take us by surprise."

The signal was already going out to the town from the tower. The town sentry reached out and began to ring a bell, arousing the townspeople and the folks living in cabins closest to Willsburg.

Mark came awake in the pre-dawn darkness. He had his arm around Lori and was curled around her body. "Lori, the bell's ringing. I have to go. Please, please stay here. Just this once. I know you're still hurting. You don't need to take part in this battle." He was surprised at her answer.

"I promise. But if they break through, I'll be ready for them."

He climbed from bed and met Matthew in the living room.

"What's the racket?" Matthew asked him.

"You may have joined up with us one day too early. That's the alarm. Clay's guys are on the way. We've been waiting for their attack all summer and half the fall. This isn't your fight."

"Are you kidding? That skirmish the other night was the first time I've really felt alive since the war."

They grabbed their weapons, stuffed magazines in their pockets and slammed through the front door. Lori slowly got out of bed, slightly disoriented and still in pain. She went into the living room where she sat in their only chair, facing the door, an Uzi in her lap.

***

Mark and Matthew met two dozen others in the main street of town. James Bascomb was already instructing the others. It had been decided ahead of time that the women would be the messengers. Some people would beef up the guard shacks in case attacks came from the rear. Everyone knew what their role was in advance.

"Jeanna and Karen, you two get up to Ted and Beth's and tell them it's on. Then go up to the north guard shack and let them know to be ready in case they're trying to sneak into the valley from other trails. Hit the other three cabins up there on your way back. Make sure they heard the bell."

"Candy, across the river. Tell them we've already headed south. Chris and Savannah, tell Lucas and Stephen and make sure the six cabins to the south heard the alarm. Everyone else, let's roll!"

Others had run up during the instructions and thirty men took the road that led south to the defensive barricades. It was a mile and a half and they made it in twenty minutes. They had erected a line of barricades, each eight-feet wide and four-feet high and stretching out like a dotted line for almost a mile wide. It was a half mile north of the rock, starting at the road by the river and running west. They didn't think an attack would come around the west side of Platte rock, due to the guard shack at the ramp covering this access, so there was a half mile with no barriers on the right. Each shield had a six-foot wide, metal back in the center to try and prevent bullets from penetrating the wood barriers, and were held up by two poles that extended from the upper corners to the ground. They were staggered forward and back to allow men to go through the line and move from barrier to barrier.

Mark and the others spread out along the width of the valley. He and Matthew were about one third of the way from the river side. He thought this was likely to be the hot spot of the battle.

The moon was less than half, its crescent casting ghostly shadows on the field. Mark heard other men arriving in the dark and their muffled greetings. He wondered what Clay was waiting for and then heard a sudden volley of gunshots. They all tensed and raised their rifles, pointing to the east side of the rock. Then a tremendous number of rifles began firing.

Mark told Matthew, "They're aiming a suppressive fire at the guard shack to keep them from picking off the soldiers as they advance around the rock. Once they're past, Sheri and Tyler won't be able to fire at them from their vantage point. The Anasazi Tower is too far away to effectively aim at them, although they might get in a lucky hit. That means they'll be here soon."

And they were. In the dim light of the moon, Mark saw movement to the left of the rock. A body of men came around the rock and veered west until the rock was at their back. He could vaguely see three groups separate and take cover behind the scattered rocks. One went right, one stayed at the left of the rock and the third took the middle. To his surprise, a mule drawn wagon swung around the rocks and took position in front of the center group. He heard someone yell a command and the center group of men moved forward. *Why are the others holding back?* He wondered. The first group was fifty yards from the front barriers.

"Hit the switch!" James called out.

***

Clay, with Einstein and Lloyd beside him, had given the order to move out from the ranch. Stewart and B.J. were standing directly behind Clay. The wagon, pulled by two mules that had wandered onto the ranch property one day, moved forward and Clay jumped into it with Jinx and Jackson. The creatures kept pace alongside. They went straight up the dirt road for two miles, until they came to the intersection with the smaller road that crossed the river to the bridge.

It was 4 a.m. and the moon was dim. Had Clay waited a few more nights there would have been no moon and their movements would have been unseen. But once the Remnant had rescued Lori, there was no stopping Clay from his revenge. When they were just outside the entrance to the valley, he told the driver to stop the wagon and the men formed up behind.

"One more time," he told them as he climbed down into their midst. He directed his comments at his two lieutenants. "We attack in a 'vee' formation. Lloyd's guys to my left and back a little, Einstein's to my right. My guys will fire continuously at the shed on the rock so they can't fire down at us. We just run right on by them. The idiots won't be able to reach us with their fire. Whoever is in the shed will be neutralized. We swing around behind the rock. Their freakin' barriers are a half mile away but they should be unmanned. Everyone should be home in bed. Even if they somehow found out we're coming and they're at the barricades, they're a bunch of pussys. They don't know how to fight and our guys do. We'll overwhelm 'em." He raised his voice. "My guys, move out." He jumped back in the wagon and they moved forward, following his men by thirty yards.

They saw muzzle flashes from the rock and a volley of shots whizzed by. There were a few seconds with no gunfire, and then Clay gave the order.

"Return fire!"

His entire army surged forward at top speed and the twenty men that had been designated began firing at Sheri and Tyler. They had no choice but to keep their heads down as the invaders ran across the fields and swung around the gigantic rock formation.

As they ran by, Tyler stuck his rifle out the slit and fired several rounds in quick succession. Two of Clay's men were hit and went down, but a lucky shot toward the shack caught Tyler right in the forehead, the only spot that was vulnerable. Sheri gasped as his dead body flew backward onto the floor. Angry beyond belief, she stuck her own weapon out the window and fired until her magazine was empty. She crouched in the corner, bullets sometimes flying through the small opening as she swapped out the empty mag for one of her two remaining full ones.

As Clay's army came around the rock pile, Clay could hear firing from the guard house on the other side of the river but the chances of any hits from that far away were minimal. They spread out in front of the rock, taking cover behind smaller boulders and large bushes. Now it was time to storm the barriers, and then they would move on to the defenseless town. The wagon driver swung the mules around toward the barricades.

"Charge!" Clay yelled.

***

The night sky lit up with the lights from a dozen emergency beacons they had saved for this eventuality. Clay's forces were literally caught in the headlights. The Remnant opened fire, blasting away with everything they had.

It was a massacre!

A score of men fell on either side of the wagon and the creatures slunk back from the lights, each taking several hits as they crouched behind the rocks. The mules spooked and turned sharply left even as the driver fought to maintain control. The harness snapped and the panicked mules continued back toward the rock at full speed as the wagon, no longer pulled by the mules tilted and fell, spilling the three men onto the ground, twenty yards in front of the barrier. They lost their rifles as they tumbled forward. The driver, jerked off the wagon by the mules, hit the ground and tried to crawl away but was cut down by heavy fire. Jackson and Jinx were each hit multiple times and flew backward to slam against the overturned wagon as it ground to a halt in the dirt.

Clay jumped up untouched by a single bullet, as the Remnant recognized him, holding their fire. He turned and looked back at Einstein and Lloyd, whose forces remained hidden in front of Platte Rock.

"You BASTARDS! You fucking TRAITORS!" he screamed. The other two commanders stood with white flags waving, easily visible, even though the light from the beacons barely reached that distance. Clay swung back around, breathing in gasps, eyes so wide the whites were visible all the way around. He was trembling with anger.

Mark stepped out from around the barrier. He was aware that others had joined him in front of the barrier, but he was completely focused on Clay.

The man he had thought of as a brother.

"It's over Clay." He felt conflicted, strangely deflated.

"You're right Mark. It's done." He held out his arms. "You won. I'll leave this place, and just go back to California. You'll never see me again. I promise." He had calmed down and was realizing they held his life in their hands. His eyes widened as he saw Mark raise a mean looking .45 Caliber Smith and Wesson and point it directly at him.

"Mark, come on. You kicked me out of the shelter and turned Dad against me. It wasn't my fault. You and me... we grew up together! You're like my brother." He turned and looked to Mark's right, where Mark was surprised to see Chris standing beside him.

"Chris, for God's sake! You didn't stop them from kicking me out. Your own brother! What was I supposed to do? I know. I should have just left but you all hurt me so bad." Tears were now running down his cheeks. "I'm going to leave. I don't think either of you will shoot me in the back. I don't think you can shoot your brother."

Mark hesitated as Clay raised his eyebrows in a questioning look... and Mark's heart broke, as the gesture revealed Will Hargraves in his son's face. Clay turned his back and took a step, then suddenly, and very quickly, swung back around, a handgun pointed at Mark's face. Triumph lit his face. Mark had lowered his guard with the paralyzing flash of memory, but others had not, and gunfire erupted on either side of Mark as a round whizzed past his ear.

Clay looked surprised, as bullets slammed him back and he dropped like a puppet with its strings cut. Shocked, Mark looked left and saw Marci standing with her rifle still pointing at Clay's still form. Swinging right, he saw Chris with a large caliber revolver held in both hands, also pointing at Clay.

Terry Holcomb walked by his daughter and kicked a handgun, from where it lay by Clay's outstretched hand, toward Mark. He walked by a stunned Mark, who stood with his gun lowered, and said…

"Never hesitate!"

There were two ear-splitting roars, and the infuriated monsters charged at the crowd of people standing in front of Clay's body. This time there was no hesitation, as Mark and everyone else opened fire. An arrow appeared in B.J.'s throat and dozens of rounds pummeled the creatures as Stewart's face disintegrated before their eyes. The Devols finally went down just a few feet in front of the humans, their hands outstretched, touching Clay's body.

Now there was only one left in the valley, watching them from atop the ridge above the Anasazi Tower.

Chapter 28

They buried Clay next to his father. Tyler Forbes was laid to rest a few yards away, with Tom and the others that had died since entering this valley. As with all the other funerals, a light rain was falling and the afternoon was dismal. The attendees cried when they buried Tyler, but not even Chris nor Mark shed any tears for Clay. Only Helen. She remembered the little boy growing up in the Hargraves household before he turned into the man they buried that afternoon.

They had collected all the guns and ammo off the dead bodies, then piled the corpses on the remains of the two Devols, dousing them all with gasoline. James had tossed a match onto the stack of corpses and the mound went up in flames, creating a massive bonfire that burned into the night, until all that was left was a greasy, obscene stain on the valley floor.

Most of the attendees of the funeral left by the southern trail, to travel the shorter distance to Willsburg. Mark put his arm around Lori and they walked over the fall's bridge to head back home in solitude. When they reached the fork in the trail they went north a few yards to a copse of trees where they were sheltered from the rain. Mark put his arms around her, his head bent low beside hers.

"Are you ready to talk about the baby?" When he'd taken her home the day before, she had gone to bed and not risen until the bell rang calling him to battle.

"He hit me Mark. He hit me so hard I couldn't breathe. Doc says the blow is what caused the miscarriage. I'm so sorry." He could feel her shaking and knew she was silently crying.

"No, Lori. It's not your fault. I'm glad he's dead. He caused so much misery. Why didn't you tell me you were pregnant?"

She looked up at him with tear filled eyes. "I was going to surprise you. Oh Mark, I was so happy about the baby."

"I know. It'll be okay. Since this damn war we just have to take one day at a time and see what happens. Let's get back. I just want to spend the rest of the day with Ashley and Kevin."

***

"We never really intended to fight with Clay against you guys," Einstein told the group gathered in the Town Hall. James and the council were there, along with a score of others that wanted to hear from the enemy commanders. "I was a businessman before the war and I knew an ally was always better than an enemy. From the day they came to Cimarron my plan was to contact you guys to see if we could work together to get through the winter. When Lloyd came down from Red River we talked, and his ideas were the same as mine. We held back and didn't participate. None of our guys fired on your people."

Ruben scowled at him. "Why the hell didn't you stop him? You let him attack us! Tyler would still be alive."

"He had those monsters on his side. One word from him and they eat you alive. Lloyd didn't join us until a month ago. Even though we didn't want to fight you, it wasn't our place to interfere. We were pretty sure he was wrong, and that you weren't as helpless as he thought."

Lloyd chimed in, "We just found out you folks were here. It wasn't our fight. I'm an insurance salesman, not a soldier. I've got thirty families, half with kids, and another twenty, single folks that managed to survive the war and radiation, but we're running out of food. Red River had a population of under a thousand. Our town was a ski town. It hasn't taken long to go through the food in the stores and houses. If you don't help us we're going to die."

"You know," Ruben said, standing up and moving toward Lloyd, "we don't owe you, just because you didn't attack us!"

James stood and held Ruben back. "Settle down Ruben. They haven't done anything to us and we can't just let them all die."

Walter stood. "Can I have the floor?" James nodded at him. "Well, seems to me that the more people live in New Mexico Colony, the better chance we all have of surviving. One thing we need, for sure, is more workers. You guys have any resources at all? What can you do?"

"Unfortunately, most of our people are service oriented. Waitresses and bartenders, hotel clerks, bankers and business people. There was only one family in town that had prepared. But even they didn't take it seriously and didn't practice their skills."

Terry interrupted him, "Yeah, well that's a common problem with preppers. I call them arm-chair preppers because they read all about it and even buy supplies, but most of them never learn skills or practice. Since May, the valley people have been learning quickly. I could help your people learn some skills they'll need."

"That's very kind, but we need food and shelter. We had a garden during the summer but something was wrong and the plants didn't produce seeds. Bill Sykes, the prepper said they were hybrids. He says you need old-fashioned seeds to grow plants that make seeds and can grow season after season."

"We have heirloom seeds and have saved seeds from our summer harvest. We have plenty," Chris told him. "But you can't plant until next year."

"The people in Cimarron don't have any food left either," Einstein said. "But if you can help us, a lot of them are miners. There's gold and silver mines around here but there's also iron mines north of Eagle Nest. During the winter my people can live in Eagle Nest and fish the lake. I'm told it gets a solid two feet of ice in the winter but we can ice fish. We'll trade our fish with you folks for other types of food and next year we can start up the mines. You're going to need iron ore for your blacksmith you told me about. If we stay in Eagle Nest, can you help us with blankets and firewood?"

"There's a tackle stop that probably has warm sleeping bags. I don't know what stuff Clay and his band used. We can go down there and find supplies to get your folks set up to stay warm."

"I can cut them a few cords of firewood," Lucas offered. "They can try to find houses that have fireplaces. They may need to double up just like we have."

"Yeah, and Angel Fire, a town down south had a population of, maybe a thousand," Lloyd told them. "I bet some are alive. There was a medical clinic so they might have a doctor. We should send someone down there to check it out. It's only about ten miles south of the lake. If you can help us all through the winter, next year we can set up trade routes and barter between the towns. We're not asking to move in here with you guys. The population of Red River will need to move down to Eagle Nest too. At least for now. Red River is in a canyon and there isn't a lot of room to plant crops. We just need help to make it through till next spring."

"We'll need more wagons to hauls stuff between towns," James pointed out.

"There's one in Cimarron at the Boy Scout Camp," Einstein said.

"I'll make more, if Lucas can get me the wood," Farnsworth added.

Until meeting the survivors from Will's shelter, the remaining populations of the surrounding towns had lost hope. With no way to grow food or keep warm, they were waiting to die in the fierce blizzards and freezing temperatures of the winter. Now, for the first time since the war, they thought they had a chance at survival.

"Taos had a population of around six thousand," Matthew said from his position at the back of the room. "It has a lot of supplies. I stayed the summer there and I don't know what happened, but there's no one there. I'm wondering if, because of its more exposed location, it got more radiation. There are a lot of bodies, like they all died suddenly. Eventually it could be cleaned up and used for a large number of people. It could end up the capital city of the colony."

"I wonder if it got hit by the Red Mercury radiation," Micah said. "It's supposed to kill life without blowing up the buildings."

They all sat and thought about that possibility, when a commotion was heard outside.

"Mark! James!" Doug threw open the door and rushed in, skidding to a halt. He was breathing hard.

"We've got another body!"

***

They all ran out into the waning light of the late evening and saw one of the mustangs carrying a body draped over its back, being led by Al.

"Who is it?"

"What happened?"

The crowd gathered around the horse and the body was untied and lowered to the ground.

"Me and Paul were on duty in the ridge guard shack. He went out to pee and didn't come back. When I went to find him, he was part way up the ridge. His leg's missing. It was one of those things!"

"Are there guards in the shack?" Dave asked.

"Yeah, we just got relieved by Tony and Eric."

"That's it!" Jimbo blurted. "We have to get that thing once and for all. It can't kill any more of our people. We need to get a bunch of guys and go kill it."

Mark remembered a nightmare from before the war. He was being chased by one the creatures before he even knew they existed. It was his problem, his cross to bear.

"Nobody's going after it," he said. "Only me. It's me it wants."

"Are you crazy?" James said.

"We'll find it and I'll lure it out so you guys can cut it down."

"Where do you think it hangs out? We blew up all the entrances to the shelter."

Bud Nagle was listening to the discussion and limped over to where the men stood over Paul's body. "Did you blow up the cave on the side of the hill? The one that I crawled out of?"

"What cave?" Mark asked him.

Glen stepped forward. "There was a helicopter pad on the edge of the plateau. It would bring parts and supplies in, and they would be hauled down the road to the cave. It was a kind of back entrance, so the stuff didn't have to be taken through the shelter when the power plant was built. There's a road from the north and one from the south that's steeper. It runs up a small canyon that makes an indentation beside the falls. A large ledge sticks out in front of the cave. It's a little left, and up above, the big exit cave we came out of when we left the shelter. I thought it caved in when the power plant collapsed."

"No. When the cave-in happened I was in the tunnels. The place is a maze and there are phosphorescent markings on the wall so the workers could find their way down into the power cave. I followed them out. I was hurt real bad and I could smell those things in the warren of tunnels. I still don't how I got out of there without them finding me. I went up the road to the north and down the trail from there."

"That's where the sucker is then! Let's go kill it." Jimbo squinted over at Mark.

"Take the body to Doc's. We'll bury him tomorrow morning and then go after the Devol."

They went back into Town Hall to formulate their plans for destroying the creature.

That night, for the first time in many months Mark dreamed of the creature, the same nightmare he'd had in August three days before the war that changed all their lives forever. He was back in the darkness, the thing gaining on him in the water-filled tunnel. This time, however, it caught him and as the fangs sunk into his neck he came awake, screaming in the darkness of his cabin with Lori grabbing, and holding on to him for the rest of the night.

Chapter 29

Twenty men and two women were on the plateau above the cave. Terry had chosen the ten, best marksmen based on their training, to line the cliff on the south side as close to the top of the falls as possible. This ledge looked across the small canyon and they had a good line of sight to the steep road leading up from the ledge. The ledge and cave were easily visible from this angle and Mark was surprised they hadn't ever noticed them before. The other riflemen were spread out along the cliff directly above the ledge and to the north. Mark was to lure the beast up the steeper south road since the shooters had a better angle there.

He and Lori had their first big fight that morning after the funeral. They both had lived through many dangerous times in the past year but she didn't see why he needed to be the one acting as bait for the Devol.

"Because I'm the one it wants. It killed Paul but left the body for us to find. It's trying to lure me out just like I'm going to lure it out. I don't understand it Lori, but there's a connection between me and the thing. I could tell when it looked at me in the shelter. It's like it recognized me and I was responsible for its plight. There was unbelievable hate in its eyes."

"We can all go to the cave and draw it out."

"No, it would go deeper in the warren. We would never find it. I have to go alone so it will come out and we can ambush it."

"You don't have to go, dammit! I can't lose you!"

He hugged her to him for a long time. "I have to go. Everyone's ready. Lori? I need a huge favor. If it gets me... will you shoot me? I don't want it to eat me alive."

She collapsed on the edge of the bed. "Oh God Mark. Please don't do this."

"It's my job."

The climb up the east ridge took an hour but they didn't want to rush it and be tired for the battle with the creature. The riflemen took up positions along the edge, looking across an abyss at the road leading down to the ledge. Lori stayed with this group hoping to be the one that finally freed Mark from the creature. Mark and the others went north, where several spread out above the ledge and to the north above the road.

"Be just our luck," Jimbo told Terry and Matthew. "It probably doesn't live there, or it isn't home."

Mark went down the abandoned road alone. It was filled with ruts and rocks, and weeds had sprouted around them.

The plan was to lure the creature up the south road to give the marksmen a better shot.

He slowed as he neared the clearing in front of the cave. It was thirty feet from the entrance to the edge, which was lined with large rocks. Other rocks haphazardly spread across the shelf, having fallen from the cliff above during the earthquakes. Quietly slipping forward, he saw that there was a clear path to the road on the far side of the ledge. He didn't have a rifle, just his Smith and Wesson. He would rely on the others to bring it down before it caught him.

Reaching the bottom of the road where it leveled out at the ledge, he moved to the outside of the shelf to give him a better view of the opening. He was no tracker, but he could see bare footprints leading into the cave and quite a few behind the rocks at the edge. He glanced over the rocks and saw the graveyard below and the town in the distance. He shivered as he realized the Devol had a perfect view and had probably been watching them for months.

Mark realized the men were anxious and he needed to get on with it, so he slowly moved forward around the rocks and approached the opening of the cave. He couldn't see very far into it and he couldn't hear anything inside. Going directly to the opening, he peered in as far as he could see. There were remains of a wooden door or barrier and he was unable to see beyond that. He thought about going in, getting closer so it would hear him, but thinking of Lori and the kids, he decided to try to attract its attention from here first.

Just as he started to yell, he felt that touch of dizziness he recognized as an aftershock. Dirt and small rocks dusted him from above and larger rocks struck the ground behind him. He reached out and put his hand against the side of the opening to steady himself. The shaking ceased but he heard the sound of cascading rocks around the south corner. He was turning to investigate, when he heard a faint sound of movement coming from the depths of the tunnel.

Startled, he moved back a few steps. In an instant, the darkness in the back of the tunnel materialized into an enormous on-rushing monster.

He'd forgotten how gigantic it was!

Fortunately it had to bend over as it came at him and he was able to turn and run before it reached the entrance. It blasted out of the cave and paused for an instant, as its eyes adjusted to the brilliance of the mid-morning sunlight that had flooded the ledge only moments before, when the sun climbed above the ridge.

Like a frightened deer, Mark leaped over rocks and slammed around the corner onto the steep road… and skidded to a stop. The entire road had disappeared in a rock fall that still slid down the hill as he teetered at the edge. Dust obscured his view, and the view of the riflemen farther along the canyon. Choking on dirt, he swung around to the outside of the shelf to try and get around the creature. It stood twenty feet away, its red eyes glaring with malice, its fangs dripping with mucoid saliva as it anticipated tearing this man apart.

There was no escape. Arby stretched up to its full height, a full eight feet as it had continued to grow over the past months. It began to sway, a sinuous waving. Mark was temporarily mesmerized, staring into those savage red eyes. The creature twitched and he knew it was coming!

Making a dash for the edge of the shelf, he felt his arm grabbed in an iron vise and he was jerked from his feet. Holding the .45 in his left hand he fired it at the creature, temporarily surprising it into releasing his arm. It knew the power of a rifle but was unfamiliar with a handgun. It released Mark, leaving gashes down his forearm, but before he could get by, it charged at him again.

He was only a few feet in front of the edge. Mark faked a turn to the left, and just as Arby reached for him again, he threw himself on the ground and rolled toward the onrushing creature. Tripping over him, it tried to check its path but hurtled toward the cliff. It twisted impossibly in the air and grabbed Mark as it hit the rocks at the edge of the shelf. He was pulled into its embrace as it flew over the edge. Wrapping his arms around a boulder, his cheek slammed into the rock, scraping off skin as he hugged with all his might. The monster smashed into the side of the cliff as its arms slipped down his body to grasp his thighs. It was screaming and clawing at Mark when its foot slipped into a crevice. Momentarily secure, it tore into his buttocks with its fangs and Mark gasped in pain… and released his hold on the rock.

Strong arms grasped his as gunshots went off near his ear, deafening him. Intense pain shot through his back and arms as he was jerked back over the rocks and fell to the ground, writhing in pain. But he could hear the tormented screams of the monster as they diminished in volume with distance… and suddenly ceased.

The nightmare was finally over.

***

Three days had passed and Mark regained consciousness in his own bed. Lori sat by his side, sound asleep, and he could hear the sounds of the kids whispering in the front room. Lying in the dark, not sure if it was night or dawn, he tried to recall what he'd been dreaming. It faded too quickly but he didn't seem frightened or distressed. He hurt from his head to his toes, his shoulders aching from bearing the weight of the beast, and searing pain still emanated from his backside. He was sure he would never live that down.

"Lori? Honey, can I have some water?"

She jumped to his side and held him in the darkness. "Mark, you idiot! Trying to take on that thing alone. You wonderful, brave idiot." She rose and brought him a glass of water, holding it to his lips so he could drink.

"Not my fault. Earthquake."

"As soon as your escape was cut off, Einstein, Matthew, Terry and Dave took off like a shot for the other road. They grabbed you and shot the bastard right in the face until it let you go."

He tried to sit but the pain kept him from moving. "How long?"

"Three days. You were at Doc's until this morning. They took out the I.V. and moved you here because they ran out of saline. Dr. Jim said he thought you'd be awake soon, since you almost woke up a couple of times."

"Is it dead?"

"We burned it. It's done. I'll put the kids to bed and be right back."

When she returned and crawled into bed beside him he was sound asleep.

Chapter 30

After the first blast of winter subsided in mid-October, the valley experienced a warm, Indian summer. Having been imprisoned for months by Clay's band of outlaws, the residents were now enthusiastically exploring their surroundings. Sam and Willy Yancey rode down to the ranch and expressed their desire to own and operate it. The council agreed, but it was decided they could only have the southwest quadrant of land, that comprised close to a thousand acres. The boys had their two horses and two of the mustang mares. They had donated the stallion and the other mares to the community and the mustangs mares were boarded at the Wright's ranch at the upper end of the valley. The rest of Paradise valley would be sectioned off for additional family residences.

The Yancey boys had rounded up the mules and the wagon had been repaired. Using the Jeep, the old Camaro and the wagon, and making dozens of trips, the residents of Red River and Cimarron were brought to Eagle Nest. Lacking enough houses with fireplaces, some of the families doubled up. Next year they would build additional residences with fireplaces. Three of the shelter families had originally come from Eagle Nest, invited by Dave and Lenny when they had passed through town and they had returned to their homes.

Sending a team to Angel Fire, they found almost one hundred survivors. They were sick and hungry and probably wouldn't make it through the winter without help. It took two days before they would even meet with the delegation from Willsburg, worried that the little they had left would be stolen. The citizens of Willsburg explained that they would help them cut wood and provide supplies to keep them alive during the winter and in the spring they could help them get crops going and build warmer homes. They wanted to set up trade between the towns. Three of the families with very sick kids wanted to go back to Willsburg since their doctor hadn't survived the war.

"You are telling us," the Minister said, "that you're going to give us food to get us through the winter?"

"Do you like potatoes?"

***

"Hi guys." A team had returned from Eagle Nest and walked through the door of the Town Hall carrying boxes with more liquor bottles. "This is the last of it," Jeff said. "Clay's gang drank most of the liquor in town. I'm setting up a still though, so Dr. Jim and Aaron can have ethanol as a disinfectant. I'm going to learn to make whiskey and beer."

The room erupted in cheers.

Sheri had been ecstatic when one of the men returned with her bike.

"Where in the world did you find it," She asked Mike.

"Found it in a garage behind the house that Clay stayed in. Fifteen of us had a lot of fun knocking down that old house, for the Holcombs. The lumber can be used by the residents to burn in their fireplaces."

They all worked feverishly to ensure the residents of Eagle Nest and Angel Fire would be ready for the coming winter. Two of the mustangs were trained to pull a wagon and they were used to ferry supplies to the two towns even though it shorted Willsburg on some items. Angel Fire still had warm clothes and sleeping bags in their sporting goods store and they found every last can of food in town and delivered them to the school auditorium, which would be used as a community kitchen. They scrounged for propane to use in the stoves.

The residents of Willsburg taught the others how to get gasoline from the underground tanks and provided them with one of their generators. Obtaining a battery from the hardware store, they tried every vehicle in town and found one old car that ran. It was designated for emergencies but made Angel Fire seem much closer to Eagle Nest and Willsburg. They were barely ready when winter howled into the region and isolated them once again.

Mark hoped they had done enough. If they made it through this winter and the Remnant could teach them what they'd learned of survival skills, he felt they would be okay in the future.

***

A new blanket of snow lay sparkling in the light from the full moon. Mark's breath came out in white puffs in the freezing night air. Sitting on his bench, bundled in warm clothes, he could look out on the town and the whole valley. The town looked like something out of a Thomas Kinkaid painting, with smoke streaming upward from chimneys and lights from the oil lamps and fireplaces shining through windows. In front of the Town Hall, colored lights of a Christmas tree could be glimpsed, attached to the branches of the living tree they planted in the summer and reflecting off the snow. A single storage battery under the tree powered the lights.

"It's beautiful isn't it?" Lori said as she slipped onto the bench beside him.

"Incredibly so. I never noticed beauty like this before the war. Oh, I saw beauty in the ocean and in the forests and mountains where I ran, but I never really appreciated it like I do now." He put his arm across her shoulders and held her against him.

"I know. I never thought I would enjoy a simple meal or the kids playing outside in the meadow. Would you go back if you could?"

"That's really hard to say. There's so much I miss about my old life. I miss flying my old planes. But with you and the kids this is so much more meaningful. If I could take you back with me, maybe."

"I would never go back to my old life. But, like you said, if we could be together and have things the way it was before, well, I don't know."

"Bud Nagle's talking about getting the power back on in Taos. They have sub-stations or whatever. I don't fully understand it. Lucas wants to build a grain mill on the river and Bud says we can even use the river to make electricity. Next year some of the Red River folks want to go home and if they can't grow enough food they want to set up businesses to trade for what they need. The New Mexico Colony may be one of the main regions for civilization to come back. Matthew says we need to build a whole wagon train, and in the spring, we can go to Taos and bring back a lot of things we've run out of or never had and some families may even want to move there permanently."

"People with kids will probably want to stay here since we have teachers and doctors."

"Yeah. We can make it comfortable here, but we'll never know when the Chinese are going to come marching up the valley." He shifted uncomfortably, trying to keep his weight off his right butt cheek that still ached two months later. He had endured weeks of kidding about the bite in the ass.

"That's very true. It scares me but I don't know what we can do about it."

Continuing their conversation, they discussed what they would do for a living, now that the major dangers had been eliminated. Until now they mainly had worked security but there hadn't been any more sightings of Devols. The town still maintained sentries, but the east ridge and north guard stations were unmanned, as were the ones at Platte Rock and the Anasazi Tower. Only the one at the ramp was maintained in case people came down from the west. Six more people had arrived before winter set in.

"I miss the ocean and the California beaches and mountains. I wonder what's happening out there. What it's like on the coast."

They sat still for a while just enjoying each other's company and the idyllic winter scene.

"Mark, we're not staying here. Are we?"

He looked over at her. "No. I can't. I have to know what the rest of the country looks like but I don't want to take you and the kids into danger. I just don't know what to do."

"Don't worry about us. We will go anywhere you want us to go. As long as we're together we can face anything."

"It's dangerous out there. It won't be easy."

"Yeah, like we've had it so easy since we left the shelter."

He hugged her. "Don't say anything until spring and we're sure."

"Okay. We need to get back to town. Santa's coming and the kids are at the Town Hall with all the others."

Chapter 31

The table in the Town Hall held five bottles of vodka, since the only thing Jeff had to make mash with was potatoes and the rest of the liquor had been consumed over the past few months. Most of the production from the still went to the medical clinic. Next year they would have whiskey, Jeff had promised. Sam Yancey and Matthew sat at the table, each with a glass of vodka in front of them. Matthew's back was to the wall, ever alert, and he glanced up as Ruben entered the room.

"That's a fine looking colt you got," Sam told Matthew. "How's about I trade you Jasper for him? Jasper's only four years old and he's a fully trained cow pony. Real smart. I'll take that little one and train him up to be just as good as Jasper. In a couple years he'll be improving the bloodline of those mustangs. You got two more foals due in March."

Ruben joined them at the table. "Hold on a minute. I think the council needs to make that kind of decision."

"You're kidding right? Those horses belong to us."

"Yes, but we have to decide what's best for the community."

"Pardon my French, but that's bullshit. Me and my brother already donated a half a dozen mares and the mustang stallion to the community." He was beginning to bristle and Matthew stepped in to calm things down.

"Ruben, there's always been debates about individual rights versus the needs of the community. In this case I think The Yancey boys and I have given our share to the community. Now I think you need to get out of our private business transaction." Sam and Matthew just sat and stared at Ruben until he became uncomfortable. He angrily scooted back his chair and left the building without even having a drink.

"Sam, you have a deal, but he can't leave his mother yet. You boys can move them to the ranch until he's weaned and then bring back the mare. Fair?"

"Yeah, that's more than fair." He reached out his hand and Matthew shook it firmly.

As they slowly sipped their drink, Jeff came in carrying a wooden box with a dozen bottles of liquid.

"Hey guys. My first batch of beer! You want to try one?" Both men shrugged and accepted the bottles handed them and pulled the corks. Jeff popped the cork on his bottle as all three men took a big slug. Matthew choked on his and the other two guinea pigs simultaneously spit theirs out, all over the table and each other.

"Damn! I guess it's back to the drawing board."

***

During the winter, school was held in the Town Hall. Dr. Laskey, Barbara and Sandy had a full curriculum, that differed from what they taught before the war. They still taught reading, writing and arithmetic, along with history and literature, but the afternoon classes were all vocational, teaching the children skills, and how to make things. Sandy taught part-time, as the baby was only eight months old. Sarah cared for the baby while Sandy worked, and it was difficult to get her to give the baby up when Sandy came for her. Having no breast pumps, Sandy took a lot of breaks and walked over to Sarah's cabin to feed the baby the old-fashioned way.

Work went on and cabins continued to be built. It was a lot slower going as storms blew into the valley every few days. The major bottleneck, even during the summer had been transporting the logs from Lucas and Stephen's lumber mill to the job site, and now that the ground was covered by snow most of the time, it was almost impossible. The Jeep mired down in ground so muddy, even the four wheel drive had trouble when the vehicle was loaded with lumber.

"I wonder how the people in Angel Fire are doing?" James said at the town meeting. "Eagle Nest seems okay. They're providing us with fish from the lake. Einstein says it's freezing cold at night but they have plenty of blankets. Nobody's starving anyway."

"I wish we had a way to communicate with them. Did anybody try to find ham radios or shortwave?" Johnny asked. "If they had radios we could talk to them. It doesn't seem I have anybody else to talk to."

"We didn't have time. We barely laid in their supplies before winter hit. Next year Johnny."

It seemed like "next year" was becoming a major theme. Next year they would be planting the apple, pear and cherry trees that Chris was raising in the Greenhouse. And the asparagus. Next year they would plant grains and cotton in the fields around Platte Ranch that the Yancey's didn't own. Next year they would use some of the oak trees on the east of the river between the ranch and Eagle Nest, to make better furniture and to use in their soap since ashes from hardwoods made better soap. Next year, they would put in covered sidewalks and build more businesses. Next year, they would finish the rest of the cabins and the families that doubled up this year would be able to spread out into their own homes. Next year they would dig a new well and maybe even find a way to get running water.

But Mark knew that next year, he, Lori and the kids would be gone.

***

"It's a girl!" Dr. Jim came out of the back room and told the crowd gathered in the waiting room. "They're both doing well."

Mark high-fived Samuel who wasn't sure what he was doing and slapped Mark in the face when he missed his hand. Mark laughed and hugged Lori and Sheri. Dr. Jim went outside to let the others, that couldn't fit in the clinic, know about the baby. This was the fourth child he'd delivered in the past three months and so far they all did fine. He knew the day would come when there would be a complication that he didn't have the equipment to handle but for now he was batting a thousand.

Aaron came out of the room with a tiny bundle in his arms. "Chris says I can show her to you for two minutes, then she wants her back."

They all took turns holding her, and when Aaron took the baby back to Chris, Mark watched him go, wondering if that would ever be him.

***

Spring came earlier than the year before and decorated the valley with sprays of wildflowers and mantles of green grasses and leaves. Mark and Lori sat on the bench atop Sentinel Hill, the warm sun on their upturned faces.

"Man, oh man, that sun feels good. It's been a long cold winter," he said.

"Yes, and it's still only April. It's like we're being forced to make a final decision about leaving. When are we going to tell the others?" She leaned against him, holding his arm, her head on his shoulder.

"Today, I think. We don't have to leave until we're sure the last frost has passed, but that way we have plenty of time to get ready."

"Do you think anyone will go with us?"

"We'll find out tonight."

***

"I called this meeting to discuss something important and I thank those of you that came from outlying cabins. It looks like a pretty good turnout. Reminds me of the meetings in the Greenhouse when everyone showed up."

He sat in a chair on the platform at the back of the main room. Now he stood.

"Lori and I have decided to leave the valley, go back to California and find out what's going on out there."

The room erupted in conversations.

"No, Mark. You guys can't leave," Chris told him. "If you go, I'm going too. You're all the family I have left. Me and Aaron will have your back."

"Chris, that's great but you can't take the baby on a trip like that!"

"Just try to leave without me!"

Samuel looked stricken, but he knew he would be more of a burden on the road and that the Remnant would need him more than ever without Chris.

"What are you thinking Mark?" Walter said. "Will you come back?"

"I haven't thought farther than leaving."

"I have a family here. I can't go with you."

"I know, Walter. It's okay."

Sarah shot to her feet. "Walter Thompson. Don't you use me and the boys as an excuse. If you want to go you just say so and I'll go with you. It's up to you but I'm not going to hold you down." He put his arm around her and kissed her on the head. "We'll talk about it, okay?"

"Well, I'm damn sure going with you," this from Jimbo. "I want to know what's happening out there too."

"And me," said Sheri.

"Me and my brother will go with you a ways," said Sam. "We want to find some more stock. If things get real rough we can help you shoot your way back here. Otherwise we'll stay with you for a while and then come back to our ranch." The boys both had girlfriends and wanted to settle down.

"What route you taking?" Terry asked him.

"Don't know, but it will probably be easiest if we head east around the mountains, then north to the Colorado border and west all the way to the ocean. We'll want to avoid Las Vegas."

"I'd like to go with you as far as Raton. Just to see what shape it's in. We might continue on or come back. I don't know."

"Man, you can't leave. We need you!"

"Pete and Jerry can run the meat processing as good as me. You guys have really learned a lot. You'll be fine. We'll be back.

I have a feeling my oldest daughter won't be going. She'll stay with Tucker."

"We'll leave when we're sure the frost is past. I think another month. We will need some of the wagons or will have to build some more. I need the mules and provisions."

The crowd of people stayed late, talking about Mark's plans, who would go and who would stay and what they thought the conditions would be on the outside.

When he and Lori went home, he wondered for the thousandth time whether he was making the right decision.

***

In early May, just one year after being ejected from the shelter, three couples participated in a triple wedding. Mark and Lori, Chris and Aaron, and Tucker and Marci. Brian presided over the nuptials. Chris had told Aaron she wanted to be an honest woman now that she was a mother.

Lori and Mark had never thought about marriage until they heard about the wedding and asked if they could join in. Chris was thrilled.

Skillet, Helen, Ernest and the other cooks prepared a feast for the occasion, including baking a large cake for all to share.

The brides all wore jeans and denim shirts and had flowers weaved into their hair. Chris wore her hair pinned up in back and it reminded Mark of the party Will had thrown in his mansion in Newport, the night before the war. The men dressed up with jeans and long-sleeved, white shirts they'd found in the Greenhouse. That pretty much finished off the clothing that had been stocked in the building. The party went on late into the night as the Remnant wiped out their meager supply of alcohol.

After their lovemaking on their wedding night, Mark asked Lori one last time, "Are you sure you want to go with me?"

"There's no way I would let you go off on your own. I want to see what's happening out there too."

"I'm worried about the kids."

"Me too. But if anything happened to you I couldn't take it. I would spend the rest of life looking down the road, hoping to see you returning. At least if we're with you we can face it together and I'll never wonder what happened to you."

"Then we'll continue this adventure together," he said as he pulled her close.

Chapter 32

The wagons were packed, the horses saddled and the wagon train had drawn up next to the bridge spanning the swollen river. Chris sat in the front wagon with three and a half month old Karen at her breast. She had a space carved out of the piles of tied down crates, a sleeping bag under her and a large goose-down pillow cushioning her back from the box she reclined against. A wool blanket covered her from the waist down to protect against the chill.

"Baby? You comfy in there?" Aaron rode back to check on her for the third time. He rode one of the shaggy mustang ponies, a brown and tan mare. He wore a hat and his jacket, leather gloves and a scarf around his neck.

"I'm just as fine as I was five minutes ago. Thanks for asking."

He laughed and rode toward the front of the wagon where the two horses were chomping at the bit. These horses had only been trained recently to pull a wagon and they seemed restless and nervous.

"Easy Ethel. Easy Fred." He stopped his mount alongside to try and quiet the team.

Mark saw the oil lamps of a large group of people walking from Willsburg, across the meadow toward the wagons. The sun wasn't above the western cliffs and the darkness hid the river that roared down its channel. The trees across the river were shrouded in morning mist and a light drizzle was beginning to fall. It was late May, just two weeks over one year from the time they abandoned the shelter, to start a new civilization in the Hidden Valley. Aaron wondered again if they were doing the right thing. He had a wife and a newborn daughter to consider. But they'd talked through all this before and knew that they could never be happy until they found out what was happening out in the world beyond their sanctuary.

The townsfolk, all wearing hats or ski bonnets and gloves, and wrapped in heavy coats had reached the back of the wagon train. They all had rifles slung over their shoulders or handguns in holsters strapped around their waists. They had toughened up and most were lean and leathered. Mark swung down from Jasper and tied the horse off to the back of the wagon. He walked over and hugged each person in turn; Walter, Sarah and Jerry Thompson, Jim Wiggins, Samuel and Rana, and thirty other well-wishers that had become family over the past year and eight months, since the nuclear war had thrust them into this mad adventure called survival. Aaron rode back to the throng and dismounted, as he too said his goodbyes to his friends. Many of the Remnant had stayed in town having said their goodbye's the previous evening and not wanting to face the emotional leave-taking. Helen and Ernest couldn't physically face the trek and had said their goodbyes to the little girl they had helped raise and to the man they had known since he was a teen. They weren't in the crowd.

"Hey Jerry, take care of my cabin. Someone can use it while we're gone but when we come back we want to move back in."

"We'll watch over it Terry. You're a great neighbor."

Most of the crowd went to the front wagon to say goodbye to Chris and wish her luck. They knew it wouldn't be easy to make this trek with a baby. Some gave her small handmade gifts for Karen.

Lori, with Kevin and Ashley in tow, crossed the bridge. They'd visited the school where the other children, along with Barbara and Dr. Laskey had gathered to say goodbye in relative warmth. Barbara bawled and clung to Lori and the kids, unwilling to allow them to leave until Lori pried the children away from her and they hurried out the door. Jeremy waved a tearful goodbye.

"You take care and God bless," Barbara called after their retreating backs.

Mark was watching them anxiously as they approached the wagons. Lori's eyes were red and he felt heartsick for her, knowing how close she had become to Barbara Thompson. She jumped into the second wagon and he handed her Kevin while Ashley climbed onto the tailgate and tumbled over into the back.

The morning brightened as the sun rose in the east although it was still hidden below the ridge. Mark and Aaron remounted their horses and rode over to the group of folks that would be leaving with them. Sheri stood beside her bike, and six men who had no mounts were standing in a group waiting for the word to leave. Greg sat atop Tulip. Jimbo fired up his motorbike and Terry started the Jeep. His family were in their seats and anxious to get the pain of departure over with. Cody waved to Megan, who waved back from the roof of her father's house. Only Marci was missing, having married Tucker two weeks before. She had said goodbye to her parents and siblings the night before and was in her cabin, lying in her new husband's arms, sobbing, as he tried to comfort her.

Matthew and Einstein came riding from the south, where they had scouted ahead to ensure the way was safe. They would ride out again when the caravan was underway.

"Everything looks clear Mark. We can get started. Is every one ready?"

"As ready as we'll ever be." He pulled his collar tighter around his neck and adjusted his hat to try and keep out the rain. Looking back at the crowd, he waved, then turned and called out, "Let's move!" as Lori, Skillet and James flicked the reins, and the horses jumped forward. All three drivers had to haul in the reins to keep them in line and the wagons settled into a steady pace. The men on foot took up positions on either side and Matthew and Einstein took off ahead to scout for danger. Jimbo rode ahead to keep from spooking the horses with the drone of the motorcycle's engine, and the Jeep fell in behind so the wagons and footmen could set the pace. Mark and Aaron rode alongside the teams pulling the wagons with their loved ones, just in case the horses didn't behave.

Looking back, Mark saw the waving residents disappear in the rolling mist that followed them down the valley. As they came alongside the lake they spotted Pete and Sandy standing on the far side, barely visible in the fog, waving to them as they passed them by. They had left the baby snug in her bassinet, custom built by Farnsworth.

The three wagons were replicas of the Conestoga wagons that had carried the early settlers across a virgin land to settle and found the United States of America. The only thing shattering that tableau was a modern Jeep Wrangler four-door, an old motorcycle and a modern touring bike.

The hunters had been successful during the early spring and there were containers of jerky and smoked meats, as well as some canned goods that hadn't been eaten in the winter. They had dehydrated foods prepared by Izzy and five gallon buckets of the freeze dried and dehydrated foods left over in the Greenhouse. Marilyn, Glen and Kate tried to get them to take more but they didn't want to leave the citizens of Willsburg short. They already had given quite a lot to Eagle Nest and Angel Fire.

Once the road had cleared to Angel Fire, a group had traveled down there and checked on them. They took more food that hadn't been eaten during the winter by the residents of Willsburg or Eagle Nest. It wasn't a minute too soon, as the folks in Angel Fire had finished off their provisions.

Six residents had perished. Four, including one child, had died from pneumonia and one man died of a massive heart attack. They didn't know why the other woman had died.

A team would meet with them to get their crops planted and teach them to hunt. To begin with, they would trade their game to Willsburg for other supplies and provisions. Later, they would learn to become as self-sufficient as the Remnant had become. They would be ready for next winter.

The Yancey boys came galloping along the river from the direction of their ranch. They had taken their stock to the Wrights to care for until they returned. As the wagon train reached the bridge leading over the river they fell in on either side to provide protection. The wagons traveled through the oak studded meadow and turned south toward Eagle Nest, where Einstein waved at his people as they passed through town.

Now they were beyond their known world, heading down the highway in the direction of Cimarron. Mark saw a figure walking toward them about a quarter mile away. He noticed Matthew and Einstein coming up behind the man. As they got closer, Mark could see it was an old man with a backpack looking fearfully over his shoulder at the two horsemen.

"It's okay buddy. We won't hurt you."

"I don't have but a few pieces of food. Please don't take it. It's all I got."

The front wagon drew alongside him. "There are people in Eagle Nest that will take you in if you're looking for a place to live," Mark told him. "They have food and work if you need it. And seven or eight miles past that is a town called Willsburg up in Hidden Valley. They'll take you in too. Just ask the people in Eagle Nest for directions. Or, if you want you could even come with us."

He seemed shocked to be treated so well.

"Where you folks bound?"

Mark looked over at Lori sitting in the wooden seat, winked at her and said to the old man…

"We're going home."

***

Watch for Humanity Abides – Book Three
The Search for Home

Coming in early 2014

Read about the *Humanity Abides* series

Shelter
Emergence
The Search for Home

at:

carolannbird.com

https://Facebook.com/humanityabides

About the Author:

Carol has had a life-long interest in all things relating to survival. Even as a child in San Diego, she carried around a small canvas bag with a bottle of water and a piece of fruit, a pocketknife, a flashlight and a deck of cards. Later she enjoyed backpacking, where she could carry around a lot more stuff and even got to stay out overnight! More recently she enjoys being a "survivalist" and pondering what life would be like in a post-apocalyptic world. Joining the Army at the age of eighteen, she was the first woman to attend the U.S. Army Chemical School, and was trained in CBR, or Chemical, Biological and Radiological laboratory techniques. Carol has participated in two 10 day backpacking/survival trips and is a certified scuba diver. She has a private pilot's license and has completed several marathons and many, many races at shorter distances. She graduated from California State University Northridge with a Bachelor of Science in Biology/biotechnology and has worked as a Clinical Laboratory Scientist for most of her adult life. Carol has three daughters and a son, and lives in Colorado Springs with one of her daughters, a granddaughter and a grandson.

Made in the USA
San Bernardino, CA
13 October 2013